LIARS' PARADOX

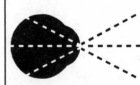
This Large Print Book carries the
Seal of Approval of N.A.V.H.

A JACK AND JILL THRILLER

LIARS' PARADOX

TAYLOR STEVENS

THORNDIKE PRESS
A part of Gale, a Cengage Company

Farmington Hills, Mich • San Francisco • New York • Waterville, Maine
Meriden, Conn • Mason, Ohio • Chicago

LIBRARY OF CONGRESS CIP DATA ON FILE.
CATALOGUING IN PUBLICATION FOR THIS BOOK
IS AVAILABLE FROM THE LIBRARY OF CONGRESS

ISBN-13: 978-1-4328-5930-5 (hardcover)

Published in 2018 by arrangement with Kensington Books, an imprint of Kensington Publishing Group

Printed in the United States of America
1 2 3 4 5 6 7 22 21 20 19 18

To my Patreon supporters, whose friendship, generosity, and love for my work keep me writing.

Chapter 1

Jack
Age: 26
Location: Austin, Texas
Passport Country: USA
Names: Jonathan Thomas Smith

Quiet gentrified neighborhood and a cloud-covered sky at two in the morning, a perfect mix for breaking and entering. Would have been, anyway, if the house itself hadn't been lit up like an Omani oil field, every window eating shadows from the neighboring yards in the same way flare burn-off stole night from the deep desert dunes. So, he sat in his car three houses down, hidden in the dark beneath a thirty-foot live oak, watching the front door and debating the options, none of them good.

Bringing in a target was so much easier if it could be dead.

Or at least unconscious.

Especially *this* target.

Her cherry-red Tesla angled out from the curb ahead, obnoxious and sloppy, rear end jutting into the street. A hundred thousand dollars of machined luxury squandered on a vodka-downing, pill-popping, cocaine-snorting, foulmouthed waste of talent who was no closer to a degree now than she'd been at twenty-three, because finishing meant the party would end. God forbid.

Shadows passed behind curtains in the lit-up house.

Hints of *thump, thump* bass bled into the street, just low enough that sleep-deprived citizens wouldn't be inclined to call the cops.

He drummed his fingers in a slow pattern against the steering wheel.

Limited possibilities played to their final ends.

Timing forced him to choose between the hard way and the harder way.

Jacking her car first would be the hard way.

He stepped into early fall air, listened to the city dark, and nudged his door closed.

The neighborhood and the neighborhood dogs ignored him.

He walked to her car, dragged his fingers from tail to nose along the cherry-red curves, and patted the sleek rooftop. The Tesla was how he'd found his party-girl needle so quickly in a haystack of millions — more precisely, a little tracking device stuck up inside its wheel well, which probably, legally, made him a stalker.

He touched the driver's door handle.

The machine opened for the stolen key fob tucked inside his pocket. He popped the hood and trunk, ran a flashlight over empty cargo areas, then let himself in behind the wheel and passed the beam along showroom-clean carpets and spotless leather.

Eight months in and she still hadn't left a pen cap, a scrap of paper, or a whiff of fast food to mar the interior. The OCD-level tidiness made him uneasy in the same way not knowing how she'd paid for the car made him uneasy.

He'd asked her about the money.

She'd brushed him off with typical snide contempt.

He'd let that slide the first time. The second, he'd accused her of working favors, and she, in turn, had told him to go fuck his high horse. But he knew, and she knew that he knew, there was no other way to bring in Tesla-sized money the way working favors did. He should have cared about that, but he didn't, not really.

What made him mad was that she played

him for a fool, trying to bend his mind around her little games the way she did to everyone else. As if he didn't know.

He tossed the flashlight aside.

The practical half of him didn't want this job tonight.

The vindictive half really sorta did.

He peeled the boosted car into the street and out of the neighborhood.

Behind him the shadows against the curtains in the *thump-thump* house were none the wiser. Behind him, the house flared on.

He left the Tesla at the Walmart Supercenter on Anderson and made the time-depleting two-mile return on foot, back to the quiet neighborhood where the target house still lit the street, back to the live-oak shadows and his car, where he pulled the tool bag from the trunk, dropped it onto the rear seat beside the license plates, dug into the bag, hefted a pair of cuffs, and debated. What he really needed was the tranquilizer, but bringing her in unconscious had the potential to turn things to shit real fast.

He zipped the bag closed.

Quiet gentrified neighborhood and a cloud-covered sky at three in the morning, not ideal for a raucous kidnapping but would have to do.

He crawled his wheels forward to where the Tesla had been, left the trunk open and engine running, and headed for the narrow porch, counting steps and counting seconds, amped on excitement and dread.

Three guys lived here, college students at UT Austin. Quick and dirty background checks had given him the basics.

He hadn't looked for more, because more didn't matter — it wasn't the guys he worried about.

In his head the strategy wheel spun.

The front door coursed with beat, drowning any possibility of catching nuance from the other side. He tested the lock. The handle moved freely, sparing him the issue of breaking in or bluffing his way to the other side.

He slipped into the foyer, eyes scanning for movement, ears struggling to hear beyond the bass line, fingers wedging cardboard against the frame to keep the door from closing. He twisted the handle's thumb lock.

Noise trying hard to pass as avant-garde music covered his footfalls.

Three steps took him past a wall segment and into a living room decorated in late bachelor not-give-a-shit. The strategy wheel stopped on *unexpected element of surprise.*

On the couch to his right, what had been gray shadow against the shades became living bottle-blond color. His target, shirtless, straddled and played lip tango with a half-naked Lothario whose hands wandered in places they didn't belong.

She never heard him. Her guy friend never saw him.

He reacted to the gift without thinking, moving fast, because speed was the only way to maintain the upper hand, leaned in behind her, slapped a cuff on the nearest wrist, grabbed the other, yanked both hands behind her back, and locked her in.

One second.

She rotated to free the leg pinned between body and couch cushion and registered his presence in a long, slow blink. She was high. Dulled reflexes would save him.

Two seconds.

She rose to strike out.

He got an arm around her waist.

Three.

He pulled her off her lover; snatched her shirt, purse, and shoes from off the floor; and hefted her, ass in the air, over his shoulder, his arm around her thighs.

Voice and movement and confusion followed in a jumbled sequence: Lothario scrambling off the couch. Lothario yelling, "Hey, asshole!"

Five seconds.

The weight on his shoulder pitched from side to side. His free hand grasped the cuffs, held on to that handle for life, and he swung for the door.

Six.

Lothario lunged after them.

The blonde bucked and twisted and hissed, "Put me the fuck *down!*"

He made it to the entry and the cardboard wedge and over the threshold before Lothario reached him. He snagged the front door, pulled it shut, and kept on moving.

Behind him the locked handle rattled, and Lothario, slowed by the unexpected, gifted him seconds.

He hustled down the sidewalk like a laden drunk, focus narrowed into tunnel vision with the open trunk at the end, counting, counting, counting, only vaguely conscious of anything beyond the rocking weight that crushed him.

Eleven seconds.

He reached the car, dumped her shoulders first into the trunk together with shoes and shirt, and slammed the lid before she could straight-arm block him from shutting it.

The door to the house opened.

Lothario stood on the steps, shotgun in hand.

Jack pointed a finger at him. "This isn't what you think."

A high-pitched Hollywood scream pealed out from the trunk.

Lothario pumped the gun.

Jack dumped himself into the driver's seat, tossed the purse aside, threw the car into reverse, hit the gas, and tore backward toward the nearest corner.

Lothario, in the middle of the road, cut a swarthy, shrinking, headlight-blinded figure.

At the nearest intersection, Jack swung the car around, pointed the nose in the right direction, and drove, jaw clenched, at just over the chest crushingly slow speed limit. The screaming in the trunk turned into swearing.

The swearing turned to threats.

And the threats turned to an attack on the interior of the trunk.

He focused on the road.

The taillights had been reinforced long ago to keep her from kicking them out, and he'd rewired the trunk release for the same reason. Not that he'd known this day would come, but like swiping her spare key fob shortly after she'd bought the car, he'd always been the type to plan ahead.

He turned the radio on and thumbed the volume to max.

Yelling from the back rose louder than the music, every word punctuated by a punch and kick. "You're dead, John. Dead, dead, dead. I will destroy you. *Dead!*"

He checked mirrors and switched lanes.

Death and destruction were serious considerations. The more immediate concern was getting across the city without drawing unwanted attention.

The assault against the back picked up tempo.

The car rocked with each hit.

He had the package. Delivering it would be a whole different matter. The streets weren't nearly as empty as they'd need to be to keep this up the whole way. He lowered the radio volume and yelled toward the rear. "Shut up for a minute. I'm letting you out. I just need to find a place."

She punched the backseat and kicked the trunk lid and howled.

The mental strategy wheel flung round and round, scanning through options while he crawled along at forty miles an hour.

He passed a strip mall.

The mental pointer seized up and flung right.

He'd hoped to get a little farther into

nowhere before uncaging the tiger, but this was as good a place as any. He swung hard into the alley behind the dark storefronts, bumping over speed cushions and into potholes, squeezing between dumpsters and a brick retaining wall that separated commercial from residential.

If death and destruction were in the cards tonight, he wasn't going easy.

Left hand on the wheel, right hand beneath the seat, he released a Baby Eagle, pulled tight into an open space, yanked the emergency brake, and was out and moving before the chassis fully settled.

CHAPTER 2

Jack
Age: 26
Location: Austin, Texas
Passport Country: USA
Names: Jonathan Thomas Smith

He stood six feet off the tail, weapon trained on the car, and popped the trunk remotely. The lid shot open. She followed it up, eyes locked onto his, and slipped to the ground with the grace of a jungle cat leaving a tree.

She was out of the handcuffs, which he'd expected, and still naked from the waist up, which he hadn't. She faced him with a crowbar pulled from beneath the floorboards, and the only thing keeping her from taking a whack at him was the 9mm he pointed in her direction.

She hefted the bar from hand to hand and inched closer.

"You crossed a line tonight," she said. "This wasn't funny."

17

"Wasn't meant to be funny. Had to be done."

"Sure it did. Where's my car?"

"Walmart on Anderson."

Her lips curled. She growled and swung hard.

He dodged. The swipe cut close to his chest.

He added another foot of space between them.

"Asshole," she said.

"Whore."

She puckered her lips in a sarcastic pout. "Oh, that hurts, coming from a twenty-six-year-old virgin."

"The stuff you don't know."

She crab stepped to his left, looking for an opening.

He tracked her with the gun.

"Where's my purse?"

"I have it."

"Give."

He nodded toward the front seat.

She took another step toward him.

He said, "Not any closer."

"Or what? You're going to shoot me?"

"If I have to."

She snorted and, with full dramatic flair, raised the crowbar and tossed it at his feet. He tap-danced right to avoid getting hit.

"Keep the purse," she said. "Suits you and your missing pair of balls better than it ever did me." She reached into the trunk for her shirt and shoes and pulled the shirt over her head. "Don't think this is over," she said. "Not even for a minute."

She turned and, barefoot, started walking, package and prize slipping away.

He raised his voice to match the growing distance. "We need to talk."

Her free hand waved him off with a middle finger.

He needed her in the car. Chasing her down wasn't an option unless he was willing to lose teeth or body parts, which he wasn't. The tranquilizer was still a no go. And continuing on without her was definitely out of the question.

He eyed the semiautomatic in his hand: tempting, but also no.

All he had was the truth, and truth had only ever been fuzzy at best.

"Clare called," he said. "She wants to see you."

Jill stopped.

He counted thirteen seconds before she rotated around.

She stood in the alley, twenty feet down, one hand on her hip, shoes dangling from the other, perfectly frozen while her electric-socket hair caught stray wisps of light.

Jack opened the passenger door and moved aside to make space.

Wordless, she stalked back, staring — glaring — the whole way, until she stood uncomfortably close between him and the car. She said, "What's she want?"

"Don't know."

"What *do* you know?"

He nodded toward her purse on the passenger seat and, wary of every twitch and sigh, never truly able to predict which way she'd flip, said, "Only that I had to get you, and get you to her before three."

She lifted her wrist, fake glanced at a non-existent watch, and let out a sarcastic gasp. "Well, look at that. It's after three." The glare returned. "You fucked that right up, didn't you?"

"Had plenty of help. I'll be sure to share the credit."

Jill tossed her shoes into the front. "What a good son you are."

"You know I didn't ask for this."

"Didn't turn it down, though, did you?"

He sighed. "Please don't make it worse than it already is."

She said, "Just a poor innocent bystander, clean hands, clean conscience."

He didn't respond.

She notched her voice into mockery. "I had nothing to do with it," she said. "I swear. I was just doing what I was told, because I don't have the *stones* to tell Clare to fuck off and get someone else to do her dirty work."

He nodded toward her purse again. "Please?"

Her shoulders sagged, her body deflated. She turned for the seat and in that moment of forfeit punched an elbow back hard up into his face.

He shifted out of instinct, but a fractured second too late.

The thrust missed his nose and crunched into his orbital bone.

White pain and fire seared into his head.

She grabbed his wrist and chopped down on him. The Baby Eagle skittered from his hand. She fisted his hair, kneed his groin, hit a jockstrap, and never paused, twisting and jabbing again before he had time to counter. Excruciating, brain-numbing agony ran up his arm, into his shoulder, and brought him to his knees.

He swiped her ankles, pulling her off her feet.

She tumbled onto him, and they rolled in the narrow alley, he struggling to use his weight and height against her, she too

21

nimble, skilled, and aggressive to allow him the upper hand. He scrambled for the weapon.

She climbed on top of him and got to it faster.

Her hands shook for the same reason his lungs screamed.

She pushed the barrel into his chest.

He let go of her neck and froze, caught within the trap of unpredictability.

She might not kill him, but he didn't put it past her to put a few holes in him.

"Clare wants to see us *both*," he said. "Not just you."

Jill kneed into him, using his stomach for leverage to get to her feet and, for the second time, knocked the wind out of him. She stood over him, thighs scraped bloody, skimpy clothes torn, and lined the sights between his eyes.

He put his palms out in surrender.

Seconds of indecision ticked out long and broken.

"Bang," she said finally. "I win."

The air went out of him in a long exhale.

She said, "But this still isn't over."

She released the magazine, racked the slide, and caught the round. She dropped the bullet on his chest, tossed the weapon pieces onto the backseat and, without another word or even a glance, slipped into the car and slammed the door, leaving him on the pavement, staring into light pollution, alone.

Silence descended, silence and thirst and throbbing pain.

He knocked his head against the asphalt and swore between clenched teeth.

Swore at that damn phone call and its monotone demand. Swore at Clare's inability to value anyone's interests but her own, at her paranoia and delusion, at her insistence they get there immediately, even though she knew full well what short notice would cost him. He swore at his inability to say no.

Jill opened the window, rested her chin on the frame, and looked down. "You look like shit," she said. "We're late. Get in the car."

Jack dragged himself up and dusted off his jeans.

He paused and smiled at her for no other reason than to unnerve her, then retrieved the vehicle plates from the backseat, secured them in place, limped for the front and, wincing, slipped in behind the wheel.

The clock on the dash said 3:18 a.m.

They still had more than an hour of driving.

He smiled again, this time for real.

They were late, and there'd be consequences for being late, and his shoulder was
torn to hell, and he'd gotten his ass beat,
but, God, that had all been worth every bit
of being able to throw her in the trunk.

He took the car from alley to street.

Jill, beside him, sat sullen and quiet.

In the silence and adrenaline dump, the
road noise turned hypnotic, guiding them
toward MoPac, where they could pick up
speed on the usually traffic-clogged expressway, which this late at night might actually
be an expressway.

Ten minutes in, Jill ruined the trance.

Arms crossed, face toward the window,
she said, "I happened to really like that guy."

Jack kept his focus on the road. "Two
weeks," he said. "Two weeks tops before you
ghosted and turned him into another casualty."

"He was different."

"Sure he was. They always are."

"I had a solid thing going, John. Then you
come barging in like a violent ex-boyfriend
and fuck it all up."

Jack reached for the entertainment system
and drowned her out with Bach.

He had no regrets.

Pulling her off lover boy, hauling her out
of that house, it'd been the biggest possible

favor he could have done for the guy — that he could have done for any guy.

Jill leaned toward the dash and shut off the music.

He glared and turned it on again.

She turned it off and placed her hand on top of his, preventing another yin-yang go-around. Tone soft, tender, she said, "John, come on, be serious for a minute."

He caught her in his corner vision.

The jungle cat had morphed to mewling kitten, all big, brown, innocent eyes and soft, purring edges, the same manipulative act that suckered one boy toy after the next along her trail of broken hearts. Made him want to throw her out of the car.

He swung hard to the shoulder and slammed the brakes.

The seat belts grabbed, and her head whiplashed into the headrest.

She brushed hair out of her face. "What the fuck was that for?"

"How about *you* be serious?" he said. He twisted toward her. "Straight up, if I'd walked in and asked all nicey-nicey, you'd have come?"

She didn't answer.

"Exactly," he said. "Therefore, conversation over." He leaned back, checked over his shoulder, nudged the gas, and pulled onto the road.

She said, "You could've called or texted like a normal person."

"Right. And you would have detangled from lover boy to answer."

"Maybe."

"Bullshit. Three hours driving from Dallas, and I still gotta deal with Clare at the end of this, and you think picking a fight was my first choice? Don't flatter yourself. I tried calling all the way down and got nothing but voice mail."

She hiccuped for a beat, then reached for her purse and dug around for her phone. She tried to power it on, failed, and tossed the device back into her bag.

The unspoken thickened the air like dark water vapor.

Clare didn't own a phone, and Clare didn't make phone calls.

Not often, anyway.

Not unless it was urgent enough for a considerable trip to the nearest neighbors or town. But Clare *had* called and, unable to reach Jill directly, had sent Jack to do the fetching. Jill's right knee bounced and her thumbs picked at her cuticles.

Jack looked away.

Vulnerability on her was such an ugly thing, and the lines in their relationship so much cleaner when she was a bitch.

"There's a charger in the glove compartment," he said. "Use it. Odds are your boy's already dialed nine-one-one. We don't need the drama. Let him know you're okay."

Jill shoved the bag down by her feet. "I'll deal with it later."

"When?"

"Later."

"When later?"

"I fucking said I'd take care of it, okay?"

A bark of laughter gurgled in his throat.

That kind of offended promise from any other brazen flake would have been an insult to history and intelligence. From her, it was straight up button-pushing manipulation to grab control and hold him hostage.

Engaging would only feed the troll, and then she'd win.

He said, "Charge the phone."

She huffed and pulled the charger from the glove box, plugged the phone in, and shoved everything into her purse. Her knee bounced harder, and her fingers picked steadily at her nails. She said, "Makes no sense for Clare to go through all the effort of finding a way to call and then not tell you why."

"I gave up on trying to figure her out years ago."

"You're hiding something."

He'd told her what he knew, which was all of nothing, but if she wanted to believe otherwise, he wouldn't squander that opportunity. He said, "You should've kept your phone charged."

She turned for the window and watched lights and shadowed shapes go by. She said, "Tonight. I don't get it. The Tesla was clean. I got rid of the tracker."

"Put a new one in last time you took it in for servicing."

"Lies, John. I was there the whole time."

"Correction. You were there ninety-nine-point-nine percent of the whole time."

She turned toward him, eyes dark and angry, and it was hard to know if that was because he'd managed to stay a step ahead of her, which was the same as winning, which made her the loser, or if she was mad that he'd been tracking her movements.

"Don't get ass hurt and hypocritical," he said. "I know you have my car wired."

CHAPTER 3

Jack
Age: 26
Location: Near Blanco, Texas
Passport Country: USA
Names: Jonathan Thomas Smith

They pulled off the dark county road about sixty miles northwest of San Antonio as the crow flew and rolled to the edge of Clare's property at half past four. An unmarked turnoff nearly indistinguishable from the landscape led into 530 Texas Hill Country acres owned by a Belizean subsidiary of a Panamanian company established by a Swiss law firm in Liechtenstein on behalf of unnamed clients.

Complexity soothed Clare's need for anonymity.

Jack followed the dirt and gravel track at a bumpy crawl, guided entirely by starlight and headlights through untamed woodland, past rusted cattle gates and multiple NO

TRESPASSING signs, around potholed bends, and through thickening brush until a reflective gnome's face lit up at the base of a bur oak.

Those who belonged here knew what the gnome meant. Anyone else barreling up the dead-end private road ran a fifty-fifty chance of getting their tires blown out — or worse — depending on Clare's mood and how well she could see the intruder coming.

Jack slowed to a stop at the tree and flashed his high beams.

Mirrors dangling beside the gnome served the same purpose for daylight hours.

Time ticked on with no response.

He flashed the lights again.

Jill said, "Maybe she's sleeping," which was a stupid thing to say. Clare had triggers all across her booby-trapped land, ensuring there'd be no sneaking up on her, not by ground and not by air. They both knew she'd been alerted to their presence from the instant they crossed the property line.

Another minute passed.

In the far distance, a flashlight beam swung left and right.

Jill said, "That was weird."

Jack searched through the dark to where the light had been, hunting for a plausible explanation for the change in routine.

Instinct told him to abort.

Without a way to contact Clare they had no choice but forward. Better, then, to abandon the car and opt for stealth on foot.

He reached for the key to kill the ignition.

Jill looked at him and laughed.

His hand stopped, suspended between choices.

Her laughter turned manic, desperate, and painful.

She tipped her face toward the roof and between breaths said, "Late-night phone call. Urgent demand. No explanation. This is goddamn testing all over again."

He winced, unsure of which was worse: that even after so many years of knowing better, a small change in pattern had been enough to throw him right back into Clare's paranoid-level thinking, or that Jill was probably right.

She pressed palms to her head. Through clenched teeth, she yelled, "Motherfucking hell, when is she going to stop?"

He shook his head, as much in answer to his own questions as to hers.

Probably never.

There'd been a time when he believed Clare's decision to settle meant she'd finally let go of conspiracies and imagined threats — that her reality might normalize, if even

31

a little — but no. Nine years later, and the only difference was she now stayed safe from the figments chasing her by entrenching instead of uprooting every few months and running her kids from place to place across the globe.

Same tinfoil, different hat.

Jack flicked the beams and nudged the gas.

Adrenaline dripped into his system, tingling beneath his skin.

If this was Clare returning to the old ways, anything was possible.

Jill crossed her arms and kicked the dashboard.

He said, "My car isn't the one screwing with your head."

"There's no point to this," she said. "Just turn around."

He slowed and glanced at her. "You want out?"

She howled through gritted teeth and kicked the dash again. Which meant yes, she desperately wanted out, but she couldn't say no to Clare any better than he could. He would have raged right along with her if it'd have made any difference. Nothing made a difference.

No matter how long they stayed away, Clare summoned, and they were both thirteen again, two kids trying to make sense of the world, two kids feeling the agony of abandonment each time she left to chase another pipe dream or bogeyman, two kids craving hard-earned approval and affection and remaining all too familiar with the pain of rejection that followed each failure in meeting her exacting standards. She'd claimed it was all for their own good, claimed it was because she loved them and one day they'd understand that everything was meant to keep them alive. He'd long since learned to write off anything that came out of her mouth as bullshit, but by then the damage had been done. And here they were again.

The road wound up and around, stretching the distance between the glow-in-the-dark gnome and the point where the Earthship, half buried into the hillside, first came into view.

Earthship.

He still couldn't say the word without conjuring mental images of UFO sightings, crystals, and aura readings.

The house was anything but.

To those who knew, *Earthship* described a self-contained home that captured its own water, generated its own power, and processed its own waste. Its outer walls, constructed of sand-filled tires, created a heat

33

sink that kept the interior a steady year-round seventy degrees, no matter how hot or cold outside, and a greenhouse built into the design provided a year-round food source. But to Clare, *Earthship* meant a comfortable way to stay off the grid indefinitely while being surrounded by two feet of bullet-stopping power.

Bio-sustainable genius deserved so much better.

Wide south-facing windows came into view on the distant hill, glass eyes filled with clouded moonlight holding court above a long stretch of wild brush and thirsty trees. The road itself had another set of curves before it straightened for the front door, which allowed Clare plenty of time to sight in on any target dumb enough to approach by way of the easy route.

Jill spotted the glint and groaned.

Jack's stomach clenched in the same way Pavlov's dogs had salivated.

The injuries, the scars, the competition, the hair-trigger reactions came rushing back, all the times they'd come close to dying and the times they'd killed, the hardcore training, the psych-outs, and the blindsiding tests in a childhood spent on edge, never knowing what Clare would throw at them or when.

Jill said, "Right when I think I can forgive her and accept her for who she is, she pulls another stunt like this. . . ."

Her words hung in the air, suspended by a blinding flash that lit the hillside.

In the butterfly blink it took to process the light, the Earthship's windows vanished in a fireball.

Reflex took over, all those years wrapped into a single breath.

Jack pulled the emergency brake.

The shock wave rocked the car.

Anxiety drained away like water through a plug. He rolled out the door and crawled for the backseat, where he'd stashed the tool bag. Sand and tires and burning wood rained down off the hill, crashing onto the road and into the brush, sparking mini fires.

He reached the back door, yanked it open, and stared straight through to the outline of Jill's torso — Jill, reaching in to take what belonged to him.

He lunged for the tool bag.

She seized the strap and, riverbank predator snatching prey from the water's edge, dragged the whole thing after her.

Voices, indecipherable voices, carried low on the wind from the direction of the explosion. Priorities refocused.

Jack grabbed the handgun and magazine

from where Jill had tossed them, snapped the ammunition into place. On the other side of the car, Jill knelt, knife in hand — his knife — slicing fabric off the seat that had cushioned her seconds earlier, and his bag lay open, disgorging its contents on the ground beside her.

He wanted to punch her in her stupid face.

Not because she destroyed his car, but because, without any guidance from him, she knew exactly where to cut to access his stash and, without tools of her own, she'd stolen his to do the cutting.

Footfalls on the gravel — boots in the distance — headed in their direction.

Jill pulled rifle pieces from their foam-encasements.

He hissed at her. "Hey, jackass!"

She paused long enough to toss the knife his way.

He snatched the blade.

His fingers worked fast, fueled by repetition and training, freeing metal from the backseat cushions, assembling the pieces, twisting, inserting, snapping with the ferocity of muscle memory drilled into him year after year after year.

Jill, rifle in one hand, purse in the other, scurried off the road.

A fusillade of bullets responded to the

movement, hitting the car, blowing out the windshield, then tires. Muzzle flashes placed the weapons in the thicket between Earthship and vehicle.

Jack scrambled to the other side of the car for the tool bag. He stuffed the strewn contents in, swearing with each lost and wasted second.

Staccato gunfire, louder voices, boot steps closed in.

Jill's distraught laughter rang in his head.

This is goddamn testing all over again.

Mind working faster than his limbs, he replayed the nuance in every word of Clare's brief call and every action of the night. Thoughts and strategy seized up in a tangle of possibilities so convoluted that he could only make sense of them as two mutually exclusive extremes bolting in opposite directions: either Clare had blown her own house up or someone else had.

Every tangent turned hard corners from there, and both roads led into hell.

He zipped the bag, hefted it over his shoulder, and hurried into the rough.

A high-caliber barrage shredded through the car and tracked him in the dark.

He switchbacked and hairpinned, leaping low hanging branches, dodging tree to tree, and still the bullets kept coming, whining past his head and spitting wood and dirt around him. Wild countryside under a clouded sky at nearly five in the morning should have been perfect for evading marauders.

Whoever the hell was out there had thermal imaging.

He gained on Jill, a shadowed blur under a covered moon.

Sequins or sparkles, or whatever those things were on what was left of her shirt, caught and reflected the occasional glint of skylight. He followed as she slunk between trees, heading south to where the terrain sloped up and rocks along the bend created a natural ridge that provided cover where they could hide and return fire.

They'd been there a dozen times over the years.

There were similar strategic blinds across the property, along with Clare's traps, and hidey-holes, and emergency stashes of food, water, and ammunition.

He and Jill had sweat and bled and fought from every one.

Possibilities and their divergent paths flashed warnings in his brain.

Either Clare had blown her home up or someone else had.

Nothing on this property would do them

any good if tonight belonged to Clare.
But the alternative was that much worse.

CHAPTER 4

Jill
Age: 26
Location: Near Blanco, Texas
Passport Country: USA
Names: Julia Jane Smith

Rifle to her shoulder, she swung the sights left in a slow grid, scanning the dark, trying to separate shadow from shadow, hoping for betrayal in a gleam or movement or snatch of reflected light. She got nothing but darkness — darkness, and the dry stench of dust and burned rubber and the final wishes of smoldering fires that had never fully caught — darkness, and the sound of jackboots crunching gravel toward the car.

She'd counted three of them, all heavier, bulkier, and slower than Clare.

The same Clare who, through Jack, had ripped her away from a perfect evening. The Clare who, for reasons no one but the voices in her head would understand, had dragged her into another training session.

Clare — *that* Clare — had hired goons for this hit.

Least she could have done was show up for her own damn live-fire war game.

Jill notched the rifle down and reversed right.

If the boots were smart, and she hoped they were, they'd push her and Jack hard and keep them running while the dark held them disadvantaged and vulnerable.

Another hour or so and dawn would arrive as the great equalizer. There'd be no challenge in daylight.

Her finger scratched the trigger guard.

Jack slid in beside her. "Anything?" he said.

"Three," she said. "You?"

He sat on the ground, back against the stone, and said, "Same."

She repositioned the rifle barrel into the jagged gap between the rocks, exposing her heat signature where the foliage was thick enough to distort what would have been an instant target into something that warranted coming in for a second look. She said, "You spot Clare?"

He thumped his tool bag down between his knees. "Nope."

"The mercs might be distraction," she said. "Keep us focused in one direction while she pops us from another."

He unzipped the bag and dug through it. "Could be."

His tone held the same irritation she felt, and probably for the same reason, but clipped sentences meant he was angry and the only way she'd get whatever else was in his head was if she apologized for taking his stuff and then asked nicely.

That wasn't going to happen.

She returned to the sights and scanning the darkness all the while her purse, just out of reach, sung to her with sweet, distracting temptation.

She brushed her lips against her hand, caressing the chewed-up webbing between thumb and forefinger, memento to battery acid and permanent reminder of the first time panicked on-her-feet thinking hadn't gone according to plan. She'd been eight freaking years old, trapped alone in the dark and chased by monsters before she'd even had a chance to unpack her bags.

That had been Clare a lifetime ago, on their first night in Sofia, Bulgaria.

And that had been Clare everywhere else, before and after.

Here they were again, same monkey, different circus.

The purse and its contents sang louder and sweeter.

Jill glanced at Jack, then back at the night.

A little fortification would go a long way toward making this wack episode tolerable: a quick hit, a special something-something to speed the time and get this over with so she could take the experience, throw it in a sack, toss it off a bridge, and drown it to death, same as she did to every other PTSD memory tied to Clare.

Her fingers stretched toward that relief.

Beside her, Jack pulled a vacuum-sealed pack from his bag, tore it open, and shoved a T-shirt at her.

Reverie interrupted, she batted him away.

"Reflections," he said. "You're a liability."

She glanced at her top, slid down beside him, traded him rifle for cloth, and shrugged into the shirt. What she really needed was shoes. The strappy pieces of shit looped around her ankles wouldn't get her a whole lot farther. He knew that. And he also knew she knew his Barefoots were still flattened down in their own space-saving pack at the bottom of the bag.

She motioned for them.

He plopped a pair of rubber-soled socks into her outstretched hand.

"Seriously?" she said. "I could have taken the shoes when I had your stuff."

"You should have," he said. "Now you can get them from your own damn bag."

She gripped the socks.

She hadn't carried a tool bag in years — hated that she'd ever had to carry one, hated everything the bags represented — and even though having gear on hand had saved their asses down by the car, she hated the sting of betrayal that came from knowing Jack still hauled his around like he was Clare's little bitch.

Her *own damn bag* was, like, seventy-five miles north, stuffed somewhere in the back of her closet — probably didn't even have shoes — and the only reason she knew where to find the damn thing was because Clare had insisted they update burner phones a few months back and had made her trade the old one for new. Now *that* shoulda been a big fat clue that there'd soon be stink in the air.

Jill shoved the socks on over her sandals.

Jack put a finger on her arm and stilled her.

He said, "Where are the dogs?"

She cocked her head to listen.

The only sounds rising above the night were those from the road.

The silence was wrong.

Clare had a pack of Kangals and Anatolians that ranged the property, 130-plus-pound, fiercely protective guardians with keen hearing, thirty-five-mile-an-hour speed, and booming vocals that kept Clare and her menagerie of animals safe from coyotes, cougars, bobcats and, of course, human predators. Even if she'd put the dogs up to prevent them from getting shot, they'd have gone nuts from the gunfire. They should have heard them.

Jill returned to position against the rock's natural divot, returned to scanning the grid.

Jack reloaded his bag and strapped up.

The quiet lagged on, and quiet was the worst. Once the shit started flying, things got easy. Waiting for the unexpected, knowing it would eventually come — that was what messed with your head.

To the night, she whispered, "Come out, come out. . . ."

A branch snapped below the ridgeline.

Not Clare. Clare would never be that pathetically stupid.

Jill rolled away from the gap and dragged the rifle back with her. Jack tapped his arm and motioned past ten feet of open space to the series of outcroppings that marked where the downhill slope began.

Jill gripped the rifle and grabbed the purse. She knew the drill. They needed to know where the enemy was, and needed to know what skill level they were up against.

They'd been there, done that often enough that explanation wasn't necessary.

She counted, took a breath, and bolted into the open as live bait.

The night reacted with a quick burst of automatic fire.

Trigger-happy gunmen didn't speak highly of Clare's choice in hirelings.

She scrambled and rolled.

The bullets followed, chunking into stone.

She crab crawled toward the end of the outcrop, where she could take a shot of her own and the night went quiet.

No dogs. No sounds from the brush. No gunfire.

She held position, waiting for muzzle flashes, and received only darkness while the boots, silent and invisible, advanced.

She had no patience for the dragged out cat-and-mouse shit.

She yelled, "Hey, short-dick monkey-ass scratchers, over here!"

Darkness. Silence. Nothing.

She stood, torso above the rock for the briefest second to add a flash of light for their head mounts, and ducked again. Loud and singsongy, she said, "Hope she's paying you pussies good, 'cause tonight you're gonna get pounded!" An angry burst replied from the left, an ego-filled grave marker.

Jack's rifle answered with steady, controlled reports, once, twice.

The muzzle flashes went dark, stayed dark.

Grunts from the cannon fodder said he'd hit *something*.

Jack set the rifle aside, struck a match, lit a fuse, and pushed a Tasmanian Devil into the open. The firework sparkled and shrieked and exploded in multiple heat flashes, flooding the immediate area with colored light that would feel like a migraine in a mosh pit to anyone using thermal imaging to search for them.

He scurried from his blind across the open distance between them and pushed her on back into the open again toward a boulder in the near distance.

They had the high ground. They'd tagged enemy location. And the boots, wary of another heat flare, would move a little more cautiously now, and that bought them time.

This was kids' stuff.

There had to be some new trick from Clare still coming.

She followed Jack down the natural curve, using fortification in the hill's flow to stay out of sight, flitting from outcropping to tree to crag, guided by moonlight and memories — far too many memories — in a race around the bend to the bottom.

The hill evened out into a tree-filled dip that marked the north turn toward the nearest of Clare's buried hides. Jack cut sideways for a hunting track that ran west.

Not the opposite direction, but definitely out of the way.

Jill caught up and nudged him north.

He touched her wrist, letting her know the redirection was deliberate, and he pushed forward at an unfair pace that left her sock- and sandal-clad feet at the mercy of the elements and her bare legs and arms torn by every branch that cared to snag her.

She kept up without a word or whimper.

To complain or ask him to slow would be the same as admitting he'd won, and she'd never give him the satisfaction.

He plowed on for another ten minutes and then stopped, turned in a small circle, and scrambled off trail into the brush, heading more or less toward the creek, where water only flowed during the rains. He zigzagged, pacing like a treasure hunter running a metal detector over the sand — a treasure hunter who'd lost his goddamn mind — and she was losing patience — and they were losing time.

Jack dropped to his knees and crawled into a thicket.

She waited, confused.

He hissed at her, and so she went in after him, musty earth pressing against her hands, decaying foliage fresh in her lungs.

Leaves and branches grabbed her hair. Bugs flew into her mouth and nose.

Jack found whatever he was looking for.

He pulled hard and shoved up.

"Go, go," he whispered.

She reached him and scooted past for a rectangle in the ground.

It was small, like a coffin for two.

Tandem burial.

This wasn't Clare's. This wasn't marked on any map.

She hesitated. Jack pushed her, and she tumbled in. He tossed his tool bag down past her feet, fell in beside her with his rifle, and pulled the lid down over them.

The already dark went pitch black.

The quiet went deafly silent.

Ragged breathing filled the space.

They were two phlegmatic monsters in the closet.

Time passed. Her heart rate slowed, and her senses acknowledged what they'd been too busy to recognize before: the coffin, this thing they were in, smelled of moldy wood that had been left in the dirt for years, yet a fresh breeze brushed across her face.

She twisted a hand over her shoulder, found the outline of a screened vent, traced upward, bumped into foil-lined fiberglass twelve inches above her nose, and it dawned on her then what this was. The airflow vents weren't just for oxygen, but also to dissipate their heat signatures, making them virtually invisible to the outside.

In times like these, twins or not, she truly hated her brother.

Jack had built this hide on Clare's land without Clare knowing and had put it here God only knew how long ago and for what reason.

She'd never ask him to explain.

Nothing he said would clarify in a way that made sense, because this was Jack, and this was what he did, what he'd always done: he planned for the inevitable, and he planned for the absurd. He was worse than Clare. Sure, she'd started him on this path, but he'd taken psycho contingency planning to a whole other level on his own.

Jill elbowed him in the ribs, a cheap shot, because no matter how badly Mr. Responsible wanted to return the favor, she was crazy enough to escalate, and he wouldn't risk an attention-drawing fight.

She jabbed him again, because she could.

He ignored her, and time began its slow, slow march toward dawn.

Her left hand loosened its grip on her purse.

The temptation was still there, just as sweet, maybe a little stronger.

Her fingers twitched, and her insides craved.

She wanted the benzos now, something to put her out so she didn't have to smell these smells and breathe this air or remember the many ways the past linked to the present. In her mind's eye, she unzipped the purse, found the Xanax bottle, popped the lid one-handed, and got that pill to her mouth. But in real life, she couldn't.

Not with Jack beside her.

He'd know. He already *knew*, but knowing and experiencing were different things, and she didn't want him to know in *that* way.

She didn't need his judgment.

That she cared what he thought made her hate him more.

Sound filtered in through the ventilation shafts.

Outside, somewhere close, the boots tromped through the brush. She could feel each step, dulled by insulation, and knew it was gut instinct and imagination filling in for lack of sight.

She and Jack were feet underground, buried alive under dirt and wild grasses.

They could die here and never be found.

Panic and claustrophobia might have risen had the scenario not already been so familiar. Different year, different country, but she'd been here before.

This was déjà vu.

CHAPTER 5

Jill
Age: 5
Location: Córdoba, Córdoba Province
Passport Country: Argentina
Names: Julieta Maria Suarez

Everything was dark, same as since Clare closed the lid, and soft and silky but smelly, like old, wet clothes. She and Jack could fit just so side by side, if they kept still and quiet. They had to stay here a long time. That's why they'd practiced so much, every day a little bit more in the wooden box beneath the house.

It was hard to keep from moving for so long, even with the practice.

Clare said the box was a coffin, and a coffin was where people went when they died, and that she should play pretend like she was dead.

Jill didn't know how to be dead, and she didn't want to ask Clare, and, anyway, she couldn't, because Clare left a long, long time ago.

Forever ago.

Jill was hungry now and thirsty, but she knew from practice that if she ate all the food and drank all the water, there'd be nothing left for later. Last time she'd cried from being hungry. Clare said it was her own fault for having poor self-control, that she deserved to be hungry, and if she didn't stop crying about it, she'd go hungry for a week to teach her to be stronger. Jill had made herself stop crying.

Now she knew how to wait and be hungry.

This time she'd wait until she couldn't stand it, maybe even another five whole minutes. She closed her eyes and pretended she was blind.

She opened her eyes.

It was the same kind of dark either way.

She thought about that, closed her eyes, and opened them again. She couldn't see anything. Maybe she was blind for real now. She didn't want to be blind. She held her breath so she wouldn't cry and wiggled closer to Jack.

If she was blind, then Jack would keep her safe and everything would be okay.

Jack's hand moved, and she saw the light on his wrist.

The light made it feel like there was more air to breathe and chased the tears away. She wasn't blind for real! She snuggled closer to her brother.

Clare had given them glow-in-the-dark watches to pass the time. The watches had a special mark, and when both hands went dark, it meant they should come out. If Clare hadn't come back yet, they'd have to push the lid open and crawl up to the house and carry the tool bags to the grocery store at the end of the street. Only that grocery store, because it had the special phone that could call all over the world, and they would call the number written in permanent marker on their thighs.

Jack patted her shoulder. Then the earth shook.

Jill grabbed on to him, and he grabbed on to her. They waited, and it shook again, and dust fell down onto their faces. Then came the sirens, lots of sirens, and soon enough there were people yelling, all of it far off and away, just loud enough that they could hear and knew that something bad had happened.

Jill's throat hurt. She couldn't swallow.

Maybe Clare was dead, and they were just saving this box for her.

She squeezed her eyelids tight and pretended to be blind again.

She would be blind for all her whole life if that meant Clare would come back.

CHAPTER 6

Jack

Age: 26
Location: Near Blanco, Texas
Passport Country: USA
Names: Jonathan Thomas Smith

Stale breath and body stink stifled the air, made worse by the way captivity slowed time to a crawl. Nights like these used to be a matter of course, he and Jill holed up in hiding or planning or biding time, entwined like twins in the womb, just as they'd been entwined before birth and entwined in subconscious memory and entwined throughout the years since. The regularity had toughened him, had made his mind stronger than anxiety, boredom, or the need to piss.

But that was then.

Rubbing shoulders with his sister now, breathing her breath, and sweating her sweat just rubbed him raw. He wanted out, wanted away from the squirming and spoiled-ass complaining, meant to ensure he stayed as miserable as she did.

Noise from the hunt outside had faded.

His watch said predawn had already begun its slow march into the sky.

Reason held him firm, told him the longer they waited, the better off they'd be. And that same reason burned him from the inside out.

The night had been wrong. All wrong.

Clare had nothing to gain by starting this crap again — even when viewed through the lens of her delusional worldview — not after last time, when trap and assault had turned their twenty-first birthday celebration into a war that ended with Jill putting a deliberate bullet in Clare's thigh and threatening to kill her in her sleep if she so much as considered coming at them uninvited again.

The aftermath had forced a cease-fire of sorts.

The surprise attacks stopped and the guilt-inducing demands to visit became fewer, providing an opportunity to break free from Clare's orbit and yet they returned, couldn't help but return, seeking out bloody, life-threatening competition across thousands of raw acres the way cubicle slaves pursued paintball and laser tag, because nothing else offered the adrenalized pressure release that hunting and hiding from another human predator provided.

A graduate degree in biochemistry hadn't done him any better than part-time student, full-time party girl had done for his sister — wasted time, money, and talent, all of it — because a kid who'd fired his first automatic weapon at the age of five, who'd teethed with his fists as an outsider in Jakarta's dirt slum streets, who'd learned to use wit and strategy for safety, and who'd grown up knowing better than to trust the one person he should have been able to rely on, could only ever play pretend in a world of safe spaces, trigger warnings, and microaggressions.

He'd never fit behind four walls or abide taking orders from fools, might stay stuck barely above broke freelancing in the gig economy because nothing else gave him the freedom he craved, might never find a way to turn a string of short-term relationships into something deeper than surface attraction, and might be forever consigned to having many acquaintances and no true friends, but, Clare be damned, even that was better than going back to the way things were before.

To break free of her now, he had to finish out the night, and the night kept bringing him back to the explosion. Either Clare had blown her own house up or someone else had, and he wasn't sure which was worse.

Thumping in the distance stopped the pendulum swing.

Jill's head ticked up. She whispered, "Helicopter."

Explosion.

Silent dogs.

Clare's absence.

Helicopter.

One more thing that didn't make sense.

He knocked the latch, shoved the lid aside, and like some monster rising from a swamp in a B-rated movie, crawled, bedraggled and dirty, from the earth.

Early morning underbrush light blinded him.

Jill shoved his bag out and clambered up.

He dragged sweet, clean early morning air into his lungs, and listened. The thump came in from the south.

It didn't take a genius to guess where it headed.

He grabbed his gear, slung the rifle strap over his back and, with his sister breathing down his neck, squirreled through the brush. He reached the trail, rose, and ran, winding through the trees, jumping fallen logs, and dodging branches, chasing the projected flight path.

The helicopter passed overhead.

He raced against time, too slow and too far away.

Inconsistencies wound round his head, pounding, pounding with each foot beat:

Explosion.

Silent dogs.

Clare's absence.

Helicopter.

The blades descended.

He ran faster, second-guessing the decision to wait in the hide as long as he had, hating Clare and the way she made him doubt his instinct and his senses, hating that even after all these years she still could.

His chest burned. His legs burned.

No amount of weekly endurance training could keep him fit the way Clare's daily onslaughts once had. He hated the weakness.

The blades went up again, this time heading east, and he slowed, heart pounding, lungs seizing, and he knew that no matter who had blown up Clare's house, the hope of a normal life had gone up with it and this thing, whatever it was, already had him.

CHAPTER 7

Holden

Age: 32
Location: Buttfuck Nowhere, Texas
Passport Country: Canada
Names: Troy Martin Holden

He stood at the clearing's upper edge, loaded stretcher at his feet, toothpick in his mouth, grinding disgust into splinters and watching the blemish in the sky grow larger.

They were thirty minutes past sunrise, four hours behind schedule, half his team was dead at the hands of a target he was required to keep alive as an explicit part of the contract, and somewhere out in the rough were two complications that had gone abracadabra, *poof,* into the night like vanishing magic.

He couldn't afford loose ends and didn't have time to crawl the godforsaken land chasing ghosts.

He flipped the toothpick and ground harder.

Ten years, five continents, innumerable contracts, and not once had he come close to a mess like this — not even in Buenaventura when he was young and wet and stupid, and *that* had been a disaster.

He spit out the splintered wood and dropped another toothpick into place.

The bounty, high as it was, wasn't damn near high enough to account for what he'd just walked into. She'd expected them, *had* to have known they were coming.

The helicopter *whomp* grew louder, and the blemish bigger.

The Bell 407 flared above the landing site.

Sand kicked up beneath the blades, gusting over shredded tires and the charred innards of a house that had disemboweled from the earth and turned hilltop into caldera. The explosion's timing gnawed at his insides the way his teeth made use of the pick. Another few feet closer and they'd have all been smears in the debris field.

The helicopter skids settled, and the rotor blades wound down, leaving the single pilot exposed behind the glass of his shiny cage.

Baxter, standing guard below, clomped toward the bird.

His face and biceps were red and raw with

burns, and his finger twitched near the trigger guard of the M16 cradled in dirt- and soot-smeared arms.

They were all a little twitchy now.

The transport's arrival should have signaled a plan gone right, should have meant they could get the bounty on its way and haul ass back to civilization, but with half the team dead by ambush, they weren't taking chances.

The big guy reached the helicopter, pulled the cabin doors open, and peered inside. The pilot, none too happy, emptied out of the cockpit.

Baxter patted him down, disappeared into the cabin, and a minute later motioned him back in and waved an all clear. Holden tossed the toothpick into the dirt, reached for the stretcher and for the gagged and straitjacket-bound body it carried.

Honey-brown eyes, dark and soulless, met his.

Hair on his arms lifted in warning, just as it did every time he looked at her.

She was small, possibly old enough to be his mother, with the sinewy frame of a woman who'd never grown soft by city living and who might out-endure him on a trail while wearing a fifty-pound pack, but what made his hair stand on end, he'd realized, wasn't what he saw but what he didn't.

Her face held no defining features. She could have been any combination of races within a wide range of ages and staring into that void he knew that he observed a phantom, a shadow capable of slipping unnoticed between the world's social layers.

This was a creature who shouldn't have allowed herself to be taken alive but had, and he scanned the length of her body, searching past the mud and blood, wondering for the first time who she was and why he'd been sent to hunt her.

Irritation shoved curiosity aside.

He knelt and checked her bonds.

In a world where only the best survived, selective ignorance was life. He never knew — never cared to know — because knowing turned targets into humans, and humanization opened up weakness and invited mistakes.

He tugged the strap at her wrist.

Her gaze, electric with intensity, tracked him.

He recognized the look — the promise from one hell-bound soul to another — the kind of promise that had no expiration date and knew no borders, a promise one didn't take lightly, even when made from a position as helpless as hers.

He cinched the strap across her chest tighter as a precaution.

The corners of her bloodied lips twitched in laughter against the gag.

With that laughter, the night's inconsistencies rushed back to the fore — the ambush, the calls she'd made, the car arriving shortly after his team had, the timing of the explosion, the ghosts in the night — all tempting him for a blinding second to undo the muzzle and let her spit in his face if it meant extracting some iota of understanding. Instead, he moved to her legs and tightened those straps, too, then grabbed hold of the handles and stood.

Rafi, at the stretcher's feet, raised the bottom half.

Holden refused to acknowledge the man.

First mistake on this messed-up mission had been pulling Rafi onto the team for extra manpower at the last minute. Second mistake had been keeping him. Last night's bullet would have done better to find his head instead of his thigh.

Without Rafael Vega and his macho ego, their immediate concern would be ID'ing and disposing of two bodies instead of being forced to waste time and resources figuring out where they were, who they were, and why they were here.

Holden gripped tight and strode for the clearing just fast enough that Rafi and his gimp leg struggled to keep up. He shoved the stretcher headfirst into the belly of the bird and stepped aside. Baxter and Rafi clambered up. Holden hesitated at the doors, then shut them, pounded the panel, stepped back, gave the pilot the thumbs-up.

He watched as the blades rotated faster and the skids left the ground.

He had no words for this.

There should have been four heading up to guard delivery.

He should have been able to keep Baxter behind to tag team on tying off loose ends. Instead, he had one man and an idiot to accompany the transport, and he was left to exfiltrate alone and mop up a mess that split his focus between a phone call urging him toward Louisiana and building a trail to find the ghosts.

Holden hefted his pack and weapon, and slipped into the brush.

There wasn't a single reason events should have turned out as they had, not if the information he'd been handed was accurate.

If.

He'd never had reason before to question the data or its source.

Now questions burned with doubt, fevering in betrayal's possibility, and words that had been shouted in the dark played round inside his head.

Having fun yet . . . ? Hope she's paying you good. . . . Gonna get pounded. . . .

His thoughts twitched with paranoid suspicion the same way Baxter's finger had twitched at the trigger guard.

On a marionette stage, all were disposable save those who pulled the strings.

A fat branch on a bur oak became a hide from which he could watch what was left of the hill. He sighted in on where the house had stood, weighing the odds that the ghosts hadn't come on behalf of the target but rather because he was theirs, and that of all the loose ends left to be tied on this contract, he was the last.

Only one person had the power to send surrogates to kill him.

Holden pulled the phone from its zippered pocket. He powered on the device, opened the encrypted channel, and filled in the requisite update.

Acquisition successful. Bounty en route to drop. Contract fulfilled and payable.

He slipped the unmistakable accusation

68

between the lines.

Packet incomplete. Bounty alert to status and waiting in ambush. High likelihood associates at large. New contract required for further action.

He hit SEND, tucked the phone away, and returned to watching the hillside.

Time marched on.

Mosquitoes and biting gnats drew blood from his skin, and he ignored them.

The sun rose higher, and with its ascension came more heat, and with the heat, impatience and the acute awareness of passing opportunity.

The phone in his pocket vibrated. Debate chewed through him.

Noise, any noise, would carry far.

Balanced on the branch, phone pressed between ear and shoulder, Holden took the call without speaking.

A mechanical voice filled the silence. "You've never been one to whine," it said. "Shame, Christopher, that you'd start now."

Holden raised the rifle and peered through the scope. In a low whisper, he said, "I took a contract based on specific parameters and a risk-reward calculus."

The voice, derisive, if computerized

speech could be derisive, said, "Neither had I pegged you as a crybaby with a penchant for drama. This new you is surprising."

"Half my team is dead. Your so-called *isolated target with no known associates and no access to telecommunications* placed three calls prior to contact and had armed professionals on-site at the time of the hit. She was waiting for us."

There was a hiccup of silence, not even a full beat.

"You accepted a contract, Christopher, one that called for no witnesses and no trails. Complications are your problem, not ours."

Holden's brain crawled into reptile mode. "I want what you left missing from the bounty packet."

"For your sake, we'll pretend that insult was unintentional."

Holden chose his words carefully.

On this answer, the Broker would rise or fall.

"Bystanders and accidental witnesses are one thing," he said. "Tracking down a team of trained assassins is something else. Taking them out doesn't come free. Provide the missing information, tell me what I'm dealing with, and renegotiate, or I'm out."

"That was a lovely tantrum, child. Anything else?"

Holden didn't answer.

The Broker said, "Final payment releases when you report back clean. Rescind now and forfeit the balance. This discussion is over."

The connection went dead.

Holden gripped the phone.

His skin burned hot with betrayal, begging him to call Baxter, to reroute the drop and hold the bounty hostage until the Broker paid what was due.

Experience and cunning warned him off. Open confrontation would get every killer from here to Timbuktu hunting his ass.

The honey-brown eyes and their dark promise flashed inside his head.

He tucked the phone away as if the thing was toxic.

There were other ways, subtler ways.

He'd buy time and feign the appearance of ignorance by cleaning up this contract, he'd get paid, and then he'd create his own form of payback. But, for that, he'd need to know who this bounty had been and to whom she mattered.

Movement arrested his attention, a flash of unnatural color from across the clearing. His breathing slowed. Eye to the scope, he swung a slow scan, searching through the

71

crosshairs for what natural vision had brought, and stopped short on a male face between the trees, looking him dead on as casually as if he'd walked up and said hello.

Holden moved his finger past trigger guard for trigger, and in that nano-slice of time, the face vanished.

Adrenaline surged with the unexpected.

Holden tossed his gear to the ground and scrambled down after it.

He didn't get to where he was in life by showing up unprepared in a kill zone.

There were two of them out there, and he was position-compromised.

He had already been ambushed once today and wasn't about to let it happen twice.

CHAPTER 8

Jack

Age: 26
Location: Near Blanco, Texas
Passport Country: USA
Names: Jonathan Thomas Smith

He stalked the clearing's edge, winding between trees and through the brush, hunting for color, movement, anything that didn't belong while nature held its breath, suspending the woodland in the post-scattered hush of birds flown and timid creatures hiding.

The attack was over, the area deserted.

Man and metal had taken flight.

He'd reached the lower perimeter in time to watch the helicopter vanish over the horizon, and he'd stood in awe of the barren destruction that spanned the stretch between him and what had once been Clare's home.

Questions had begged for a closer look.

Instead, he'd turned away.

This wouldn't be the first time Clare used strange distraction and upturned strategy to throw them off. Too many years as a pawn in too many of her stupid games told him the hill would be watched by an unseen enemy waiting for curiosity to pull him in. So he'd moved on, circling and searching.

Jill had gone in the opposite direction, working the same hunt from the other side.

The big bur oak came into view, a vantage across the open space that he'd used more than once for pursuits of his own. He studied the branches, scanning higher until he found what he expected, and knew he was right.

Hired hunters were so predictable.

He pushed on, tree to hill to brush to dip, scouting for others.

Silence met him, silence and the constant buzz of insects and the slow return of birdsong and the subtle sounds of nature coming out of hiding. He reached the oak, and Jill, leaned up against it, arms crossed and cocky, as if beating him there had meant winning a round. She handed him a strand of black nylon thread and jutted her chin toward an upper branch.

She'd have done one better by staying clear of the site altogether.

He crouched and traced his fingertips against indents in the earth.

Only one pair of boots, come and gone.

Jack stood.

His gaze traveled between the trees, out to the clearing.

The marksman wouldn't have abandoned a clean line of sight like this unless he'd been compromised or believed he was outmatched, and for that, he'd have had to have been working alone. That was one more detail added in the round-robin chant of inconsistencies that kept his brain itching.

Explosion.

Silent dogs.

Clare's absence.

Helicopter.

Single shooter.

The breeze blew. The humidity rose.

Jill said, "I'm tired of this shit."

Jack didn't answer.

She turned for the clearing. "I'm taking a look."

He watched her stride into the open, naked legs scabbed and garish in the daylight, waited until she'd gone halfway before following in a hot, thirsty slog across wasteland that had until last night been vibrant and life-filled irrigated pasture. He reached her near the hilltop, and they stood in silence, staring over the twisted, charred remains of appliances and bathroom fixtures at the bottom of a gutted crater.

Memory laughed at the present, jarring in its impossible contrast. Last time they were here, it'd been Christmas.

Clare had been a shadow against the windows then, waiting on the doorstep, with a moth-eaten sweater sagging off one shoulder, an AR-15 in her hands, and muck boots on her feet, looking like an older, harder version of Jill, with a deeper tan from all the time spent outdoors. She'd smiled, set the assault rifle, butt down, against the wall, and thrown her arms wide, as if she'd expected they were just as happy to see her as she was to see them. He never did understand that. He'd kissed the top of her head, fragrant with tree sap and sweat.

All he smelled now was dirt and smoke, and all that remained of the house and the hand-built furniture — the result of years of callus-causing labor that Clare credited with keeping her stable — was shredded and strewn across the homestead.

The rest of the place hadn't fared much better.

Her forty-year-old Bronco, usually parked under a metal carport, lay on its side at the base of the hill, front smashed and windows blown out. The carport itself was a twisted mess of severed legs and missing pieces a hundred feet back.

Sand covered the ground in a fine patina that made it difficult to see tracks, but even still, there didn't seem to have been any movement other than foot traffic, which meant Clare hadn't likely left the property to make her calls, and that, in itself, was the biggest inconsistency of all. One didn't just decide after nine years of paranoid off-the-grid living to use a cell phone from home — not without anticipating the consequences — and for Clare that would have meant abandoning the homestead.

Jack uncapped the water he carried, glugged down most of it, and offered the rest to Jill. She curled her lip, as if drinking after him would give her the cooties.

He tucked the bottle away and his gaze tracked over the barn, which was still standing, fully open and visibly empty. Same for the coops and pens.

Jill said, "We should have her committed."

The words jarred his train of thought, and it took a second to rewind.

He said, "A hospital couldn't hold her. Not even *that* kind."

"Then, we could get her arrested."

"She'd find her way out of prison, too.

She's already been a fugitive for twenty-seven years, so it's not like *that* would change anything." Jack tossed a pebble into the crater and watched it bounce to the bottom.

He said, "What if this whole thing wasn't training?"

Jill's expression turned dark, shouting with hate and hurt.

Jack nodded toward the empty, dust-covered pens and coops. "She got rid of the animals. I can see her letting them go if she thought she had to run again." He motioned beyond the farthest coop to a brown-gray lump lying lifeless in the dirt. "I can't see her killing Mack."

Jill followed the direction of his finger, bit her lip, and drew blood.

Mack had been the first of Clare's dogs and her favorite. She would never have taken the others and left him here, but if he'd been alive during the firefight, they would have heard him, which meant he was dead before they'd got here.

Jill crossed her arms and turned back to the crater.

"No," she said. Her eyes rose and met his. "No, that's exactly the kind of narcissistic, delusional, Munchausen thing Clare would have done."

"She loved that dog more than she loved us."

"That's not saying much. She never loved us."

"She did in her own kind of way."

"Stop defending her."

"I'm not defending her."

"Then shut up. Just. Stop. Talking."

"Why? Because it's easier to believe she was crazy than to believe she was right?"

Jill growled, kicked the dirt, picked up a rock, and threw it into the pit.

Jack knelt, tossed another pebble in, and let her have the silence — took the silence for himself, really — because the conflict tearing at her also tore at him.

Believing Clare was sick had always brought sense to the madness and excused the pain. To broach the idea that this wasn't Clare's doing was to admit that maybe Clare had been telling the truth, that she wasn't psychotic and delusional and, worse, that her actions weren't the by-product of a pathological mind, which meant they had a mother who knew exactly what her actions had cost them and had made them suffer, anyway.

No child, no matter how old, wanted to face *that* prospect.

Jack traced a finger through the dirt and

followed that thought into the present.

There wasn't a chance in hell that a group of armed, funded, and well-trained men had shown up on her property by random chance. Something had pointed them here, and if that something wasn't Clare herself, then what?

Jill sat down with a huff and thumped her purse into the dirt beside her.

Jack looked at her, then at the crater, and then at her again.

She caught him staring. She stared back and said, "What?"

"Did you do this?" he said. "Did you bring this down on her?"

"What the fuck's that supposed to mean?"

"You know exactly what it's supposed to mean."

"Humor me, jackass."

"Clare might be a whacked-out nutjob, but the one thing she's been straight up consistent about our entire lives is leaving no trail and keeping us invisible. Then you start working favors, driving flashy cars, and blowing money like a trust-fund baby, and next thing we know . . ." He paused and thrust his hand in an arc around the destruction. "Boom." He stood and towered over her. "What. Have. You. Done?"

Jill lurched to her feet and matched him

posture for posture. "So now not only do you side with *her*, you blame me for whatever shit she's pulling?" She shoved his chest and followed that with another push. "Have you lost your goddamn mind?"

Jack took a step back to maintain footing.

He said, "Answer the question."

"This has nothing to do with me!"

"Pretty defensive for someone who's not guilty of something."

"Fuck you, John."

"Thank you for making my point."

She came after him, raging, unthinking.

He sidestepped, held up a finger in warning, and said, "Touch me again . . ."

She stopped. Chest heaving, fists clenched, jaw tight, she glared.

He backed out of reach, crossed his arms, and glared right back.

Last thing she wanted right now was to be on her own.

She could pretend she didn't give a crap about what happened to Clare, but that didn't make it true. Unresolved issues didn't vanish when the root cause did.

He was the brains, she was the brawn.

She was impulsive, and smart enough to know it, and smart enough to know that she needed his ability to think and reason. He didn't have a lot of cards to play, but the one that mattered was worth a lot.

Jill turned her back, and he turned his to her.

He dug the burner from the tool bag and powered it on.

If Clare was going to contact them, the burners were how she'd do it.

The phone booted. No calls. But she had called, hadn't she?

She'd been adamant that they get to her by three.

He said, "Where's your burner?"

Jill, her back still to him, said, "Together with my shoes, dickwad. Where else do you think it'd be?"

He tucked the device back into the bag.

First step in clearing out the variables would be to get to her burner.

He turned and motioned toward her purse. "Let me see your phone."

"Why?"

She'd charged it while they were driving and hadn't powered it on since. He said, "We've got enough on our hands without having to deal with the cops, too."

"I said I'd take care of it."

"Do it, then."

"I'll get to it."

"Now."

"Why?"

"Because if you don't, I'll walk off this property and leave you to figure out how to deal with this crap on your own."

"Go," she said. "I don't need you."

Jack picked up his rifle and shouldered his bag. Four strides into his descent, she yelled, "Fine!" A phone thumped hard between his shoulder blades.

Jack knelt, picked up the device, and plodded slowly back up the hill.

He held the phone out to her. She grabbed it back.

He watched over her shoulder while she wrote a text, and waited to confirm she'd sent it, and said, "Get your stuff. We're walking."

CHAPTER 9

Jack
Age: 8
Location: Zurich, Switzerland
Passport Country: Austria
Names: Johannes Steiner

The apartment was huge — a whole bedroom and a full bathroom and a living room and a kitchen — and the water in the taps came out clean enough to drink without boiling first, and there weren't any bugs in the food. This was like a fairy tale, except without a happy ending, because they'd leave soon, and there was no telling where they'd go next.

He went back and forth like that as he paced the hallway — eight steps forward, eight steps back — and then he eyed the watch on his wrist and paced some more.

Jill sat on the couch with her legs scooched up, watching him over the top of some stupid book about a wizard boy who wore circle glasses. *Boring.* All her books were boring compared to encyclopedias, which was why Clare had got him *Encarta,* a whole library on a few computer disks, which he didn't have to leave behind the way his sister did with her dumb paper rocks.

Jill said, "She's not coming back."

Jack ignored her.

Maybe Jill was right, maybe she wasn't. With Clare, there was never any telling, and he wanted to be sure she was *gone* gone before he turned on the television.

Jill said, "You're being a baby."

Jack stopped. "You're the baby," he said. "All grumpy because we're going to move again."

"You don't know anything."

He smiled just to tease her. "I know more than any stupid little sister."

Jill stuck out her tongue. "You're the stupid one. And the little one."

He stuck his own tongue out and went back to pacing.

He didn't really know if he was older.

At least once a month they'd asked Clare who'd come first. She'd never said, so he'd made Jill believe it was him, and that was almost enough for him to believe it himself. Maybe he couldn't be sure about that, but he was absolutely sure they were leaving soon. Clare hadn't said so, and she didn't need to. It's how it always was: Clare traveled to do favors, and when she returned, they'd pack up and leave, sometimes in the middle of the day, sometime at night, sometimes as soon as she walked in the door, sometimes a day or two later, but they always moved.

Jill was silly for thinking it would be different this time.

There wasn't anything different.

Clare had left with a kiss, a pat on the head, and the promise to be back in three days. Sometimes she returned when she said she would, sometimes she only pretended to leave. Sometimes she was days late. Once she was a whole week late.

When they were little, they sometimes used to cry when she didn't show up, but they weren't little anymore. There was food, and they had books and schoolwork, and the tool bags were stashed in the coat closet beside the front door. They knew what to do in an emergency and knew not to leave the house unless there was one. Not because Clare didn't trust them to take care of themselves alone outdoors, but because sometimes two kids without an adult attracted attention, especially if they didn't look like they were from around here, and attracting attention was the worst of the worst of the worst things they could possibly do.

He checked his watch again and groaned on the inside.

Twenty minutes of pacing had really only been eight minutes.

He had to wait at least a half hour. A whole hour was better.

Jack placed his ear to the front door and listened.

The stairwell was quiet, but Clare was quiet, too.

She made sure you could never know if she told the truth, that way you were always guessing. Sometimes she said she was leaving as a trick to test their reflexes and training. The worst tests were always the ones he didn't see coming.

He paced some more. Twenty minutes.

She was probably gone for real this time.

He gave in to impatience, sat cross-legged in front of the television, and turned it on. CNN International showed images of bombing raids in war-torn Kosovo.

From the couch behind him, Jill said, "Silly Mommy's boy."

"Shut up."

"Your anxiety is pathological."

He turned around and glared. Jill used a

lot of big words she didn't understand, because she thought she was smarter than him.

"I don't have anxiety," he said.

"You're still pathological."

"You mean pathetic."

"Pathological, pathetic, silly Mommy's boy."

"Shut up."

She said it louder, like a chant. "Pathological, pathetic, silly Mommy's boy."

He got up, crossed the room, and punched her in the mouth.

He hadn't meant to, really, it had just sort of happened on its own. He pulled his hand back and stuffed it in a pocket.

Jill smiled a gloating smile. He wanted to punch her again.

"Drawing attention," she sang, smiling bigger. "Drawing attention, drawing attention, silly Mommy's boy, drawing attention."

Jack sulked back to the floor in front of the television.

Jill would tell Clare what he'd done and would gloat when Clare gave him training. Or Jill would keep quiet and hold it over his head. Either way Jill had won. He'd let her.

That made him mad.

Jack slept in front of the television. He ate

in front of the television. For more than a day he waited and watched, and finally, patience paid off.

The station went crazy with news of an airplane that had crashed near Canada. Important people had died on that plane. Jack would have needled Jill. He would have said, "See, I told you. I told you every time Clare does favors or hands us off to someone else for training and goes away, there's a big event on the news." But he didn't want to make Jill mad, so the conversation stayed between him and the television.

CHAPTER 10

Jill
Age: 26
Location: Near Austin, Texas
Passport Country: USA
Names: Julia Jane Smith

She pressed her palms against her thighs to force her fingers into stillness, tipped her head to the window, and tried to ignore the world by watching the world go by. This made twenty hours of forced sobriety, and if ever she needed to dial down the real in real life, she needed it now.

The screams from the purse beside her feet were only getting louder.

Another fifteen minutes. She could hold out for fifteen.

They'd be at her apartment, and she'd have privacy and a bathroom to herself.

Her knee bounced. She stepped on the purse to make the jitters stop.

Jack didn't notice either way.

He was focused on the road, both hands on the wheel, holding the speedometer steady at exactly two miles over the speed limit in an F-150 almost as old as they were. The truck had come courtesy of Clare.

They'd detoured first to two of her hidey-holes, cleared them out of money and ammunition, and then followed the dry creek downstream and northwest across acre after acre of abandoned and overgrown terrain to the old Hatcher homestead, where they'd found the Ford under a dusty tarp in the teetering, weatherworn barn, which was pretty much all that remained of the once thriving working ranch that had been in the Hatcher family trust for generations.

To the untrained eye, the dust, the tarp, the truck — the entire barn — had sat abandoned and forgotten, just like the burned-down ranch house and the land around it. But a closer look showed the vehicle's registration was up to date, the engine had been rebuilt, and the tires were good — courtesy of Clare — who'd also left a tank's worth of gas in old metal jerricans, and the keys stuffed inside a broken hay-filled mason jar on a pile of scrap. Folklore said the reason the Hatchers never rebuilt and why the land never sold was that the whole place was haunted.

The gossips weren't wrong, not exactly.

As far as Jill was concerned, it'd been Clare who'd burned the place to the ground. Didn't matter that the fire had happened when she and Jack were still learning to read, or that they'd been living in Beirut — or maybe by then it was Monrovia — nothing in Clare's life was coincidence, especially not when it involved acquiring properties with connecting boundaries.

Jack had once called her out for stashing things in the barn, had asked her what kind of attention she thought she'd get if someone discovered her stuff. Clare had smiled one of those sly "never really know what she's thinking" smiles and had said the beautiful thing about trusts was the lack of public access to the details inside the trust documents.

Jack had eventually figured it out.

The Hatcher homestead technically belonged to Clare, even if no record of the sale existed, because she hadn't bought the land. What she had bought was the Hatcher family trust or, more specifically, she'd bought a change of trustees and beneficiaries, and, by doing that, she'd also bought invisibility and silence.

The Hatcher homestead would stay haunted as long as Clare was alive. By Jack's reckoning, that might not be long.

According to him, the signs all pointed to Clare getting ready to run again.

The hides would have been her final move and she hadn't gotten to them before whatever happened had happened. To him, finding the stashes and the truck untouched was one more indication she'd been taken off the property against her will.

Jill didn't buy it.

Clare was known for stashing supplies in the same way squirrels hid nuts, and there were less than worst-case scenario reasons for her to have left the hidey-holes alone.

Even in the remote chance this whole thing wasn't Clare fucking with their heads, she had multiple getaway arrangements and owned other properties — probably some they didn't even know about. In land alone, Clare had to be worth tens of millions, yet she lived like a hippie, and her cars and trucks were always pieces of shit.

Like this one.

Inconspicuous Clare would have said, "People would rather look away than see the poor. The poor are invisible."

Maybe out where she lived, or if she'd been trying to make a run across an unmarked portion of the Mexican border, but not in Snootsville, Austin, which was where

93

Jill called home. So while Clare was off somewhere plotting her next move, her dear children were left to deal with the issue of drawing attention in a very visible truck.

Jack turned down the street that led to her apartment.

Joggers and dog walkers and moms out with kids watched, eagle-eyed, as they passed, as if home entertainment systems everywhere depended on them. He swung onto a side road and pulled to the curb, put the truck in park, and stuck out his hand.

"Keys," he said.

She scrutinized him, half-convinced she hadn't just heard what she'd heard.

His fingers motioned "gimme," and his eyes had that faraway look he got when his mind went into hyper-focus and he lost the capacity to see anything other than his way. She said, "My keys. My house. My tool bag."

He said, "Don't trust you. No offense."

"Offense taken, anyway, jerk face. I'll get my own damn bag."

He shook his head in a slow, self-righteous side to side that made it hard not to reach across the seat and slug him. He said, "You know I've got my own set. Give me yours. Make it legit."

No matter what else he thought was happening, if he believed she'd turned lapdog, he was sorely mistaken. She pulled the purse off the floor and pawed through its dark caverns in search of the clump of jingle-jangle, grabbed the keys, and thrust them high in angry protest. He grabbed them.

She didn't let go. He yanked them free and in that distracted second, her other hand stabbed the hypodermic into his thigh and pushed the plunger.

His mouth opened, and his eyes went wide. From shock, maybe, that she'd done it, or that he hadn't seen it coming. He said, "That was . . . how could . . . you're a shortsighted . . . impulsive . . ."

"This comes as a surprise?"

She capped the needle on a syringe that had been meant for her. If he'd done a proper stock count in his bag, he'd have known she had it.

He blinked, and shook his head, as if somehow that would clear the cobwebs.

She slipped out of the truck, walked around the hood to his side, and opened the door. "Come on, big boy," she said. "Let's get you settled before it all kicks in."

He leaned away from her. She snagged his arm. "You'll be just fine," she said. "Think of all the fun we'll have when you wake up."

She tugged him toward her and his body followed out of the truck, already uncoordinated and off balance but still trying to show her what's what. She opened the suicide door and nudged him up onto the rear seat, pushed his shoulder and tipped him over, tugged a plastic-wrapped blanket out from beneath the seat, tore it open, and draped it over him.

"Night night, John."

His eyelids drifted closed.

He was so much easier to like when he was asleep, all sweet and relaxed and almost normal. She stuffed the syringe back into the pocket of his tool bag, the same pocket from which she'd swiped it while cutting weapons out of his car.

Mr. High-and-Mighty wasn't the only one capable of thinking ahead.

He'd remember some of this and see her putting him out as dumb luck for the same reason he'd been disgusted with her by the bur oak. Yeah, she'd messed up the site around the tree — deliberately — after she'd done her own tracking.

She knew there'd been only one guy. And she knew he'd headed north toward the Millers' land.

Jack would have known, too, if he'd bothered to ask. He never would. Smartest guy in the room was too dumb to realize how far his overconfident head was shoved up his own ass. Maybe one day he'd figure out the joke was on him. Jill closed the rear door, reached into the front and plucked the keys from the ignition, grabbed her purse, lowered the windows a touch, and locked him in.

The day was getting hotter.

Early fall was a joke when the cooler temperatures didn't kick in till mid-November, but the truck was in the shade, and she'd be back before he overheated.

She jogged for the nearest building, slipped around to the rear, through a privacy gate, and into a postage-stamp garden. This was home for now, the bottom floor of a three-story town house owned by a former friend's mother, who considered six months' rent in cash twice a year a completely valid reason for avoiding messy formalities like lease contracts and identity and income verification.

She let herself in, shut the door behind her, and breathed in the fresh linen scent of privacy. Then dumped her purse out in the foyer, pawed through the contents for the lipstick tube, and pawed some more.

Hands shaking, she turned the purse upside down.

A paper clip, a gum wrapper, and a few stray pennies joined the pile on the floor.

Mind disbelieving, she went through the items again, slowly, one at a time.

The lipstick tube was gone.

The pill bottles, gone.

Everything, gone, gone, gone.

She sat on the floor and howled.

Motherfu . . . son of a goddamn . . . she was going to kill him.

She stomped to the kitchen, pulled a chair from the table, and dragged it to the bedroom closet. She climbed to the highest shelf, pulled the blue duffel bag down to the floor, opened it wide for the dopp kit, hooked a finger into the kit's smallest pocket and snagged the baggie. She tore a hole getting it open.

Sweet relief spilled onto her hand, and she snorted it right up her nose.

Focus and clarity washed into her.

Her insides relaxed.

She yanked clothes off hangers, tossed them into the duffel, dumped the dopp kit back in, and zipped the bag shut. As an afterthought, she dug through a pile of shoes on the closet floor for the tool bag at the back and pulled that out, too, then ran the shower, jumped in long enough to wash off the dirt and stench, and tugged into too-tight jeans that stuck to every inch of her wet legs.

She checked the time.

She'd been inside for more than ten minutes.

She might as well have been away for an hour, but she'd still not done what she'd truly come inside to do. She pulled a phone from the duffel's outer pocket, took a deep breath, and powered it on. Her idiot-savant brother had been right about one thing: she *had* been working favors. No apologies for that.

Not after losing her entire childhood to a delusional mother whose version of a tinfoil hat was to drag her kids across the continents; train them to hide and hunt, kill and survive; put them in situations that tested those skills; then cut them loose to find their own way in a world they could never fit into.

Now she was supposed to just what?

Barista at Starbucks, like the past had never happened?

Work for pennies when her set of skills could pull in the big money?

No thanks. No thanks to Clare, and no thanks to asshole Jack, who'd bought into the delusion until they were sixteen fucking years old, always connecting Clare's whacked-out they're-coming-to-get-us conspiracies with random world tragedies, until Clare finally abandoned them for good and he had nothing but nothing as thanks for believing in her all those years.

So yeah, she'd been working.

She'd been careful in a way that only training under Clare all those years could make a person careful. There was no way she'd brought this back with her. Just couldn't have. But Jack's accusation needled and needled, and she needed certainty.

Jill eyed the phone.

She couldn't call the Broker from here, not even with the phone encrypted and the signal bouncing around the globe. And she couldn't do it with "Mom loves me best" breathing down her back, either, and she had no idea how long Jack would be down.

Jill stuffed the phone into her pocket, jammed her feet into a pair of Jungle Glove slip-ons, grabbed the duffel and the tool bag, and strode for the door.

Outside the garden gate she spotted spinning cherry lights and stopped short. A neighborhood patrol car had claimed one corner, and a city squad car the other.

The cop, already outside his cruiser, was moving for Clare's truck.

Jill's insides roiled, every cell screaming with memories from the past: attracting attention was the worst of the worst of the worst things she could possibly do.

She breathed out one life and drew in another.

Old Jill, the Jill who'd cared what Clare thought, the Jill who'd tangled herself into knots trying to please a mother who would never be pleased, the Jill who'd hurt and tried harder — that Jill had been killed dead at thirteen. In that other lifetime, an encounter like this would have been impossible because Clare would have never been foolish enough to let it happen. But this wasn't then, and Clare wasn't boss anymore.

Jill jangled the truck keys.

She started forward, calm and amused.

Jack was out cold in a truck loaded with guns and money, and the bag slung across her shoulder carried at least five years' hard time worth of drugs. Innocence and a beatific smile spread across her face.

This was the type of shit she lived for now.

CHAPTER 11

Jill
Age: 13
Location: Fortul, Colombia
Passport Country: Venezuela
Names: Julieta Maria Suarez

She moved forward, belly to the ground, inching toward the pot and its precious water trove while the rich bite of living soil and earthy rot filled every breath.

Footfalls a few meters away stopped her.

She froze, head tucked beneath a hood for camouflage.

She hadn't realized the searchers were so close.

No one had called her name today, there'd only been the *whack, whack* against the undergrowth, which was probably why she hadn't heard him until he was right there. A stick slashed foliage to her left and then above her, knocking leaves aside.

There'd been others who'd passed by her

hide, but she could tell from the way this one moved with a shitty rifle slung under his arm, a machete in one hand, and a cane in the other that this was Santiago.

She kept perfectly still, heart pounding so loudly she was certain he would hear it, too. The crappy rubber-soled boots moved on just a little more.

She breathed soft and slow, waiting him out.

He kept going, stabbing the ground, shoving into undergrowth.

She slid a leafy branch aside, checked for poisonous creatures, and crawled again.

Her shaking fingers stretched out and snagged the pot. She tugged it to her mouth, drank down the collected rainwater, and laughed on the inside.

This was day eight, and he'd passed right over her.

Her clothes were filthy, and she reeked, and she'd had to use a knife to cut the tangles out of her muddy hair. She was hungry — not too much, considering the stupid search parties had been tromping around like elephants, chasing animals away from her traps — but she would last another day, maybe another week, even longer if Santiago would call off the search and leave her alone.

Because of him, she had to stay hidden most of the day, and because of him, it took forever to collect drinking water, but she was doing all right. She wasn't one of those stupid kids she'd read about in books who ran away from home with the crappiest things. She had a weapon and enough ammunition to get her through a good fight. Not a lot, because ammunition was heavy and she was on foot. She'd brought fire-making tools and water purification tools and a canister and a tarp and extra socks and good boots and a map and a compass and enough food to last a few days and give her time to get her traps settled and filled.

Trapping in the wet forest was a new thing she'd learned, thanks to Santiago.

At least he'd been good for something.

And now he was out here with a bunch of the rest of them, beating bushes, trying to find her and bring her back.

If he caught her, she wasn't going willingly.

He'd have to drag her in.

Anything, even starving out here, was better than going back on her own two feet.

But if she could wait them out, then the fuss would eventually die down, and she could move more freely and head toward Fortul and from there make her way toward

Europe. She knew Europe pretty well. Money wouldn't be a problem because Clare had left drops in every city they'd ever lived in and had made sure she and Jack knew how to access them.

The thought of leaving Jack made her sad. She would have preferred if he'd come with her, but she couldn't risk him trying to stop her. She was done with suffering in camp.

Clare had gone again — big surprise — handing them off to someone else for the second time in five months. "Safekeeping" was what she called it, same excuse she always used to abandon her kids while she jet setted across the globe.

Last time she'd left them in Athens with Raymond Chance, which wasn't so bad, because Ray was fun and they knew him pretty well already, and Athens was a cool place. But this time she'd hauled them into the Colombian interior, introduced them to the tyrant known as Santiago, and taken off fifteen minutes later.

She'd been all full of fake smiles, too, trying to reassure them that while Santiago might be a stranger to them, he wasn't to her, and that leaving them here was for their own good. She'd said that one day they'd understand, which was what she always said, and she'd hugged them good-bye, told them she loved them and to never forget it, and then left them to spend a month in the jungle with a jerk and his band of uniform-wearing, gun-toting gorillas.

Yes, gorillas. She knew the difference between ape and rebel.

Santiago was old, maybe around the same age as Clare, a round-faced guy with a big ole belly and a thinned-out beard. He looked like he should be jolly, not a dictator. But no, he had them up before dawn, out hauling water and collecting wood, and he kept them scrubbing, polishing, digging, and burying, like they were his personal servants. And God forbid they should finish early, because then he'd make them do drills until they puked. And at night, when they were wolfing down food, he still couldn't leave them alone. He'd have to talk and talk, like they cared about anything he had to say. Worst was when he bragged about the times he'd worked with Clare, like that was some kind of special honor, and made up tall tales that anyone who knew Clare would know were lies. She and Jack would be too tired to argue, they just wanted him to shut up so they could go to sleep. Then they'd do it all over again the next day.

It might not have been so bad if Clare had

actually come back when she'd promised. Even a week after she'd promised would have been okay. Jill had kept a calendar, marking down days to escape, and the day had come and passed, and then passed some more, and then another month had gone by without so much as a note from Clare, and she'd finally asked Santiago if he knew anything. He'd answered with a laugh, like it was the funniest thing he'd heard all year.

Late that night she'd rolled over, nudged Jack, and whispered her biggest fear.

"You think Clare's dead and we're stuck here forever?"

Jack hadn't been sleeping, either. She could tell because he had that faraway look, like he'd been plotting his own escape. "She'll come back," he said.

She'd snuck out exactly twenty-five hours later and headed into the wild alone.

She hadn't figured Santiago would spend a lot of time looking for her.

That had been a slight miscalculation.

Jill burrowed into her hide and nibbled on the last of her stale bread.

Since traps weren't an option right now, she'd have to wait till full dark, when everything went quiet, to try hunting. She stretched out, let delicious drowsy sleep take her, and jolted awake to a voice in the distance, an unmistakable voice.

Jill froze, heart pounding, and she searched the dimming evening light, not sure if she'd really heard what she'd thought she'd heard or if maybe she'd hallucinated.

But there it was again, this time a little closer, calling in Russian, her mother tongue, the language Clare used when she didn't want to risk Spanish or French being understood by the people around them.

Reality kicked in.

She rolled to her knees and scurried, squirreling away supplies as silently as she could, covering evidence that she'd made camp here, embarrassed that Clare might see her like this.

That voice bounced through the underbrush again, far and near at the same time, and perfectly clear. "We know you're out here," it said. "Do *not* make me track you down."

Jill hurried to finish loading her bag. She dragged the pack out after her and brushed leaves across the floor of her hide to obscure the campsite. Then she scampered into the falling night to get as far away from the voice as possible.

Her water pot was toast.

Her traps were lost.

She counted the slow, painful distance in her head and, when she couldn't afford to wait any longer, routed around a tree and came out the other side standing.

She walked a slow, slow tromp back the way she'd come.

Clare called her name again.

Jill yelled back, "I'm on my way. Can't you see me?"

The forest went quiet. Flashlights beamed in multiple directions.

Jill kept walking and let them find her.

Clare came toward her, a ghost looming in the night, with Santiago to her right, Jack at her left, and a dozen other men and women with cheap camouflage and machetes and guns at her back. She stopped when she was nearly chest to chest with Jill.

"Yuliya," Clare said. "What *have* you done?"

The words weren't a question but a condemnation and a horrible promise.

Jill withered under the glare, then squared her shoulders and stood defiant. Clare had been missing for more than a month and wanted to know what *she* had done?

Jill said, "I've been surviving, and I've been invisible, and you should be proud of how well I've succeeded, but no, you're pissed off, just like you always are."

"This," Clare hissed. She thrust her hand in an arc, pointing toward the forest. "This is attention we don't need."

Jill cocked her chin up. "You ran off," she said. "You ran off and left us. Left me and Jack with people we don't even know, and never bothered to send word you'd be late or that you were even alive."

"You can't understand," Clare said. "Hopefully, you'll never have to understand. Don't repay sacrifice and love with disrespect."

Jill crossed her arms and clenched her jaw. "You've never loved us."

Clare's lips pressed tight, and her skin changed color, and Jill knew she'd gone too far but couldn't stop now. Louder, she said, "You don't even know what love means."

Clare's right hand lifted across her chest toward her shoulder, and for the first time then, or ever, she backhanded Jill across the face.

The blow knocked Jill on her heels, and blood, warm and sticky, trickled down her lip. Her throat burned. She wanted to scream and cry and hit and yell.

She wanted to be hugged. She wanted Clare to tell her she loved her.

Instead, she stood tall, fists clenched, and glowered.

Clare studied her, and turned away. To Santiago, she said, "Get her back to camp and get her cleaned up."

Jill watched Clare go. She couldn't bring herself to look at Jack. She wouldn't be able to bear it if he mocked her, and she might crumble if he gloated.

Santiago reached for her arm with his big, meaty hands.

Jill yelped and dodged his grasp.

He lunged at her, swearing and angry, and she slid aside again.

She didn't care if Clare had returned, didn't care if the whole world hated her, she still wasn't going back of her own free will.

Santiago caught her arm, gripped it tight, and tried to grab her waist.

Jill fought, kicking and swinging.

Jack stepped between them. He put a palm on Santiago's chest.

"No," he said. "I'll do it."

Santiago let go. Jill fell backward and hit the ground hard. Jack stretched a hand to her, offering to help her up. She recoiled and scrambled away.

He followed her. "Come on," he said. "We'll go together."

"No," she whispered.

"Together," he said, stretching the word

into three strong, emphasized syllables. "And anything Clare deals you, she'll have to deal me, too. Together."

CHAPTER 12

Jack

Age: 26
Location: DeRidder, Louisiana
Passport Country: USA
Names: Jonathan Thomas Smith

Consciousness rose in disjointed segments, first with the sick-sweet smell of weed, which made him want to vomit, and then pounding in his head, which made him want to die. He fought weighted eyelids and blinked against a predawn gray just bright enough to set off the neuro-jackhammer. He squinted past the pain.

Senses engaged one by one, treating him to cramped muscles and aching joints, seat cushions and window panels inside a car he didn't recognize. Ready-to-eat meals and bottled water were on the floorboard beside his hand. His fingers fumbled and grasped plastic, and he groaned his way up to where he could saturate the desert in his mouth.

Swallowing hurt, but the water cleared some of the fuzzy and dulled the headache enough to let him open his eyes. He focused on the windshield and then through the glass, where a shadow on the hood tightened into Jill's silhouette.

A faint spark of orange in her hand explained the smell.

Beyond her loomed the outline of a large brick building, its white dome starkly bright against the sky's creeping light. Other shapes and shadows lined the streets around them, but the courthouse was enough to let him know where they were, and the gut punch of recognition made him wish he could crawl back into oblivion, get a rewind on life, and wake up somewhere else.

He opened the door and, legs still shaky, found solid ground.

He placed his hand on the car for balance. His foggy brain registered the light gray paint and then the vehicle itself — a Camry, ubiquitous and invisible, exactly what Clare would have had them drive — and he puzzled over where it'd come from and how Jill had managed to get him into it and what she'd done with the truck and if she'd left the Tesla where he'd parked it.

Jill, staring at the courthouse ahead, hadn't turned when he opened the door, and didn't turn as he approached. She took a drag and, when he was near, said, "Seemed the appropriate place to come."

Jack plucked the spliff from her hand and tossed it as far across the lawn as his stiff and aching joints would let it fly. "You're crazy for smoking that here."

She answered with indifferent silence.

He eased down on the hood beside her, engine still warm beneath him.

Jill pulled her knees up, wrapped her arms around them, and finally looked at him. He met her gaze and wished he hadn't.

She sighed and went back to staring.

Of all the places Jill could have driven, she'd taken them home — or at least as close to home as home had ever been, considering the two years they'd spent under Raymond Chance's roof was the longest they'd ever stayed in one place.

If Ray'd had a middle name, it would've been Second.

He'd had another name and another life once and, like them, had been severed from whatever came before. He was the closest they'd ever find to a living dead man.

Staying dead, he'd said, was the best way to stay alive.

Clare had dropped them off on his doorstep when they were sixteen: no warning, no promise to come back, just "By the way, you're staying with Ray now."

It mattered, he supposed, that she'd chosen someone they already knew and liked, that she hadn't left them with strangers from her past the way she'd so often done before, but gratitude to that degree was hard to feel in the face of abandonment. They'd stood on Ray's wraparound porch, backpacks at their feet, watching the tires of her Bronco bump between stands of pine along the potholed road until the taillights vanished. Reality had sunk in right about the same time the shock had worn off.

Clare would send for them sometimes — a Christmas break here, a month out of summer there — and would always ship them back to DeRidder, to the man who would become the closest thing they had to a father. Jack got why Clare had left them, but never did understand why Ray had agreed to foster. Ray wasn't what most would see as the fathering type: an ex–something or other who'd never married or had kids of his own, he was dangerous like Clare, though only half as paranoid and not as crazy.

To Ray's credit, he'd spoken a language they could understand, because he'd seen the types of things they'd seen and worse, and he'd done his best with two angry, resentful kids who were each capable of killing a neighborhood and making it look like an accident. He'd fed their need for gunpowder and poison, had endured the grief they gave him with humor and patience, and it was he who'd taught them how to navigate a boring, staid, rule-filled world they weren't raised to live in.

Jack adored the man. Jill respected him.

None of that lessened the impact of being unworthy of their mother.

With effort, Jack had managed to make it through high school. He'd stayed in touch with Ray and visited now and again, keeping away for reasons that had nothing to do with Ray and everything to do with Clare. But Jill had gone off the rails early, drinking, drugging, and burning through boys as if she were the last woman on earth.

Ray had put up with her longer than anyone else would have and had finally thrown her out at gunpoint when she was seventeen.

Jill hadn't spoken to him since.

Transitioning to a small town wouldn't have been easy for any outsider, much less for two wild creatures who'd never sat in a classroom or regularly interacted with non-sibling age-mates and for whom the local language and customs were strange and foreign. Getting through hadn't been without its troubles, and perhaps a house fire and maybe a car accident or two before trouble learned to steer clear, so it would've been easy to write off Jill's behavior as the by-product of all that.

Maybe part of it was, but mostly not.

Far as Jack was concerned, DeRidder was just another battlefield upon which an emotional contortionist had unleashed psychological warfare until she got bored. The real battle was with her mother. Everything Jill did was to punish Clare, and for that, the only option was escalation, and that was the only war she couldn't win.

Jack didn't blame Jill, he blamed Clare.

Even Ray blamed Clare.

Jack said, "You think Ray had something to do with Clare's disappearance?"

"I don't think there *was* any disappearance, but Ray's the only other person who knows where she lives, and if anyone has a clue about what she's up to, it'd be him."

"You're a brave woman for coming back."

Jill slid off the hood, stretched her arms over her head, and breathed deep. "Time to let bygones be bygones," she said.

"You bring the guns?"

"Yeah," she said. "Everything's in the trunk."

"So much for bygones."

"It's been a long drive, and I hate being back. I'm not wasting the trip."

"You let him know you're coming?"

She gave him a dismissive, withering look. The one that said she wasn't an idiot while simultaneously calling him one.

Jack turned back to the courthouse.

There were reasons to argue with her and more reasons not to.

If Ray had had anything to do with Clare's disappearance, announcing their arrival would be a bigger mistake than coming at him blind after years of estrangement, but doing it Jill's way meant they were going to need the guns.

Jack patted the hood. "Whose car? Is it clean?"

Her lips turned up. In the shadows the gloating looked evil. "There's so much you don't know," she said. "I like it that way."

A knot of angry frustration spawned inside his chest.

He said, "Where's Clare's truck?"

"With the Tesla."

"At the Walmart?"

"Nah."

"Where?"

"I got it handled, okay? Let it go."

The frustration grew, enveloping his heart and lungs and pounding his throbbing head harder, making it more difficult to think. Jill knew how to hold him hostage, knew even better than Clare how to trip him off his game.

He rubbed his thigh, still sore and bruised from where she'd jabbed him.

His only recourse in the moment was to deprive her of the pleasure of knowing she'd won, but he'd find payback, and when he did, it'd be a bitch.

He stood and walked for the front passenger door.

Jill called after him. "If you're right about Clare being taken, even if that means she's been telling the truth all these years — I'm not saying I believe it, but even if it's true — that doesn't change anything else, you know?"

He paused and glanced back. "How so?"

"Clare maybe not being one hundred percent delusional and Clare being a sociopathic narcissist — they're not mutually exclusive."

He nodded. Acknowledgment, not agreement.

The possibility of Clare having told the truth all these years changed everything. He just couldn't piece together how or why, especially not while he couldn't fit the past twenty-four hours into a coherent portrait.

He opened the door. "If I'm right, then we're running out of time."

Jill slid off the hood and trailed around the other side.

She took the wheel and headed out of town, driving south past cropland and the occasional farmhouse on Highway 27, a two-lane county road that connected a patchwork of smaller roads that cut deep into the Louisiana wild. They rode in silence, Jack shoving calorie-dense food into his mouth, while the lightening sky transformed colorless shadows into shades of green.

Jill turned east.

The sun crested and climbed higher.

She pulled off onto an unmarked track, thick with untamed foliage and unchanged by time, and crawled the Camry up a graveled stretch that would eventually dead-end in a cul-de-sac outside Ray's front door. She stopped forty yards in, just far enough that the car couldn't be seen from the paved road and hopefully far enough out that Ray's coonhounds and Catahoulas wouldn't raise an alarm.

She killed the engine.

Hands in her lap, she paused. "How's your head?"

Concern would have been nice. What she really wanted to know was if he'd cleared up enough to strategize and shoot.

He answered by stepping out of the car.

Jill followed him to the trunk and watched as he took in the disorganized mess of weapons, ammunition, and supplies mixed in between their personal things. His assessment stopped with her tool bag, the whole reason they'd gone to her apartment and the reason she'd stabbed him with the needle.

Jill pulled the burner from a pocket and handed it to him. "She hasn't called this one, either."

Jack took the phone and held it tight, the weight in his hand a miniature of the burden on his shoulders. Love and hate and obligation and want and fear and hope chased through his head. Clare was stronger, fitter, and in better shape than most men half her age. The only person he'd bet on going up against her was Jill, and that was because Jill was a lunatic trained by *the* lunatic. Clare could take care of herself.

He picked up his rifle, ran the bolt.

Clare was a pain in the ass and a horrible mother, but she was *his* mother, and it had now been a full day since he'd watched the helicopter leave her property, and still there'd been no sign of her or contact attempt from her.

He drew in the fragrance of gun oil.

Yesterday he would have sworn Ray would never do anything to hurt Clare. A lot had changed since yesterday.

Jill crossed the gravel, AR-15 in hand, and disappeared between the trees.

Jack zipped into a tactical vest and loaded the pockets.

Tension and animosity faded, just as it always did when he and Jill were working. Only the objective mattered, and the same familiarity and birth bond that allowed them to torment each other so well made it possible for them to work as a single unit: no wire necessary, no need to articulate.

They both knew what had to be done.

He headed into the marsh, toward Ray's three-bedroom cabin, testing the wind and following the dry ground. He stopped before breaking into the open and shimmied up a tree for a better vantage. Last time he'd been here, Ray had had project cars up on blocks, a shed under construction, and a carport crammed with tools and workbenches.

The place was cleaned up and empty now.

Fresh weather stain on the porch and new curtains in the windows said he was still around and suggested there might be a woman in his life.

Jack moved the scope in a slow scan across the front, analyzing, measuring.

At the edge of his vision, the curtain color shifted.

Ray might as well have looked him dead in the face and said hello.

Adrenaline surged in an immediate fight-or-flight response.

He didn't have time to think or plan. He let go and jumped, hit the ground hard, and rolled. A bullet spit into the trunk a few feet lower than where he'd been.

Silence and secrecy didn't matter anymore, time did. He scurried on all fours, caught footing, and ran for the road where there'd be nothing to obstruct sight.

CHAPTER 13

Jack
Age: 26
Location: Outside DeRidder, Louisiana
Passport Country: USA
Names: Jonathan Thomas Smith

He plowed through the underbrush, cutting an angle toward the house, racing the clock while his feet caught against vines and twisted saplings. The woodland responded to the noise with an eerie quiet, which only made the yowls from the kennels out back that much louder.

He reached the embankment, scrambled onto the road where the gravel curved for a clear view of the porch.

He waved his arms at the house and the untamed land around.

"Ray, it's me," he yelled. "Don't shoot!"

The dogs' distracting ruckus answered in reply.

He walked to the middle of the road and

there, out in the open and fully exposed, started toward the house.

Metal zinged into the gravel a yard ahead, spewing rock and dirt projectiles.

Jack stopped hard, turned, and faced the direction from which it seemed the shot had come. Overgrown foliage and the marsh faced him back.

He waited.

The morning breeze rustled through the treetops.

Jack said, "Warning received, Ray. I'm headed toward the porch, that's all."

Another bullet ricocheted off the ground, closer than the last. Sound suppression made it difficult to tell how quickly Ray was moving and in which direction.

Jack placed the rifle on the ground, then unzipped the tactical vest and let the weight drop. He lifted his T-shirt, flashed his back and stomach to the woodland in a full three-sixty and, hands up in surrender, head in the crosshairs, and mind filled with doubt, moved forward again.

Ray came from behind at the cul-de-sac opening.

A single misstep against the gravel gave him away.

Jack froze, resisting the urge to turn. He said, "It's been a while."

The muzzle pressed into his back, hot, even through his shirt.

A muddy, torn tennis shoe kicked his legs apart.

Jack said, "I've got nothing on me."

Ray's calloused hand hurried up his legs and around his waist, and a voice, deep and sandy, said, "It's a surprise to see you like this, son. What brings you home?"

"Thought I'd be neighborly-like and pay a visit."

"Front door's always been open to family, but runnin' my land with that pop toy don't make for a good impression on your intentions. You know well enough to know better."

"Don't mean no harm, Ray. Been a long time. Wasn't sure if this was still your place. Wasn't sure you'd be happy to see me if it was."

"Missed ya is more what it is, boy. You always been welcome. Where's your sister?"

"Don't know."

The muzzle jabbed into Jack's spine, and Ray's voice turned the corner from cautious to dangerous. "You two only run in pairs. Where'd she be, if you don't mind?"

A clink of metal answered for him.

Jill's voice said, "Nice to see you, Ray. Put the fire stick down."

Jack hadn't heard her approach, and, apparently, neither had Ray.

The muzzle eased slightly up off Jack's spine, but Ray stood firm.

Jill said, "I shoot, you shoot, and everyone gets dead but me."

Ray said, "Must be nice."

She said, "We didn't come to hurt you. Didn't come to cause trouble. Just wanna talk, that's all."

"A phone call woulda done you better than guns."

Jack said, "Clare's missing."

Silence filled the air between them.

Ray said, "How'd you say?"

"House blew up night before last. Helicopter lifted off the property a few hours later. Don't know if she's jacking with us like old times or if we have a problem. Rumor says you might know which is which."

"You think I blown it up?"

Jill said, "You're the only one besides us who knows where she lives."

"I had nothin' to do with whatever it is you saw."

Jack said, "Have you heard from her?"

Gravel crunched, and clothing ruffled. The muzzle lifted off Jack's back, and the air seeped out of his lungs. He lowered his hands, glanced over his shoulder, and turned, gaze tracking over the only man who'd ever understood what it was like to crawl the earth in his skin.

Ray studied the ground, his once formidable body draped in a T-shirt and jeans two sizes too big. His weathered hand traversed a coarse beard that had shed lush black for wiry gray. He was a smaller, older, and more tired Ray than Jack remembered, with thinning hair and new patchworks of sunspots mottling his leathered skin.

Passing time and wasted opportunity punched Jack hard in the heart. He should have come home long ago.

Ray said, "She called me a night ago. Hung up when I answered. Tried to call her back and got nothing, and I ain't heard from her since."

"Called us, too," Jack said. "Summoned us down but never said why. We were late getting to her and watched the end unfold."

Ray's gaze traced south, and he stared into the long, far distance, as if wandering through a maze of secrets. He shook his head. Jack's stomach dropped and his brain pounded, and he knew he'd been right about Clare, and wished he hadn't.

His voice choked in a struggle to ask *the* question. He chewed his words, swallowed them down, and spit them back up.

For reasons that ebbed and flowed with the seasons, every one of Clare's absurd demands or insane behaviors had been based on a need to stay ahead of "them." As he and Jill had gotten older and less believing, they'd challenged her — mocked her really — brushing off her conspiracies and geopolitical convolutions by demanding she elaborate on who "they" and "them" were.

"Everyone that matters," she'd say. "CIA, FBI, FSB, SVR, GRU, BND, DGSI, DGSE." And that was right about where Jill would roll her eyes and he'd zone out.

Asking the question now felt like validating a hallucination by holding a conversation with someone else's voices.

He said, "Do you know who could have done it?"

The older man looked up, clear blue eyes full of fatalistic acceptance and unspoken pain. "Son," he said, "there ain't a thing I can tell you about your mother that she ain't told you herself since you was young. Saying it again here won't make you believe it any more than you ever have."

"She said a lot, Ray."

"You know what she is. Known it since you was eight, I reckon."

"That's not helping."

Ray sighed. "Look to what you just seen with your own two eyes. No one but government brings a helicopter to claim the dead."

The words were a kick to Jack's brain. He'd gone in circles trying to make the pieces fit a portrait in which delusional Clare was the one pulling the strings.

Ray didn't have that kind of baggage.

Jack said, "Clare's not dead. Whoever got to her came in on foot, abandoned what remained of their own dead, and all but one of those alive left by air. This was six, maybe seven hired guns, using a civilian helicopter. They took Clare out alive."

Ray looked toward the sky and tugged his beard.

Jill said, "You do know something."

"Depends," he said. He ran a palm across his cheek, and his fingers followed the gray to its very tip. "There's knowing, and there's knowing. Example being I known your mother since before you could string three words together, but that don't mean the same as knowing her movements every year since. I known her long enough to recognize a repeat, though."

Jack looked at Jill, she looked at him, and they both looked at Ray.

He spoke worse gibberish than Clare ever had.

Ray said, "When's the last time she talked about your daddy?"

Jill's mouth opened. She glanced down the road, as if trying to decide if she should stay for more or wash her hands of the huge waste of time this trip had been.

Jack said, "Years. What does he have to do with anything?"

"Your mom ever surfaces to look for him, stuff happens."

"Stuff?"

"Stuff."

"What kind of stuff?"

"Last time — oh, I think you musta been right around thirteen or so, tucked away where she was sure no one could find you — best as I remember, was an ambush in Budapest that got her, or might maybe have been Bucharest. They hauled her off to a black site, had her for a week before she squirreled free. Tight call that one was, and still not sure who done it. Had a touch of government to it. Rationally, we figured Russian military intelligence, but who knows?"

"You're saying that's who did this now?"

"No, son, I'm sayin' any time she goes looking stuff happens, is all. She did call you down."

"More like demanded. Urgent. No time

to waste. The usual."

"My guess'd be she got wind of trouble on the way. Maybe wanted to warn you, let you know she was running again, or maybe try to convince you to run with her."

"We never would have."

"Yup. No question on that, not even for her."

"Why bother waiting for us, then? Why not just go?"

"Because," Ray said, and he looked pointedly at Jack, "she loves you."

Jill snorted.

Ray's cheeks reddened, and his chest rose. "Oh, you don't think it, missy. Maybe she don't always show it in ways you understand, but you been the world to that woman. Time's gittin' on, and running gets harder. She mighta suspected this'd be the last time, might maybe thought there'd be no coming back and couldn't bear leaving with no good-bye."

Jack clenched his fists. His gaze drifted to the near distance and his thoughts followed. They'd been late getting to Clare. If what Ray said about her wanting to say good-bye was true then they wouldn't be standing here having this conversation if he and Jill had gotten to her in the time frame she'd given.

He said, "What does any of that have to do with our dad?"

"None she ain't already told you more times 'n you can count."

"Help me out here, Ray. You know her history, and you know her connections. You've gotta give me something I can work with today, not twenty-seven years ago."

"I ain't being abstruse. Told you, son — and nothin's changed since — I dunno what's happened to your mom or where she's gone."

"You said 'stuff happens' whenever Clare surfaces to look for our father."

"That it does."

"Was she looking for him now?"

"None that she told me, but like I said, time's gettin' on, and with your mother, there's just no tellin' what she's up to or why." Ray shrugged. "That woman's had a lotta years to make a lotta enemies. If it was me lookin' to find her now, first thing I'd be askin' is which way'd the chopper go."

"Due east."

"Houston, then, more 'n likely. Lotsa ships in Houston. Two big airports, plus a handful of regionals."

"Easy route out of the country."

"Could be," Ray said. "Or to other parts of the country."

Ray went back to studying the ground and nodded slightly, as if plotting his way through a maze and then, one blink to the next, his head was gone, obliterated into red mist with a rifle crack that split the morning like a bullwhip wrapping around Jack's throat, cutting off his air, slicing his veins, and bleeding him dry.

In slow-motion disbelieving horror he watched Ray's body fall, and Jack was rolling, stumbling to his feet, running for the porch, body on autopilot while his insides bellowed and brayed. Jill barreled off the road in the direction the report had come.

Another crack ruptured the air.

Jack heaved into the front door, lifting the handle as he shoved, and it popped open for him, just as it always had. The window-pane beside him shattered.

He flung himself to the floor beside the couch, stretched a hand beneath fabric folds, found the casing strap, and yanked.

An old .308 thumped to the carpet, a trusty friend from Raymond's past. Jack grabbed the rifle and bolted through the living room, down the hall, and tore out the back to where the dogs, howling in their runs, pawed at the fences.

The staccato of Jill's semiautomatic fire hurried him on.

He raced along the chain-link, slamming latches, opening gates.

The Catahoulas darted first, with the blueticks right behind, tearing out of the kennels and around the corner, hunting and tracking dogs, all of them. They knew Jack, they didn't know Jill, and they'd probably head for Raymond first, but none of that mattered as far as the shooter was concerned, because unless he planned to stay in a tree until they shot him down, the dogs would find him, and dogs were trouble.

Jack followed the pack, running from the back porch to the carport and from the carport into the verdure. Most of the dogs broke off for the cul-de-sac, and he kept going, tracking his sister in his head, plunging down the opposite side of the road.

The pack quieted. Gunfire stayed silent. His breath labored hard in his ears, and then, in the distance, an engine turned over and he knew they'd lost their target. He found Jill on her knees at the base of a tree four hundred yards to the west.

"I hit the motherfucker," she said. She dabbed her fingers against the ground and pulled them back red. "The bastard hit and ran," she said. "Same MO as the asshole at Clare's place. Gotta be the same guy."

Jack leaned into the tree and slid to the ground.

Rifle across his lap, he drew air into burning lungs, and his focus drifted toward the house, toward the closest thing he'd had to family now lying dead under the bayou sun.

What little he'd had was lost forever. So many years he could have come home and hadn't.

Jill said, "We need to get out of here before this comes back on us."

His head rolled against the tree in her direction. "Shooter came for Ray."

Jill stopped and turned and took a step back toward him.

Jack said, "You, me, and him huddled close like that, it could have been any one of us first, but he took Ray. Wasn't luck of the draw and wasn't an accident."

He didn't finish the thought. Jill had been the shooter often enough to know how things worked with multiple targets and only one clean shot.

She said, "Is this on us? Did we lead him here?"

"It's on Clare. She called him."

"She called us, too."

"Yep," he said. "Whoever did this is already looking for us. Ray was just easier to find. Only a matter of time, really, before they figure out that the same people who keep showing up in the right place at the wrong time are the ones the phones trace back to."

He heaved up and stood and started a slow trudge toward the house.

Jill caught his arm. "Wrong direction," she said. "Car's that way."

He shrugged her off. "I'm not leaving Ray out there rotting for the dogs to eat."

Jill stood in his way. "We need to go," she said. "We need to go *now.*"

She was right, of course. Ray's place, rural as it was, wasn't surrounded by thousands of empty acres like Clare's. The rifle reports had been heard by someone who'd recognize them as something other than hunting or target practice, and even if they hadn't been heard, the dogs would eventually bring attention back.

Fingers would point at them, the hammer of the law would fall hard, and that was the best-case scenario if they were caught here.

Jack couldn't bring himself to care.

Hands against his chest, Jill pushed him back. "Can't let you do it, John."

He gripped her wrists and shoved her aside.

She raised the rifle and put the muzzle between them. "You're thinking with your heart, and this is not the time to have a heart. You can hurt it out all you want when it's over, but right now you need to use your brain."

Disgust rose up like bile in his mouth.

He said, "You sound just like your mother."

Jill's jaw clenched, and she shoved into him. "I'm warning you. I will take you down before I let you become a liability."

He looked at her, through her, reached for the muzzle, and nudged it aside. "You can't," he said. "I'm the only one left who knows what it's like to be you."

CHAPTER 14

Holden
Age: 32
Location: Miami, Florida
Passport Country: Spain
Names: Thiago Martín Moreno

He moved beneath the skylights, swallowed in a kaleidoscope of race, color, and social class, jostled this way and that by hurried people and waddling people and tired children and travelers with too many bags. Airports, big, fat international airports, were where the rich rubbed shoulders with the poor, and light touched dark, and East met West in ways otherwise impossible. Airports were where the folds of the world overlapped, and they were ground zero in the study of becoming someone else.

A large African in a bright green head wrap had taught him this.

He'd been seventeen then, waiting out a layover in Zurich Airport's food court.

She'd sat across from him, the African woman, with three orders of fries and nothing else, had dumped the fries onto her tray, and then slipped off her sandals, lifted bare calloused feet onto the chair at his left, and with long, red toenails pointing toward his face, had begun to eat.

The clash of cultures had left him fighting not to stare.

He'd failed.

And by failing, he'd awakened understanding.

He'd grasped then, for the first time, the way enough small details correctly assembled could warp perception and create a new reality, could provide invisibility.

That woman with her fries and long red toenails could have been Eurasian or Middle Eastern, could have been an American white man on the run, and he never would have seen beyond the details — never would have seen the details at all had he not been present within those overlapping folds — and so airports became his university, and the people in them his study major. How appropriate, then, that the schooling he needed now would come from the same hallowed concourses and corridors.

He reached the flight board and stood, scanning, because that's what travelers did.

Inside his head the kill in Louisiana looped on endless replay, those final moments again and again, and he puzzled over them as he had on the two-hour drive to Houston, and all the way through airport security, and then for the whole uncomfortable flight. Not the kill exactly, which had been flawless, but the strangers who'd shown up as he'd closed in. Two job sites interrupted back-to-back by a male-female pair.

Didn't take much in the way of deductive reasoning to put the same ghost label on both of them, but therein lay the confusion. The team he'd faced during the night had been a skilled, professional challenge. The two he'd faced in daylight had squabbled like a married couple in a strange mix of confidence and uncertainty. He would have written off the bizarre behavior as the odd coupling of a nerd and a stripper if not for the way they'd handled their weapons.

He needed a toothpick, needed to chew.

Even a coffee stirrer or plastic straw would work, but he couldn't afford that risk because chewing was the type of detail that, if observed more than once, marked the man and tore holes through the best disguise.

Boarding calls and gate changes came like

the voice of God from the Heavens.

Holden glanced at his phone to check the time, just like any passenger with a lengthy layover would do. The motion was a detail. As were the shoes that gave him an extra two inches in height, and the backpack bought off a college kid at Starbucks a week before, and the baseball cap that made him a Longhorns fan, and the Beats headphones placed over the cap, which all together removed a dozen years and gave the cameras something to look at other than his face.

Cameras — with their indelible, searchable records which, in retrospect and hindsight, provided the ability to see beyond the details — were the price he paid to slip between the folds.

He slouched with the pathetic demeanor of the kid who'd sold him the backpack, and turned for the main concourse in search of food.

The nerd and the stripper kept pace inside his head.

He'd watched them, puzzling over their actions, trying to determine if they knew he was there and if the bizarre behavior was an act to draw him out, or if, instead, they were rogue operatives trying to make a name by stealing the contract out from under him. He'd watched until the target met them, had waited until it seemed as though some agreement had been made and, unwilling to stand by as two unknowns stole what was his, he'd taken the first shot and lined up for the second.

The stripper had stopped him.

She'd spun, looked right at him, and flashed her breasts.

One blinking delay of brain freeze had cost him the second kill, and the third.

She'd tracked him down in the time it took to zip his supplies and rappel out of the tree, had opened fire, spraying blindly, and had grazed his thigh and side.

A suitcase slammed into Holden's foot.

He stumbled into the present, blushing through apologies offered by a young mother wearing a baby in a sling, then took a breath and slowed his pace.

He strolled past Shula's Steak House.

The petite blonde behind the hostess station smiled.

He backed up, then followed her in, scanning diners, watching faces, and gauging interactions all the way to a table at the back, where he sat and studied the menu until a wrist with a Rolex attached to an arm in a pink dress shirt moved into his line of sight. Its owner sat across from him.

Holden glanced up to slicked black hair

and a pencil-thin mustache over café au lait skin nearly as light as his own. Three open buttons on the shirt showcased a thick gold rope around a solid neck on a body that looked far too healthy to be creeping past seventy. Holden went back to scanning menu items he didn't care to eat.

He said, "You look like a drug dealer."

The guy said, "This is Miami. I don't got the beach body and a guy's gotta blend in somehow." The sarcasm, rich and resonant, was filled with a New England accent that had been buried under the Appalachian foothills and revived in the Bolivian highlands.

Holden said, "How's that been working for you?"

"Eh. The bosses are happy. It's all that matters."

The server arrived. Holden removed the headphones and stuffed them into the backpack at his feet. His fingers caught a small envelope on the way back out and sleight of hand slipped the envelope under his menu and then across the table while he ordered.

It was gone by the time the server cleared away the cardstock.

Holden said, "Good to see you, Frank. How long you in town?"

The mustachioed pink shirt fidgeted with his phone beneath the table. "Long as it takes," he said. "You?"

"Catching a flight in an hour. Thanks, you know, for this."

The older man nodded. Silence filled the space between them.

When history went back eighteen years and each man carried enough dirt on the other to guarantee a concrete tomb under an ice-cold pier, silence was more than enough.

Frank stopped fiddling. He brought the phone up, glanced at the screen, pulled it away for a clearer look, then tugged reading glasses from his pocket and slipped them on.

He flipped from one picture to the next and turned the phone facedown on the table. He said, "That the best you got?"

"What do you mean, *the best*? Those are damn good shots, and you know it."

Frank shrugged, unimpressed. "They're all you have?"

"All I have."

"What else you know?"

"The woman is Karen McFadden, single female, fifty-two years old, alias Katrin Schmittlein, alias Catherine Smith. Alias goes on ten names deep. Took six of us to take her alive. The younger two are ghosts encountered twice, first on her hit and then again on a cleanup. For them, I've got a VIN that's tracing to dead ends and the pictures on that card. That's it."

Frank turned the phone over and flicked the screen again.

"What'd you do these at? Four, five hundred yards?"

"Four-thirteen."

Frank nodded and shrugged, as if to say, "Not bad." He moved the phone under the table. The SD card flicked into Holden's lap.

Frank said, "Ghosts are too young. After my time. Don't got nothing on them for you, but this Karen McFadden, she's trouble. She wanted you dead, you and me wouldn't be talking right now."

"She wanted me dead."

"So you say. Who sent you for her?"

"Don't know. Was a brokered deal."

Frank winced in pained disapproval.

Holden said, "Was hoping you'd be able to tell me who'd want her."

The food arrived. Frank winked at the server, called her honey doll, and ogled her ass when she walked away. She was young enough to be his granddaughter.

Holden waited until she was out of earshot

and said, "The Rolex and greasy hair aren't enough? Now you gotta be a lecher, too?"

Frank jabbed a knife into a rare steak, sliced off a piece, and shoved it in his mouth. Chewing, he said, "Lay off. At my age, looking's all I get anymore."

Holden pushed his plate toward the table's center. "I got twenty minutes."

"McFadden," Frank said. He pointed his knife for emphasis. "Everyone's wanted a piece of that woman over the years. She started out as CIA. Clandestine operative. She was good, too. Ran deep undercover in Moscow attached to an asset valued so highly the agency kept her outside the chain of command. Chief of Station didn't even know she was in town. On a strategic level, probably the smartest thing they ever did, but for everything else, not so much."

CHAPTER 15

Holden
Age: 32
Location: Miami, Florida
Passport Country: Spain
Names: Thiago Martín Moreno

Frank sliced another red, fat-rimmed bite. "To understand McFadden, you'd have to understand the mess she came from," he said. "But it's Cold War stuff, before your time. You wouldn't know it."

Holden offered the man an extra napkin.

Frank waved him off.

Holden said, "I was young, but I remember. Work with me."

Frank chewed and nodded and restuffed his mouth. He said, "CIA ops in the USSR were bullshit. Soviets wiped their asses with us. Still do." He grabbed his soda straw and washed the food down. "We had maybe three or four high-value assets over the entire course of the war, not recruits, mind

149

you, walk-ins, and those poor bastards all ended up executed for the trouble. Meanwhile, we're being spoon-fed disinformation by guys we think we're controlling, and that's the shit that got churned into some of our most important intelligence analyses.

"The KGB ran a hell of an operation, I'll give them that. They were ruthless in ferreting out our officers. That didn't excuse our missteps, mind you. Hell, there was hardly an officer stationed in Russia who even spoke the language. Wasn't just Soviet Russia that went bad, either. Had a two-year spell in the mid-eighties where the agency lost every spy in Eastern Europe. So, along comes McFadden, fluent enough in Russian to pass as a native. She's like this . . . I dunno what you'd call it. . . . A shapeshifter. You could know her for years and pass right by her on the street and not know it was her you's seeing. If intelligence was actually up to date, if anyone had seen what was coming, then maybe they wouldna sent her or woulda gotten her out before the shit hit the fan.

"She got caught in the mess as the USSR was coming undone. One day she bleeps off the map. No one knows what's happened. Higher up the chain, they're thinking she got snatched, but there's nothing leaking out of the KGB, and later nothing from the FSB or the SVR, either." Frank paused and then, as if he was teaching high school world history, said, "Those are what the KGB morphed into after the restructuring."

Holden kept a straight face. "I keep score for a living, Frank. I'm familiar with the terminology."

The man didn't miss a beat. "So the State Department gets involved, like the CIA's supersecret missing spy is some regular Jane. The Russians swear they have no idea what we're talking about, and we don't know if that's typical denial or if she's gotten lost in the chaos of right-hand, left-hand miscommunication.

"Couple years later, she shows up in Prague for a hit-and-run. Not as McFadden, you see. She's never been reliably ID'd since she was last seen in Moscow, but a lot of old-timers swear by the MO that it's her. Could be wrong. For all they know, she died in some Soviet hellhole, and this thing, this person, maybe more than one person, has been using her legend as cover. Still, someone who fits the profile would show up a few times a year and always left a dead man in her wake."

"Political assassin?"

"Political, economical, something like

151

that, but here's the thing. A decade rolls around, and then, *bam,* she's gone again, completely vanishes. Been so long since she's left her mark that I'da thought she's dead if it weren't for seeing that photo. So if this really is McFadden, the question you need to ask yourself is why you were able to find her in the first place."

"You think she wanted to be found?"

Frank stuffed more than a mouthful into his oversize mouth and shrugged. Knife in the air, he said, "Far be it from me to tell you what that woman's thinking. Alls I know is if McFadden wanted you dead, we wouldn't be sitting here now."

"What about the ghosts? Can you get me something on them?"

Frank laughed. "I like you, kid, you know I do, but I'm a month out from a beach house in the Bahamas and a pair of twins in bikinis. I don't like you that much worth."

The older man paused. He put his fork and knife down. For the first time since he'd joined Holden at the table, he looked him dead in the eyes. "Now wait up," he said. "You got McFadden, didn't you? Delivered your target?"

Holden nodded.

"Then what's driving all this need to know?"

"Self-preservation."

"Someone put a hit out on you?"

"Don't know, but I get the feeling I'm the final loose end on this McFadden deal and those ghosts are the ones sent to take me out."

"Ah, the plot gets clearer." Frank pushed back from the table. "You're thinking someone knows she's alive and wants the rest of the world to think she's stayed dead?"

"Contract called for no witnesses and no trails. I'm both."

Frank pressed his lips together and studied the table. "Brokered deals are a dangerous thing, kid. You were raised better than to mix with that pit of vipers."

Holden smirked. "I was raised on behalf of that pit of vipers."

Frank shook his head. "Nah." He shook his head some more. "Not like this, no." He dumped his napkin on the table. "Listen, I know a guy who needs a security detail, pays real good. You decide to switch career paths, let me know. I'll hook you up."

"How about hooking me up with someone who can access NGI?"

Frank stood. Hands on the chair, he paused.

Holden waited. He'd find the ghosts with or without help, but the FBI's Next Generation Identification system, which took facial recognition to a whole other level, added a real-time scan that factored in body height, gait, scars, tattoos, and birthmarks and ran it all against a database of every immigration pass-through, law enforcement encounter, fingerprint, palm print, and mug shot, could cut a long-term search down to days.

Frank looked Holden over. "I worry about you," he said. "It's an ugly business, and these are dangerous people."

"I'll be okay."

"As a favor to an old man, try to not hit the grave before I do. Maybe put the good looks and good body to use while you still got 'em. Get out while you can. Meet a girl. Get laid. Settle down."

"Get me hooked up with NGI and I'll make your wishes come true."

"Was good to see you, kid. Thanks for lunch."

Holden smiled and watched the pink shirt leave.

The detour had cost him a day, the information on McFadden was worth ten. He paid the bill and slouched back to the boarding area, slept through the return flight, and fought with the ghosts in his dreams.

At Houston's George Bush Intercontinental he was one more body in another of the world's overlapping folds until a random glance at a random soundless television showing a random over-tanned, over-bleached newscaster brought him face-to-face with the stripper.

He paused mid-step, choked on his own surprise, and then continued in slow, cautious disbelief to stand before the TV.

Subtitles gave him the gist: Panicked boyfriend. Missing girlfriend kidnapped out of his house at gunpoint. Police sketch of no one Holden recognized. Austin law enforcement asking the public for any information.

And then the television gods gifted Holden with names:

Jennifer White.

Robert Davis.

The reporting ended. Video switched to a hamburger settling in slow motion onto a bun, and Holden turned away, feet on autopilot, headed for the exit while his mind stumbled past disbelief into anger.

He hated, hated, *hated* being played for a fool, and only a fool would walk, invited, into the trap that had just been laid out.

But that didn't mean he couldn't utilize the information in his own way.

He put the battery into his phone and

powered it on.

The bounty had been delivered. Baxter had cut Rafi loose with a threat to never show his face on a contract application again, and the big guy was kicking back, waiting for news on what next.

Holden punched in his number.

Now was the time to go hunting in pairs.

CHAPTER 16

Jill
Age: 26
Location: Beaumont, Texas
Passport Country: USA
Names: Julia Jane Smith

The bar and grill was an upscale mom-and-pop affair, just south of Beaumont, off Interstate 10, with plenty of midafternoon booth space and a clean, empty bathroom where she could dip into her purse without being disturbed. In the stall, alone, she sniffed relief, closed her eyes, and leaned back against the wall.

She'd threatened Jack with bodily injury if they didn't stop for food. She hadn't eaten since dawn, had endured the heat and the dogs and the emotional conflict of burying Ray. She wasn't waiting for sustenance until they reached Houston, no matter what Jack had planned. Not like they really had a plan.

Houston was where Ray seemed to think

Clare would have been taken.

Jack's reasoning went that the shooters would never have put the effort into taking Clare alive if they'd wanted her dead, that there were a dozen airports north and south of the Earthship that would make for simpler logistics than heading east, that the only thing east that made sense was Houston, and that the only thing that would make Houston a better option than any of those dozen airports was if they were taking Clare somewhere by ship. So he had his sights on the Houston Ship Channel and was hell-bent on getting there as quickly as he could. But the ship channel was fifty miles long, and Houston was a big fucking place.

Not a plan.

Jill opened the stall and headed for the door.

She caught sight of herself in the mirror and paused.

Her clothes were a disaster. Her roots needed doing. The shower at her apartment had worn off six hours ago, and she looked like Clare — a younger, rounder version of Clare, with the same skin, light enough to be white, tan enough for Hispanic or Asian or Polynesian, same light brown eyes that fell within those ethnicity ranges, same cheekbones, same nose — which was why her hair was always any color but natural, and why home had so few mirrors, and why seeing her face now made the past forty-eight hours feel that much more fucked up.

She moved closer and studied her reflection.

Anger and loss and hope and fear and want and need and love and hate gushed up into the stillness. She slammed the mental lid shut. There weren't enough drugs in the world to make it worth looking inside *that* Pandora's box.

She pawed through her purse for mascara and a tube of rose gloss and spotted the phone instead — not the burner phone, not her personal phone — the Blackphone that connected her to the Broker.

Unanswered questions doused her high with a miserable comedown.

She nudged the phone aside.

She'd call him. She would. Soon as she figured out how, because she couldn't just put in for an audience with a man who paid good money for dead bodies and be all, *Hey, um, any chance those guys you sent me to kill sent someone to kidnap my mom? Or did you kidnap her? Or maybe you know who did?*

She brushed goop on her lashes and highlighted her lips and cheeks, then left the bathroom and threaded between mostly empty tables, avoiding eye contact and hoping no one else could smell her the way she could smell herself.

Her brother, without the benefit of a shower, was twice as rank.

Food waited for her at the booth.

She slid onto the bench and stuffed fries in her mouth before her butt hit wood.

Jack, across the table, pushed and prodded his food, just like he used to in places where unwanted surprises often found their way onto a plate.

She shoved a fry toward him and said, "Eat."

He batted her away.

She wiggled the fry and pushed it up close to his nose.

He brushed her away again and said, "Stop."

But she couldn't.

Annoying him, provoking him, was self-harm that soothed a deeper pain.

She doused her hamburger with condiments, took a mouth and a half full and, meat juice running down her fingers, went after him again. "Eat."

He smacked her hand. "I said stop."

She smooshed a fry on his chin, because making him mad was better than the dark, brooding silence that forced her to feel and think in ways she'd rather not.

He looked up, face red and fists on the table, and his eyes kept going, tracking over her shoulder, and his expression shifted to surprise, and his mouth went slack.

"Put your hat on," he said.

She took a sip of sweet tea and dug in for another messy bite. "Why?"

He leaned forward.

Still looking over her shoulder, he hissed, "Hat. On. Now."

She turned, followed his line of sight to the television on the back wall, and there was Robert Davis, good ole all-American, clean-cut, solid, reputable, fucking Robert Davis — the first guy she'd ever considered sticking around for, the guy she'd been stupid enough to think she could pick back up with after this was over — on the news, choking down emotion, telling the world she'd been taken at gunpoint and asking for help in bringing her home.

She reached for the baseball cap beside her and slid it on.

Jack nudged sunglasses beneath her fingers.

She turned to her food, pushed the glasses on, and slunk lower in her seat.

She'd caught only the final fifteen seconds, but even that was enough for her to realize the shit storm she was in. Attracting attention was the worst of the worst of the worst, but this was in a whole galaxy of its own.

Jack leaned toward her and hissed, "Have you lost your goddamn mind, letting him get a picture of you like that?"

Jill stared at her plate, thoughts scattering like a dozen terrified cats refusing to be herded, struggling, trying to place the image and sort through missing memories for where and when the photo had been taken, trying to breathe away the disgust rising up from her belly like spoiled food. She'd liked Rob, she'd genuinely liked him, and she'd stuck around for him, because for the first time in her short messed-up life, she'd found a legitimately decent guy who was strong enough to call her on her bullshit and laugh at it and whose brain she couldn't turn to jelly. But this, this public spectacle, this begging and ineffectuality, this going to the police and media — which, from society's point of view, was probably a heroic thing — this was repellant.

Jack's judgment bored through the hat and into her skull.

This shouldn't be happening. Couldn't be happening.

"I didn't," she said. "I didn't let him take pictures."

162

"Then you were too buzzed out of your head to notice or to do anything to stop him. Pick your poison, sister dearest. This is on you."

Memory failed her, left her nothing to hold on to.

She shook her head.

He said, "You don't even remember it happening, do you?"

She couldn't answer that.

"I warned you," he said. "I told you he was going to be a problem. I told you to call him. You said you'd deal with it, said you'd take care of it."

"I did," she said. "You saw me send the text."

"Because I *made* you. Because you never *called.*"

"Whatever. It got dealt with, so this isn't my fault."

"Your face is plastered all over the television, and you want to talk about fault? This isn't about fault. It's about fixing. You broke it, you fix it, and you better fix it in a hurry because trying to find Clare is impossible enough without every do-gooder in the state calling in hotline tips everywhere you go." He sat back, crossed his arms, and glared. "I get hauled in for this, and you can kiss Clare good-bye forever, and me, too, for that matter."

Jill shoved fries in her mouth and, staring him down, worked the food the way a cow chewed cud. Jack's jaw clenched. He motioned for the server, and when he'd gotten her attention, he smiled a forced smile that almost passed as charming and circled a finger over their barely touched plates.

"Duty calls," he said. "We need to get this packed up and need the check."

The server returned the smile and headed off.

Jack tapped his fingers against the table. He said, "You need to call him. Need to call him, let him hear your voice, make sure he knows it's you, and put an end to this now."

Jill bit another mouthful off the burger, kept staring, kept chewing.

Jack, the good son, Jack, the responsible son, Jack, the son who could do no wrong had, by dragging her out of that house, put them in this predicament in the first place. And, just like always, the fallout for both their mistakes was fully her failure.

It was the same damn argument they'd had for twenty damn years, only this time instead of Clare casting blame, Jack was the blithering surrogate.

Jack, the smart one. Jack, the emotional idiot.

Jack, who never did understand why she'd rage at him as if he were Clare, never got that the reason she lashed out whenever he came to her defense was because taking her side only intensified the pain when he didn't.

"I never asked to be favored," he'd say.

No, but he didn't turn his back on it, either.

"What was I supposed to do?" he'd ask. "We were just kids. I was just a kid. I wanted and needed parental love and approval as much as any other child would, and I never threw you under the bus to get it."

And she'd feel guilty, because she loved him, and it was harsh to hold his child self responsible for adult choices, but this right here, this brought it all back.

This was what hurt the most.

Here he was, parroting Clare's bullshit, blind as fuck to his own responsibility.

He'd bought into the fucking mind-set and couldn't even see it.

But he was right about one thing, and she hated that he was right, because she didn't want to make the call to Robert now any more than she had after Jack had humiliated her by dragging her out of that house right in front of him.

They left the restaurant and drove in angry silence, Jack at the wheel.

She played worst-case scenario in her head down the freeway miles until Jack turned off onto the wide white concrete of a rest-area lot. He backed up against a wooded area, shut off the engine, and stared out the windshield.

She dug through her purse for the phone and the battery, snapped the pieces back together and, with her thumb over the CALL button, said, "If I'm going to do this, I want privacy."

Jack barked out a laugh. For emphasis, he added, "No."

She pushed away the urge to punch him in his stupid mouth.

She couldn't compete with him brain to brain, couldn't make Clare love her the way Clare loved him, but none of that mattered when she could take him down in two fast seconds, break him into submission, and beat his self-righteous no into a yes.

That had always been the reason for training hard, fighting hard, and getting her teeth knocked in by bigger assholes. Except she couldn't, not here, not now, because he'd leave, and she'd be cut off from finding Clare, and she didn't have *that* in her, so instead, she thumb-punched CALL.

The line connected.

And rang.

And rang.

Voice mail answered.

She hung up without leaving a message and heel kicked the dashboard.

Her hand vibrated. She fumbled, dropped, and caught the phone.

Baby blues under black hair smiled at her from a good-looking face that had, until two days ago, felt like hope. She swiped and answered.

Robert said, "Jen? Is that you?"

It took a second to make the switch, to move out of anger and confusion and twenty-six years of shit and get her head back to the fun-loving party girl he knew.

"Oh, thank God," she said. "I was so scared when you didn't answer."

"Are you okay?" he said. "Where are you?"

Her mind rushed through an array of possible directions in which to steer the conversation and got caught between real and fake.

She'd always been true with him.

Well, besides the lies.

Which were pretty much everything.

But besides those, she'd been authentic — as close to whatever a person like her could know as authentic — because he'd been the first guy, besides Ray, besides her brother, who'd called her on her bullshit and manipulation.

That was why she'd liked him.

And that created just a small problem in the moment.

She said, "Of course I'm okay — *was* okay. I just saw my face on TV. Rob, those poor police, those poor volunteers, and all that wasted time and money. I texted you, and I told you I was fine. This has gone off the rails. You have *got* to let everyone know there's been a misunderstanding."

The line hung dead with silence, and when Robert spoke, his tone went cold.

"Misunderstanding," he said. "Some guy comes and rips you out of my house, and you're just gone. I call and I call and I call, and you never answer, and then, finally, the next morning, I get a text — a text anyone could have written — and when I text you back, you don't answer that, either. The police can't get a trace on your phone, you've basically vanished, and I keep trying, and for two days nothing, until now." He paused and took a breath. "I'm glad you're fine. I'm so relieved I'm angry. You want to know how I am? I'm wrecked, that's how I am, and this isn't anywhere near a misunderstanding."

CHAPTER 17

Jill
Age: 26
Location: Beaumont, Texas
Passport Country: USA
Names: Julia Jane Smith

She sighed, oozed sugar and sweetness into her voice, and thickened the vulnerability. "What do you want me to say, Rob? My cousins can be over the top with their pranks and jokes. Grabbing me like that was extreme, but I wasn't ever in danger. I thought when I texted, you'd find it hilarious, just like I did."

Sarcasm dripped back, thick enough to feel. "Right. Some stranger hauls you out of my house and throws you in his trunk, and you think I'd find that *funny?*"

"When you put it that way . . ." She let the thought trail off into sorrowful remorse. "Please don't be mad. These past few days have been hard enough as it is."

Robert's tone turned harder. He said, "Some woman calling from Jen's number says Jen is fine. You could be anyone. Someone could be forcing you to make this call. I'm not kidding here. You really need to contact Austin PD and tell them from your own lips, so they can be the judge of what's what. And again, where are you?"

She nudged exasperation up a notch. "Same as I told you yesterday. Bastrop, with my friend Angela, the one whose mother got hit by a drunk driver. I've been stuck here, trying to help as best as I can with funeral arrangements and stuff. I miss you," she said. "I really am sorry for the drama."

"You could have called using Angela's phone."

Jill clenched her teeth, tipped her head back and took in a long calming breath. "Angela's been crying nonstop, doesn't eat, can't sleep, and I've been just a little distracted."

"Well, you've got your priorities."

"Come on, Rob," she whispered. "Don't be like that."

He said, "You do what you need to do. I'll let the detectives know we've had this conversation, and I'll let them know my doubts."

He paused and she waited and he hung

up on her.

Feet on the dash, face tipped up, she tossed the phone on the floor.

Silence filled the car.

Jack draped his arms over the steering wheel and rested his forehead against them.

She said, "Do you think Robert had something to do with Clare? The timing and all, putting me up on television, do you think it's to pull us out into the open?"

"No."

She would have asked him to explain, would have pestered to understand how, given everything else over the past two days, he was so sure, but under the circumstances she knew better, and so she let him be.

He said, "How clean is this car?"

"Clean."

"Need more than that from you right now."

"Titled to a New Mexico corporation with a ghost address in Hawaii. Plates, insurance, and tags go to a drop in McAllen."

He nodded, and she couldn't tell if he was relieved, impressed, or finally willing to acknowledge she wasn't a complete fool, and it didn't matter because he changed the subject. He said, "There's liquid latex in my tool bag."

"That's your plan B?"

He sat up and looked at her. "You got a better way?"

She scooted up and twisted around to grab his bag and drag it to the front.

He carried latex for the same reason Clare claimed she'd stopped traveling: each year the grid got tighter, the data aggregation better, and facial recognition software further advanced, which made it more and more difficult to remain invisible. Latex built a temporary disguise from the skin up, widening the nose, softening the eye sockets, and reshaping cheekbones and jawline. Hardest was altering distance between the eyes, but even that was doable with a keen attention to detail and a steady hand. A half hour of work could modify the landmarks and shift enough distance between nodal points to both mess with the software and change the way a face looked to the naked eye. She'd carried the stuff, too, before she pilfered her stash to become Jennifer Lopez for Halloween, and had never bothered to replace it. Liquid latex was Jack's solution to her face being plastered all over the news.

Robert's picture, which had caught her in mid-movement, wasn't incredibly clear and probably not even framed well enough for facial recognition to pick up half the nodal points, but it definitely showed enough for strangers to recognize her walking down the street. Latex meant Jack planned to ignore the Robert issue for the time being and focus entirely on finding Clare.

She was good with that.

She dragged the bag forward and zipped open the inner pocket.

The bag vibrated and rang — rather, the burner phone inside the bag — the phone Clare would call. Jill's hands froze. Her heart seized. Jack reacted because she couldn't. He ripped Velcro, grabbed the phone, and took the call faster than she'd seen him move in a long time.

He punched over to speaker, cut out pleasantries, and said, "Hey."

Clare's voice came through, Clare without a doubt, Clare alive and live in the moment, speaking to him as if he were a lover, not a son.

She said, "Baby, I'm sorry I missed the party."

In a routine so old and used so often that Jill wished she could forget, Jack said, "Make it up to me. Dinner and drinks. I'll bring a friend. Your place or mine?"

"Yours. As soon as I'm —" And Clare was gone.

A voice replaced hers, not so much a voice as a computerized rendering of human speech. "Your services are no longer needed," the voice said. "You will no longer be paid for protection, and any further action on your part will result in death."

Jack stuck to the role.

He said, "Hey, dickwad, I don't know who you think you are. . . ."

The line went dead.

Jill said, "That went well."

It was the best she could do to keep from vomiting.

In so few coded words Jack had told Clare they were together, and in return Clare had told them to stay away, but it was the other voice that had made her guts turn inside out.

Jack set the phone down and, oblivious to what they'd heard, said, "I guess we sit tight and let her do her thing."

The words were tiny bombs to her brain arteries, twisting reality into a slow-motion dream that couldn't be possible.

She said, "No."

"What do you mean, no?"

Primal screams, frustration, and fear and anger filled her head, her chest.

He didn't know what she knew.

To abandon Clare now was to leave her to die.

She wasn't ready for that, not like this,

not like this. . . .

She said, "It's so obvious. Can't you see it? Clare saw the news footage, she was hunting for confirmation that we were both alive, and okay, that's what that was."

Jack looked at her like she was stupid. He said, "This is Clare we're talking about. If there's a way out, she's going to find it without our help. This was her letting us know that she's alive so we stop looking and don't interfere and mess up whatever she's got going on."

He pulled the burner apart, took out the battery, and removed the SIM.

Jill's blood roiled in protest.

Burners were one-time use. Jack would run the car over the phone, flush the pieces down a toilet, and Clare would never be able to call again.

She couldn't breathe. She needed air. She said, "Goddammit, John. Stop and think for a minute. The stuff that happened on her property and what happened to Raymond . . . Whoever has her is going to use her and then kill her. She's just trying to keep us away from it."

Jack ignored her like she'd never spoken. More of the same. The way it'd always been. Soon as Clare offered an opinion or gave an instruction, his critical thinking stopped, and he did exactly what she wanted.

But Clare was wrong. He was wrong.

Jill's senses shut off, and fear took over: fear that he'd abandon Clare, that he'd abandon her. A guttural scream rose from far, far away, and she lunged over the center console into his seat, into his lap, fists jabbing in the short, tight space. She knocked his head back and gripped the seat belt and twisted it around his neck.

He bucked and flailed and hit her in turn, and she never felt a thing, until a knife jabbed through her shirt and broke skin. Face-to-face, breath to breath, she said, "I don't give a fuck what you think Clare said. We're going after her. We're going to find her. We're going to get her back."

His oxygen was cut off, and Jack's face turned a darker shade.

He twisted the knife deeper.

"Fuck this," she said.

She let go of the seat belt, and he gasped down air.

Her fingers caught the door handle, and she tumbled, shoulder first, down to the pavement, crawled to the bushes, and retched what little food she'd eaten right into them.

She didn't need to call the fucking Broker to find out if he knew anything about Clare.

The Broker, through Clare, had just called her.

CHAPTER 18

Rob
Age: 23
Location: Austin, Texas
Passport Country: USA
Names: Robert Preston Davis

The doorbell rang, followed by another knock, third time in two minutes, and he stood in the foyer, bare feet against cracked, aging marble, with his back to the wall.

He'd gotten this far and stopped short of answering.

He'd hardly slept in days. Couldn't remember when he'd last eaten. Hadn't shaved or showered since he forgot when. He didn't want to see people and yet desperately craved news, any news, so he fidgeted with his phone, too curious to walk away and too nervous to announce his presence by stealing a glimpse through the peephole.

The chime sounded above his head again.

Whoever was out there wasn't a sales guy,

anyone going door-to-door would have left by now. Wasn't Girl Scouts or a school fundraiser, either, wrong time of year for that. Probably wasn't a reporter. They had a tendency to trample his lawn and go looking into windows to get to him, and there wasn't any of that going on. His housemates had abandoned the place for safer territory, and none of their friends had come around since, so it wasn't them, either.

Indecision kept him frozen.

A voice spoke from the other side, nothing loud that the neighbors would hear, more like the person had pressed their mouth close to the hinges.

His stomach crawled up his throat.

More like whoever was out there knew he was here, right here behind the door.

The person said, "Just need to talk with you, Robert."

The tone was friendly, almost. Somewhere between "Let's have coffee" and "Don't make me come in there and get you."

"Come on, Robert," the voice said. "Don't drag this out all day."

His heart hurt. His mouth went dry. He wanted to fall asleep and wake up to a world where things were back to the way they'd been before he ever met Jen.

He took a breath, and opened the door to

two men in suits, big ole shadows blocking the afternoon sun. They were packing — definitely packing — and they wore the swagger of cop authority, but they looked more like younger versions of his dad's Marine Corps buddies than any officer or detective he'd encountered so far in this nightmare.

He hesitated for an awkward second, trying to place who they were and why they'd come. The smaller of the two stretched a hand forward and said, "Thanks for answering."

The guy had an accent, nothing glaring, just enough to point out that he was a transplant. He said, "We're here about Jennifer. Mind if we come in for a few?"

Robert shook the hand because it was there, but his palms flushed and his face burned and the world went a little dizzy.

Jen was dead. That was what this was.

They'd found her in a ditch somewhere. Assaulted. Decapitated. They believed he'd done it and were here to arrest him.

His jaw clenched shut.

Handcuffs and Miranda warnings would be next.

The talker pulled out a notepad and took a step closer. "We have a few more questions," he said.

Robert blinked through a slow motion blur. The words reordered into a different meaning: More questions meant these guys weren't here with answers. More questions meant Jen wasn't dead. Not yet. And they hadn't come to arrest him. Not yet.

Relief and desperation collided with reality.

More questions meant Jen was still missing, and what he needed now, most of all, was for her to be alive, very much alive, not just on the phone alive, but real-life, walk-into-a-police-station alive. For her sake and for his.

The talker said, "We won't take much of your time."

Robert's lips pressed together. His feet remained planted.

The talker tried stepping forward. "You mind?"

Hand on the door, Robert moved to shut it.

Yes, he minded. He minded very much. Going to the police had become a bad, bad idea. The asshole who'd taken Jen hadn't left so much as a fingerprint behind, and the crime-scene techs who'd crawled over his house hadn't found much to prove Jen had ever been there, either. Based on the way the questioning had gone, either the detectives were going to nail him for pulling a hoax or he was their prime suspect in her kidnapping.

There was no way to put a positive spin on that.

He'd told them about Jen's call. He'd begged them for the umpteenth time to trace her phone. They'd told him to sit tight and wait, which he was pretty sure was their way of telling him they believed this new story was even more bullshit than the first and were dead set on proving it.

The talker stuck his shoe over the threshold and blocked the door.

Robert glanced at the foot, then the face. He said, "Already told you everything I know."

The guy looked up from his pad. "Different agency. We're running a separate investigation from the outside."

Those ten words made the world tilt.

Different meant another shot at convincing someone to take his version of the story seriously. *Different* meant hope for both him and Jen.

"Texas Rangers?" Robert said. "FBI? You have a badge or anything?"

The big guy, the silent partner, the Dwayne "The Rock" Johnson wannabe with huge arms and a shaved head, said, "Yep."

He reached for his back pocket.

The talker moved forward to make space.

Robert stepped out of his way, and somehow, they were all three inside the foyer and then standing in awkward silence at the edge of the living room.

Robert glanced around, uncomfortably conscious of his unwashed hair, his clothes permeated with three days' worth of wrinkles and body odor, and the mess of takeout containers and spills littering the carpet. The kitchen, piled with dirty dishes and half-eaten food, was worse, with nothing cleaned, nothing cared for, because it had taken every bit of energy he had to endure the flow of Jen chaos and keep from breaking under the stress of not knowing what came next.

"Anything you need to help Jen," he said. "I just don't know what I can say that hasn't already been gone over a dozen times."

The talker shrugged in an almost apologetic way, which drained the tension from Robert's shoulders and made it hard not to like the guy. "You might as well run us through everything from the beginning," he said. "You know how it is between agencies. Not so great at communication."

Robert's jaw relaxed. He motioned toward the cluttered couch.

The talker said, "How about we start with your phone."

Robert's brows furrowed. His gaze drifted to the device in his hand. "The forensic team already mirrored it," he said. "You don't want to copy what they've got?"

Another disarming shrug, another self-deprecating smile, and the guy said, "It's that *other agency* thing. We're covering all the basics as a just in case. Want to make sure we've got Jennifer's number correct, confirm the time stamps on calls and texts, and get a look at the actual words she used in communicating with you over the past month."

Robert glanced from the talker to the big guy, who stood a few feet away, expression grim, badge billfold gripped tight in a dinner-plate hand, and changed his mind about asking for a closer look.

The talker said, "We'll also need any pictures, notes, gifts, anything tangible you might have that you haven't already turned over."

Robert rubbed his eyes. This was like swimming against a riptide, more and more of the same thing and still no progress. He was exhausted. He wanted this over. "Don't have much," he said. "We weren't together that long before this all happened, and of course, the other guys took a lot. You'll have to check with them for that."

The big bald guy looked at his watch.

The talker said, "Anything you've got."

Robert sighed, slouched down the hall to his room, stood in his doorway, and sighed again. He'd yet to put anything back the way it'd been before the cops turned it all upside down, and didn't have the energy to even think about it. He knelt and dug through a pile by the desk for the shot glass Jen had got him on some trip she'd made to Europe right after they first met and reached into the desk drawer for the Schlitterbahn receipt he'd stashed in with a few old bills.

He couldn't think of anything else that might matter.

The suits were still standing when he returned to the living room.

He handed his stuff to the talker and then unlocked his phone to open up Jen's texts. Something stung his neck. He slapped his skin, jerked around, and came face to collar with the big guy. He hadn't noticed the suit move, but the dude was way up in his personal space.

Robert rubbed his neck, took a step away, and glowered.

He said, "What the hell was that about?"

Mr. Strong-and-Silent plucked the phone out of his hand.

Everything went hazy.

Robert struggled to stay on his feet.

From out in the fog, the big guy said, "Some of this should be useful."

The words were warm and toasty.

Useful was good. *Useful* meant maybe these guys could find Jen.

That was his last thought before the room went dark and his legs gave out.

CHAPTER 19

Jack
Age: 26
Location: La Porte, Texas
Passport Country: Paperless
Names: Jose Manuel Valero Santos

He sat on the floor between bed and bathroom wall in a room that stank of smoke and mold and cheap chemicals. Shotgun beside him, ice pack melting against lip and darkening eye, he studied the notepad on his lap.

He needed sleep.

What he had instead was the distraction of water rattling through the pipes in the wall at his back and a night of work that had barely begun.

They were out of the public eye for now, just south of the ship channel, surrounded by industry and a permanent eau de oil refinery, in a motel that catered to day laborers and the chronically homeless,

187

where customers paid cash, the desk clerks avoided eye contact, and a young man with a lost bar fight on his face could show up without speaking a word of English and fit right in.

Where to from here was anybody's guess.

They were as close to Clare as he could hope to get them, and might as well have been a continent away. He and Jill had spent the past five hours dredging up memories that had taken them years to forget — every story Clare had told, no matter how bizarre, every motivation and excuse, every move they'd made and the reasons why, every person she'd named and every person they'd met, cataloged in a timeline of sorts — five exhausting hours, until Jill, in sullen silence, had retreated to the bathroom to wash off the road wear.

He flipped through page after page of details that had, until two days ago, been delusional fantasy. If even half the stories were true, there were a hundred reasons for Clare to go missing, and he had to find one, just one, strong enough to reach out from the past to grab her. Trying to build off Raymond's strange questions and a lifetime of Clare's paranoia was like trying to build a life raft from baling twine and bubble gum.

Thinking about it made his head hurt.

What he really wanted was to let Clare sort this mess out on her own.

She didn't want their help, she'd made that clear.

Thirty seconds on the phone had given him that.

Jill wouldn't have any of it, wouldn't listen to reason, wouldn't acknowledge that by interfering they could make things worse. And so here they were. Not because of her fists or her threats to beat him half to death to force him to comply, which she was more than capable of making good on, but because Jill was panicked and slowly falling apart.

If forced to choose between saving Jill or saving Clare, it always had been and always would be Jill. That's what this really was: saving Jill.

Clare could handle her own affairs. If there was a way to get loose, she'd find it with or without their meddling. The phone call had made that clear, too.

You will no longer be paid for protection.

That was so typically Clare: kidnapped — possibly tortured — in a position of weakness and at the mercy of people who hated her, and she still managed to spin bullshit into gold to get exactly what she wanted while giving up zip in return.

She knew her kids were alive, and she had gotten her message through.

In exchange, her enemies believed her kids were mercenary protectors. Even so, the second part of the guy's sentence kept coming back.

Any further action on your part will result in death.

It was a brush-off that ranked their threat level somewhere between an irritation and inconsequential — bugs to be squashed if they got underfoot — and that kind of dismissal could cut two ways. Either the people who had Clare truly viewed her so-called protectors as extraneous enough to settle with a warning, or they'd let her make the call in reverse manipulation and there was more coming, he just couldn't see it yet.

Jack pulled the lamp off the cigarette-burned nightstand and, under its dim wattage, flipped through the pages of notes, hoping for the latter. This was kamikaze hide-and-seek, and anything the other side threw at him would be better than what he had at the moment. Shouting from beyond the front door broke the logic progression.

He set pen and pad on the floor, gripped the shotgun, hugged the wall on the way to the window, and nudged the curtain just enough to get a glimpse of the lot.

Three gangbangers in sagging pants and torn T-shirts pushed each other around in an unintelligible argument that seemed to go nowhere. He let the curtain drop.

The car was still there, original plates swapped out for spares from his tool bag on the high chance a scanner-fitted patrol car rolled through the property, and the car was the only thing out there that mattered.

He returned to his place by the wall and, attuned to the sounds in the bathroom, paused. He checked his watch. Twenty minutes since the water had turned on, and the only things he'd heard were the rattling pipes and a constant spray.

He swore under his breath and strode for the door.

He'd known better than to leave her alone, especially now.

Knuckles to the flimsy wood, he rapped and waited. He called Jill's name and, with only more water and rattling for an answer, gripped the handle and heaved hard.

The frame splintered, the door popped open, and steam hit him in the face.

Jill, on the floor, with her back against the tub, looked up.

Her eyes were red and mascara stained her cheeks. Her cavernous purse lay open beside her. Three empty mini vodka bottles littered the floor nearby, and her right hand, limp in her lap, gripped a pill bottle. She sniffed and ran her sleeve under her nose and smiled with the dead-sick glaze of narcotics.

Jack knelt and unclenched her fist, pulled the bottle away, and read the label. Anger rose, fearful, vengeful anger — at her, but mostly at himself.

He'd known this was coming and had still let her out of sight.

He gripped her shoulder and shoved the bottle up in her face. "Is this what you took?" he said. "What's on the label? Is this what you took?"

Her drug-sick smile twisted and her eyelids drooped to half-mast in time with a slow-motion head drop.

"How many?" he said.

She struggled, elbows against the tub, to heave herself up off the floor and get away from him. Hand on her shoulder, he shoved her down.

"How many?"

She sniffed and wiped her nose again. "Two." Her words were slurred. "Maybe three."

Given her habits, the opiate-alcohol combo wasn't enough for an overdose, but she'd be out for a good long while. He stuffed the bottle into his pocket, got in her face, and searched her faraway eyes. He wanted to hit her. Instead, he grabbed her, shook her and, volume rising, said, "The fuck are you doing to yourself?"

Jill sniffed. "You used a bad word," she said. She giggled. "You never use bad words. Only I get to use them." Her voice cracked. "I'm telling Clare."

"You're killing yourself," he said.

Her lashes drooped, and her lids closed.

The moment swallowed him. He shook her harder, shook her until she looked at him again. "This has to stop," he said. "You're killing yourself, and you're killing me."

She looked away, drifting as far from him as she possibly could.

He slid to the floor beside her, grabbed her, and pulled her tight.

Her eyes rolled over, locked on to his, and tears spilled down her cheeks.

"I want my fucking sister back," he said. "I want you to be you again."

She leaned into him, and the tears broke into big, wet, honking sobs.

The weight of the world crushed down.

"We'll find her," he whispered. "We'll find her."

She nodded against his shoulder.

The crying slowed, and her breathing settled. Jack stood and pulled her up after him, got an arm around her waist, picked her up like an overgrown baby, and managed to get her out of the bathroom without hitting her head against the doorframe.

She was out cold by the time he reached the bed.

He let her drop and stood over her for a moment, watching, wishing things could have been different for her, for him. But they weren't and never would be. What they'd lived was what they had, and wishing couldn't change Clare any more than self-medicating erased the past. At some point everyone had to grow up and take ownership of their own life, and for Jill, that should have been years ago.

This wasn't Clare's damage anymore.

He returned to the bathroom, shut off the water, and grabbed the purse.

He emptied her crap out onto the floor beside the bed, nudging through life detritus that had, whether Jill realized it or not, become her own version of a tool bag: makeup and hygiene products, money, ID, scraps of trash, and the drugs — of course the drugs — which she rotated through in a razor-blade walk between amnesia and addiction.

He stopped at the sight of the cell phones, three of them, neatly organized in small Ziploc bags. The day phone he recognized, cover off, battery out, SIM card tucked inside a micro case with spare SIMs. And the burner was familiar, too. But the Blackphone, that was new.

The strategy wheel started up.

Technology was a moving target, but for years the Blackphone had been the securest smartphone on the market, trusted by governments, law enforcement, and high-security enterprises, and the only way to get one now was to find one on the secondary market. Far too expensive for a secondary burner.

The wheel spun faster.

Jill already used commercial call and text encryption on her day phone.

That made this third piece redundant.

Jack glanced at his sister, sprawled out on the bed, snoring away, with her hair strung out over her pillow-smashed face. He'd asked where the money for the Tesla had come from, had accused her of working favors, and now had the closest thing to proof in his hands. He turned the baggie over.

There was no such thing as a safe phone. No cellular communications device was 100 percent secure against network vulnerabilities that allowed anyone with a little bit of cash and the right kind of know-how to triangulate within feet of the device anywhere in the world, and no phone could prevent cell tower spoofing from stealing IMSI data out of thin air. But the Blackphone was a close second best. Its telecommunications software used Voice over Internet Protocol rather than cell signals, routed through servers in Switzerland. With the SIM pulled, as it was, the phone was off grid as far as the more vulnerable cell networks were concerned while still able to send and receive encrypted calls using Wi-Fi.

Jill was waiting on more than just a call from Clare.

Jack dropped the phone into his palm, brought the screen alive, and pondered the security code. Jill had denied and denied, hadn't wanted him to know, and would never have wanted Clare to know, she was working favors. But if anything ever happened, she'd want him to be able to follow the breadcrumbs to her and that would have guided her security choices.

He let his mind wander.

The strategy wheel, spinning through permutations and possibilities, jerked to a hard stop on mother dearest, the woman without whom Jill would have never begun working favors in the first place. He followed the tangent back to the beginning — their beginning — to the name they'd first learned on the day Clare had given them their French birth certificates, their real birth certificates, a name she'd never used before or since.

Of all the identities Clare had morphed through over the years, only *Catherine Lefevre* was their mother, just as *Catherine Lefevre* was the only Clare they didn't know.

Jack tapped out the letters.

The device unlocked, and he faced an empty screen without phone access, without apps, with nothing but a slate-black background, and he sighed.

It didn't mean much to get into the phone itself when Jill had utilized the sandboxed spaces — a feature that created virtual phones within the phone — each isolated from the others, each with its own user-set security level. He swiped from the top.

A drop-down bar followed his thumb.

He tapped the icon for the first space, and with no password required, the device rolled over. On the new home screen, a single customized icon waited for him — specifically for him. Black letters against a white background spelled his name, his real birth name.

JACQUES.

His face flushed and his stomach flipped with the anger of having fallen for another setup. He'd lost again, had emotionally invested, only to be made a fool so she could have a laugh at his expense, but unable to help himself, he tapped.

A note opened. He read:

If you get this while I'm still alive, do us both a favor and let me explain in person. I'm asking nicely. If you ignore me and take a crack at the other spaces anyway, you're going to make whatever's going on right now way worse. Just trust me on that. If I'm dead or missing or in a coma or locked in or locked up, then that's different. In that case, feel free to take this as notice that revenge needs doing and shit needs blowing up. Watch your back. And never forget that no matter how much of a bitch I was at times, I still always loved you.

His stomach somersaulted in the opposite direction.

This wasn't taunting. This was real. He stared at the screen, mind racing, insides rebelling.

This phone was tied to Jill's present and Clare's past. He could only imagine how, couldn't know if the connection was more than tangential, but it all wrapped together somehow, and the one person who could explain was in a drug-induced coma.

The words on the screen, chains to his brain and lead to his lungs, made it impossible to soothe the itch that so desperately needed scratching. He would have ignored Jill's written warning if not for the chance, however small, that he might lose both mother and sister to impatience.

He placed the phone on the bedside table, tugged a water bottle out of their supplies, set it beside the phone, pulled the blanket over Jill, and returned to sitting on the floor with notepad in his lap, no longer able to focus on the lie-woven tall tales, which might not have been so tall at all.

Catherine Lefevre stuck in his head.

Birth certificates stuck in his head — birth certificates that had no father. Except for the obvious DNA donation, the man didn't exist outside Clare's imagination. They'd never met him, never spoken to him, and never heard from him, yet Raymond had asked about him as if he'd mattered.

Clare had shown them a picture once, when they were younger. Told them their father was from Russia, and that when they were ready she'd give them the story of his life. She never did. Not even when Jill, as a thirteen-year-old, had threatened to run away if she couldn't go live with him — whoever he was, wherever he was — because anything was better than living with Clare.

Never short on stories, she'd refused to tell them the one they wanted to hear.

Instead, she'd looked Jill over, pressed her lips tight, and turned away with some bullshit about how, for Jill's own safety, it was better not to know.

They were sixteen, on the Mexican side of the Rio Grande, when she'd handed them a decade's worth of shifting identities and told them they were old enough to decide what to do with their documents. She'd saved the birth certificates for last, hesitating like she had something to add, but in the end, she'd shoved those down into their tool bags with the rest.

He'd known then it was a story he'd never hear.

And he'd known then Clare was preparing to say good-bye.

He'd just had no idea how soon.

CHAPTER 20

Jack
Age: 16
Location: Near the US Borderlands, Mexico
Passport Country: Paperless
Names: Jose Manuel Valero Santos

The Mexican desert in the winter was still a vast moisture-sucking wilderness, just colder. They were two days out on foot, surrounded by rock, brush, and dry creek beds that stretched on in every direction under a merciless sun, and they were dangerously low on water. Perfect, really, if dying and never being found had been Clare's plan.

Jack leaned into the backpack on the ground behind him, took a costly glug from his dwindling water supply, and recapped the canteen. They'd calculated the distance, measuring liquid against its weight against time without a lot of room for error. They'd reached *Error* more than a day ago.

It was all so ridiculously, unnecessarily stupid.

He pulled off his trail boots.

Best chance for walking out of this alive — besides a miraculous rain shower — was keeping his feet in good condition.

He swapped sweaty socks for dry and laced back up.

Jill, several paces to the right, did the same.

Neither of them had the energy to talk. Neither of them *wanted* to talk, just like neither of them had wanted to make this trip — especially not the way Clare had insisted they make it — heading out into desolation to cross the border on foot as part of the undocumented flow of immigrants headed for a better life in the United States.

They'd argued hard against the move when she first told them about it in Belmopan and had kept on arguing all the way to Zaragoza.

She wouldn't be dissuaded.

There was no point in arguing now.

It had to be done, she'd said. They were American citizens, and it was long past time they experienced their own culture and claimed their heritage.

American citizens.

That had come out of nowhere the night before last, dropped from her lips as matter-of-factly as if she'd said their jeans were blue. He'd gaped, speechless, torn between the urge to laugh out loud and the need to shove her own nonsense in her face.

That would have been the thing if she was simply a bald-faced liar.

The problem with Clare was that no matter how bizarre or inconsistent her statements got, she earnestly believed every word. In *her* upside-down world, offering French birth certificates one day and claims of American citizenship the next somehow made perfect sense, especially when wrapped within a plan to sneak paperless across the US border.

He'd called her on the contradictions.

Had bet the water in his canteen there'd be American documents waiting to be picked up on the other side, which meant the so-called American citizenship was as legitimate as any other legend they'd lived under: another identity, another role to assume, another game to play. That didn't make it real.

Unfazed, same as always, Clare had doubled down.

By her accounting, as far as their government was concerned, her kids had been born in the United States and had never left, and she wanted to keep it that way. One day he'd understand. One day he'd thank her.

He would have thanked her more if they'd just stayed in Belize.

He had no desire to move to the United States.

He'd met plenty of Americans over the years, had always found them loud and overly friendly, and they offered opinions on everything even when no one wanted to hear them. They were fun in small doses, visiting would have been fine, but living there until he turned eighteen was so far from what he wanted that the idea suffocated him.

Worst would be the language.

Clare hadn't even started them on English until they were nearly ten, and because English was so widely understood, they'd rarely spoken it with each other. He'd struggled, botching words and sentence structure, his discomfort made worse by his obvious accent. Russian was his mother tongue, the language of choice between him and Jill. French came next. Even Spanish would have been a better fit than English.

He'd said as much to Clare in his litany of arguments against the move.

She'd laughed and, ignoring every other point, had told him if Spanish was what he wanted, then he'd do just fine in Texas.

Her dismissal had only made him madder.

Life had been so much easier when he'd worshipped the ground she walked on and accepted every one of her twisted turns of logic as a matter of fact.

All he had now was a baseline of disbelief and second-guessing.

Best he could hope for was that this was another stress test.

Jack pulled the map from his pocket and took a compass reading. Come nightfall, he'd use the sextant to get a more accurate measure of where they were. He dotted the map, tucked it away, and watched from the corner of his eye as Clare haggled with the *coyotes:* human smugglers she'd hired in Zaragoza as guides to minimize the risk of getting caught crossing the border. They were brothers in their early thirties, lean and leathered, Sherpas of the desert who'd been making the trip for years.

They'd bragged of their connections and quoted ridiculous prices for handing them off to partners on the other side, who'd then smuggle them around U.S. Border Patrol checkpoints and even out of Texas, if they were willing to pay a higher price.

All Clare had wanted was to be guided to the best crossing and part ways.

They'd pushed hard in the other direction, selling the value of their experience on the Mexican side to avoid *Federales* and paramilitary raiders from competing drug cartels, and a list of disasters that could put them in a grave before ever reaching the border. Full of exaggerated fearmongering, they'd talked down to her, as if, because she was a transient out of Central America, she was dirty and uneducated.

The dirty part had had a little basis, considering they'd been on the road for weeks, and their gear out of Honduras had added a touch of authenticity. Central American transient had been plausible, too, when taking their foreign Spanish, dyed black hair, and darkened skin into account. But even if they'd gone with a full-blown disguise, only an idiot could have assumed they were uneducated, and these men, slimy, manipulative, greedy scum, weren't idiots. That they were nearly out of water with miles to go had far more in common with extortion than with being lost, which meant the biggest flaw in this ordeal, outside of making the trip in the first place, had been relying on outsiders for any part of the journey. And Clare didn't do *flaws.*

The volume of the exchange went up a notch.

Jack slid a shiv out of a shin strap.

He could recognize a shakedown by the time he was six, had got shaken alone for the first time in Harare when he was eleven. He knew what this was. He just wasn't sure who was shaking down whom.

Jill, too, switched from hot and thirsty to alert and twitchy.

Clare picked up her pack and hefted it to her shoulders.

The younger coyote stretched, loosening his shirt, exposing a gun grip in its holster, like he was some caricature in a badly scripted Western.

Clare moved away from him with cautious regard to potential danger.

She wasn't carrying. She'd always preferred stealth, smarts, speed, and lies as weapons, and the odds of a foreign trio being harassed while traveling a hodgepodge of ground transportation up from the Guatemalan border were too high, and the penalty for getting caught with weapons in Mexico too big, to make carrying firearms worth the risk.

Both men, loud and vocal, strode after her.

Jack stood, reacting on instinct, years of

training colliding with doubt and an unwill-
ingness to make a game of life and death.
Best as he could guess, two old S&W
L-frame revolvers made up the entirety of
the brothers' armory. He scanned the area,
alert to the unexpected that might come at
them from behind. Numbers and distance
and light and weight and lies and truth spun
wild in a struggle to understand how far
into another of Clare's tests he'd fallen.

Body language clashed with words and
tone.

These coyotes would steal a desperate
mother's last dollar, would take everything
from her children, down to the packs on
their backs. In all likelihood, the brothers
would leave them here to die in the desert
rather than waste the bullets needed to kill
them, but Clare had known this before hir-
ing them.

Revolvers out, laughing without mirth, the
brothers closed in on her.

Jill left her pack on the ground and, one
deliberate foot in front of the other, closed
the gap until she was nearly at Clare's side.

The brothers laughed at her, too, careless
with their weapons, crude in their gestures,
taunting the little baby who thought she
could rescue Mama and promising to turn

her into a woman as soon as Mommy was gone.

Jack played the shiv against his fingers. He moved closer.

The brothers, alert to him, stopped laughing.

In a rapid shift that said these men were no strangers to street warfare, they leveled their weapons at his chest and Clare's head. If they were smarter, less sexist, they'd have focused on Jill, who was creeping incrementally closer.

Clare, voice low and steady, said, "You've been paid. You're free to leave. We'll finish the journey on our own."

Little Brother backhanded her hard across the face.

Jack's stomach clenched, and his head swam.

Against his better judgment, he took another step forward.

Big Brother met him partway.

Jack stopped.

Blood trickled from Clare's lip.

Little Brother put the revolver to her forehead and ordered her to kneel.

Index finger to her chin, Clare wiped the trail of red up to its source and, defiant, taunting, placed the finger in her mouth and pulled it away clean.

Warning number two fell on overconfident ears.

"Down now," Little Brother said. "Or I kill your baby while you watch."

Clare slid a strap off her shoulder and let her pack drop. She followed the bag down far enough to angle beneath his arm and was up again faster than seemed possible. Vicious, murderous, she struck, hands and knees destroying joints and pressure points in a quiet rage of debilitating grips and jabs that knocked the revolver from his hand and brought him to the ground. She straddled him. Slammed his head back against the rocks and stopped at the lick of a cocking hammer.

Big Brother motioned her off.

"Shoot me," Clare said. "I'll kill you before I die."

Focused on her, he didn't see Jill. None of them saw Jill — not in the way she should have been seen. Her arm came out from behind her back, Baby Eagle in her hand. She two fisted the 9mm, raised the muzzle toward Big Brother's head and, walking toward him, pulled the trigger in a double tap to the brain.

The reports thundered out in waves along the empty miles.

Big Brother dropped to his knees. What

was left of his face headed for the dirt.

Jill reached him as he fell. Put a bullet in his back. Turned the muzzle toward Clare's knees and fired again in a three-tap sequence that sent Little Brother's body jerking.

Clare twitched and froze.

Pride, shock, and anger presented a rapid sequence across her face.

Jill lowered the weapon but didn't release her grip.

In gunpowder-deaf silence, Clare stood and placed a foot on Little Brother where her knee had been when Jill had fired.

Bullet holes seeped inches from her boot.

She glared at Jill's hands — rather, at the weapon gripped by them — and said nothing. She didn't need to. Thoughts scrolled across her face like a movie list on a marquee, and the words filled Jack's head as clearly as if Clare had said them out loud:

Jesus Christ, are you insane?

You brought a weapon.

Against my explicit instructions, you brought a weapon.

And hid it from me.

This is unforgivable.

Jack held his breath, kept perfectly still, afraid to move or speak or blink.

Jill raised the Baby Eagle again and

pointed it not at Clare necessarily, but close enough that the threat was real, and the statement behind the threat even more so.

She said, "I know. You were fine without my help. You don't have to thank me for saving your miserable life, but you might want to acknowledge the skill."

Clare stared Jill down, silent and unbending.

Jill raised the muzzle higher, lining the sights with Clare's forehead.

Jack said, "Julia, not here, not this way. Save the fight for another day."

Jill ignored him. He took a step toward her. She said, "Stay put."

The seconds ticked on, long and parched and painful.

Clare said, "That was excellent marksmanship, Julia."

In her voice Jack heard anguish and reluctance and pride.

Jill shifted fast, inches to the right, and pulled the trigger. The report clapped with heart attack–inducing surprise and the bullet missed Clare by a whisper so slight, she would have been dead if she'd wobbled.

She never even blinked.

But Jack saw what Jill hadn't, saw the flash of fear, and in that flash he understood why they'd made this trip and why Clare wouldn't be dissuaded.

Jill wiped down the weapon, placed the grip in Little Brother's palm, strode for her pack, and heaved it onto her shoulders.

Clare watched her go, and then, slowly, without acknowledging Jack, she leaned down, grabbed her gear, and hoisted the bag.

Finger by finger, Jack released his hold on the shiv, then moved toward Little Brother's body, retrieved the gun, and hefted it in his hand.

He watched Clare and watched Jill, both of them moving on like hikers into the desert the way they had before the stop, as if nothing had changed.

He holstered the weapon in his waistband.

Everything had changed, he knew.

Clare had created a lethal animal that had outgrown its cage.

They were moving to the United States because Clare had lost control.

Chapter 21

Jill
Age: 26
Location: La Porte, Texas
Passport Country: USA
Names: Jennifer White

Out of the fog the buzzing came, persistent and annoying, the same merciless fiend that had chased her dreams for the past two nights. Her eyelids fluttered.

Threads of light outlined a curtain, a door.

The fragrance of old cloth and mildew filled her nose, and her skin registered the heat of a body beside her in bed.

The night rolled into the present.

Annoyance turned to dread.

She bolted upright, fingers fumbling for a phone that danced closer and closer to the nightstand edge, thoughts racing through a jagged sequence.

She had to answer.

No, couldn't because Jack was beside her.

Wait, the phone was on the nightstand —
why the fuck was it on the nightstand?

Shit, shit, shit.

Jack — Jack had put it there — he knew.

She *had* to answer.

Mental thunder clapped.

She sat tall and, answering with the confidence of no fucks given, said, "What do you have for me?"

"Work, as always," the Broker said.

The words hitched in her head, and her heart squeezed with the same panic she'd tried to escape in the night. This wasn't how a bounty offer went. If he had work for her, he would have sent a code first, a link she could follow to an encrypted folder on an offshore server, the contents of which would be mirrored on her screen — no files transferred, nothing she could possess, nothing for packet sniffers to intercept, just a limited look-see at the terms and timing, enough to allow her to determine if the offer agreed with her — and if she accepted, and if it was necessary, *then* they'd move to the phone.

The Broker had arranged Clare's takedown.

He most certainly had Clare in his possession.

And now he was toying, setting her up for

215

something.

Or this was a coincidence.

Possibilities and questions and unknowns spun wild in her head, knotting into a tangle so twisted she couldn't separate one from the other.

The vise tightened. The trap closed in.

She said, "How unusual to receive a call."

"Indeed. But the work is time sensitive."

The words filtered through software that disguised his voice and had none of the nuances of human interaction, but she searched them for hidden meaning all the same.

"Send the code," she said. "I'll look."

"The matter is urgent, with a bonus for speedy delivery."

"I understand," she said. "Send the code."

The call disconnected. Blood pumped loud in her ears.

She dropped back against the pillow and stared up at the dark water-stained ceiling. She wanted to crawl back under the covers, sleep for a month, and wake up after an extinction-level event.

Jack, beside her, remained perfectly still, arms beside his body, hands folded atop his chest, the way they did when he went deep down inside his head while waiting out the night in a hidey-hole.

He said, "I read your note and left the rest alone."

She exhaled long and slow. At least she'd have the opportunity to explain in person before the shit hit the fan. She glanced at him.

He looked like hell. Probably hadn't slept at all.

He said, "Answers would be nice."

She checked the time: nearly noon. Her brain slowed to a crawl, stuck in mud, spinning through gears, searching for where to even start, and she braced against the coming judgment and condescension and the reaffirmation that she'd never be as good as he was.

The phone vibrated. Notification that the Broker's code had arrived.

She ignored one train of thought for the other, followed the link, entered her bona fides, and connected to a full bounty packet instead of the summary she'd expected.

But for what was missing, it might as well have been a summary.

The target was male.

The only thing she had to go on for age, height, and race was a single blurry picture that'd been cropped out of a larger photo taken from a considerable distance. In it, he wore sunglasses and a ball cap, which left little to see, but if this was the packet, then it was all the Broker had and all she'd get.

Other details were just as sparse.

His name was Christopher Rivera, aliases unknown, list of known affiliates just as short, list of skills longer — much longer.

This was the Broker offering her a chance to kill one of his own.

The packet provided an address. No date. No explanation as to why that specific location, simply the setting in which the target was expected to show up.

She pondered the implications, weighing them all against the one detail that made her want to vomit all over again. *Last known location: Austin, Texas.*

"The matter is urgent," the Broker had said.

She grabbed the bottle from the nightstand, cracked the cap, and glugged the water down while insanity wove a web of tangles impossible to follow or sort through.

She'd been careful.

She'd made sure not to bring work home with her.

She'd gone to great lengths to mask her location and stay anonymous, and yet here they were, with Clare kidnapped and Raymond dead and her face on television and the Broker making a joke out of it all by sending her on a hunt for the very guy who'd likely started it all to begin with. She dropped the phone on the bed, shoved the musty pillow over her head, and screamed into it.

Jack tugged the pillow off her face.

"It's not that I don't know what you've been doing," he said. "I just don't know the details or how they connect to what's going on right now."

She grabbed the pillow back, smothered herself again, and screamed louder and harder, then sat up and faced him. "They don't connect," she said. "That's the problem!"

"Of course they do."

"Not in any way that makes sense."

"Yet."

"The call I just got," she said, "that was a job offer." She shoved the phone in Jack's face. "This guy's my target. A killer with a skill set longer than my arm. A hundred and fifty grand if I can take him out clean by the end of the week. And the only piece of information I have on him, besides this shitty picture, is that he was last seen in Austin." She paused. "Austin, John. Do the math. This is the guy who took Clare, the one who killed Ray, and . . ." Her throat constricted. Her voice trailed off.

Jack said, "And you don't know if you're meant to be his assassin or prey."

"Yes," she said. "But it's more than that, so much more."

Within her tangled mess of thought, only two possibilities came close to making sense: either the Broker had chosen her because he knew she was connected to Clare, or he'd chosen her because she was closest to the kill, which meant that in spite of every precaution she'd taken to protect herself, the voice on the other end knew who she was or knew where to find her, and she wasn't sure which of those two was worse.

Jack studied the picture and offered her a third option.

"Guy with these kinds of skills is going to be top line in your dealer's little black book. Probably not a lot of people he can send to track and take him down."

She wanted that lifeline but couldn't accept it.

She said, "He's valuable. Why would the Broker kill him?"

"Could be personal. Could be he's been around too long and knows too much. Could be to eliminate the final thread that leads to Clare. Could be anything."

Jill shut off the screen. "Could be a trap

to bring us right into his hands."

"Could be. You ever carry that phone around your boy toys?"

"No."

"Ever carry it around Clare?"

She tossed the phone in his lap and, stomach rising, struggling against every word, said, "No, but the guy that this connects to is the same guy who has Clare."

Jack glowered in angry, accusing silence.

She said, "I didn't know until Clare's call yesterday, didn't know until I heard the voice at the end. It's the same voice that just called me."

Jack's glowering grew darker. "You ever have the phone on at the same time, same place, as your personal phone or any of the burners?"

The question hiccuped in her head. She searched back and thought, really thought, through the past several months. Unable to look him in the eyes, she studied the bedspread. "No," she said. "But we both know there are other ways."

Jack said, "Who's the dealer?"

Jill choked on the answer, couldn't get the words out.

What had started as a search to satisfy curiosity had opened a portal to another world that felt far more like home than the one she lived in day to day, and what had made rebellious sense in secret a year ago left her with empty shame under the moment's spotlight.

Jack pulled back slowly, as if he already knew the answer.

Seeking out the Broker to spite Clare was low, even by her standards.

"Aw, Jesus," he said.

He pressed his hands to his forehead and turned away, took a long, deep breath, glanced up at the ceiling.

She waited as the silence ticked on.

He said, "What the hell were you thinking?"

She opened her mouth.

"No, don't answer. Don't even talk."

He slid his legs to the floor, stood, and paced beside the bed.

She kept quiet, because explaining would only make things worse.

They both knew what the Broker was, if not who he was, not exactly.

The name had come up throughout the years, overheard first in late-night conversations between Clare and Raymond, brought up again in later discussions between Clare and others from her past, like that jackass Santiago outside Fortul. There'd been a powerful, larger-than-life, mysterious air to the way they'd said the name, similar to the way people used *Illuminati* or *Mafia* or *global elite,* unknowable to anyone but the knowing. She was ten when she'd asked Clare what *the Broker* was.

"A backstabbing traitor, liar, and thief," Clare had said, and she'd warned her then that one day his path might cross hers, warned her and Jack both, the same way she'd warned them about riptides, burning buildings, and hit men, preparing them to survive in the same way she'd prepared them to survive everything.

Even still, it had taken a few more years of eavesdropping for Jill to actually get it. By then she'd also understood that there was blood in the water and that Clare's distaste for this person-slash-thing was as much personal as practical, which was why, in spite of everything she doubted about Clare's delusions, she never doubted that the Broker, on some level, was real.

Jack stopped pacing.

Hands at his sides, he looked down and said, "Accept the contract."

Jill glanced up, puzzled. "You can't be serious. We have no idea what he knows or what this contract really is or what the endgame is or how well the target is supported. Meanwhile" — she glanced at the

mildewed carpet between bed and wall —
"we've got what's in this room."

"All extraneous," Jack said. "If this is the
guy who took Clare, then he knows where
Clare was dropped off and into whose
hands she was delivered. That's a heck of a
lot more than we know. The contract gives
you a legitimate reason to pursue him."

Jill traced a finger along the frayed bedspread stitching.

She said, "He had the skill to find and
capture Clare, got to Raymond before we
did, and your plan is to take him alive?"

Noise patterns beyond the door shifted.

Jack slipped toward the window, nudged
the curtain aside, and peered out.

He signed to her, hands indicating what
his mouth couldn't. "Cops. Door-to-door.
Five minutes. Hurry."

CHAPTER 22

Clare
Age: 54
Location: Somewhere on the Water
Passport Country: Paperless
Names: Unprintable

She waited in the dark, palms to the floor, back to the wall, counting the thuds and scuffles that marked a shift change above.

The floor rose and fell in a soft, rolling heave.

Groaning metal vibrated beneath fingers and cold bare toes.

She stared at the reinforced door, where, if she focused long enough, hard enough, the threads of light danced and warped.

Time marched on, infinite and unending, spiraling into forever.

She'd woken in this frigid black, dehydrated, disoriented, hungry.

Her captors had sedated her in the helicopter, stripped her down, and put her in the prison-like scrubs she wore now. She hadn't been conscious for the handoff. Three days, possibly four, she'd been in this closet-sized vault, shackled ankle to ankle and wrist to wrist by way of a chain around her middle, suffocating from the odor of her unwashed body and the stench of waste that had yet to be removed from the bucket in the front left corner.

Reprieve had come with interrogation, and then the phone call.

And there'd been darkness again, blinding her to the passage of time.

She was locked away where no human voice could reach her by chance and where, scream as she might, she wouldn't be seen or heard.

Absolute solitude. An unending wait.

This was the path to mental destruction.

The human brain, isolated and sensory deprived, atrophied like an unused muscle, beckoning psychosis. Madness rode in on its heels.

She cackled at the thought.

Laughter echoed against the walls, seconding in commiseration. She shushed the gremlins and sent them on.

She wasn't alone and wasn't without sight, not even here.

Darkness and solitude were gifts to the

senses, allowing what lay dormant to stretch like seeds reaching through soil for the sun. Every shift in sound, every smell, every motion had meaning. She knew, even cut off as she was, that she rested near the engines, deep down in the belly of a freighter at port.

A change in reverberation moved up through her fingertips.

Her breathing slowed.

Her hands heard footfalls, heavy, nearing footfalls.

She strained for the higher pitch and found the keys, jangling against a leg.

Food came sporadically, preventing her from timing an arrival, and never in enough quantity to keep her fully fueled, for the same reason the air piped in through inch-wide vents stayed several degrees too cold.

She stood and counted chain lengths as she headed toward the door.

Heat-seeking cameras watched her.

She didn't care.

She knelt and, head inches from the slot near the floor, waited.

Metal touched the door. The tumblers released the lock.

She shut her eyes against the coming light blindness.

The slot slid open wide enough for a half-sized tray and a hand to fit through.

She inhaled, pushing her senses beyond the room's stench to the labored breathing on the other side.

Fat fingers scratched along the floor, feeling for the empty tray.

Fragrant hints of onion and *selyodka* layered over base notes of diesel oil and cooking grease.

Happiness and pain rushed in with the smell — unmistakable recognition — reliable in the way only sensate memories could ever be.

She pushed the emotion away and focused on the opening, straining to place the guards. Her captors couldn't be foolish enough to trust the strength of this prison and the cameras alone, yet in the three days, possibly four, of searching for them, there'd been no voices, no movement, and still she had no sense of where they were or how many of them there were.

The hand pulled the old tray out and shoved a new one in.

Selyodka on the skin.

Vodka on his breath.

A Russian cook on a ship meant nothing by itself. But for the sixth time now, *salo* on cold bread . . .

The food on her plate told of a kitchen galley that had been provisioned for a ship and crew that had come from half a world away.

The room went black again.

She left the food and returned to the wall, to chasing light slivers in the dark, and to the memories and the questions and the silence.

Hope of a Russian destination warmed the cold.

She'd known a hit would come, but not when, and not from where.

Unknowns from the present corroded her insides with doubt. Worry bubbled into another replay of the phone call and the potential aftermath, urging her to rise and fight and flee. She quelled the protective instinct and fed the rage instead.

She would escape, yes. The overweight cook had been their first mistake. . . .

But not here, not in this country, not before the journey took her closer.

Calculation took hold.

This was the sweet spot, the information void in which all the players scrambled to put meaning to events. Two and two hadn't yet collided. She had time. Not endless time, but still enough, perhaps, before the powers that be understood her hired protectors weren't hired at all, and her children became active targets simply because they existed, and she was forced to choose between saving them and pursuing the questions she'd set out to put to rest. There was no choice.

The kids would win. They'd always won.

She shut her eyes against regret and shoved failure into the background.

She was so close and yet so far.

A quarter century of hardship and pain, of doing what had to be done to keep the twins off radar and safe, of pushing them until they broke, and in the end, she'd led them right into the insanity all the suffering had been meant to protect them from.

There'd never be a safe time for questions. She'd known it then and knew it now.

No matter which regime changed, how the political climate shifted, who died, or where power was transferred, there were some things that time would not forgive.

The twins had been thirteen the last time she surfaced.

She'd hidden them in the Colombian mountains, with arrangements for Raymond to collect them if she failed — and she nearly had.

All these years she'd waited.

They were older now, smarter, stronger, and so she'd prepared for this final ride, planning to chase the trail until it ended or she did — whichever came first — but age had made her soft. She hadn't been strong enough to steel herself against never seeing them again, hadn't been strong enough to simply vanish. She'd succumbed to emotion, broken the rules of survival, and called them home to say good-bye.

She'd miscalculated.

She'd called them home too late.

So many years of struggle, of teaching them to be strong, and in the end, the failure was hers, all hers.

She'd destroyed the Earthship in an attempt to reverse the damage, had destroyed every tangible thing she treasured, hoping to keep her children out of a trap they wouldn't see, and had added the complicating risk of toying with her interrogators to warn them off by phone, and still the twins wouldn't stay away, she knew.

Duty bound, they'd come after her and would hate and despise her, just as they despised her for so much else.

Hate.

A luxury she'd paid for with blood.

The day they stopped hating meant a day they understood through experience, and that was a day she'd fought hard to ensure would never come.

Failure lumped in her throat, making it

difficult to breathe.

Beyond the door the reverberation shifted again.

She heard the keys and, with the keys, a familiar squeak of rubber.

Her body reacted, viscerally and violently.

She stood, drew in a long, hard breath, clenched her hands within the shackles, planted her feet as wide apart as the chain would allow and, with her back straight and chin high, braced for what came next.

CHAPTER 23

Holden

Age: 32
Location: El Paso, Texas
Passport Country: Canada
Names: Troy Martin Holden

He stood at the edge of the abandoned lot, scuffing a shoe against cracks in the concrete walk, playing a coffee stirrer against his teeth, staring out over knee-high weeds and grasses strewn with broken glass, empty cans, and wind-blown trash. Torn and stained mattresses rested against the exposed brick of the adjacent walk-up, and his gaze followed those to mistrustful eyes in second-floor windows watching from behind laundry hung out to dry.

The same picture that satellite and street-view images had given.

He'd known the odds were slim to zero that a building had gone up at the address since the last image capture, but he didn't know when that capture had been, and so he'd had to see for himself. Standing here now, he found it hard not to laugh.

Ten mind-numbing, body-cramping hours in a drive across a landscape from hell had brought him to a dumping ground on a derelict street that would have fit in with the Calamar of his childhood better than any version of big-city USA. He flipped the stirrer and chewed the plastic into a ball.

To his right, three boys in grown men's bodies loitered on concrete steps, eyeing the rental car behind him, sizing him up.

He nodded their way. They nodded back.

He'd been them once, a version of them, stray-dog hungry and suspicious, with everything to prove, nothing to lose, and angrily susceptible to kindness.

He offered them Jennifer's photo.

They conferred in slang-filled Spanish.

Holden caught enough to know the answer before the ringleader handed the photo back.

He'd have spent the last of the afternoon knocking on doors and exchanging greenbacks for knowledge if he thought he'd have a chance of picking up Jen's trail. All he'd get for the effort was wasted time and money.

She'd never been here, not even once.

He returned to the rental, sat behind the wheel, and studied the picture.

Finding her really shouldn't have been this difficult. She wasn't a hit man who'd moved into town and set up a temporary legend before moving on again. Her boyfriend had hooked up with her too frequently and spontaneously for that, and too many people knew her as a hard-core party girl well acquainted with the "had to know someone to know about it" happening scene for her to have been a recent transplant. Austin had been her home for a while, yet she was as much a ghost in real life as she'd been outside Blanco, hiding in plain sight and living in the open while not existing at all.

She had no address, no number that led to a traceable phone.

He couldn't find her in property records or aggregated data. She was invisible on social media, didn't exist in credit histories. And clues to family and friends had all led nowhere. Thanks to her knight in tarnished armor, he *did* know how she smelled, the way she smiled, and what made her laugh. And he knew her poison of choice, the drugs she took, the clothing brands she wore and, more importantly, the car she drove, which was why he was now six hundred miles away, in front of a non-existent address, sitting in a rental car, looking at her picture.

There were so few Teslas on Texas roads that finding hers had been easy.

The techs at the Austin service center had seen her on the news. They'd known who she was even before he'd come asking and had gotten him plate and VIN numbers. Those had given him the vehicle's registered address, which was what he'd followed to this trash-filled lot where his greatest lead had turned into the biggest dead end.

He was back to working back channels to gain access to the Tesla's electronic data, back to chasing location leads through license-plate scanner databases.

He ran his thumb over the face in the photo and contemplated. She was a tough catch, a formidable opponent.

The challenge made him smile in a way nothing had for a long time.

Any buffoon with the right hardware could point and shoot and blow things up, but that type died off fast. In this line of work longevity required invisibility, the mastery of self and surroundings, the ability to turn hits into accidents and random acts of violence — skills that took time to develop, took training and learning through mistakes, the kinds of mistakes that made for early shallow graves. This Jennifer, whoever she really was, was too young to have reached this caliber on her own or to have come out of nowhere. She'd been trained hard, and that made him like her more.

Seemed a sorry waste to have to kill her.

Light flickered in his peripheral vision.

Holden set the photo on the passenger seat and watched without watching as a gang of eight, tatted up and turf protective, headed toward him.

He knew their walk, had seen the same purposeful stride herald protest violence and street-level assassination and mob justice. And he'd been them once, too, street thug and lawless, before Frank had found him and taken him under his wing.

His mistake in the moment was forgetting that familiarity and recognition were one-sided. He no longer appeared as he'd once been. This wasn't home. He was an intruder who'd stayed in the neighborhood beyond the pretense of tolerance.

He buckled in, moving slowly, methodically, to avoid the appearance of flight, which would incite the instinct to chase. He pulled the car from the curb.

The men ahead stepped into the street, blocking the way.

He veered toward the center line.

The gang fanned out, filling the street, and edged closer, betting with their bodies that a well-dressed outsider in a new, plain-vanilla, low-end Cruze would be too much of a coward to create casualties by driving through them.

To a point, they were right.

Unlike them, he had nothing to prove by fighting.

In his world, killing bystanders and creating collateral damage were signs of an amateur's sloppy thinking. In his world, only the weak felt shame in avoiding a battle wherein every dead or wounded body brought unneeded complications and potential exposure. He nudged the gas and closed the distance, counting weapons and watching eyes, measuring footfall to footfall, waiting until the last possible moment to break.

Shouts carried above the engine and into the car.

The checkered flag inside his head went down.

Pedal to the floor, he swerved left over the curb, onto the sidewalk.

A crowbar swung hard for the windshield and missed.

He fishtailed between light poles and aging concrete.

The passenger mirror exploded into shards of plastic and glass and he plowed past, onto the street behind them, and through a red light, with not even enough tension to get his heartbeat up. In the rearview the lot faded, the men faded. With them, Holden's smile faded.

The prospect of another ten-hour drive across hell rose before him, and dread descended. He'd rather sacrifice an identity to catch a flight back than make that trip again. He reached the next intersection, took a hard right, and shifted into the speed of traffic. The light ahead turned yellow. He slowed, redirected the GPS to the airport, and there, with his hand stretched out, with Jennifer White moving in and out of his peripheral vision on the seat beside him, he froze.

He'd seen that face before.

The traffic cleared. He cut over, pulled into the nearest parking lot, and stopped. Grabbed the picture, laid it flat, and studied it hard, looking down, as if he stood over her.

The angle of her face, the way her hair drifted into her eyes made it difficult to see the connection exactly, but yes, he knew this face. He'd seen an older version on the bounty before he'd shoved the stretcher into the helicopter.

He reached for his phone, scrolled through photos, and pulled up the images from Louisiana that he'd shown to Frank. Taken from a distance as they were, their resolution was too low and her face turned too far to the side to have seen the obvious then, but the harder he looked now, the clearer the relationship became.

He stared through the windshield.

Hands on the wheel, desert sun beating down through the windshield glass, he rewound back to the night he'd lost three men, to the phone calls he'd traced, to the vehicle that had arrived right before the explosion, to the chase through the brush for two professionals who'd vanished into the dark, and to the look on the bounty's face — the promise — before he'd shoved her into the helicopter. And he pondered the way the ghosts had arrived on his heels in Louisiana, forcing him to switch from creating an accident to taking a kill shot. Step-by-step, he rearranged the truth as he knew it, everything filtered through one simple change that put each event into focus.

The ghosts were connected to the contract, yes, but they weren't hit men.

They hadn't come for him. They'd come

for *her.* They were McFadden's children.

Realization ran headlong into memory, and he stumbled over the Broker's words on that call outside Blanco, Texas.

He'd been mocked, his concerns written off. These were children that the Broker, apparently, knew nothing about.

The irony made him laugh out loud and scared him just a little.

If even the person who made a business of knowing things was unaware of the kid's existence, did she exist? He stared at the picture again and fit the pieces into a tighter puzzle — what Frank had and hadn't said — the clues Robert had dropped — what he'd figured out on his own.

There was a mother, an assassin mother, but no father.

Jen would have grown up on the move, born to kill, trained to survive, never in one place long, always present and never belonging. Robert's stories about her took on new meaning — the drugs, the partying, the manipulative mask — so many decisions and choices made day after day in a perpetual effort to avoid the need to feel.

He and Jen, they weren't so different.

She was him, a version of him, a version of him if he'd had a mother.

He stopped mid-thought and, in a moment of frustrated violence, tore the picture in half. He knew better, knew so much better.

Humanization opened up weakness and invited mistakes.

He shredded her face piece by angry piece.

This had gone far, far past humanization.

He tossed the photo remnants on the floor, pushed into cold hunter mode, and started for the airport again, driving by rote, mind zigzagging through options in a race to stay ahead of the unknowns.

Vibration from his pocket intruded as a guilty reminder that he was hours overdue in contacting Baxter. He'd called the big guy in to go hunting for the face on television and had left him in a single room with a doped-up, panicked kid and nothing but daytime television and cheap fast food. It was enough to drive anyone to self-destruct, much less an adrenaline junkie who thrived on action, movement, and wide-open spaces. He owed the man a call, if for no other reason than to talk him off the ledge of stir crazy.

Holden glanced at the phone.

The caller wasn't Baxter.

He stared down the road. The call vibrated on and the sting of betrayal and mockery, of being taken for a fool and set up to fail, simmered hot beneath his skin.

He'd have to answer eventually.

To ignore the Broker completely was unwise and dangerous.

Holden swiped the screen on the final ring.

The computerized voice, efficient and without introduction, said, "Your target's associates have been located for removal."

Holden's focus darted toward the picture pieces on the floorboard.

That the collector and curator of knowledge had already located those he still hunted wasn't impossible, but the timing was off.

He said, "Who are they?"

"Hired guns. Loose ends of little consequence."

The Broker's words exploded inside his head, sending the mental pendulum on a wild swing between betrayal and gift and back again.

Mercenaries were never *of little consequence.*

That these particular killers were the kids of the target he'd just taken was its own universe of importance. Even factoring in the genuine possibility that the curator and collector of knowledge had known nothing of McFadden's children then, and that he knew where they were but not who they were now, they still weren't *of little consequence.*

He said, "No consequence, little consequence, it doesn't matter. You should have had everything in the packet from the beginning."

"Oh, dear boy," the Broker said. "And to think I'd believed your whiny excuse finding had been a temporary lapse. I suggest a thank-you, and that you get on with cleaning up your mess."

Holden waited.

There'd been a time when wounded pride would have blinded him to distraction and misdirection, and he'd have responded to the snide condescension with chest-thumping self-importance and braggadocio, oblivious to the way egoistic outbursts announced his own weakness and need. But he wasn't that boy anymore.

He heard past the mind games and mental bait.

This was a philanderer accused of indiscretion picking a fight to focus attention anywhere but on himself. This was the Broker showing his hand.

Of little consequence, indeed.

A man's threats were his actions, and those would come soon enough.

The Broker said, "There's a bonus for quick, clean elimination. Assuming you're still man enough for the task."

Holden said, "I'll finish the job. Send the link."

"There is no link. Only an address."

"Then the link to the address."

"No links. Write it down."

Holden rifled for a pen to transfer the information the old-fashioned way, found a receipt, and wrote, and when he'd finished and confirmed what he'd heard, he took the Broker's manipulation and twisted it backward.

"I assume you've verified these targets," he said.

Silence, louder than words, rose in place of an unasked why.

The knowledge was much too valuable to give away whole, but worth every penny of the suspicion and chaos that parceling it out could provide. Holden said, "My own digging has led elsewhere. These are targets you want alive."

He ended the call before the Broker could respond and studied the address.

Peckinpaugh Preserve. Spring, Texas.

He tore the paper into pieces and turned

the information into a stick of gum.

The location was north of Houston, according to the Broker. Not far from where the bounty had been sent, according to what Holden already knew.

He pondered the entwining possibilities.

He'd been wrong about the ghosts, specifically, but not wrong in his conclusion.

Priorities reordered inside his head. What had started as a high-value extraction had gone completely off the rails.

The rules no longer mattered.

He glanced at the remnants of Jen's photo, and the look on the bounty's face before he'd sent her off wound round and round inside his head.

He'd asked Frank all the wrong questions.

McFadden, her kids, their history — he'd been looking at them backward.

There was more to this story, far more, than just a contract.

He was willing to bet his future that in the same way Frank had filled him in on McFadden's past, McFadden could do the same for the Broker.

He wanted what she knew.

He picked up the pieces of Jen's photo and held them in his hand.

Want congealed into plan.

McFadden had already been delivered;

she was off the table, but her kids were fair game. He needed to get paid, and for that, he needed them dead, but information could come first.

Perhaps.

Faking a killing or two would be the better complement to payback.

The phone vibrated, as he'd expected. The Broker back with unfinished business. He had no patience for another conversation and thumbed the device to turn it off. Baxter's number caught his eye instead.

Holden answered.

The big guy said, "You good to talk?"

"Maybe. You doing all right?"

"Depends. How'd you feel about our young friend having just received an invitation to visit downtown bright and early tomorrow morning?"

"He still their main squeeze?"

"Looking more and more like he's their only squeeze."

"Invitation, huh?"

Baxter snorted.

Holden sighed.

At this stage, the cops wouldn't be calling the kid into the station to ask him more questions, they were calling him in because they planned to arrest him and wanted to make their job easy. Holden pinched the bridge of his nose and, for the second time within the hour, fought the urge to laugh.

He couldn't afford to lose Robert to law enforcement, but there'd be warrants issued when the kid didn't show up. He dug a dispenser out of his pocket, shoved a tooth-pick in his mouth, and ground down deep into thought. The Broker was coordinating a hit to ensure he died and stayed dead.

McFadden's children, out hunting for revenge, wanted the same.

He was about to walk a tightrope between lunacy and mutiny, and his link to Jennifer, the one thing he had available to draw her in, was sixteen hours from becoming a high-profile fugitive.

CHAPTER 24

Jack

Age: 26
Location: La Porte, Texas
Passport Country: Paperless
Names: Nameless

He stood behind the door, fingers resting against the hinges, measuring and timing the gaps between vibrations. Another thud, another room, another minute fewer until the uniforms making their way down the corridor came knocking.

The men out there were skipping vacant rooms and passing over those where the occupants were out, a batting average only possible if the information had come from the front desk, but that they didn't seem to know which room held what they were after indicated the front desk hadn't called them here.

So they were cops, or they were assassins playing the role.

And they were here because someone had seen and recognized Jill, or because her Blackphone had led them, or for something else with god-awful coincidental timing.

Jack glanced toward the bathroom.

Jill had grabbed his tool bag and taken it with her in the rush. His things in her hands made him nervous. He would have fought to keep them with him if there'd been time, but priority always went to survival — that kind of training would never die — and at the moment, survival meant liquid latex and a quick change of face. So he'd let her have the bag and had gone for the weapons, shoving the armory out of sight in an instant decision to disarm rather than arm — a turn through the strategy matrix that might yet come back to kill them both.

Fists pounded one room over.

Furniture scraped and scratched. Stage whispers carried through the wall, and the next-door bathroom door opened and shut.

Authority had a way of scattering the undocumented.

A deep drawl in horrific Spanish bellowed, *"No buscando papeles."*

A few seconds passed. The neighbors answered.

They had a minute at best, and Jill was still painting on the layers.

250

The strategy wheel spun hard, clacking through a limited quantity of knowns and vast array of unknowns. If he'd predicted correctly and the uniforms outside were legit law enforcement, he didn't have to open the door or answer questions, but standing firm on constitutional grounds threatened more action and more attention than playing along.

If he'd predicted wrong, he was probably already dead.

He checked over his shoulder again.

For this to work, Jill had to answer the door.

She was the one who crawled into people's heads, made them see what wasn't, got them to behave as she wanted. They had their mother to thank for that, the one who'd refused to be pleased no matter how hard Jill tried, the one who'd rewarded Jill's best with impossible expectations and harsher demands.

Jill hadn't been able to make Clare love her, so she'd tried filling an unfillable void by making everyone else love her instead, morphing into whatever people wanted or needed until she owned their hearts, and he'd hated it every time — hated the gullibility, hated that people refused to see past her charade — and he'd fought her, needling and scheming and provoking, forcing her true self to the surface to shove reality in their faces.

They'd only loved her more.

He'd lost, always lost, and tired of losing, he'd switched to putting ideas in her head, winding her up and setting her loose for his own benefit, and she'd gone right along with it, because to the unwanted child, any attention was love. He'd been under Raymond's roof, watching her downward spiral, when he understood, but by then he was too late. They were all too late.

Jack felt the footsteps through his fingertips.

The pounding transferred to his shoulder.

The bathroom door opened, and Jill rushed out, bare-legged, in his dirty T-shirt, hemline at high thigh, hair tousled from two nights' worth of sleeplessness, eyes red and puffy, nose wider, cheeks fuller, chin fatter. The latex wasn't dry, but under the circumstances, it leathered her skin. She was Jill, but nothing like in the picture on TV. She was older, had lived harder. She looked like shit, and he approved.

He scurried for the duffel, snatched the strap, and dragged the bag after him into the bathroom. She tossed the bedding, wrapped a sheet over her shoulders, and headed for the door, huffing, swearing, and muttering with each step.

The lock turned. Her voice, a husky octave deeper and thick from a three-pack-a-day habit, said, "What in God's good name d'ya want?" The chain caught. She said, "Oh." Paused and then added, "My apologies, Officers."

Muffled voices followed.

Jill said, "Give it. Let me see."

She fumbled with the chain. The door hinges squeaked.

She said, "I ain't seen her, honey, but if her home is looking to adopt, I'm available." She guffawed and coughed and said, "Listen, sugar, I'd invite you in to chat some, but I ain't slept more'n an hour or two, and I gotta get some rest before my next shift."

More talk followed, and then the door closed and the chain was latched, and a few seconds later Jill's nails tapped lightly on the bathroom door.

Jack opened it.

She gave him a chin salute and motioned him out of the way.

He said, "They had your picture?"

She slipped in behind him. "Same one shown on the news."

He grabbed the tool bag and stepped out of the bathroom.

She shut the door on him.

He dumped the bag on the bed, and thoughts zigzagging in a race through a mental maze, hands working by rote, he ran an inventory to ensure she hadn't stolen anything. He set the last filled hypodermic aside and shoved everything back into proper pockets and places. They were done here. He'd been right about the uniforms, and now they had an assassin to find and kidnap and follow to Clare.

He reached for Jill's purse and dug for the Blackphone.

The Broker had given her an address, a picture, and the promise of a bonus if she took the target out quick and clean. The scenario ate at him, churning up inconsistencies that refused to let go. If he could see the setup flashing its neon warning in the dark, a man with the ability to kidnap Clare would certainly see it, and the only reason a man like that, on the hunt to clean up loose ends, would willingly detour into a potential meet-greet-shoot was if he'd been offered the right motivation.

This Christopher Rivera had to believe he'd find his missing targets.

Jack brushed his thumb against the phone screen and hefted the weight, struggling against the questions he'd asked less than an hour earlier.

He couldn't ignore the possibility that Christopher or the Broker had connected the face on television to the individual who controlled this phone. The dots were hard to follow if Jill had kept the phone away from Clare and away from boys and away from the burners, like she'd claimed, but that was a mighty long series of *if*s.

The Broker very well may have engaged Jill to take down a top-tier assassin for the simple reason that she was one of a few with the skills to do it. And he'd have convinced Christopher that the targets he was hunting would be there.

And the irony of it all being true would be a bitch.

But even then, a schemer like the Broker would never pit equal strengths against each other and leave the winner to fate. There'd be more.

The trap he couldn't see was where the danger lay.

This was Clare 101.

He dropped the Blackphone into his tool bag and dumped the rest of the phones in after it. He'd pulled SIM cards and batteries out of all them, including the burners — especially the burners — but even bricked as they were, they left him feeling exposed and naked. He'd have run them over and flushed the pieces if they weren't handcuffs keeping them connected to Clare.

Jill stepped out of the bathroom, hair brushed, clothes cleaned, face bright and made up, but still not Jill. Her gaze drifted from the bed to his bag, and she stopped.

"All your stuff's still there," she said.

Her tone was mellow and nonconfrontational, but he knew where this was going, and he watched her eyes, wary of her hands and feet.

Her focus cut to the purse. "I've got stuff missing."

"Stuff? That's what you're calling it now?" He reached for his tool bag and swung it off the bed. "What do you want me to say? You knew what I'd do and backed me into a corner."

"Where'd you put it?"

"Down the toilet."

Her eyes narrowed. She scrutinized him, and he fought hard to maintain the truth within the lie. She said, "You're not that stupid."

"No, not stupid, just desperate."

All of which was true. He had no idea how bad her problem was, wouldn't risk pushing her into withdrawal right when peak performance mattered most. He'd just left out the part about where to find the little he'd held back.

She moved in close.

He said, "Focus on the mission. Focus on what matters. This wasn't about you, wasn't about me. It was about priorities and finding Clare."

Her hand snapped around his wrist. "Give it back, or I'll break your fucking thieving fingers."

He tugged free. "Before or after we find Clare?"

"Don't use her as your excuse."

"I'm not the one who needs excuses."

She came at him, the old Jill, the one who needed to fight just to fight and who took her frustration out on him just to prove she could. She punched the heel of her hand into his chest, took the air out of him, made him dizzy.

He said, "You can have the drugs, or you can have me. You can't have both."

She hesitated, and in that hesitation, he plunged the hypodermic into her thigh.

She grabbed his hand, fought for control of the syringe, pulled the needle free, and shoved him against the wall, fingers like talons pinching nerve points.

He waited through the pain, waited for her to weaken, pried himself free, and pushed back.

No matter how badly she claimed to want to find Clare, priorities had a way of shifting when addictive need kicked in. He couldn't risk taking her with him and couldn't risk leaving her alone.

"It's not that I don't trust you," he said. "I just don't trust you."

She shoved him again, kicked, and lost her balance.

He guided her to the bed and nudged her down.

Speech starting to slur, she said, "You're going to regret this."

"I might," he said. "But I'll regret it less than if I hadn't."

CHAPTER 25

Clare
Age: 54
Location: Somewhere on the Water
Passport Country: Paperless
Names: Unprintable

She woke choking, gasping, thrown from dreams of drowning, trapped beneath the ice to a body racked and shivering in the pitch-black vault, thrown from forgetfulness into painful silence and acute awareness. The ship wasn't moving.

Possibilities for the delay rose blacker than the room.

Stillness had become a special form of torture.

She tamped down the rising dread and tucked frigid fingers beneath her arms.

Her clothes, still damp from the most recent hosing, permeated her skin and infected her bones with a chill made worse by the constant air seeping in from the vents.

She rolled onto her stomach into a push-up and pressed through set after set, forcing blood into her extremities, wasting limited energy for the sake of warmth. And she stood and took short hobbled steps to the door, where the last tray of food sat untouched.

Austerity, living hard and training hard, had kept her tough, made sleeping in the rough tolerable, prepared of sparse nutrition a feast, and tamed darkness into friendship. But here, where day and night were one and torture arrived in stop-starts as random as sleep, the cold took a slow, hard toll.

Ear to the slot, she strained to catch sound from the other side.

Silence reached out from beyond.

She pulled stale bread off the tray, took a bite for her watchers, and carried the rest back to the wall. More than food, she needed sleep, and sleep was an elusive mirage. Her captors made certain of that. She tucked her feet into her pant legs, pulled her arms as far into her sleeves as the chains would allow, and nibbled on the bread while her hands twitched in a repetitive motion against the cuffs, just as they'd regularly twitched throughout the days and nights she'd been here.

Time and scheming played shadowed games in the dark until the squeak, dreaded and familiar, rose from beyond the door.

She sighed and stood.

Her clothes weren't even fully dry and they were already at her again to torture her with water and with the voice, that god-awful voice on speakerphone, demanding answers she would never give and taunting her with truth mixed into lies.

With patience, she'd morph from prisoner to punisher, but not yet.

This dark vault wasn't her end destination.

She was a prisoner in transit, a trouble-maker whom unwatched transport guards punched and pummeled because they could, because it satisfied a perverse need.

A razor-thin margin separated daring from danger, and the ability to discern one from the other was what divided the living from the dead.

Reacting was danger, overcompliance was danger, manipulation was danger when a quarter-century wait could end only if the journey began, and the ship had yet to leave port.

She needed the ship to move, needed the

journey to begin.

She inched toward the center of the room, counting space and measuring time.

Hands clenched, she faced the door and waited for the freezing rush.

The squeak stopped. Metal jangled. The lock engaged.

Some patterns couldn't be helped.

The door swung open. Light flooded the room, and a torrent of cold hit her with the force of ten thousand needles, a fire hose stream that knocked her feet out from under her and drove her away from the door, as if she'd be fool enough to attempt an escape when they were most prepared to prevent one.

She screamed against the pain and didn't care that she screamed, and she fell hard and slid backward, fighting to find air outside the force pinning her to the wall.

The water shut off. The world went silent.

Arm up to shield her eyes, she watched the shadow at the door, a hulking, blurry shadow that moved slowly into focus and separated into two distinct bodies, henchmen with tools who knew nothing and were nothing and meant nothing.

One held the hose, the other carried a wireless speaker.

She struggled to her feet and turned to

face a spying eye in the corner. She no longer had anything to gain by silence. To the infrared watcher, she said, "Hello again, Boris."

Mechanical laughter crackled through the speaker.

She bowed theatrically.

She'd known this was him. How could she not?

In the world's dark underbelly where assassin supply was matched with illicit demand, there was only one king, and regardless of who had ordered and paid for the hit, the torture and interrogation reeked too strongly of personal vendetta to have come from anyone without a shared history.

Tone dry, sarcastic, she said, "What could you possibly want from me now?"

He said, "Your bodyguards."

She huffed, leaned back against the wall, and slid to the floor. "Already gave you them."

"But then, you've always been a liar, haven't you?"

The corners of her lips tweaked. With those nine little words, he'd rewritten history and turned the past inside out.

She said, "Never so good a liar as you."

"I've seen them," he said. "They're not what you've claimed."

The words thundered into her ears and down to her chest.

Relief breathed into her.

If he'd truly seen them, this would be a different conversation.

She pressed her lips in grim contrition and, in silence, thanked him for telling her that her children were still alive and free.

The computerized voice said, "Last opportunity, Catherine."

"For?"

"The truth. About them."

Questions were danger, revealing more of the asker than the asked, and he'd already revealed too much.

She said, "Yes, I hired protection. I imagine you'd do the same if you'd heard rumors that old friends were out looking for you."

"Contractors skilled enough to meet your standards aren't easy to come by, especially without telecommunications access. How did you recruit them?"

Questions revealed what he didn't know. What he needed to know.

She said, "Through a broker."

He waited, waited so long she thought he'd fallen asleep, waited until the smirk drooped off her face from the exhaustion of holding it in place, and said, "I'd have thought the last time would have taught you the joke's not nearly as funny as you think it is."

Her shoulders slumped from apparent dejection, and she sighed. "They're just a couple of kids I brought back from Colombia."

"The more you lie, the worse you'll suffer."

"Fine. I found them through Craigslist. Happy now?"

"How high a price are you willing to pay to drag this out?"

Questions revealed the truth in power dynamics.

He could hurt her. Torture her. He could hold on to her and stretch the wait into unbearable torment, but he couldn't kill her. Someone, somewhere, had invested heavily in a capture, not a death. She was worth too much alive.

She turned her face toward the floor and stayed silent.

He said, "And here we circle back to where we were when last we met — me seeing the bigger picture, and you, dim-witted and naive, screwing yourself over. Perfect bookends to your sad life, don't you think?"

Questions revealed ignorance.

"Perfect," she whispered.

Her gaze drifted toward the speaker and

265

then back to the camera.

He hadn't come for truth, he'd come for control, to reinforce the power he had over her. Had she dropped to her knees, pleaded for her life, and spilled her soul onto the hard, cold floor, the end result would have been the same. She said, "You poor, poor man. You've become a living, breathing version of the liar's paradox."

"Better than rotting in a putrid cell."

"It's been a long day . . . night . . . whatever. I'm tired, and you're still a bore."

"Give me names, Catherine. Biographical details, histories."

"I'd tell you all that if I thought it would settle anything, but it won't. That's the problem with you, Boris. You've lived lies, double lies, triple lies, betrayal, and back-stabbing for so long, you can't even recognize truth when it's wrapped in a bow and handed to you as a gift." She shifted forward. "You know, I know, and you know that I know that you see everything out of my mouth as a lie. Sets up quite the psychological game." She paused, then pitched her voice to a precise mimic of the computerized speech and added, "Don't you think?"

The speaker hissed with the emptiness of a disconnection.

She drew a deep, deep breath, grabbing

air before the hose turned on, and in that breath, she stretched for a glimpse of what stood behind her tormentors.

Machines. Tools. No corridor walls.

This vault was at the back of a larger room.

Arms to her face, she protected her head from the bruising power while the man with the hose moved forward in a slow, steady march, rubber boots squeaking against the floor, wading pants repelling the harsh cold.

Two feet away, he shut off the torrent.

His partner reached for her.

Her body rebelled in protest, every part of her demanding she attack in defense. She struggled, kicking and flailing enough to force him to work for his keep, tamping down momentary self-preservation for the sake of long-term gain.

Illusion was her greatest power.

Their complacency was quicksand to their minds.

The speaker man grabbed her by the hair and dragged her to the room's center.

The hose guy turned on the flow again, flooding her face with a stream so strong the water forced its way up her nose and into her throat.

The cold paralyzed her and stole what little oxygen she'd grabbed.

She couldn't breathe, couldn't fight.

She relaxed and allowed the flood to swallow her.

She would not die on this ship.

They couldn't afford to let her die.

They brought her up for air just to drown her again, every plunge followed by a demand for answers that wouldn't change no matter how hard they pushed.

The truth had many faces, and she'd given them one.

With each wretched, gasping breath, she held on for another.

CHAPTER 26

Clare

Age: 25
Location: Moscow, USSR
Passport Country: Ecuador
Names: Maria Catalina Molina Nieves

There weren't words to describe the Moscow winter in a way one who'd never lived it could understand. This cold had to be felt to be known. Bitter and biting, it blew through wool and goose down, stole body heat out from between synthetic fibers, and turned fur into a necessity that even the poorest found ways to possess. The Russian winter had defeated the armies of Napoleon and Hitler when horses and cannons, then rifles and tanks had failed to do the same, and it felt like it would defeat her now as she trudged along the icy street, collar turned up, hat swallowing her ears, fingers encased in lined gloves, maneuvering within the bleak pedestrian crowd, because Boris had called to let her know he was in town and had invited her to visit.

Eyes were on her, they were always on her. From the hallowed prestige within Moscow's music conservatory to the endless lines in which she waited for bread and eggs and milk — toilet paper, if she could find it — colorless, humorless lines for every basic necessity, they watched her.

Suspicion ruled daily life, for her, for her friends, for most of the population, because if the intelligence agents or the police weren't spying, nosy neighbors were quick to make reports. Even at home, in the narrow one-room *khrushchyovka* apartment four flights above the neighborhood post office, she had no privacy. Not that she had proof her apartment was wired — because to look would arouse suspicion — but she was a foreigner, and all foreigners were suspect, and her friendship with Dmitry made her especially suspect, so she lived and behaved as if it was.

Teeth chattering from the cold, she reached the corner in time for the bus.

She rode to the center of the Yakimanka District and walked into the wind for a series of grim five-story concrete apartment blocks. She let herself into the nearest of them through the middle entry and took the stairs up, unwinding her scarf as she climbed past broken lights and peeling paint in a stairwell nearly as derelict as her own, though here the stairwell was wider. The flats were bigger, too, with only two doors to a floor instead of four.

She stopped on the second landing, at the apartment on the left, and knocked.

Hinges creaked, and the door opened to a familiar face with milky-tan skin and light brown eyes beneath a mop of lush black hair. He was in his late forties, if she had to guess, trim and tall and wide shouldered, exuding the good looks and charisma to which even stonehearted commissars weren't entirely immune.

Her stomach churned with nausea and disgust at the sight of him.

He hugged her, and she hugged him back with formal politeness for the sake of the listeners and watchers.

Her mouth smiled, but not her eyes. She said, "You look well."

"Come, come," he said and invited her in.

He knew her as Catherine, as Maria Catalina. She knew him as Boris, though surely, he had other names, just as she did. And he was watched intently, just as she was watched, every interaction scrutinized and analyzed, partly because of who he was and his frequent travels, but mostly because of his association with her. Because of Dmitry.

She stepped over the threshold into the same cloying heat found in every building during the winter, shed her outerwear and exchanged boots for slippers and, following him into the living room, said, "How long will you be in town?"

"Only a night, maybe two. I have business in Quito that requires quick attention."

She forced elation into disappointment. "So sorry to hear it."

"Don't be, don't be. Have a seat. I'll make tea."

She'd have preferred to be anywhere but here, alone in this room with him, but she didn't have the luxury of options. She cleared architectural books off a chair and sat, uncomfortably comfortable in the familiar surroundings. His home, furnished with a mixture of old handcrafted quality pieces and the newer mass-produced Soviet industrial crap, was bigger than hers, with more windows, a larger balcony, and a wider hallway, but still austerely Russian.

He set about making tea on a two-burner stove, and she did her best to avoid looking at him. He laughed at her, the type of laugh that listening devices — both CIA and KGB — would interpret as friendly, but that he and she both knew was taunting.

He brought two cups to the seating area and handed her one.

She held the cup, relishing the warmth, but wouldn't drink anything he served.

Amused, he watched her and said, "Tell me about school." So she did, and from there the conversation drifted to other things, mundane things, all for the eyes and ears.

He invited her to meet with friends in the evening, and she begged off, saying she couldn't. "Then lunch," he said. "Let's do lunch tomorrow."

For that, she had no choice but to find the time.

This was the way it always was with her and him.

According to their legends, Boris's connection to her Ecuadorean parents went back to before she was born. There wasn't anything important about this conversation now, just as there likely wouldn't be much importance to whatever they discussed over lunch, but that was the point of these frequent inconsequential visits between student and family friend. The routine had been going on so long that they'd slowly become invisible, and within that invisibility, the sleight of hand took place, though not without suspicion or incident.

Boris had been hauled in by the KGB more than once, questioned, and let go.

His legend was impeccably backstopped, as was hers.

She had her straitlaced, unforgiving, community-pillar Omaha parents partly to thank for that. They'd pushed her hard to excel from the time her tiny hand was strong enough to hold a bow, and in so doing had provided a path out from under their late-night-yelling, liquor-swilling, serial-philandering roof. She'd been eighteen, naive and starry-eyed, determined to make her own way in New York City. Had found disappointment, hunger, and had been facing homelessness when a newspaper ad offering full-time work for the right classically trained violist led down a rabbit hole, in which she'd vanished.

Two years of training and language and culture immersion later, she'd established a new identity in Moscow-friendly Ecuador and, under the agency's guiding hand, applied for the opening at the conservatory where freedom had turned to handcuffs, and handcuffs to prison.

Metaphorically speaking, she'd been sent undercover into a supermax facility, where, for the sake of authenticity, warden and guards, judge, jury, and public all believed her guilty. Without a lifeline to proof of innocence, the truth would cease to exist. Boris was that proof, her only link to the chain of command.

Through him her orders came, and through him she sent information back, and yet she couldn't trust him enough to drink his oversweetened tea. Her life and safety had become dependent upon a man whose motives and priorities, she suspected, had diverged diametrically from hers.

Boris rested his hand on her shoulder and, making small talk, crept his fingers lower until they cupped her breast. She shrugged away and stood.

In flawless Ecuadorean Spanish, the common language of their shared legend, he said, "Your family misses you. Take a break from your studies. Travel with me."

The words made her heart skip a beat. "My parents sent for me?"

"Let's surprise them," he said.

She turned away, bitter with disappointment.

The agency wasn't calling her in. This was Boris propositioning her, asking her to break protocol and put her life and mission at risk. She said, "You know how mother is, crazy with details, needing everything to be just so. This isn't the type of surprise that would please her." She paused, caught Boris's eye and, voice strained to make the point, said, "I could write ahead. That would provide plenty of time for her to make arrangements."

Boris touched his nose and tipped his finger, as if both to compliment the cleverness and to acknowledge the threat. He drew close to her again, arms out to embrace her.

She took another step away and, putting distance between them, turned for the hall. "It's getting late," she said. "I'll be missed at school."

He walked with her toward the door.

Heart picking up tempo, she forced her breathing to remain steady.

Boris was a dangerous man — not just to her, but in principle — and she was about to walk a bridge she couldn't uncross. She risked cutting herself off from support, risked being branded a traitor, risked having no way to defend her name or her decisions and, worse, risked being turned over to the KGB for torture, if not death. Palms sweating, she turned to face him. "You've been good to my family," she said. "You've known me since I was a child, and for that, I'm grateful, but you have no right to touch my body as you have been. Please stop."

Boris's mouth opened, and his face blanched. Tone light and teasing, he said, "What a silly girl you are, telling silly stories."

"I don't want to inform Father," she said. "I will if it's the only way to make you stop."

Boris's lips turned up in a nasty snarl that belied the sweet tone of his voice. "If I didn't know you as such an innocent girl, I would imagine these ugly words were threats."

"Is truth ugly?" she said. "Are promises threats?"

She reached the coatrack.

He said, "Don't think I don't know how you put out for your boyfriend."

She grabbed hat and scarf and clenched her teeth.

By *boyfriend,* Boris meant Dmitry, a fellow student at the conservatory, beautiful and gifted and as fascinated with her as she was with him. She'd been handpicked to appeal to his personality and tastes and had been trained to adjust in ways she lacked. For nearly a year she'd studied beside him and flirted with him while living life with all the normalcy of every other student at the conservatory. She hadn't been told why he mattered or what she sought to gain from his friendship, but he was the son of the minister of defense, so she could guess. *Get close to him,* were her instructions. *The closer the better.* She'd done her job well, and it had turned into a physical relationship, and somehow, by Boris's twisted logic, that made her a whore, and because she was a whore, she was no longer a person with a right to her own preferences or desires.

Boris reached for her, pulled her into him, and so sweetly said, "You think you can go crying to Mommy and Daddy? Wrong. They'll never believe you. You breathe one bad word about me to your parents, and I'll tell them you've run off. I'll ensure they cut off your allowance and take away your housing, and make sure they learn in very sordid detail what an ungrateful little bitch you've been. I own you. What I want is mine, and you'll give it to me."

She shoved him back. "I won't."

He reached for her again, and she kneed him, grabbed her boots and coat, pushed out the door, and ran, tripping in her socks down the stairs, skidding into the foyer door.

She fumbled, shoving her trembling limbs into her boots, trying to get her hat and scarf on and to get the coat wrapped around her, all the while the heavy *thud-thud-thud* of his clogged feet tromped slowly after her.

"You can't hide from me," he sang. "You can't run. No matter where you go, no matter how long it takes, I'll find you."

Hat askew, boots finally on, she rushed out the door with laces untied.

Her lungs iced up. Breathing hurt.

The cold bit into every part of her body.

She fought the wind to get her arms into the coat, to get the coat wrapped tight around her, and to pull the gloves onto her shaking fingers. She found a modicum of warmth, and head down, body racked by shivering, she walked-ran toward the bus stop, took a look, and kept on walking. She didn't expect Boris to chase her on foot — he'd first have to return to his apartment and change shoes and bundle up, and an actual chase would be too conspicuous and would draw unwanted attention — but she wasn't about to wait at the bus stop and give him the chance to stroll up and say hello.

She fought the urge to look behind her and instead searched the hardened faces of those who walked toward her for any glimpse at or reaction to unusual movement at her back. And she continued on, utilizing window reflections across the street, and when she was confident that he hadn't followed, she turned off the sidewalk to enter the metro and followed the stairs down into a lesser cold where she traded frozen gray mush and diesel-fumed air for stale piss and burned metal and oil.

On the platform she leaned into a pillar and caught her breath, then loosened her coat, reached her hand up under her shirt, pulled down the micro recorder, and de-threaded the mic that had been pinned to the inside of her collar. Heart beating hard again, she hid the electronics in her fist and then shoved them deep down into her pocket.

Boris had come so painfully close to brushing against the wires.

Worse was that she still wasn't sure if she would have been better off if he *had* discovered them and thus saved her from the predicament she faced now.

There were no easy solutions.

Desperation had driven her here.

She could live with Boris's unwanted sexual advances, unprofessional and irritating as they were, but not with enduring day after day along a razor-blade edge of guessing and double guessing, wary of how every word and every movement might be misinterpreted by those who watched and listened, while also running scared from the one man into whose hands her life and safety had been placed. It'd been six months — six long, silent months — since she'd had contact with anyone from her team.

Packages from Ecuador continued to arrive every few weeks, filled with treats and basic necessities and handwritten letters, which were inevitably copied and read before she received them, but there was nothing in those boxes beyond the routine of maintaining her legend. Boris was the conduit through which everything flowed, and Boris wasn't playing straight, had possibly already sold her out.

She had no proof, nothing but a rising tension and small coincidental incidents as evidence to suspect him, much less outright accuse him. He knew that as well as she did, just as they both knew his warning that no one would believe her wasn't about his groping.

Without a way to substantiate her concerns, he'd easily charm his way out of the finger-pointing, and she'd still be forced to rely on faith that the details she received from him were true and that what he reported back was accurate, and she'd be more dangerously trapped than she was now, but he wouldn't be able to charm his way out of what she'd just recorded.

She needed him investigated, and while

evidence of moral turpitude wasn't anywhere close to proving he was double-dealing, it'd be enough for someone to give him a closer look, and hopefully, that push would be enough.

The train rolled in. She scanned the platform and then stepped on.

Eyes were on her again, they were always on her, just as all mail she sent was opened, and every call she made listened in on.

Her travel was monitored, and everyone she spoke to, questioned.

Catching Boris on tape had been the easy part.

A weapon served no purpose if she had no way to use it.

Chapter 27

Holden
Age: 32
Location: Dallas, Texas
Passport Country: Canada
Names: Troy Martin Holden

He drove three hours before making the call, up from Austin, into downtown Dallas, far enough away from Baxter and the kid to blur the line of connection, and would lose a day to a never ending suburban landscape because the poison of mutiny had taken hold.

He needed to know.

Needed to know he was right before choosing the highway of no return.

A soaring skyline rose with the horizon. Two lanes widened to three, four, five, rose up into layers that divided, entwined, and circled the glass and steel towers.

He'd traipsed the globe, had traveled through the world's largest cities, and hadn't come across a road system yet that touched the size and scope of Texas's high-rise interstate interchanges — and they still weren't enough to contain the traffic.

He followed the curves, bumper to bumper, between merging eighteen-wheelers and texting drivers, down from dizzying heights and across multiple lanes to reach an exit that led into the downtown matrix.

GPS guided him through one-way streets and eventually to parking.

Flying would have made for a quicker, safer trip, just as a pay phone would have made for a simpler call — a two-for-one opportunity since about the only place he could find a pay phone that didn't draw attention these days was in an airport — but he'd already been in too many of them over the past weeks and couldn't afford to burn another ID. A disposable phone in a hotel lobby, one number among thousands, would work as a close second best.

He pulled a blazer and fedora off the backseat and slipped them on. They were details, like the baseball cap and the Beats headphones had been details.

He walked mostly empty sidewalks to the Westin and pushed through glass doors into a din of bodies and matching lanyards and the giddy rush that inevitably followed a room of hundreds just let out for lunch. Phone in hand, he hit SEND on a pre-dialed number and wove through the crowd, counting rings. He made it halfway before Frank answered with the same authoritative hello he used no matter who called.

Holden, voice light, as if picking up from where they'd left off on a shared joke, said, "Hey, Pops. Been to Bogotá lately?"

Frank said, "Gawd no. What's going on, kid?"

"Not much. You busy?"

"Little bit. Let me call you back in twenty."

The air went dead. Holden pushed on to the back of the thinning crowd.

The problem, always, with calling Frank was the number of listeners. The precautions weren't to keep Frank protected from Holden's line of work, although that was a legitimate concern, they were to avoid drawing attention to Holden from those listening in on Frank's side.

Frank needed to find a hotel of his own.

Holden checked his watch and set the timer.

Twenty minutes meant twenty minutes exactly.

He found the stairwell, followed the stairs down to where the cell signal was spotty at best. He tore off the blazer as he went, folded the arms, tucked the collar down, and turned the whole thing inside out and in on itself. Blazer transformed to leather backpack, hat went into it, strap went over his shoulder, and he pushed out of the stairwell into a well-lit concourse.

The pedestrian underground connected a swath of downtown office towers, hotels, shops, and restaurants and made it possible for him to avoid more than one pass in front of the same camera — made it possible to get lost and disappear. He wandered, browsing, eating time in a roundabout path toward the Crowne Plaza, then headed up and into the lobby and waited on the sofa, newspaper in hand, eyes passing over words at a legitimate pace while his mind stayed stuck on Jen and the empty lot in El Paso.

His best efforts to derail the thoughts inevitably took him back, back to what he knew of her life, back to wanting to fill in the blanks, back and back, just as they had the entire drive up. He wanted to find her, wanted to find her bad.

Want was a problem.

He'd seen what want, the passion of need, could do. Want had killed his mother. Want had forced him to watch her die before the gunmen stuffed a bag over his three-year-

old head and tore him, clawing and screaming, away from her body.

Want had killed the biological father he'd
never known.

His parents had wanted, and want had
caused them to take what they shouldn't
have, and he in turn had structured his life
around the absence of want, always in
ambivalent motion, always going, never connecting, because want was a beguiling,
dangerous animal.

His pocket vibrated, twenty minutes to
the beat.

Frank said, "I've only got five."

Holden said, "Remember that travel al-
bum I showed you?"

"Sure do."

Holden folded the newspaper, left it on
the coffee table, and made a slow path to
the front door. "Found out that the lady I
was interested in, she has kids."

The line went quiet, which was good.
Meant that Frank knew he was talking
about McFadden and the ghosts and the
pictures they'd discussed over lunch in
Miami and that he was just as puzzled over
the new perspective as Holden had been.

Frank said, "There always were those rumors."

"What kind of rumors?"

"Maybe the not-worth-repeating kind. What else?"

Holden stepped between thoughts and returned to what had pushed him through the three-hour drive for a five-minute call. "Been thinking about that lady," he said. "Been thinking about how she connects to that pit of vipers you hate so much. She knows the guy who runs it, doesn't she? There's history between them."

Frank's voice, cautious, guarded, and very slow, said, "Those are bloody, chummy waters, kid. Really wouldn't advise you to swim there unless you're well prepared to get between a shark and his food."

"Can you be more specific?"

"Do I wanna know why you're asking?"

"Probably not."

Frank hesitated. Holden knew the pause, the delay of risk calculation, of Frank afraid of where the information would take him, of heartbreak, and of the parental wish to protect the child, followed by the conscious decision to let the boy be a man. He ran a hand over a couple days' worth of stubble, thick enough that Holden could hear the gesture over the phone, and said, "You good to party?"

"Cleaned up and ready to go."

"Burn the phone when we're done."

"Always."

Frank said, "The two of them go way back to when she was working undercover in Moscow. He was her contact — handler, if you will — her one line to the outside. Official story is just one day to the next, *bleep,* both of them are gone. Unofficially? He was working both sides. He sold her out to the Russians, and she outed him to the agency. It's an incestuous story full of bad blood and hatchets that never got buried."

"You know who he is? Know anything more about him?"

"Not any more'n I know who she is, which means I know crap. Can't help you find him, if that's what you're asking."

"Wasn't, but thanks." Holden checked his watch, gauged the minutes left, and picked his battle. "Tell me what you know about her kids."

"A few years after she disappeared, a guy walks into the Paris embassy claiming to be high-ranking GRU — Russian foreign military intelligence — says he wants to trade sides. Chief of Station sits him down for a chat, checking him out, wants to see if he's legit. Somewhere in that conversation the guy drops her name, talking like he knows her and talking about a kid — singular — like it's common knowledge she has one.

289

Might not have gone anywhere, except the station chief knew exactly who McFadden was, and with her name, plus mention of a kid, his bullshit detector goes off. He starts pushing. The guy gets mad, stops talking, has a change of heart, like maybe Mother Russia ain't so bad after all."

"That's it?"

"All I got."

"But you said there'd always been rumors."

"Sure, the way she up and left, no trail, no trace, no nothing. Turned her into some kinda Loch Ness Mothman Bigfoot alien. Then someone comes along, claiming they seen her since she disappeared, and the rumor machine cranks up to a whole new level. Watercooler whispers got louder, story grew. Was all bullshit, though.

"Apparently, not all of it."

"You're better off believing it was. This thing with him and the woman, it's ugly and personal. Personal is what gets a man killed. *Capiche*?"

"Any way to track down the guy in Paris?"

"Not a chance in hell."

"Any better odds on getting me access to NGI?"

Frank hesitated. "I'm, uh, still putting out feelers."

Holden sighed on the inside. The lackluster noncommitment said that even if Frank did have the connections to get him what he wanted, the contents of this conversation had killed any chance he'd use them.

Frank said, "Look, I gotta go, but do me a favor, will ya, kid? I didn't make all those trips, spend the years running from Calamar to Bogotá, trying to find you, dealing with the shit I dealt with in keeping a promise to your old man just so you could hit the grave before I do. Let me go out knowing that I upheld my end of the deal."

The request was a guilt punch in the gut.

Holden reached into his pocket for a toothpick and fought the urge to chew. He forced levity into his voice. "I get it, Pops. You get to die first."

The lie felt like poison, but Frank didn't hear the lie.

"Good," he said. "Good, good."

If he'd been present, he'd have run his thick fingers through Holden's hair and knocked an affectionate knuckle on the side of his head.

"Forget all this history," Frank said. "It only leads to trouble. Find a sweet girl, settle down, and maybe make me some grandbabies."

Holden smiled for real. "Oh yeah, grandbabies coming right up."

The call dropped. Holden shoved the phone into a pocket.

Settling down might come, eventually. In the meantime, it'd take every resource he had, and every bit of smarts, to ensure Frank got his favor.

CHAPTER 28

Clare
Age: 26
Location: Bière, Switzerland
Passport Country: France
Names: Catherine Lefevre

She stood behind old leaded panes half hidden by bright red and green geraniums in wooden window boxes, stood looking out over forest and vibrant manicured pastures, which, for all she cared, might as well have been Moscow's cold, bleak concrete.

This window in the second-floor hallway was the only one in the old farmhouse that provided a view of the front door, so it was here she waited, watching for the mail from noon until the postman drove by. It'd been two weeks — no, three — nestled in a hill above quaint charm not far from Lake Geneva, four weeks of fading hope, growing desperation, and a heightened sense of torment with each new sunrise.

She chewed her thumb and fought the urge to pace.

God, she needed a cigarette.

She'd never intended to turn smoking into a habit. Long winter evenings short on entertainment, nights of small friend-filled gatherings fueled by alcohol and black-market tobacco had seen that she had.

The *putt-putt* of a small engine carried over the hill.

Her heart rate picked up.

She pulled her thumb from between her teeth, steadied her shaking hands, and focused on the road, the winding road, afraid to breathe, waiting for the first flash of color to signal a vehicle headed for the farmhouse.

The postal car came into view.

The car pulled to a stop in the tiny parking niche, and the same little man she'd watched drive by day after day carried letters to the door.

Sick, wet dread uncoiled inside her chest, a living, waking thing that entwined her heart and squeezed to the point of tangible, physical pain.

She turned away from the window and paused, suspended between the compelling need to hurry down the stairs and the crushing anxiety begging her to stay, soul holding out in defiant resistance, refusing to accept what her mind understood weeks ago, because the truth hurt more than she could bear.

Dmitry wasn't coming. He'd never planned to join her.

Or . . . or he'd been prevented from it.

The distance between those two possibilities split her in half.

She oscillated minute to hour to day between hating him and hating herself. No middle ground existed: either he'd abandoned her and was alive and well, in which case she wished him dead, or he'd truly loved her, but the worst had happened, and only a despicable human being would cling to that kind of hope.

"Wait for me," he'd said.

At the time, making the trip out of Moscow had seemed the only sane choice.

The regular calls and frequent visits from Boris had stopped completely after her confrontation, and months had passed without a package from Ecuador. She had no way of knowing if her packet with the recording had reached its destination, no way of knowing if Boris had gotten to Headquarters first and, because of him, she'd been cut off.

She'd debated making a run for the US

Embassy.

Without proof of citizenship, she had no guaranteed entry, and if they turned her away — which was likely — she'd be worse off than if she'd never gone. Even if they did let her in, she had no way to prove her bona fides. The best she could hope for was detention and interrogation while they confirmed her identity stateside. And if Boris had fulfilled his promise, and the agency, believing him, had branded her a traitor, she'd be arrested, and imprisoned. And if none of that was true, she'd have blown her cover for nothing.

The predicament had borne down with crushing weight, offering no clear way out, building tension into something unbearable which had finally surfaced in a rare bout of tears, made worse because Dmitry had walked in on her crying.

She'd turned from him to face the window, but not quickly enough.

He'd stood behind her and wrapped his arms around her. "Whatever it is," he'd whispered, "I won't let you hurt."

Those few words had changed everything.

He'd tipped her chin toward him so she could see his face, and in that brief flash she'd understood, understood that she'd been right about Boris, that he'd already sold her out — understood that Dmitry knew what she was, and had probably known from the beginning — that it hadn't been the training or being handpicked to appeal to him that had caused them to come together but that, as part of a disinformation campaign, she'd been his target as much as he was hers, and that he was the only reason the KGB hadn't yet rolled her up. CIA and KGB, she and he, target and target.

She couldn't breathe, couldn't think.

Suffocating, she slipped out of his arms and pressed her head against the cool window glass. Dmitry reached for her and pulled her back. Inside her chest, in her heart, she fought his embrace as if she'd discovered infidelity, and yet she craved his comfort all the same. KGB and CIA, lover and lover, target and target.

No one had predicted that for both of them, work would become personal, and that a relationship full of lies would become tender and trusting.

Desperation thickened. The trap closed in. Words she'd never planned to utter spilled out of her mouth. She whispered, "I'm pregnant."

For two months, at least, she'd hoped for an opportunity to communicate the turn of events with her team, half relieved she couldn't — because it wasn't their decision to make — and half terrified of being left to decide on her own. Abortion was the only option, and easy enough to obtain in a country with the highest abortion rate in the world. She expected Dmitry would say as much.

Instead, he held her in a long, long silence and, finally, using the term of endearment she'd taught him and by which he'd called her ever since, said, "*Querida,* how long have you known?"

She couldn't face him directly.

Truth within the lie, she said, "A few weeks."

He took her hand, walked her to the radio, and turned the music up, as was his habit when he wanted to speak privately, a move she'd always ascribed to the paranoid over-cautiousness that permeated this harsh monitored world but now had a different meaning. He pulled her close. Lips beside her ear, he whispered, "Let's run away, you and I. We can make a life away from this."

She wanted what he offered more than anything, but she was a realist. She said, "We'd never get through the airport."

"No, no, not like that. We go on holiday formally, with proper paperwork and permission, and from there we make our own way."

She offered a half smile and rested her head on his shoulder.

The same suggestion from anyone else would have been preposterous. There was no getting out, no going on holidays, not for the average citizen. But he, with his family connections, had already traveled extensively.

A short getaway would hardly raise eyebrows.

"Where could we go?" she said. "Where could we go and never be found?"

Where could they go and never be found by her people?

Where could they go and never be found by his?

Money was a concern, too. Her paychecks were deposited into an account back home, and a decent amount would have accumulated by now, but if she ran, as Dmitry proposed, there'd be no way to access that money without being traced and found.

She'd saved while in Moscow, squirreling away what she could from the small monthly stipend sent to her under the guise of an allowance from her Ecuadorean parents, but currency restrictions made converting rubles into deutsche marks or francs a dodgy black-market affair, one that she hadn't been willing to risk.

Dmitry solved both issues.

It took him over a month, but he worked through the red tape and the bureaucracy of being able to travel legally and made use of connections to borrow a family friend's chalet to put a temporary roof over their heads.

The night before they were set to fly, his aunt died.

He had to delay his departure, and she wanted to change her plans to match his.

Lying on his bed, head on his chest, their tickets and exit paperwork in her hands, she said she'd wait until they could travel together. He traced his fingers over a belly that had become harder and harder to hide.

"Go," he said. "I'll join you in a day, maybe two, but you go."

She studied his confident smile, searching for a hint that her trust had been misplaced, and found nothing. He took her to the airport the next morning, walked her to the boarding area, and waited with her through to the last call, and when waiting was no longer possible, he handed her an envelope with twenty thousand Swiss francs and whispered, "I'll follow soon. Wait for me."

She had no idea then or in the days that

followed that this would be the last time she'd see him. She flew to Geneva as they'd planned, found the house empty and available. She let herself in with the key he'd given her, and made herself at home.

One day stretched into three.

An express post envelope sent from Milan arrived with another twenty thousand francs, no note, just the money, and she felt the sinking awareness then, her instincts warning her to pack up and leave. Instead she tried to reach him.

Calls to his flat went unanswered. Calls to their mutual friends revealed he'd quit school and no one had seen or heard from him since the day she left.

Three days turned into a week — a week of being cut off, with no one to turn to, no way to return, and this home above Lake Geneva the only thing left to connect her to him — a week of knowing she should leave but being unable to take that step, because leaving meant losing him forever, meant spending the rest of her life torn between the illusion of love and the bitter belief that all she'd ever been was a high-value instrument played by a master of strings.

One week turned into two.

Her return ticket expired. She squatted at the house, lights off, bags packed, and ready to flee, jumping at every sound along the road in a constant swing between hope and despair, certain only that each passing day multiplied the risk of being grabbed.

And now mail had come again.

Through the window she watched the postal carrier return to the car and continue up the steep, twisted road. Barefoot, uncomfortably swollen, and off balance in a body that no longer felt familiar, she trod down the old wooden stairs, reached the front, flipped through the two letters added to the growing pile in the box, and put them back.

Nothing for her.

The autopilot of self-preservation pushed her to the hallway bench.

There was no way Dmitry would have gotten the exit paperwork without KGB approval. That they'd been content to let her sit out the month meant they'd wanted her here. Self-loathing grew thicker with the thought. She'd been an easy accomplice to their plans, whatever those plans were, cutting off her own avenue of escape, turning herself into an enemy of the state, outplayed, outwitted, because, fool that she was, she'd believed Dmitry.

Boris had done this. His scrawl was so obvious in the signature.

She worked water-fat toes into her shoes.

Love and loss churned in the turbid poison of survival and fantasy revenge.

She stood and, brushing her fingers along the wall, walked toward the back door, toward the unknown, in which she had only herself to trust and more life than her own to protect. Certainty drove her forward.

Events that had brought her here weren't over.

Leaving wasn't part of their script.

The past would one day catch up, and when it did, she'd have to be ready.

She pulled her suitcase from the coat closet, everything to her name in that one small bag, closed her eyes, and whispered the forever good-bye.

Today was the day she ceased to exist.

CHAPTER 29

Jack
Age: 26
Location: Spring, Texas
Passport Country: USA
Names: Jason Francis White

He walked off suburbia's edge into a wilderness hemmed in by freeways and toll roads, franchise restaurants and chain grocery stores, off a dead-end street in a crossover- and minivan-filled neighborhood onto land that had never known the developer's scythe, following a dot to dot to the man he believed had taken Clare.

The Broker's bounty packet, as Jill called it, pointed a half mile northwest to Peckinpaugh Preserve, where Christopher was expected to surface: twenty-five acres of hiking and biking trails that wound around a lake and through natural forest as part of an expanding greenway project that connected parks and older reserves, which, combined, encompassed thousands of acres of suburban wild.

He headed for it backward.

Branches and lush undergrowth scratched his skin and snagged his clothes.

He shoved forward, patiently, methodically, slowed by the weight of gear he'd acquired in the hours since leaving Jill, creating a path to the beat of Marxist guerrilla philosophy that had been forced into his head.

The fighter chooses when and how to fight.

He strikes. And runs. And returns and strikes again.

Santiago's lectures had meant nothing when he and Jill had been squatting beside buckets of dirty water, washing and peeling root vegetables in the Colombian mountains.

They held meaning now.

He'd come ahead of the battle to choose when and how to fight.

Jack checked his watch and then his position, course corrected, and continued on from thicket to creek, and across the creek and onward, until rich underbrush opened to a gentler, tamer wild thinned under the hand of civilized upkeep. Clare's voice chased after Santiago's:

You need to know your opponent to outthink him.

Understand your enemy and you'll know his plans before he does.

Hard advice to follow when one had no idea who the enemy was.

Jack stopped thirty feet in from a trail.

This was as far into the preserve as he'd go.

He scouted potential vantage points, found what he wanted, shoved his hands into half-finger gloves, unhooked climbing rope from his pack, looped it over a branch, and clipped carabiners to his climbing belt.

He had an hour and a half left, two hours with any luck.

If Jill woke before he returned, she'd be gone, and he'd be forced to fight two wars instead of one. He tied a Prusik to one side of the rope, locked the carabiner on his climbing belt to a loop at the end of the other, and headed up.

They'd had weapons and ammunition, had their tool bags and two decades of experience, but taking Christopher alive required more. Acquiring more had required invisibility. Invisibility had required time. He'd left the motel on foot, marbles of tissue beneath toes and heel to alter his gait, hat and glasses on to hide a clear view of his face.

A half dozen new burner phones, prepaid debit cards, and a few generic clothing items inside a forgettable backpack had started him on the long chain of disguises and ID shifts that had got him to where he was now: hauling eighty pounds of equipment to a sniper's hide in the middle of a suburban wilderness.

Their old phones — all of them — were on the move somewhere in the city.

He'd hated letting go of his only connection to Clare, but any two known devices connecting to the world from the same location would create all the dots the Broker needed to know them and track them. Thanks to Clare, the Broker had his burner's number. He couldn't guarantee the Broker hadn't acquired the Blackphone number and no matter what Jill said, he couldn't guarantee the Blackphone hadn't been running at any point that either of their burners had been.

He had to keep those phones moving.

He also needed a way to get them back.

A temporary phone, a prepaid credit card, and the Uber app had been the easy, if messy, solution. He'd left his burner on, volume off, had left everything else in pieces, had tossed his bags in the trunk, had shoved his burner down with the emergency tire beneath the floorboard, and had stashed the rest of their old phones beneath the backseat. A solid tip to the driver and a request for a possible off-the-books pickup had gotten him the driver's number.

It was the best he could do under the time constraints.

Those same time constraints propelled him to hurry now.

Forty-feet up was high enough.

A haul line and pulleys got the gear up after him. He secured his kit and rappelled down, retraced his steps out of the preserve, into the greenbelt, back to the neighborhood where he'd left the rental parked between two homes, and out before the neighbors figured out the car didn't belong to the other guy's guests.

The motel room was as he'd left it, and Jill was already restless.

He packed while she came to, dividing weapons and ammunition and enough food and water to get them through a three-day wait. He retrieved the X-Caliber, a two-thousand-dollar gauged and scoped CO_2 projector that he'd found in the barn together with Clare's truck, the kind of thing ranchers and game wardens used to tranquilize one-ton animals from a safe distance.

The accompanying case should have held five rapid-delivery devices. It only had three. He couldn't guess at what Clare had used the first two for, certainly not for four-legged animals. He loaded the first of the syringes and dosed for 250 pounds.

Three delivery devices: three opportunities to make a hit.

One would have been enough if he could guarantee that Christopher was coming alone or that he'd recognize him on sight, but if there'd been more than one man alive after taking Clare, there'd be more than one at the preserve, and split-second survival choices didn't make good bedfellows with switching out weapons — especially not in a civilian-filled park where every movement was a potential mother or child begging for disaster. He strapped the rifle to his bag, cinched it down, glanced up, and met angry eyes watching from the edge of the bed.

Adrenaline hit with a defibrillating jolt.

He had no idea how long she'd been there.

He flinched, fought the urge to scramble, and offered her a bottle of water.

Her eyes tracked to the water and then to him.

She was calm, the dangerous kind of calm that came before wreaking unthinking damage because she was too highly charged to care about outcomes.

He scooted back, out of reach. "You win," he said.

She shifted off the bed, feet on the floor, as if he'd never spoken.

He stood and, louder this time, said, "You. *Win.*"

She kept coming.

Hands up, defensive, he sidestepped. "Name your price. Call a truce."

She paused, lips flat, eyes seething.

He said, "I don't have time to fight you, I sure as hell don't have time for recuperation, and I need functional bones and joints to find Clare, so . . ."

She snatched the bottle, uncapped it, and took a long swig.

"You want a truce?" she said. "Give me back the shit you stole."

"Come on, be reasonable. I can't undo what's already done."

She took another swallow, glared at him while she drank, and capped the bottle. "The problem with you, John, is you forget that being the smartest guy around doesn't make everyone else an idiot."

"I've *never* thought of you as an idiot."

"Yeah? So maybe don't ask for a truce and then insult my intelligence. We both know you didn't flush it all."

He'd have argued if he thought he could win, but she'd called it right. Doubling down would only double the hurt at the end. He knelt for his bag, ran a finger between the bottom and an inner pocket, pulled out a pill pouch, and tossed it toward her.

She motioned for more. "All of it."

He opened his mouth in protest.

"Give it, or I take it," she said. "Your call."

This was him in the truck, demanding her keys, forcing compliance for the sake of compliance, knowing full well he didn't need it, because he had keys of his own.

He'd earned this and hated every bit of it all the same.

He fished the rest in tiny portions from hidden seams and pockets and dropped each packet into her outstretched hand. She clenched a fist around the goods, turned for the bathroom, stood over the toilet bowl, and he watched, dumbfounded and silent, as she opened each bag and flushed the stash away.

His face reddened. His palms went damp with the sucker-punched anger of having expended time and emotional effort over something that hadn't been real, of having lost another round due to manipulation. He met her halfway out the door.

She straight armed him in his chest to keep him back.

Teeth gritted, he said, "What the hell was that about?"

She jabbed a finger into his chest and moved up into his face. "I am *not* your fucking crack whore, John, and you're delusional if you think that shit matters enough for me to let you use it to control me."

He smacked her away. "*Control you?* What kind of messed up are you? I held on to that in case you needed it to be okay, to stay well."

Her eyes narrowed. Her lips tightened. She shook her head in slow, chiding correction. "Don't confuse self-righteousness with love. This shit we do to each other, the gamesmanship and one-upping, tracking, tagging, sabotaging, that's one thing." Finger to his chest again, she jabbed harder. "No matter how much you think you know what's best, you do *not* get to play God with my life. You do *not* get to make choices for me."

He caught her hand and stared her down, but god damn, he hated when she was right. He pulled her into a hug and held tight until the tension ebbed and her arms wrapped around his waist, and they stayed that way until she whispered, "Truce."

He let her go. She shrugged away.

She slugged him hard in the stomach.

His eyes smarted. Voice cracking, he said, "What the hell?"

She pinched his cheek and smiled into his face, goo-gooing like he was a tot in diapers. "So you don't get any ideas about me being less than a cold, crazy bitch."

He clenched his jaw and fought the urge to punch her back.

She turned for the supply stash he'd already assembled, dug for Excedrin and, with far more swagger than having woken from artificial sleep should have allowed, said, "Let's get going, buddy boy. Christopher's not going to kidnap himself."

He made her eat and waited until dark to leave and led her off a different street into the same suburban wild. They worked in silence, familiar in their roles, turning camouflaged hammocks into shooter's nests on opposite sides of the lake, setting cellular motion-activated game cameras above critical trail junctions, and they waited out the night, watching the entrance and verdure for a man who'd just as surely be searching for them.

Midnight brought the damp and drizzle of low-lying fog, which coated equipment and supplies and turned sunrise into a drawn-out affair that only partially helped improve visibility. Cars and minivans entered the parking area. A trickle of joggers and bicyclists braved the weather, each as suspect as the last, until a familiar body in a zipped-up jacket, overdressed in more ways than one, turned strategy upside down.

The last time Jack had seen that face, it'd been in his headlights as he careened backward down the street with Jill in the trunk. His head hurt to see it again now. And he crawled a mental reverse to the Blackphone and the Broker and Jill's denials, and in the frustration he let it go because searching for the unfindable led to madness, and in the moment it didn't matter because they were here and Jill's boyfriend was here.

Christopher wouldn't be far.

The boyfriend walked from the small parking area to the trailhead, each step stiff and awkward, beads of sweat pooling along his hairline, but what caught Jack's attention was the white-knuckled death grip on a phone.

He swung the spotting scope toward Jill.

She sat in her hammock, back straight, watching the entrance, seeing what he'd seen, and then, as if reading his mind, she swung the glass in his direction.

Clare had never allowed them to wear a wire while training.

"Relying on technology makes you lazy," she'd said.

According to Clare's philosophy, electronics were worthless during weeks on the run. And, since they didn't have the luxury of choosing when and where they might engage, unless they were planning to wear an earpiece daily, she didn't want them wearing one at all. So she'd taught them to sign, and they'd taught themselves Morse code, and there'd been nights, as they'd crawled through the dark, when her argument fell apart completely, but it was on those nights that they'd learned to compensate.

Jack spoke with his hands.

Jill needed to call the boyfriend. This was all on her.

She dug for the new burner he'd given her, and he scanned the area, watching for movement as she dialed.

She swung out of the nest and rappelled to the ground.

He pulled his gear together.

Clare had been right about a lot of things he'd never wanted to admit, not then, not now, not ever. He hoped to God her training proved to be right on this, as well.

CHAPTER 30

Rob
Age: 23
Location: Spring, Texas
Passport Country: USA
Names: Robert Preston Davis

His hands were wet against the steering wheel, clammy, sweaty wet, gripping tight, guiding the car along the narrow road where trees and underbrush hedged both sides. Everyday city life had turned into rugged wild.

The isolation added to the weight crushing his lungs.

Each tire rotation brought him closer to the possibility of dying, but if he stopped, the whole *possibility* part would vanish and he'd absolutely be killed.

Sweat dripped into his eyes. He blinked against the sting, lifted his shoulder to wipe his face against his shirt, and stared straight ahead, trying not to think.

Drive. That's all he had to do. Drive and park.

Drive, park, and walk.

He was lying to himself, but the lie kept him moving.

Truth was, he was screwed no matter what he did.

He was a wanted man, thanks to Jen, a fugitive driving a stolen car, about to enter a nature preserve with ten pounds of explosives strapped around his chest, thank you, fucking Jen. He'd have been better off if she really had been kidnapped, and he would have wished her dead if he didn't so desperately need her to stay alive. Whoever she was, really was . . . No, he didn't want to know, didn't even care.

He was so over her and done with this already.

The parking area came into view, and then a little white building at the end of the lot that would have seemed welcoming on any other day but right now felt like the gateway to hell.

He eased the car into an empty spot, turned off the ignition, and sat in silence, staring at the phone, staring through the windshield, staring at nothing, while his brain fritzed and fried. They were out there, the assassins, the kidnappers, watching his every step, listening to every sound he whispered. One wrong move and the same guys who'd never put a violent hand on him or sworn or raised their voices, the same guys who'd fed him well and made sure he was comfortable and, aside from keeping him doped up and holding him against his will had been more decent than a lot of people he called friends, would turn him into hamburger.

Their flat indifference terrified him more than the vest itself.

At least psychopaths who fed off their victims' fear, or animals that toyed with their prey before they ate it, or irrational and jumpy criminals on the run would have made some twisted sort of sense.

For these guys, he was just part of a job that needed doing.

"Do it right," they'd said, "and we'll let you live. Ignore the instructions and . . ." The smaller one, Christopher, the talker, had opened his hand in a simulated *bang*.

So he'd driven. He'd parked.

He had no choice now but to walk.

He left the keys in the ignition and stepped out of the car with the careful trepidation of a man strapped into a band of explosives against his will. He made his way toward the information booth one foot at a time, then past the booth to the trailhead, focus on the ground, cautious to avoid eye contact out of fear the desperation would give itself away. "Turn left at the first trail," they'd said, so he turned left.

"Keep the phone out, clearly visible," they'd said, so he did that, too.

Jen would find him, and she'd call him.

They hadn't offered any explanation as to how they knew Jen would be here or why or how they knew she'd call, only that she would, and that when she did, his job was to draw her to him and keep her out in the open as long as possible.

A jogger headed for him, earbuds in her ears, shirt drenched from the sprinkling rain, or maybe it was sweat. He watched, nervous and heart pounding, as the woman drew close and passed him, and he kept watching until she was out of sight.

Dangerous, dangerous thoughts churned through his head.

They'd said he could go when this was over. He'd argued with them. The only way he'd really be free was if Jen proved to the detectives that she was alive.

"You'll be fine without her," they'd said. "Without a body, there wouldn't be evidence, and without evidence, no conviction."

They'd laughed when he choked.

"We don't want to kill her," they'd said. "Just want to talk with her."

Like he hadn't heard those exact same words through his own front door, and yet here he was, bait strapped to a bomb and cut loose to swim between feuding assassins.

What could possibly go wrong?

Oh, just everything.

If he followed the instructions, if they were right about Jen being here and calling him and coming to him, then they'd get to her, and there'd quite possibly be a body and evidence, and he'd have been right there, fully present and accounted for, and guilty as sin. Even if he did live, he might as well be dead.

The vest grew heavier, grew into eighty pounds of threat dragging him down, turning his feet to lead and his body into deadweight. Desperation and fear swirled and congealed into one simple goal: stay alive.

And, if he lived, prove his innocence.

He reached a junction, a lonely junction.

His spine tingled with the creepy sensation of being watched, and he turned a slow circle, looking for whoever was out there. If his kidnappers were hunting Jen, that meant she was hunting them, and possibly hunting him as a by-product.

He walked on, phone held out where it'd be impossible to miss.

If he followed the instructions through to the end, he was already dead.

The dangerous thoughts surfaced again.

CHAPTER 31

Jack
Age: 26
Location: Spring, Texas
Passport Country: USA
Names: Jason Francis White

He shadowed Jill through the spotting scope, scanning ahead, around, tracking until fog and foliage swallowed her, and then, in a race against time, he strapped on his gear and rappelled to the ground. They'd set up for a protracted hide-seek-hunt, had planned, if necessary, to use Jill as bait to draw Christopher to them, had planned for a hostage scenario, and a dozen variants of psychological warfare.

You need to know your opponent to outthink him.

Understand your enemy and you'll know his plans before he does.

Christopher had gone a level up.

He'd gone after Robert and brought him

as a bazooka to a gunfight.

Anything intimate, personal that Robert knew about Jill, Christopher now knew.

Christopher knew his enemy.

Jack slunk through the silent damp, stepping over fallen trees and skirting low-hanging branches, scanning, scanning for an enemy he could feel but not see.

His jacket vibrated with a photo alert.

He crouched for cover and pulled a mini tablet from its case.

From camera two, he had a blurred image of Jill with Robert in tow.

Jack checked GPS location on the pet tracker she wore.

She was on the move, heading toward the creek that marked the preserve's border.

He changed his trajectory and pushed faster through the quiet undergrowth to keep behind her, hunting the fine line between guarding her way out and veering off course so those in pursuit couldn't set ambush.

Another vibration followed.

He stole a glance at the tablet and, in that glance, froze and knelt and pinched and zoomed. Fair skin, angled cheekbones, and cropped blond hair filled the screen.

Crazy eyes and a hungry mouth smiled for the picture.

Heartbeat rising, the prospect of failure climbing, Jack ran a signal check on the other cameras.

Of the six he'd placed, only one still had power.

Strategy shifted.

He shoved the worthless tablet aside and cut for the open trail that led toward the lake, ran for the remaining signal and its promise of collision with the enemy.

The whine of death stopped him cold.

Bark chunked off the tree ahead.

He rolled hard, shrugged out of his pack to free up mobility, and crawled deeper into the brush. The high-pitched mosquito song of live fire moved past him at thousands of feet per second. Clare's voice looped in his brain in an endless replay of course correction.

He'd been moving forward to confront the enemy.

The rounds had come from behind.

He'd missed something.

This wasn't an ambush. Was something else.

He checked Jill's GPS. She was moving faster.

He ripped the pet tag off his belt, bit down on it, cracked the plastic, and yanked the electronic guts free. Jill would destroy hers when she realized he'd gone dark.

They were running off script now.

The shooting stopped.

He held himself motionless, eyes closed, listening.

A whispered rustle betrayed movement. He rolled hard to the left.

Dirt spit from the ground beside him. He swung in the direction from which the shot had come, took aim on instinct, and pulled.

The CO_2 cartridge hissed.

Silence ruptured with a bull moose bellow.

A fast-moving shadow charged out of the underbrush, two hundred and sixty pounds of angry muscle rushing toward him with a barrage of suppressed fire.

Jack tossed the X-Caliber aside.

He'd broken a cardinal rule, had headed into the fight without knowing his weapon, trusting that stealing from Clare's stash meant she'd already done what needed doing. He scrambled for his kit, cursing Clare with every ragged, dogged breath.

His hand found the stock of Raymond's .308.

He ripped the rifle free, swung the barrel.

The charging giant paused mid-step, dropped to his knees and, a full eight dangerous, breath-holding yards from where he'd started, toppled over.

Jack crawled forward, checked the guy's breathing, and listened to his heart. He'd hit the ground hard, but he'd live, which might be a mistake.

This wasn't Christopher, wasn't the guy he'd wanted to take alive. This was six feet, four inches of fat-free, bulked-up muscle wrapped in a package of discipline cut with the hard-core dedication required to eat thousands of protein calories a day and not much else — the kind of mind one didn't fuck with lightly, the kind of man, if he had to bet, that Christopher would have as a partner.

Jack patted down his legs, torso, arms.

He checked ears and wrists and neck.

No identification. No electronic tethers.

He filched a Desert Eagle from the guy's hip holster and stashed the .50 caliber beast in his bag. Serial numbers would probably lead just as far into nowhere as the pockets had, but they were worth a try. He untied the big boy's laces and, time ticking away far faster than he'd accounted for, pulled boots off feet to check for hidden items.

A flash, a sparkle, in his peripheral vision caught his attention.

Years of training shoved him like physical hands.

He rolled aside. Logic followed after

movement, processing the glint as sunlight reflecting off glass across the lake. A round hit just beyond where his head had been.

He squirreled backward away from bullets that kept coming — not at him, but at the body on the ground. The big guy shook with each impact.

Blood spread from three torso wounds.

Jack watched, paralyzed, confused.

The face on the game camera flashed in his head: brash, brazen, foolish.

Delayed realization kicked hard against the shock and sent him scrambling on hands and feet through the brush. Adrenaline surged, powering mind and body in a race to clarity. Fear twisted up his legs, into his gut, and along his spine — real fear, felt for the first time in a long time.

He'd known a schemer like the Broker would never pit equal strengths against each other and leave the result to fate.

He'd expected a thumb on the scale to guarantee a winner.

Had seen a third party sent into the fight as the Broker's most plausible strategy.

He'd planned on outcomes that favored either side but hadn't expected the Broker would send crazies — thrill seekers — to annihilate them all.

He caught his footing and slashed in the

direction Jill had gone, noisy and careless, throwing away caution and stealth to draw attention to himself. She'd put herself in a position of weakness, had trusted him to guard her back, and he'd just inadvertently given psychopathic bounty-hunting gunslingers a long head start on the one person he loved enough to protect with his life.

Chapter 32

Jill
Age: 26
Location: Spring, Texas
Passport Country: USA
Names: Jennifer White

She slunk between the trees, tracking movement and shadows and nature's whispers, winding her way toward the target in the same way she'd stalked prey during so many hunts of the past.

She'd taken the bait, she'd made the call.

She was full in now.

She crouched low, paused, and listened.

The shooter was out there, somewhere in the foggy quiet, Christopher, the man who'd taken Clare, who'd killed Ray, the man she'd been contracted to kill, out there watching for her and watching Robert as surely as she watched Robert and watched for him.

In her head, Clare said, *Yes, you found the*

trap. Yes, you avoided the trap. Congratulations, Julia. You're dead, anyway.

Robert turned onto the trail she'd told him to find and came into view, body stiff, expression grim, trying and failing to appear relaxed and normal.

Her conscience, what little conscience she had, twanged with guilt.

She'd been careful, had kept her separate lives separate, hadn't been the one to point killers and kidnappers to him, but it was still because of her life of lies that Rob was here, and she didn't want his blood on her hands.

He moved off the trail to a narrower path, each slow step placed carefully, as if he was afraid of falling. She slipped behind him, shielded by foliage, following the earth's natural bend. Clare's voice, sarcastic and strident, kept pace.

What were you thinking? You weren't thinking! The enemy gave you what you expected, and you were so busy avoiding the obvious, you were blind to the invisible.

Find the trap. Seed the trap.

No. No, no, no. Use the trap against your opponent.

Dead again, Julia.

Go. Do it over. Do it better.

Jill pushed the voice away and pushed

herself forward, following Robert from a distance, frustrated by the pace. They had a quarter mile to go, and at this rate, it'd be nightfall before they finished.

He rounded a bend, and she moved in closer.

Three feet away, so close she could nearly touch him, he froze.

She stopped, waited for him to turn, waited for him to search out whatever noise had startled him. He didn't, and neither did he start walking again. She was too close to call him. Too close to do anything other than prod him forward.

She said, "Oh, for fuck's sake, Rob. Walk."

His whole body turned, back ramrod straight, one awkward high step at a time, until he faced her. Sweat dripped from his hairline, and his knuckles were white from gripping the phone. His fear made her nervous in the same way successfully completing one of Clare's tests made her nervous, like she'd missed something critical and the blow was yet to come.

She took a cautious step forward.

He flinched, and she stopped.

He glanced down at his jacket.

She followed his gaze and reached for the zipper.

His head backed as far away from her as

his neck would allow.

She tugged the zipper down.

Thin red tubes surrounded his chest, taped together and wired from tip to tip to form a crude suicide vest, which, for a second, left her hovering in the space she imagined existed between hearing a land mine's click and obliteration.

She knelt. Her fingers followed the wires.

Last time she'd done this, she'd been the one strapped in, wired with just enough explosives to pop a hole in a canister of pepper spray, definitely enough incentive to make failure untenable. She'd paid attention and had failed, anyway, because, as Clare had pointed out while she lay gagging and weeping on the ground, the lesson had never been about disarming an explosive but about ensuring she knew how it felt to realize death was inevitable. She had that same realization now, in reverse.

Admiration rose, a perverse, guilt-inducing form of betrayal.

She wanted to meet the mind who'd assembled the contraption.

She looked Robert dead in his terrified eyes and said, "I can't disarm it."

His face went white, and it seemed for the briefest flash that he might pass out.

Whoever had built the thing had run

perfect psych ops on him, ensuring compliance, guaranteeing he'd look like a paranoid nutcase if anyone else got to him before she did. She stood and dusted off her hands. "There's nothing to disarm, Rob. It's just a prop. Take the fucking thing off and let's go."

Robert stood, mouth open, soundless, and didn't move.

Hands on his shoulders, she turned him around, released the Velcro beneath the jacket, unclipped the wires that served as over-the-shoulder straps, and let the vest drop. He eyed the assembly like it was a venomous snake he wasn't quite sure was dead. She stomped on the tubes for his benefit. Powder burst out.

She dipped her fingers into the white and held them up to her nose. "Flour," she said. And when he still didn't move, she took his hand and, finger by finger, loosened his death grip on the phone and flung the eight-hundred-dollar brick into the lake.

Mouth open, he turned toward the water in wordless protest.

She didn't have time to explain that the phone's microphone and camera had likely been activated remotely so that someone could listen in and watch, or to discuss the vulnerabilities of the SIM itself and the way the networks could be tapped to use the device as a homing beacon.

Hand on his arm, she nudged him forward. "I'll buy you a new one."

His focus traveled to his jacket. Sound gurgled from his throat, revealing the strain on vocal cords that had gone unused for too long. "Wait," he whispered. He tugged at the jacket, trying to get it off. "GPS," he said.

She held out her hand.

He tangled in the sleeves and finally broke loose.

She snagged it, and her fingers traced the seams and found the thumb-sized lump sewn in along the left side. She balled up the jacket and tossed it into the bushes.

He said, "There's another one somewhere in my jeans."

She held out her hand again.

He looked at her, glanced around, and shook his head.

"Jesus, Rob, it's not like you've got anything going on down there that I haven't seen before."

"I don't care. I'm not taking them off."

She knelt and ran her hands down his legs and found the bulge on the inseam, by the hem. "Need them off."

"I'm not walking out of here without

pants on."

She didn't have time to argue with him. She ripped a knife off her belt, flipped it open and, before he could react, jabbed the point inward.

He winced.

She said, "Don't move."

Two clean slices separated the chunk of fabric from the pants. She tossed the fragment after the jacket and folded the knife shut.

Robert took a cautious step backward.

He said, "This is where we part ways."

"Yeah?"

She stood slowly, the way she would have in the presence of a skittish animal, and slipped the knife back on the belt. She watched him, measured him.

She'd freed him from imagined death and freed him from surveillance, and had been so focused on keeping ahead of Christopher that she'd skipped right over the possibility Rob would turn into an ungrateful bitch and refuse to go along with the plan.

She said, "Where you gonna go?"

He checked over his shoulder and shuffled another six inches in retreat. "Don't know," he said. "Away. As far away as I can get from you and the two lunatics chasing you."

Two lunatics. That was a nice touch of intel.

She moved in closer.

He scooted backward, jumpy and primed for flight.

She said, "They're not going to be happy with you, not after you ignored their instructions. They're gonna come after you. You're safer with me."

"You?" He spit the word with spiteful sarcasm. "Is that some kind of sick secret-agent, spy, assassin humor?"

"Longer we stand here, the closer we get to dying."

"Oh. Dying. Let me tell you about dying. The police have a warrant out for my arrest for *your* murder. School administration is throwing around words like *liability, misconduct,* and *expulsion.* My parents are blowing up my phone, wondering why they can't reach me, my friends are starting to think I'm guilty for the same reason, and then two special ops guys kidnap me, tack explosives to my chest, and send me out as bait to pull you in." His tone tipped toward hateful. "Thanks for the offer, Agent Salt, but you've already ruined my life. I'd appreciate if you just got the hell right out of it now."

"I can fix all that," she said.

"I'd rather you didn't."

Tone soft, even gentle, she said, "Come on, Rob."

She reached for his arm. He batted her away.

"Stop that," he said. "Just quit, okay? I liked you, Jen, the person I thought you were, but that wasn't you. You've done nothing but lie since we first met, and if I never see you again, it'll be too soon."

The words stung a little, mostly because they were true, and she wasn't used to rejection, but he'd earned the right to say them. She said, "After tomorrow you never have to see me again, but right now you need to come with me."

He glanced over his shoulder again, searching for his escape. "No," he said. "No, I really don't. What I need is to get as far from you as possible before you wreck my life any more than you already have."

She watched him go for a step or three, torn between making the effort to charm her way back into his good graces or taking the easy road of force.

Unnatural noise in the near distance settled that for her.

She went after him, grabbed his shoulder, and gripped hard.

He recoiled, and she dug her nails in. "Don't fight," she said. "I'll knock your ass out and drag you with me if I have to."

"You hit first, I'll hit you right back."

She laughed. She couldn't help it. "You'd never have the chance."

He smiled, sarcastic, mocking, and she saw the party girl reflected in his eyes.

Didn't matter how much he'd learned or what he'd experienced in the past week. He'd never take her seriously or see her as a physical threat, and she couldn't blame him for that. She'd worked hard to perfect that persona, and she'd done a good job.

She said, "I gave you fair warning, but I'm not gonna do it a second time."

"Whatever." He started walking again. "I'm done being your pawn."

She quick stepped and blocked his way.

He moved to get around her.

She grabbed him. He shoved her.

She two-knuckle punched him in the throat.

He dropped to a knee, gagging and gasping, and when he could breathe again, he tipped his face toward her and said, "For God's sake, why can't you leave me alone?"

The words gurgled out in equal parts accusation and plaintive plea, and on some level, not wanting to see him hurt, she wished she could give him what he wanted right here, right now. She hooked an arm in his and helped him stand.

To her left — far, far left — the undergrowth shifted with a hint of blur.

She swore under her breath, spun him in the direction she needed him to go, and quick marched him forward, trusting Jack to guard their backs the way he'd promised because she had no choice.

She passed the trunk of a two-hundred-year-old oak and changed her mind. Trust was fine when the plan went right. Blind trust in the middle of change got a person killed, and something had changed.

She pushed Robert up behind the tree.

The noise was there again, wind through the leaves, moving stealthily in their direction, and this time Robert heard it, too. She covered his lower face with her hand and leaned up close beside his ear. "If you want to stay alive, don't move, don't say a word. Don't even breathe." He nodded.

She took her hand off his mouth, dropped her backpack to the ground, and dug for the handset and checked Jack's GPS position.

He was off route, had stopped moving, and was nowhere near close enough to get between her and whatever stalked her.

Clare was in her ear again.

The trap you can see isn't the one to fear.

This was the jungle forest. This was life with Clare.

She'd been here before a hundred times, and she could beat this. She reached for the semiautomatic, held a finger toward Robert, and shook her head.

Not a sound.

CHAPTER 33

Jack
Age: 26
Location: Spring, Texas
Passport Country: USA
Names: Jason Francis White

He charged toward the open trail, running for where the foliage was thinner and he could move faster, and ran parallel to the trail, weaving into camouflage and out again. A splash of color change within the green tripped him into a fast trajectory change and then plunged him to a stop. Dead ahead, branches whispered against nylon.

He crab crawled in the direction the color had been.

Blood in his ears played a bass-line beat to the soft patter of moisture falling from leaves, and the scent of loamy earth filled his nostrils, taking him back to nights he and Jill had spent crawling through the dark, facing off against a small army they couldn't hear or see.

The stakes had been lower then — pain, not death. Torture, not bullet holes — but for a twelve-year-old, they weighed about the same. And, in answer to every wound and bruise and broken bone, Clare had told them if they were lucky, they'd never have to thank her.

He'd lost many times over as she'd pushed them ever harder, but he'd never lost by making the same mistake twice.

Burn him as it might, he thanked her now.

He'd played this game before.

He slid forward, belly to the ground, head covered, fingers probing the earth, collecting stones and pebbles. He edged against a fallen log.

A twig snapped somewhere to the left.

He tossed a pebble against a tree trunk. Waited.

He pitched a second to its right.

An amateur would have fired at the noise and given away position, but even crazies weren't that stupid. No, just as he and Jill had originally planned to use Jill as a decoy to lure Christopher, he used himself now, drawing attention to himself like an idiot, providing the enemy a source to bead in on. This was what Clare had trained him for.

All those years of sneaking through forests and across rocky terrain, of running with Raymond through the Louisiana bayous, days and nights and weeks and years of life ruined and wasted for this — a variant of this — because she believed a day like this would come.

The fourth pebble brought him the movement he wanted.

The *hiss-pop* of suppressed fire followed.

A bullet hit the log to the right of his shoulder. He tracked the position in his head, rolled, and pulled the trigger. The rifle crack split the empty morning.

He ran the bolt, moved to his knees, and fired again — movement, motion, controlled repetition — unmistakable noise until he'd emptied the rifle's small magazine and the woodland sounds hung suspended between the church-bell gongs ringing inside his head.

His senses stretched, desperate for feedback.

He was vulnerable, was in the critical moment when perceived success could so easily reverse to deadly trap. He crawled forward again, past silence, past stillness, crawled right into a body shaking and drowning in its own blood.

The guy was early twenties, maybe six

feet, a smoker with skin that had seen sun and teeth that had seen meth. He wasn't Christopher and wasn't the face in the game camera picture, but it didn't take a genius to figure out which team he belonged to.

Jack smacked his weapon out of reach, grabbed hold of a foot, and dragged the guy backward to where trees and underbrush sheltered him from another distanced shot.

He searched legs and torso, tossed knife, handgun, and cuffs aside.

Precious seconds fled. Desperation rose. He straddled the guy, gripped his shoulders, and shook. "How many?" he said. "How many of you are there?"

The throat gurgled what sounded like "Fuck off."

An earpiece dangled from behind the guy's collar. Jack ripped it from the shirt, found the receiver, plugged the audio jack back in, and shoved the bud into place.

In his ear a male voice called for a check-in.

An older voice replied.

Semiautomatic fire chimed in from the near distance, three quick taps.

Jack paused. His head ticked up.

The first voice requested a response.

None arrived.

Monologue sputtered into swearing and

then went silent.

A wave of cold, clean relief breathed into him.

Whoever had been following Jill wasn't following anymore.

Jack rushed through pockets and moved to shoes. The bleeding body beneath his hands trembled harder.

A bullet to the head would have been the merciful thing. With Raymond dead, Clare kidnapped, he and Jill in the cross fire, and his body covered in dirt and running on exhaustion, he was two days and one position giveaway tapped out of mercy.

He gripped Ray's .308 and backed away.

A hint of shadowed movement sent another adrenaline spike coursing.

Jack dug into his pocket for ammunition and slowly, soundlessly, chambered a round. In his ear, the radio remained silent.

Leaves rustled to the right. A light breeze covered the movement.

He inched backward along the ground to where he'd left his kit, shifting, scanning, searching for whatever watched him now.

Ten yards out, a blur straightened and lengthened.

Low light distorted facial features, but even in the dim Jack knew him.

He glanced toward the X-Caliber, measuring distance, speed, seconds. By the time he grabbed the weapon, Christopher would be gone.

Jack rose, rifle stock to shoulder, and they stood, weapon against weapon, target against target, killer to killer.

Need and loss clashed in a fight over Raymond and Clare and Jill.

Voice raised for distance, Jack said, "I didn't kill your friend."

The shadow said, "Just as I didn't kill your mother."

The words sent strategy colliding against time.

Jack sighted on Christopher's thigh. Desperation tangled in probability and threatened to break through resolve. Inside his head, his own voice begged the man to move, to do anything that invited a kill shot.

He said, "Is my mother alive?"

"I hope so."

The syllables tripped over each other, bouncing around Jack's brain like words spoken from a marble-filled mouth.

"Where did you take her?"

Christopher lowered his weapon until his arms hung loosely at his sides. He said, "It's an ugly day to die. For us, there's tomorrow."

"Just tell me where you took her."

"Houston."

"Where in Houston?"

Christopher turned without answering.

Jack dove for the X-Caliber and swung back. Eye to the scope, he searched through empty space and pressed forward, chasing a phantom.

He stopped at the spot where the enemy had stood, and he turned.

Christopher had had a clear line of sight to him but hadn't taken the shot. Could have, but didn't. Jack continued the circle, searching through the fog and dim.

This hadn't been a handshake, or a truce, or even an enemy who'd killed an enemy becoming a temporary friend.

The quiet swallowed him. Urgency laughed at him.

He needed to move.

The firefight, brief as it was, had been loud. And the trees, thick as they were, wouldn't hide these secrets for long. Every clue, no matter how obscure, and the trail, no matter how well hidden, could eventually lead back to its source. He needed to clear out the nests and erase their presence before the greenbelt crawled with attention.

He returned to his kit, and his hands packed and strapped, while his mind structured and reorganized. "For us, there's tomorrow," Christopher had said.

The man would have to get in line.

The Broker wasn't finished. The crazies weren't gone yet.

And he, too smart for his own good, had given them a map right to him.

CHAPTER 34

Clare

Age: 54
Location: Somewhere on the Water
Passport Country: Paperless
Names: Unprintable

The squeak returned, demon in the darkness, claws to the brain, ripping her out of hard-earned sleep, flinging her with a thud back into cruel, silent stillness. Her eyelids opened. On the floor, face to the wall and away from the door, she panted against awareness. This new interruption had come too soon, too close on the heels of the last.

Shoulder aching, body hurting, she rolled to face the ceiling.

Sleep deprivation coaxed paranoia to life.

The urge to run rose from deep, deep down, gurgling and spewing the need to chase after answers, toxic with the fear of having already lost them, of having already lost everything for nothing. Panic taunted her from the darkened corners, laughing at her for misjudging so badly, promising the only way off the ship would be by her own doing, chanting in rhythm to the *squeak, squeak, squeak* of rubber dragged against concrete until it stopped right at her door.

She sat and, facing the thread of light, pinched hard on the web between thumb and forefinger, squeezing until fire filled her hand and seeped up her arm, squeezing until fear and anxiety fled in the face of pain.

Metal touched metal. The slot near the floor slid open.

She shielded her eyes against the light and watched, transfixed, as the pudgy hand stretched in and fingers searched for the tray she'd incrementally moved farther and farther from the door each time it arrived.

He grunted, and lowered double chin and soft neck and puffy eyes to the hole. He redirected his aim and reached in to his shoulder. The watch on his wrist glinted, just as it had each time the tray had entered, dancing in the light the way the walls danced inside her head.

He snagged the plastic and, muttering, dragged it out.

Voices followed, not hushed, merely muted by distance, and the key engaged, and the door swung open and she braced for a stabbing cold that never came.

Silhouettes of a fire hose and two bodies filled the doorway, both too thin to be the pudgy tray stealer. An unfamiliar voice, commanding and strongly accented, said, "Stay where you are, or the hose turns on."

Even in delirium, she understood this was new, understood they'd come for reasons other than to torment her for the sake of torment.

She lowered her arm and placed her shackled wrists in her lap.

Lights in the room powered on for the first time.

She winced against the pain they brought.

The tray stealer stepped inside, glanced at the shadows behind him and, with a shaking outstretched hand, continued toward her one sideways foot at a time, as if he expected she'd make a grab for him and devour his soul. She measured him, weight against height, fear against action, playing guessing games over what outside that door terrified him enough that he preferred cowering his way to her side.

He stopped three feet away and shoved papers in her direction.

She shifted toward him, legs straight, shackles tight, and made an exaggerated show of reaching for this thing he offered and being yanked short.

He took another step forward.

She toppled over, forcing him closer.

He lowered a knee and offered the papers toward hands pulled taut at her face.

Her fingers fumbled, trembling with cold.

He pushed the pages in farther.

She read his watch, both date and time.

Knowledge reconfigured inside her head.

The sensory input brought air to her lungs.

Two in the morning. She'd been in this hole nearly six full days. No matter who had put the hit out on her, they never would have intended to keep her suspended in time the way she'd been. There were other factors in play.

Pudgy hands shoved the pages into her own.

She glanced at them and, refusing to react, handed them back.

The fat hand yanked away and retreated, empty, and her gaze followed the pale, soft skin as it melted toward the door with ten times the speed it had entered. Metal slammed behind him, the lights powered down, and the room went blacker than the black it had previously been.

For the cameras, she tipped back over, head to the floor, and shut her eyes.

The pages, photos taken from the crosshairs, had been delivered without accusations or lies, without threats, and without commentary, because none were needed.

Boris had found what she'd fought for a quarter century to keep hidden.

Two pictures, two thousand unspoken words, making clear that as a special gift to her, he'd put a contract out on her children, ensuring that whether she lived or died, her legacy would be wiped from the earth.

The sleepless demons dancing in the dark had been right in their taunting.

Peace was an illusion. There'd be no answers, not now, not ever. The thing she'd feared had come to pass, and there was nothing left now but to face that fear.

Acceptance filled the spaces between her heart and lungs.

She had time, a small amount of time. If her children were already dead, she'd have been handed a different set of pictures. She shut her eyes against the dark.

Her stay here was over.

The data she'd collected, footsteps and shift changes, routines and engine-room noises, came together in a three-dimensional picture. From between her cheek and gums, she pulled the shard of hard plastic she'd worked off the food tray on her first night in. Hour after hour, she'd sat with that piece between her fingers, rubbing it against the floor, whittling it to size, small enough to fit the handcuff keyhole, rigid enough to maintain its shape.

She bit down on it now, bent the plastic at an angle, and lay with her face to the wall, hands shielded from the cameras, in the same sleeping position she'd taken time and again. She worked the piece into the pinhole lock methodically, patiently, twitching as she'd twitched against the shackles for six whole days.

Time rolled on into a sea of focused movement while her fingers, bent hard toward her wrists, failed and failed and returned to fail again. The pictures drove her, her children's faces through a scope, and the promise that had been made all those years ago.

You can't hide from me. You can't run.

No matter where you go, no matter how long it takes, I'll find you.

He'd kept that promise, had found her twice, and she'd suffered then far more than she suffered now, but she'd never allow him the same for her children.

This time, she'd find him, and she'd destroy him.

Somewhere within the sea of focus, the manufactured hook caught, and her left hand slid free. She worked the lock against her feet, hurried now because her functioning hand wouldn't be familiar to the cameras in the way her repetitive twitching movements had been. Feet free, her right hand came next, and when that was finished, she sat against the wall facing the door, staring into the sliver of light, hands and feet positioned just as they'd been for hours every day when the shackles had kept them there.

Food would come eventually, and feeding time meant freedom.

CHAPTER 35

Holden

Age: 32
Location: Humble, Texas
Passport Country: Paperless
Names: Nameless

He sat beside the bed in the quiet dark, slouched in the same position, on the same sofa chair, holding the same vigil he'd held since bringing Baxter in. Heavy curtains blocked most of the afternoon light, and the air conditioner's hum held the room in a cathedral stillness reverent with pain, remorse, and supplicant pleading.

If he'd had rosary beads, he would have used them.

Instead, he picked at his cuticles and studied Baxter's face, counting the time between each strained exhale to the endless slow-motion replay that relived every step, every bullet over and over, as if willpower alone could stop time and rewrite the morning.

He'd been forced to cut into Baxter on the forest floor.

Calling on emergency responders would have betrayed his friend's wishes in the worst possible way, and he hadn't been able to carry the sleeping giant out.

In the annals of battlefield dressing, his work wasn't the worst.

He'd watched men bleed to death. He'd watched men heal. He'd gotten his own hands bloody in making miracles out of shattered bodies in wars where there were no hospitals or licensed surgeons. He'd worked with far fewer supplies than what he'd been able to source from a drugstore and steal from an emergency care center.

A headlamp and a tarp doused in antimicrobial wash had become the operating table, and he'd dug for metal and irrigated wounds beneath the cries and calls of searchers hunting through the trees in response to the battery of weapons that had been fired.

The holes had bled little enough, were positioned high enough, to give him hope. He'd stitched them closed and waited for Baxter to wake. Getting out and into the car had been hell, getting to a room even worse, but now Baxter slept, floating on stolen opiates, which eased the pain, and hooked up to an IV for hydration and antibiotics.

There was nothing more he could do but watch and wait and pray infection didn't set in, and in that waiting, his thoughts turned dark and brooding.

From one blink to the next, things had deviated into shit.

Robert had performed exactly as expected, following Jen rather than drawing her to him. They'd let him run. So long as he stuck with her — and they were certain Jen would see that he did — they'd be able to track her. That was the beauty of playing against an opponent trained for the same job.

He and Baxter had backtracked along the path she'd taken, knowing that the brother, hunting them, expecting them to follow her, would run to them. They would have missed him if they hadn't known what they looked for.

Baxter found him first. That's where the plan went wrong.

The horror played out in Holden's head, beat against beat, to the second before Baxter fired.

The brother had shifted. The round went wide.

Hunted became the hunter.

The brother returned fire, fast enough, accurate enough that he would have killed Baxter if that's what he'd wanted, but he didn't.

Holden didn't realize it then, not at first.

Baxter's yell sent birds scattering, made suburban soccer moms out riding with their bubble-wrapped kids look around and search the sky, sent Holden crawling through the underbrush for a clean line of sight, prepared to kill and lose everything they'd gone to collect if it meant protecting what mattered more.

He was too late.

Baxter went down and never got up.

He sighted in on the brother's thigh, curved finger reaching for the kiss, and in one beat, one veritable blink, everything changed.

The brother's head ticked up and he scrambled backward, and impact thuds carried through the silence, pop after pop, and Baxter's body jerked, and a scream filled his own head.

Against experience, against knowledge, his body rushed him forward.

Through foliage, across daylight, he spotted the glint, and he knew, knew what the brother had seen. He reached Baxter and checked vitals. Relief and frustration and risk boiled into rage. He wanted to stay. For his brother, he *needed* to stay.

The mission compelled him forward.

Revenge compelled him forward.

The Broker had played him like a windup toy, offering the ghosts to misdirect his suspicions and sending a contract crew in to clean the whole thing up.

Whoever they were, they'd die.

He grabbed his gear and, in a silent race beneath the trees, tracked after the brother.

The cool, reverent present jerked Holden out of the wooded memories.

Car doors slammed. Voices rose.

He strode to the window and through parted curtains watched an older couple traipse toward the pool with three small children in tow. His heartbeat settled, and he returned to the bed, to Baxter's ashen face, to the closest thing he had to a brother, the only person besides Frank close enough to consider family.

They'd been fifteen when they met, he and Baxter. Back then he'd been a rangy, feral street kid fresh off the plane from Bogotá, and Baxter, an overweight couch potato and apartment-complex bully. Ego and posturing had pitched them into more than one fistfight.

Bruises and blood had forged a friendship that grew into brotherhood.

Holden ran his fingers through his hair.

He'd known pain, known suffering. He'd been hungry, abandoned, and cold. He'd lost men and lost family, and he'd felt none of that the way he felt this pending loss.

He hadn't seen the trap.

McFadden's children hadn't seen the trap.

The Broker would have come out the winner if not for the brother.

The brother.

The mental replay hitched there, always hitched there, with the brother on his knees on the woodland floor, hands searching Baxter's body. He'd used a CO_2 rifle.

The siblings, too, had come for reasons other than death.

They wanted him alive, just as he wanted them alive, all for the same woman.

He checked the IV running into Baxter's veins.

Plans for retaliation scorched through his own.

Violence, forced to simmer under the pressure of saving life, bubbled over with the need to take it. He'd been thirteen, an orphan and chained monkey, when he plunged a blade deep into the man who'd fed, clothed, and housed him, and for twenty long minutes he had watched as the life he hated most pooled and congealed on the tile floor. He'd since watered the earth with the blood of forty-one men, but only with that first had he derived pleasure from death.

Hell-bound soul that he was, he'd know that satisfaction again.

But for that, he'd have to leave Baxter.

The window of opportunity was fast closing.

In this gladiator arena where winner took all, staying meant losing everything for nothing. He'd get the siblings, he'd get paid, and they'd lead him to the Broker.

CHAPTER 36

Clare
Age: 54
Location: Somewhere on the Water
Passport Country: Paperless
Names: Unprintable

Darkness embraced her, darkness, her friend. Comfort to the comfortless and sight to the blind, darkness translating sound and vibration into mental images. She saw him coming, coming with food, coming for freedom.

She drifted, weightless and formless, waiting in primordial calm.

Metal jangled. The lock engaged.

Some patterns couldn't be helped.

She stood, hands and feet positioned as they'd been when shackled, and she shuffled forward as she'd done and done and done.

The slot opened.

She broke the pattern and kept going, blissful and euphoric in movement.

Someone would notice and would come to stop her, or wouldn't. Either way.

The tray slid in.

She grabbed the hand.

Grappling hooks to skin, she dug a week's worth of nail growth into flesh and swung fast, rotating her body around, flinging the free end of the leg shackles around the wrist, wrapping the chain tail up her forearm. Bare feet against the door, she straightened her legs and dragged the arm inward until the shoulder stuck.

He fought, and the harder he fought, the tighter the chain cinched. Screams filled her ears the way stench filled her lungs.

"I'll tear your arm off," she yelled. "Open the door."

He couldn't, she knew that. He didn't have the key, and even if he had, there wasn't any way to reach the lock while pinned to the floor as he was. But he believed her — that's what mattered — and he screamed louder, begging and pleading, raising an ungodly commotion.

Doors slammed, a tumult of voices arose, and the tug against the chain grew heavier, as if men had laid hold of body and legs to pull him free.

She worked her fingers around his wrist, loosened the watch clasp, then let go of the chain, and one heartbeat to the next, the watch was in her hands and the arm was gone.

She slipped the band over her ankle and secured it.

The food slot slammed closed.

She swung the shackle chain up into the nearest corner, snagged the camera, and yanked it out of position. She turned, flung for the second and missed, costing her precious seconds. She tried again, connected, and pulled.

Fatigue consumed her. Lack of sleep and lack of food turned arms to weights, depleting conserved energy faster than she'd anticipated.

She'd survived worse for longer, but she'd been younger then.

Noise shifted outside the door, and within that shift came the squeak, the beautiful squeak, with its wonderful promise of freedom, the reward for accurately predicting a move they shouldn't have made but did. A voice bellowed from beyond the door, commanding her to get back against the wall.

Smarter, better would have been to deprive her of food and water until she was dehydrated to the point of incapacitation and then drag her ass back into chains, but they couldn't. They couldn't take that risk any more than they could risk controlling her with firearms, and so they'd come with the fire hose, their only weapon, a weapon they sorely overestimated. She'd seen to that.

She spun the chain, let it loose, and snagged the third camera.

The key worked into the lock. The lock tumbler rolled.

Time spliced into micro-slivers and disassociated presence.

Senses on overdrive, adrenaline feeding her blood, she watched the chain snake upward. Light from the opening door fractured shadows with dizzying color.

The chain rode high. She yanked it back, got close enough to knock the fourth camera off position. The water came. She dropped down and slid for the door, slid beneath the force that powered into the room, slid feet first, invisible to the electronic eyes and hidden by the spray.

Momentum, lubricated momentum, took her hard into the hose-holder's legs.

She knocked him off balance. He lost control of the jet.

Water whipped from side to side, a wild cobra escaped from the flute master's basket. Legs around his torso, hands to the sides of his head, she gripped and flung herself left, taking his neck with her. She let go before he dropped, and she rolled to her feet.

A baton crashed down into the space she left behind.

Chain in both hands, she swung prisoner's nunchakus, lashing right and left, clearing a path around machines in a room that had become crowded with too many bodies.

Metal snaked around a neck in a strangling coil.

She yanked and pulled him into her, relieved him of wallet and keys, slammed his head into the wall, shoved him aside. She grabbed the items, shoved them down her shirt. Momentum, dry momentum, took her into another bowling pin. Elbow to nose. Cartilage crunched. Blood kissed her face.

Hands across his chest and into his pockets, she found a phone, grabbed it, stashed it. Lighting shifted. Shadows changed shape.

She rolled away from a crowbar.

Two more men stood in the doorway, batons and Tasers in hand.

She scrambled up, vaulting foot to tool chest to machine to wall, over their heads, chain between her hands in a dragnet. She snagged a chin, and gravity took the head backward with her. He hit the floor hard, went out cold. Foot to his chest, she propelled into his partner, grabbed a wrench off the tool chest and, with every last ounce of energy, beat him until his body went limp.

Time unspooled, film spilling from a cartridge run amok.

Water sprayed wildly and furiously around the machine room. She squatted beside the nearest body, stripped the jacket off, and was up and moving down the passageway before her arms found their way into the sleeves.

A ladder welcomed from ahead. Pounding boots echoed from behind.

She ran, and hand over fist, she climbed up through a hatch and onto a catwalk that circled one of the ship's holds. She sealed the hatch behind her, crouched on the walk, and pulled the items from her shirt.

The wallet held eighty-three dollars, a start.

She dropped it, checked the phone.

Smartphone. Password protected. Worthless. She dropped that, too.

She examined the key ring.

No ignition key, no easy way out, but the other keys might be useful in getting through padlocks and secured hatches in her run off the ship.

She glanced at the stolen watch.

Two minutes since freedom, a hundred to go.

The wall vibrated behind her.

She worked the shackle chain off her waist, mind conjuring sounds and movement that may not have existed, body begging to stay and rest. A wisp of fresh air stirred across her face, and she pushed on, following the catwalk through a stale, dank, dark bitter with salt and rust toward its source. Another ladder led up.

Shouts filled the cavern below. Air horns promised a ship roused to life.

She forced weary legs to climb up through one hatch, around, and then up through another — one level, two, maybe three — while justice and revenge and love and hate and past and future drove her closer to the sky.

She reached the end, cranked the hatch open, and slithered onto the main deck.

Halogen lights atop the ship's tower stole dark from the night, and spent diesel and fetid water hit her nostrils with each burning breath. She lay seven yards off the rails, panting, dizzy, facing a thousand feet of murky black between her and the ships and industry lighting on the channel's other side.

Twenty years ago, she'd have braved the

danger of crossing a shipping lane at night — might have even now if she'd been fed and rested — but she was lucid enough to realize that in her current state she'd drown. She belly crawled around the coaming, timing the boots and shouts and searching.

The docks stretched on in an endless expanse where ships larger and smaller, fore and aft, were loaded and unloaded in a port that never slept.

She scanned for a way off, a way down.

She had a minute, maybe less, before they found her, and when they did, they'd use more than water. Escape had a way of scratching a bounty out of the asset column and turning it into a liability easiest to write off with death.

She turned back the way she'd come and bolted for the rails.

Shouts followed after her, and with the shouts came the *clap-pop* of live fire from a suppressed weapon. Elbows in tight, hand over her mouth and nose, other hand bracing that wrist, she plunged fifty stories down.

The water hit with bone-jarring power.

She sank and kicked and broke the surface fifteen feet out from the ship's hull.

The whine of bullets punctured the water.

She dove and swam, fought waves and

wake that would slam her into sharp rusted metal, and crawled for the bow, around the bow.

The dock rose six feet above the waterline.

Waves that had rocked the ship washed her toward the concrete.

Exhaustion consumed her. Hypothermia danced around the edges of borderline temperatures, and the channel threatened to take her where the Broker's men had failed.

She swam for the next ship's stern.

Salvation arrived by way of a line tied to a bollard and left dragging in the water. She grabbed the nylon and held on to catch her breath, then wrapped the line around her waist and arms, placed weary feet against barnacle-crusted concrete, and climbed from water to dock. She slumped sideways over the metal containment rail and lay gasping, staring up at the hulking bulk of the ship beside her.

Inertia set in. Her eyes closed against her will.

She wanted sleep, wanted to sleep for a year.

Men running down the gangway kept her moving.

She rolled onto her stomach and into a crouch, waited for an opening between crane and shipping container, and limped on cut and bleeding feet for the cover of the nearest building.

CHAPTER 37

Jack

Age: 26
Location: Houston, Texas
Passport Country: USA
Names: Jason Francis White

He drove the night, prowling the streets, tiger on the hunt, coiled energy and the vicious need to pounce pushing him toward an apartment complex that would bookend the day between battles. He was late, far later than he had any right to be, still covered in dirt and sweat, burning into midnight because staying off grid while disposing of and hiding evidence had chewed up minutes and spit them out as hours.

Urgency propelled him.

Urgency and unknowns, guilt, and the escalating need to scrub his conscience clean. Clare was still a blank space in the fog. He hadn't seen or spoken to Jill since she'd swung out of her nest to take Christopher's bait. Reports executed with her trademark timing and the subsequent radio silence would have been enough to reassure him that she was alive if they'd come yesterday. But today wasn't yesterday. Today was certainty transformed to second-guessing, and instinct turned to self-doubt.

He'd been outwitted and outplayed.

He was an eight-year-old kid up against Clare again.

Too smart for his own good, blind to the blind spots, he'd kept the burner phones moving to buy distraction, had planned for reversal, for hostages, for a third party, and for intervention that favored either side, but he hadn't planned on leveling up past "Clare crazy" to a psycho insanity that would burn the world down to win, even if winning meant dying in the self-inflicted flames. And, in that lapse, he'd turned an innocent bystander into human collateral on a debt that could only be paid by blood.

Failure made him angry, and anger pushed him hard.

The only strategy against madness was greater madness.

He pulled into the alley beside the complex and stopped where aging trees shaded aging asphalt from light pollution, holstered a knife, shoved a handgun into the small of his back, swiped a packet of ninja rocks from the tool bag, and left everything else behind. He'd come for the burners. He'd retrieve them one way or the other.

He'd followed their movement until they stopped in early afternoon and powered off. Luck would say he'd mistimed battery life, but even his eight-year-old self knew that hoping on luck was for dead men and losers.

He needed the phones as a lifeline for Jill, for Clare.

More than that, he needed them as a lifeline for his own conscience.

The Broker wanted blood.

The crazies wanted blood.

So be it. He was coming for blood.

There'd been at least one shooter in his ear at the preserve. The question now wasn't if crazy had chased this lead. It was: How many of them had come along for the ride? They'd have shown the Uber driver his picture. They'd have learned he'd gotten the guy's number. They'd have turned the burners off to maintain the upper hand and force him to make that call. This was assassin's hide-and-seek.

Jaw clenched, gut clenched, he scaled the wall between alley and complex, dropped to the other side, and moved through shadows, scanning balconies and well-lit stairwells, inhaling the smoldering remains of grill fires and catching the straggling wisps of beer-fueled conversation, hunting for familiar vehicle plates.

Clare's voice cycled through his brain, warning him off.

Threat is easy to find and elude in the quiet, but it hides without worry in windows and on rooftops, along busy streets.

She'd dragged them through forests and across savannas, left them in the care of others all in the name of training. She'd taught them how to handle multiple weapons, how to fly, how to sail, how to dive, and how to survive the elements, but the worst of her efforts had put them in urban settings where she'd forced them to slip from one disguise to another while on the move, and that hadn't stopped until they were able to outwit her.

He'd been five the first time, on Zeil, Frankfurt's downtown shopping street. Clare had knelt beside him, handed him a slip of paper with a number on it, and told him he had to convince someone — anyone — to give him money for a phone call.

Without that, she'd said, he'd be lost forever.

She'd pushed him into the crowd.

His baby-fat fingers had grabbed for her, he'd been swallowed by a whirlwind of legs and color, and then it was him, just him, alone on the cobblestones, surrounded by strangers hurrying by. He'd fought the tears and failed.

That had been the first formal lesson in learning to rely on body language, facial expressions, and the outward signs of socio-economic status to size up a potential mark to get what he wanted. Those same lessons were with him now as he hugged the shadows, listening to the accents in late-night voices, feeling laughter's rhythm in the outdoor movement, smelling a melting pot of foreign culture, all of which spoke to neighbors who knew their fellow citizens, of socializing done as much in person as online, of residents who stayed aware to protect each other against the law and crime alike.

This was everything he'd been taught to avoid.

The apartments, small and tight, would turn any fight deadly fast.

Attention would come quickly. Invisibility would be difficult to maintain.

Training insisted he cut his losses and abandon the phones, told him that closing ranks, staying invisible, and protecting his family were higher priorities than returning to save a man he'd met once from the backseat of a car.

He shoved training aside and continued out into the open, chasing color and shape beneath covered parking, searching for the familiar Corolla. He found the car, door and windows locked, near the end of a forty-foot line of covered spaces that abutted a grassy incline toward a pair of three-story buildings.

Dirt-crusted streetlamps mounted end-middle-end cast enough light to provide tenants the illusion of safety and to keep him out of the shadows. He slipped between vehicles, alerted to potential witnesses by the hint of weed drifting down from a quiet group on lawn chairs two stories up and over, and to potential interruption by nearby laughter and louder music.

He fished the packet of ninja rocks from his pocket — aluminum oxide infused ceramic that had been chipped off spark plugs — lightweight, easy to carry, illegal in some states, and capable of shattering glass far faster and quieter than a crowbar or hammer.

He leaned back for leverage and flung a piece hard at the driver's window.

Tempered glass split into a thousand pieces.

The clock inside his head began counting.

Gloved hand through the empty frame, he unlocked the door.

One second.

He released the trunk. Opened the back door. Searched beneath the backseat. He touched plastic, snagged plastic, retrieved and stashed the Blackphone and personal phones.

Nine seconds.

Movement passed through shadow up beside the far breezeway, and shadow turned to form, and form slipped from breezeway onto the grass, moving fast in his direction. He swung around for the trunk, searched beneath the floorboard, around the spare tire, around the emergency tools, and in the crevices on the chance road wear and motion had knocked the burners deeper down. They were missing. He knew they would be but had needed confirmation before killing.

He dropped the lid with a near silent click and ducked around a Jeep Cherokee parked to the left.

Seventeen.

Shoes and legs hurried between wheel wells and paused beside the driver's door. Realization turned to muttering, and muttering turned to swears. A cell phone screen lit up, casting a Gorilla Glass glow on windows and asphalt.

Jack slipped out of hiding, knife in hand, blade obscured behind his forearm. The guy glanced up, made eye contact. Jack knew the hair, the eyes, the face, had seen the same angled cheekbones in the picture taken by the camera at the preserve. Recognition coursed in kind, tightening posture, sending a hand reaching for its weapon.

Blade low, Jack rushed him, stabbed his leg, slashed up, and pulled him tight into a choke hold with the speed he'd have needed to take down his sister.

Knife tip to neck, mouth to ear, he whispered, "Up we go."

The man struggled. Jack held tight.

Hands reached for Jack's arm, dug into his jacket, slipped, and swung back, punching and clawing for his face. Jack pressed the blade deeper in warning. Flailing hands gave up on his face and sought control of the knife. Jack squeezed harder, squeezed while his opponent punched and yelled through a jaw forced shut, squeezed until blood flow failed and the guy choked out.

One minute, twenty.

Jack opened the driver's door and shoved the slack body in, head over the center console, hips onto the seat. Knife tip to his opponent's fingernails, he scraped against the chance a random scratch had carried off a piece of him, then put blade to neck and jabbed for the carotid.

The guy would bleed out before he woke: one less killer, one reason fewer to run. Clare would have been proud.

He retrieved the ceramic shard and shut the door.

One minute, fifty.

He strode up the grass and into the breezeway, up the stairs two at a time to the third-floor landing. They never should have holed up here. He had the driver's name, had his plates, had his number. Any idiot with an Internet connection could have found the address, but burn-down-the-world thinking made for happy triggers and sloppy long-term strategy.

He slid over the guardrail, leapt from third-story ledge to adjacent deck, dropped to the balcony rail beneath and, balanced there, waited with his back to the wall while voices from the inside carried out too softly to place, but loud enough to separate and count. He booted up an unused burner.

Two minutes, forty.

They wanted him to call. He'd give them what they wanted.

381

He dialed the driver's number.

A ringtone sang beyond the blinds.

Shadows danced against the light. Voices rose in excitement.

A familiar accent choke-whispered a cautious hello into his ear.

Jack turned his face away so his voice wouldn't carry and lilted into the slur of good times and drink. "Hey, man. Sorry to call so late. I was one of your rides today. Got your number in case I needed pickup tonight. You available?"

Muffled talking filled the other end of the line. The driver's voice shook, and his words arrived slowly. "I am not free," he said. "But maybe you left some things in my car?"

"Things?" Jack smiled like a drunken fool, because smiles carried over the phone. "Nah, dude, I've got all my stuff. Must belong to someone else."

"You don't lose some phones?"

"Got everything with me, man. Appreciate it, though."

"Wait please," the driver said.

Another pause. More muffled speech. Another strained sentence.

"Yes, I can do pickup. Where you?"

"Don't sweat it, man. I'm good."

In his ear, hesitancy turned to desperation. "I come get you."

Jack hit MUTE and flung a ninja rock into the balcony glass. The door shattered. Yelling rose over the clash. Suppressed reports hissed out from the room, spitting and popping with the craze of a tweaker's panic. He ended the call, pulled the handgun from the small of his back, waited until the shooter's magazine emptied and rattled bickering filtered through the pane, then gripped the eaves and swung through the vertical blinds.

Seconds slivered into silence and served up rapid-fire knowledge.

Living room. Furniture. Door.

Two threats. One hostage.

The world crawled to a standstill, and he moved in half time, stepping forward with each trigger pull. Bullet to the chest of the man facing glass and swapping out magazines. Bullet to his head. Shift. Bullet to the hostage's thigh.

The driver yelped and slumped, redistributing weight, adding confusion.

Bullet to the head of the hostage taker.

Silence.

Three minutes, fifty-five.

He two-fisted the weapon toward the kitchen, the hallway, got no movement. He knelt, and felt sideways for a pulse on the man who'd held the hostage. He glanced at the driver, who sat beside the body, jaw clenched, hands gripping his thigh, which was bleeding onto the carpet.

"Are there more?" Jack whispered. "Any more of them here?"

"One outside."

"Roommates? Where are your roommates?"

The driver looked back toward the hallway.

Jack didn't need the words. Didn't want to know, didn't want to see. He leaned in toward the driver's leg, nudged the loose pants aside, and traced the bullet trajectory.

He'd gotten lucky, hadn't hit an artery and had missed bone.

The driver winced, and his eyes, full of questions, accusation, and pain, traveled up to settle on Jack's face.

Self-scorn heaped upon guilt. Jack let the material drop. "I'm sorry," he said. "It was the only way to keep them from killing you."

The driver, breathing through clenched teeth, nodded.

Jack said, "Where are the phones? The ones they found?"

The driver scooted sideways to lean into the wall and motioned toward a backpack slouched against the aging sofa. Jack reached for the bag, unzipped, and searched through crap he didn't recognize to get to what he did.

Four minutes, twenty.

He stuffed the handgun in with the rest of the stuff, shouldered the strap, retrieved a printout from the Broker's bounty packet, and held it open so the driver could see it. "Call nine-one-one. Tell them there's been a shooting. Tell them you're hurt. Eventually, there'll be questions. The police will want to know who came through that window." He moved the image of Christopher's face, shielded by hat and glasses, closer. "This guy did. You understand?"

The driver nodded again.

Four minutes, forty.

Footsteps pounded in the breezeway.

Shouts rang out from near the front.

Jack refolded the picture, stuffed it into the hostage taker's sock, and collected phones from pockets and hands. He said, "Which one of these is yours?"

The driver reached for the smartphone. Jack took it and tossed him one of several disposable plastic flip models. "The guy in the picture has yours," he said. "You took this one from that dead guy after he left."

Another nod.

Jack dumped the rest of the phones into the pack, left the weapons where they lay, and let himself out the way he'd come.

Five minutes, fifteen.

He slipped over the rail and swung down to the patio beneath the balcony.

Disgust gurgled in his gut.

He'd despised Clare, always had, for the way she'd used others to reach her end goals. Hypocrite of hypocrites, he'd been no different when pushed.

The wording of Jill's accusation poked holes in his worldview.

Don't confuse self-righteousness with love.

She'd been talking about his attitude toward her, not Clare, but the fundamentals were the same. He understood now, for the first time, understood Clare's dilemma, understood that she had cared about collateral damage, and just like him, she'd cared about protecting her family more.

Voices rose behind him, around him, sounds of threat that carried to him on the wind.

His feet hit the ground.

Approaching sirens screamed out far in the distance.

He skirted around brick and over concrete, moving just slowly enough to avoid drawing attention, reached the wall, went over the wall, and speed walked to the car.

He tossed the backpack into the passenger seat, plugged key into ignition and, lights off, moved down the alley. He made a slow turn out onto near empty streets, drove, and kept driving to put distance between himself and the crime scene.

Time dragged long, painful nails down his diaphragm, and he counted the miles as he moved away from Jill, driving in the opposite direction in which he wanted to go, because from a distance was the only way he could safely turn the burners back on — *safely* in terms of the Broker, *safely* in terms of law enforcement, who, if they did their job properly, would search for any digital trail to follow out of that complex.

Minutes bled the clock dry. An hour allowed him to pull off the road.

He closed his eyes against the wait while the phones booted up.

The tone of missed calls sent his pulse racing.

He scrolled through the numbers.

He didn't recognize any of them, but he recognized the timing gaps between Clare and Clare and Clare and more Clare.

Failure mounted into frustration and fury.

He had another round of time-devouring evidence to destroy, urgently needed to find a way to make and maintain contact, and this phone, and every other he carried, was exposure, handcuffs, and an ambush waiting to happen.

CHAPTER 38

Clare

Age: 54
Location: Galena Park, Texas
Passport Country: Paperless
Names: Nameless

Head down, hands in her pockets, cracked concrete at her feet, she shuffled past payday lender, furniture rental, and repair store, past security bars and sleeping storefronts, into the light of a doughnut shop already alive at four in the morning and under the blinking neon signs of an empty gas station.

Car tires turned into the lot behind her.

She fought the paranoid urge to turn and look.

She'd reached delirium hours ago, maybe days, and was running on fumes in a body exhausted by adrenaline surge and dump and surge, stopgap fueled by vending machines and two hours of rest pulled from a

twenty-four-hour Laundromat, which had
been interrupted by knife-wielding hood-
lums who'd tried to relieve her of the little
money she carried. She'd relieved them of
phones instead and had come to within a
hopped-up junkie's inch of breaking an arm
to relieve the smallest of his shoes.

She needed protein, needed sleep, but
couldn't stop, because once inertia set in,
she'd be done. One foot after the next, she
trudged on in Nike Airs that were as much
a relief to raw and tender feet as the phones
were a relief from drawing attention while
making calls. She checked the time and
resisted the urge to dial again.

She'd called Jill twice, tried Jack three
times.

The numbers were active, but the calls
had gone directly to automated voice mail.

Calls to Raymond, too, had rung on, unanswered.

Dread, thick with desperation, set in
behind paranoia.

She'd been wrong, wrong, and couldn't
understand. If the kids had been dead, the
pictures would have shown as much, but
they hadn't been. They'd been alive, alive in
the crosshairs, alive with a promise that
hadn't yet been fulfilled.

Heel to toe, she walked an unending,

exhausting line to nowhere. Daylight would come soon. She'd have to find a way off the streets.

Repetitively, reflexively, she checked the time again and chased back the anxiety. She had two hours, three at the most, before these phones became a liability and she'd be forced to abandon them and find others. Images and thoughts and fear bounced wild and uncontrollable within a mind fighting to maintain a grasp on reality.

Another ten minutes and she could call again.

CHAPTER 39

Holden
Age: 32
Location: La Porte, Texas
Passport Country: Paperless
Names: Nameless

The beacon led out of Humble and into Houston, led in long, jagged cuts through the city, then southeast toward the coast, where it blinked off for good. Holden followed, heading toward war, everything he'd need carried with him in a twelve-year-old Kia bought off a guy for quick cash.

He had parceled out forty-eight hours' worth of hydration and medication, had left a preset timer and instructions clear enough that even a patient in the throes of dementia would understand them, yet the burden of leaving weighed heavy on his soul.

If he didn't return, odds favored that Baxter would die.

He kept off the highways to avoid data-

sucking, driver-tracking license-plate scanners, opting for the lesser evil of missing
front plates and city traffic cameras. Vehicle
registration still pointed to the guy who'd
sold him the car, but fifty moves ahead and
looking back, the plate scanners had the
potential to trace his movements after the
fact, and he didn't need that headache.
Avenues and side streets declined steadily
into depressed neighborhoods so culturally
opposite the clipped, manicured northern
suburbs that the two might as well have
been in different countries.

The sights and smells soothed him. His
shoulders relaxed.

He'd fit into whatever social stratum the
job called for, but returning to the misfits
and the downtrodden was like wearing a
comfortable jacket or unwinding in a favorite chair, and that was the last thing he'd
have imagined in that dirt alley in the hills
of Ciudad Bolívar when Frank had stood in
front of him and offered him a fairy tale.

Not that this, here, was poverty, exactly.

Paved streets and a functioning civic
foundation, cell phones, running water,
streetlights, cheap food, and secondhand
shoes all touted the promise of the American
Dream. In that slum of slums at Bogotá's
southeastern edge, homes patched together

from plywood and cinder block and scraps of tin made the houses he passed now seem like proper mansions. He'd laughed when Frank had presented an orphan's daydream, grown aggressive when Frank persisted, and stopped cold when Frank called him by a nickname dredged out of buried memories. He'd listened to a tale of an American father who'd spent years after his lover's death searching for a son, until he'd met the same fate.

Frank had offered him the chance of life as an American citizen, and Holden had grabbed hold of the dream, but he'd known even then that there were no fairy tales, only lies wrapped in good feelings, and that happy endings weren't even endings, merely where the stories were cut and the reader moved on.

Years of using wits and hands to stay ahead of powerful people whose sadistic hatred of him deepened with each inch he grew had hardened him effectively enough that he'd done well for himself as a fourteen-year-old in neighborhoods where the violence rivaled that of the worst urban ganglands.

Taking Frank's offer had been his version of moving on.

He'd known the promise of a better life

couldn't change watching his mother die, couldn't change being hauled out of her home in Cartagena and across the country to a fortress in the hills outside Calamar where he'd been left to fend for himself like a stray dog, wearing rags, stealing food, and had been a spoil of war brought out as entertainment for guests and enemies alike, but it had turned the page.

He couldn't remember the first months, the ones in which he'd wandered the tiled halls and covered porticos, soiled and hungry and crying for his mother, the ones in which he would have starved to death if not for the kindness of maids who snuck him food from the plates they served, the ones in which he would have died from infection if not for those who had the least to give who bathed and clothed him from what they could spare from their own homes. He couldn't remember but wished he could. Wished he could hold on to the worst of the pain.

Unable to have the memories, he'd grabbed hold of hate.

Frank had tried to temper his rage with explanations, had told him his father had been a part of a joint task force, a Hail Mary operation that had targeted a kingpin's youngest mistress in a reach for insight into where the international links in drugs and politics were the weakest. As if somehow a noble beginning could make sinners whole.

There was no forgiveness when want, dangerous want, drove the liaison far past the operation's finish line. They'd gone careening over the cliff of danger. One three-year-old son later, his mom was dead, and he was a captive trophy. Another two years after that, his dad had met the same fate: two casualty blips on the relentless drug-war radar.

His parents had made their choices in spite of the risk.

What was unforgivable was that they'd brought a child into that nightmare.

Frank had never spoken of them again.

Life was better that way.

Holden pulled to the curb across the street at the edge of a mildew-stained, roach-infested motel — the type of place where occupants saw nothing and proprietors saw even less, the type of location he'd have gone to disappear, which said as much about Jen and her brother as it did about him.

This was where the tracker had led. This was where he'd find them.

Robert had been the first diversion to get him here.

Jen would never have come out into the open — not even for a hostage boyfriend — but the hostage boyfriend had shifted the power dynamics, and by forcing the kid to carry the phone, he'd provided the illusion of lesser evils, which had saved him from a protracted hunt.

GPS trackers sewn into pants and jacket had been the second diversion.

The ones in Robert's soles had been the third.

Shoes were critical when on the run, would be the last to go. They'd been backups to the backups, in case Robert fled and he was forced to hunt him down, and they'd also buy him time if Jen made it out before he was ready. And, if Jen found them, they'd be the distraction to keep her from seeing that what he'd really wanted all along was her number.

But that was before the shooting had started, before Baxter had flirted with death, before well-laid plans had flipped upside down. He'd never intended the trackers to stay live through surgery on the tarp beneath the trees, or into the hours of bedside vigil, but they had, and he'd monitored them, brooding in the dark as they'd moved across the city, until they blinked off for good and he knew he was out of time. Protocol vulnerabilities had let him turn Jen's phone into a beacon whenever the device was on — which it wasn't, not right now — but it had been, and would be again, and these quick intervals continued to point right here to this motel. Holden scanned the parking lot and studied the room doors.

Jen knew he had this number, knew there was a chance he'd come looking, could have used the calls to draw him in the way he had her, could have, but the timing between signals had gotten shorter, and those brief active bursts, communicating like Morse code in the dark, had more in common with stealth than snare.

If he'd read them right, she was waiting on a call, trying to make a connection, and was growing desperate. There was only one person she'd be in a panic to reach.

Which meant her brother wasn't with her.

He pondered the implications and weighed them against options.

She'd be guarded, trigger happy, and dangerous.

He'd needed a team of six to take the mother alive, and that was only because, for whatever reason, the mother had allowed it. That wouldn't happen here, not even if Jen was alone, not even if she had Robert to slow her down, not even if he had five men.

This was invader against defender, and she matched him on skills and outclassed him on weapons. He didn't need to see her inventory to know that.

He traveled light, always had, preferring strategy over brute force, and invisibility over shock and awe, nothing like the laughable assassins of Hollywood who transported fully assembled firearms by air — packed in carry-on luggage, no less, as if X-rays and security checks in a terrorist-watching world didn't exist — into countries where being caught with one was an instant invitation to years behind concrete walls. In comparison, the three pieces he carried now felt like wanton excess: a handgun for short range, a high-precision rifle for distance, and a high-velocity semiautomatic for spray and pray.

They were unregistered, all of them, ghost guns built out of parts purchased at shows or bought online, with receivers — the only part of a firearm treated by federal law as a weapon — milled by his own two hands. They had no serial numbers, no registration, no background checks to provide his biometric data a permanent home on lookout lists that didn't officially exist, and their ballistics were guaranteed to never link to a crime he hadn't committed. Ghost guns were legal in a way stolen weapons, filed serial numbers, and black-market purchases could never be, because US law didn't require licensing to build a weapon for personal use, and that was all this was. He watched the motel as minutes turned into quarter hours, balancing professional patience against strategy against sand in the hourglass bleeding out of Baxter's life.

A bullet into a door — hopefully, the right door — would create action and movement, and through movement he'd know if Robert was present, and if Jen was with him, or if the calls that had led him here were merely enticement and a time-sucking distraction. He slipped the hard case from the back, stepped into the cooling night, and followed the cracked sidewalk toward a chain-link fence.

Fence led to opening, opening to empty lot, empty lot to dumpsters, and dumpsters to a flat industrial rooftop. He assembled the rifle in a reverent ritual, metal to metal, fully conscious of every contact, present for every twist in prebattle meditation, and sighted in on a door bottom, high enough to cause a reaction, low enough to avoid killing anyone in the room.

Headlights interrupted the timing.

A vehicle rounded the motel corner, and

he paused to allow potential witnesses and casualties to move on.

The car stopped three spaces over from where he'd intended to put the round.

A young man and a middle-aged woman stepped out.

Dim, moth-attracting light illuminated their profiles, and his brain jolted with recognition, his mouth went dry, and his scattered thoughts wove between each other in a twisted race to put meaning into order.

CHAPTER 40

Jill
Age: 26
Location: La Porte, Texas
Passport Country: USA
Names: Jennifer White

The television scene changed, casting a kaleidoscope of soundless color over otherwise darkened walls and dilapidated furniture. She rocked on her heels, ignoring the urge to check the clock, ignoring Robert splayed out on the bed, and biting back envy over his blessed oblivion in sleep. She counted a slow thirty, crossed the room again, stood behind the door, turned, and waited.

Robert's eyes blinked open and met hers.

He dragged a pillow over his head and rolled his back to her, which was just as well. It kept her from wanting to smother him.

They'd cleaned up, she and he. They'd

visited a police station and fixed his immediate problems and retreated to this cramped box of a room, and they'd been here for too many hours, interrogator and prisoner, talking, arguing, dancing around the old construct of lovers. He wanted to leave, and she wouldn't let him, and they both knew her claims about safety and protection were more lie than truth.

She needed him to lead her to Christopher, the killer.

Just as Christopher had used Robert to get to her, she'd use Christopher to find Clare. That had been the plan, anyway, when she'd gone after Rob, but there wouldn't be a plan — wouldn't be anything — without Jack. She hadn't heard from *him* since the preserve and hadn't seen so much as a glimpse of him since she'd checked his location and found him off course and off plan.

She'd waited for him, had waited until waiting had become too risky.

He should have been here long before her, considering all the time it'd taken to sort Rob's shit out, but here they were at four in the morning and still nothing.

If he didn't make contact, didn't show up by sunrise, then he was dead, and Clare was as good as dead, and she was alone — truly alone — isolated in a way that no one, not one other person, could possibly comprehend.

Maybe that was the real reason she held on to Robert.

She clenched her fists and pushed hard against anxiety.

She wanted to open the door and run to where she couldn't feel anymore, and that made her angry at Jack for playing God with chemical escape.

In that, she was already alone.

All this time, everything he knew, and even he didn't get that sixteen fucking years of living on a knife blade, of never knowing what was coming, of constant adrenaline had created its own addiction — that she didn't medicate to get high or stay well, but to placate urges that would otherwise get her killed or put her behind bars — that she dosed to escape the nightmares and the memories and the aching quiet, like now, when anxiety rose to crippling levels as she worried about Jack and worried about Clare and worried about what she couldn't know and couldn't see.

She should have squirreled the damn goods away instead of flushing them. That would have been some magical foresight if she'd predicted that indeed the shit would hit the fan and it'd be her, not Jack, on the outs, waiting for the dust to settle.

Jill pulled the burner from her pocket, shoved the SIM and battery in, booted up, and returned to the call log. She should have destroyed the thing hours ago but couldn't bring herself to do it. Jack had become Schrödinger's fucking cat, and this was her only way to open the box and find out if he was dead or alive.

The call went straight to voice mail, just as it had every time she'd dialed.

She pulled the phone apart and shoved the pieces back into her pocket.

In the lot outside, car doors shut. Her senses jumped to alert and possibilities sequenced in rapid order: motel neighbors, law enforcement, contract killers.

She couldn't check the eyehole, wouldn't risk cracking the curtain. She reached for the AR-15 resting against the wall, side-stepped for a clear line on the door, and fought against anxious hope in a fourth possibility.

More than one set of footsteps killed that hope fast.

This wasn't Jack, and wasn't the neighbors.

She glanced toward the bed.

Robert, for all his civilian helplessness,

had recognized the threat even in his sleep. He sat straight up, pillow clenched tight, eyes wide, and focused on her.

She nodded him over.

He rolled off the bed into the narrow space against the wall.

The footsteps stopped outside the window.

She readied for the kick or barrage of bullets. Instead, fingers tapped lightly against the glass, loud enough for the sound to carry inside but not so loud that the neighbors would wake, tapping a familiar pattern that paralyzed her limbs and yet forced them to move.

She rushed the door, ran the chain, and twisted the dead bolt without looking.

Jack pushed in, laden with matériel, face bruised, clothes torn and bloody. Clare followed right behind him, both of them entering the room like ghosts walking out of the darkness. The door shut. Time compressed into a capsule of questions. Anxiety, already out of control, threatened to jump the firebreak.

Her brain reached for Jack, to grab him, hug him, yell at him, knock him hard on his ass, and demand to know where he'd been — and *what the holy fuck!* — but her body stayed motionless, gaze locked onto Clare's haggard frame, which was draped in an odd assortment of clothing that spoke of escape and theft long before Jack had gotten to her. Clare met her eyes, reached for her, pulled her tight, and held on in a hug.

Relief and pain and ache and fear fanned jealousy and shame and twenty years of craving into a gusting blaze. Jill loosened Clare's grip and put some space between them. Noise from the bed broke the silence.

Robert's face peeked up from the other side. Slowly, he stood.

Clare stalked into his personal space.

Robert backed into the wall.

Clare said, "You're the boyfriend."

Robert cleared his throat. "Was," he said. "Was the boyfriend."

Clare scanned him from face to feet and up again. "I can see the appeal." Her eyes let him go, and he bumped into the light on the bedside table.

To Jill, she said, "The boy's tired. He should go home."

Jill fought the urge to bite back. In a single sentence Clare had assessed and gutted her strategy, relieved her of command, and made herself Robert's hero. Yes, Clare was found. Yes, they didn't need Robert anymore. And yes, he was now a special kind of baggage, but it should have been her call to cut him loose, not Clare's.

Jill motioned Robert over the bed to the ratty chair in the corner and waited until he'd taken a seat. Worse than having her authority stripped in front of him would be drawing attention to that fact by fighting Clare to get it back.

She chose the lesser of humiliations.

To Jack, she said, "You still driving the rental?"

He nodded and then, following where the question led, dug into his pocket and tossed her the keys.

Jill turned her back to the room, knelt beside the chair, and leaned in close so only Robert would hear. "I can take it all back," she said. "I can walk into any police station, hand over proof that you collaborated with Christopher to kidnap me, and undo everything we fixed today. I don't want to, but I will if I have to, so you need to listen very, very carefully."

Robert nodded.

She dangled the keys above his lap. "These go to a rental that's parked outside," she said. "Return the car. Drop off the keys. Then get yourself back to Austin. I don't care how you do it — fly, drive, walk — but what you don't do, ever, is talk to anyone about today. That's it. Car. Home. Quiet. Manage those successfully, and you go on with your life without ever dealing with me or any of this again."

Relief bled into Robert's posture and out his lungs.

He reached for the keys, and she let them go.

A hint of sorrow tainted the relief.

"I know," she said. She touched his cheek. "I'll miss you, too."

She walked him to the door and to the car and stood aside for Jack, who reached through the window with directions to the airport car rental lot scribbled on a scrap of paper — old-fashioned navigation — since Robert's phone rested beneath fifteen feet of water. She watched him until the tail-lights turned out onto the street.

With their fading, the inferno broke loose.

She followed Jack into the room, moving between the beat of his steps. Years of never being good enough, of Clare favoring him while punishing her, hours of being forced to wait through anxiety-induced hell, of being left behind so Mr. Goody Two-shoes, who'd been so willing to abandon Clare, could be the one to save her, built up pressure, tore through her core, and exploded into her hands.

Didn't matter that Clare was here, watching, didn't matter that rivalry propelled her toward self-immolation on Clare's critical pyre. She swung around and sucker punched her brother with an elbow hard into his face.

CHAPTER 41

Jill
Age: 26
Location: La Porte, Texas
Passport Country: USA
Names: Jennifer White

The door slammed. Jack stumbled. Jill drove him to the floor, pounded a boot on his chest, leaned hard onto him, and said, "Least you could have done was answer your fucking phone."

Jack grabbed her ankle and twisted.

She held on to balance and pressed harder into his chest. Through gritted teeth, he said, "Been just a little busy trying not to get my head blown off."

His words were wind, background noise, a comma between movements.

She stomped his hands. He let go. She stepped off his chest toward the bed and faced Clare. Fists clenched and volume rising, she said, "Was this whole thing your

411

doing? It wasn't enough to destroy child-hoods and wreck lives? You had to give insanity one final push?"

Clare glanced up in cold, indifferent silence, and Jill's core melted down.

This wasn't what she wanted, wasn't sup-posed to be how it happened. No, not Jack the good son — *again* — saving Clare, while she, the unwanted, pushed Clare further away and made her hate her more. No. Op-portunity and hope crumbled into a dark, gaping hole. Words from the past cycled through her head.

Bravo, Julia. You win the melodrama award.

Does the princess have anything to add to the outburst?

Can we move on now?

Clare slid her feet to the floor. Softly, gently, she said, "The last thing I wanted was for you to get pulled into this mess. I'm sorry it happened, Jillian."

Uncertainty rose, suspicious and guarded.

Clare had only ever used her birth name in moments of affection, and Jill could count on one hand the times those had hap-pened. She said, "All you've ever done is pull us into crap we don't want to be a part of. Somehow this is supposed to be differ-ent?"

Clare stood, tugged her close, and kissed

the side of her head.

The affection felt worse than indifference, felt like the earth caving beneath her, felt like tumbling into the hole, with nothing to grab to stop the free fall.

Jill shrugged away.

Jack dug a packet from his tool bag and, as payback for punching him, tossed the Blackphone on the bed where Clare couldn't help but see it. Jill didn't care. Flinging her connection to the Broker out into the open and forcing *that* conversation might make Clare angry, but at least it would push them back into familiar territory.

Only it didn't.

Clare reached for the phone, ran her thumb over the glass and, as if she already knew what it represented and what Jill had done, said, "On some level, I always knew you'd find him or he'd find you. How many contracts have you taken?"

Jill hesitated. "Two," she said. "Not counting this one."

Clare's expression softened into the same wistful smile that always showed when Jack had made her especially proud. "I'm sure you were spectacular," she said. "You're very good at what you do."

Jill's throat seized and sarcasm got stuck

on the way out.

Clare's fingers traced the plastic. "It's a Faustian bargain, working for him, you know? You get a sense of purpose and identity and a way to excel in a world in which you don't belong, and he takes your soul bit by bit." She offered the device to Jill. "No matter how careful you are, he'll learn you and toy with you, and when he grows tired of you, he'll burn you."

Jill took the phone. "You worked for him?"

"Worked *with* him before he became the power broker he is now, and worked bounty contracts to stay current on his operation as his influence grew. There's history between us and we both have reasons to neither forgive nor forget."

Jill listened past her own history and, for the first time since she was twelve, considered the genuine possibility that everything out of Clare's mouth wasn't a lie or manipulation. She said, "He's who you've been hiding us from?"

"One of many."

Jill waited. Jack stayed quiet.

Clare said, "Every decision, every job, came with obvious and hidden costs, and I weighed each and every one against my reasons, but the costs were cumulative, and I had a lot of time to make a lot of enemies.

There's probably not one among them who wouldn't kill you to get to me, and the Broker, knowing who'd pay the most for that information, is at the head of that line."

Jill hefted the phone and directed it toward Clare like an accusing finger. "I didn't bring this down on you, if that's what you're getting at."

"No, my weakness brought this on *you.*"

Jill stopped, hand outstretched, still pointing the phone.

Ray's words came tumbling back. *She mighta suspected this'd be the last time and couldn't bear leaving with no good-bye.*

Realization connected to understanding.

She turned away, fought the urge to throw the phone, turned back, and jabbed in Clare's direction again. "Are you fucking kidding me? After all the shit you put us through, running, hiding, fighting, you decide to just up and *tell* them how to find you?"

Clare's eyes rose and met hers directly. "It was time, Jillian."

Jill gaped, waited, and found her voice. "That is so. Much. *Bullshit.*"

Bullshit enough that even Jack didn't buy it. He moved in beside her, crossed his arms, and said, "How about just this once, Clare, you skip past innuendo and go for substance? How about you start with telling us how our dad fits into any of this?"

Clare's lips twitched, a nearly invisible micro expression that would have been invisible to anyone else but to them said Jack had surprised her. She said, "Well, if that's not completely out of nowhere."

It was the same maddening deflect-accuse-attack-deflect course she always followed when backed into a corner.

Jack said, "No, not completely."

"No?"

"No."

Clare waited and, when Jack refused to be baited into defending himself, said, "I take it you paid Ray a visit."

The name rolled off Clare's tongue like she'd just had lunch with him or something, like Ray wasn't dead.

Which meant Jack hadn't told her. Clare didn't know.

Not a clue seeped into Jack's tone or body language. He said, "We wouldn't have bothered if we'd known it was you who'd invited the shooters in."

Jill fought the urge to survey the carpet.

Clare studied his face. Dark circles and hollow cheeks belied her clarity of focus. Her eyes narrowed, and she said, "Where's Ray? Right now, where is he?"

Jill took a defensive step forward. If the messenger was going to get shot, better it was someone used to it. She said, "Ray's dead."

Clare stopped breathing. Seconds passed. Her expression hardened. She said, "How'd it happen?"

"Sniper."

Clare let out a long, slow exhale, closed her eyes, and when she opened them again, she was different, in the same way a revolving door presented a different pane of glass to the sidewalk. She said, "Ray was smarter than most gave him credit for."

Jack said, "So he was right? This has something to do with our dad?"

"Maybe. I don't know. I don't know who put out the hit."

"But you *were* looking for him, just like Ray said."

"It's more complicated than that."

Jack's fists clenched in a rare show of anger. "We've earned the details, Clare. Through blood, sweat, and hell, we've more than earned them."

Clare chewed the tip of her thumb, walked toward the wall, crossed the room, and paced back. The visible discomfort, as unusual and out of place as kindness, set Jill on edge. She glanced at Jack.

The hand by his side motioned for her to stay quiet.

The upstairs pipes rattled.

A door down the hall opened and shut.

Clare stopped and turned. "The world was different then," she said. "We had two superpowers waging a global ideological war, fighting through surrogates and proxies and dancing around nuclear annihilation. We were young, young and patriotic opponents in that war, Maria Catalina and Dmitry, CIA and KGB, manipulating each other for information. But we were on his territory, his game was better, his sources were more reliable, and my point man was a backstabbing, double-dealing traitor."

Jack said, "The Broker."

Clare nodded, lips pressed tight, and she returned to pacing.

Her words picked up tempo with each stride. "My country abandoned me, left me trapped. Your father got me to neutral territory, and then he abandoned me, too. Favor or manipulation, I still don't know. When I fled, I became an enemy of the state, and when he left, it forced me to run. If I'd stayed, his people would have taken you from me to ensure my obedience, if not loyalty, and they'd have raised you and indoctrinated you as human weapons in their long-game strategy."

Clare turned to Jill, reached for her hand, held it tightly, and studied her fingers. "You were minutes old the first time your little fist grabbed my thumb, grabbed my soul. Minutes old, and evil was already hunting for you. I had no way to predict how long you'd be mine, but I knew I'd never allow my weakness, my heart, to be the reason you were stolen or killed, knew I'd do whatever needed doing to hide you and make you strong, strong enough to survive without me."

Jill pulled her hand free and put breathing space between them.

Clare let her own hand drop. "You wanted to know your father, wanted to live with him, demanded it really. I've looked for him over the years, tried to find answers for both of us, but like Ray said, it always ended badly, and asking questions put us all at risk. Keeping you alive, protecting you, that was my priority, so I waited as agencies changed hands and the years ravaged memory and priorities, waited until you didn't need me anymore, and waited until time and luck started running out and I couldn't wait any longer. I've lived enough, seen enough, and escaped death enough, so yes, I let the past find me, and yes, it has something to do with your father because I'm not capable of going to my grave without putting the lies to rest, but I never intended for it to rope you in the way it has, never imagined we'd be having this conversation."

The weight of knowledge returned the room to silence.

Sunlight crept beneath the curtains, hinting at morning's arrival and the need to clear out and keep moving. Jack uncrossed his arms and returned to the foot of the bed, as if Clare's explanation satisfied his need for answers. He shoved the items he'd taken out of his bags back in. Jill watched him and then glanced at Clare and back at him, and frustration and pain and memories wrapped around her throat, making it impossible to breathe or speak or think and, most impossible of all, to understand how this was enough, how it was okay.

The question, so strong in her head, came out as a plaintive cry.

"How?" She cleared her throat. "How could you possibly do what you did to us and claim it was love?"

CHAPTER 42

Jill
Age: 26
Location: La Porte, Texas
Passport Country: USA
Names: Jennifer White

The weariness of time bled into Clare's body, and the room's shifting light added twenty years to her tired face. Hands slack at her sides, she said, "I've hurt you, Jillian. Made undoable mistakes, and I am truly, genuinely sorry."

Jill stood in mute silence and, when the tumult of emotion finally settled into coherent thought, said, "You don't get to do that. You do *not* get to deprive a child of approval and motherly love for twenty-six years and then, with a few hugs and a sentence of apology, get to pretend it's all better."

Clare's head shook slowly, sadly. She said, "I'm not asking for forgiveness. I've hoped I might find it one day, but I have no right to ask. I just want you to know that I'm aware of how wrong I was and that I own it."

Jill turned away and turned back. She wanted to believe, wanted so badly for this to be real, would have accepted the apology for what it was if Jack, the favored child, Jack, who had nothing to lose — who'd never had anything to lose — hadn't been standing five feet away, watching the whole thing. She said, "You seem to forget there were two of us. All this talk of love and protecting might make sense to John, but all I hear is noise. I worked so damn hard for a smile, Clare. For a touch of approval, for you to tell me I'd done well. I killed myself to please you and was never fucking good enough."

She swiped a hand toward her brother. "I outperformed him ten to one and still failed, but John? Oh, you loved him. And when I cried for fairness, you told me I was petty and egotistical and narcissistic, imagining things, and full of self-pity. You told me I was the problem and to stop whining. So don't come to me now and offer bullshit and call it love."

Clare's expression made another rotation through the revolving door, and it took a second for Jill to realize that this new thing was pain, genuine pain. Clare reached for

Jill's face, cradled her cheeks in her palms and, so earnestly the words hurt, said, "There was never anything wrong with you, Jillian, nothing you'd ever done to cause me to treat you the way I did, and although it's difficult to believe, I loved you more than life."

She let go of Jill's face and grasped her arms. "The world out there is a hard, hard place for a woman. Out there we have to be twice as good to be considered half as capable as a man, but *this* world" — her forefinger drew a circle in the air — "this world is so much worse. It attracts the worst, and I was terrified for you, terrified of what I'd brought you into and the abuse you'd suffer for no other reason than your sex. You had to be stronger, smarter, better than the best, and I had to be the one to get you there, even if it meant driving you away, even if it meant shutting myself off and letting you suffer. I didn't know any other way. I pushed you harder than anyone had a right to push, and by the time I realized the damage done, you hated and despised me, and I hated and despised myself, and we were too far gone to undo everything and start over, so I did the only thing I could and removed myself to set you free."

For the third time since Clare had walked through the door, Jill pulled away, but the words had sucked oxygen out of her mental fire. She whispered, "I didn't hate you. You hated me."

Clare shook her head, and tears welled. "No." She reached for Jill's hand, and when Jill refused to let her have it, she withdrew. "Not then, not now, not ever," Clare said. "Every step I've made, everything I've done has been to protect you and keep you safe, you and your brother." She sighed, and she sat. "There were so many things I couldn't tell you, and the more danger I faced, the farther away I had to put you to keep you hidden. It killed me, destroyed you, and yet here we are, anyway, my greatest fear fully realized in flesh and blood. I'm so incredibly sorry."

Jill sat on the bed, three feet from Clare, as close as she was willing to get to her for now.

Years of anger and hurt were impossible to rewrite in a single conversation, but the effort mattered, Clare acknowledging her faults mattered, and on some level, she understood that as fucked up as things had been, as twisted as it seemed, in her own way, Clare had meant well. She stretched her hand across the sheet, touched Clare's fingertips, and pulled away.

Jack said, "The guy who came after you, is he part of your past, too?"

Clare's face changed again, revolving from emotion to business. "Contractor," she said. "I know him only by reputation. He started young, real young, does the work because it's work — isn't one of the head cases in it for the thrill — and he's good, probably the best on the Broker's call list. He'd be a tough matchup, would push your training hard, I think."

"He already has."

The old Clare, the strategic Clare, swung around to face front. "He's coming back," she said, "and he'll keep coming back unless he's stopped."

"Not just him," Jack said. "There's a third party in this mix now. *Was* a third party. They killed his partner, and almost got him." He paused in slow contemplation, then paced toward the front door. "Something's off, something we're missing." He turned and stopped. "This guy had me, had me right there, and didn't take the shot. He didn't want me dead."

"A temporary truce to fight the enemy of his enemy doesn't make him your friend. Just means he had something more pressing to deal with and already had a line on you, knew how to find you when he was ready."

Jill's hand went for the burner pieces in her pocket.

Jack said, "You called from the room?"

She said, "Couldn't risk Robert running off."

He rolled his eyes. "You should have told us as soon as we got here." He knelt and pulled a pair of Jill's pants and one of his shirts from a bag, tossed the clothes to Clare and, to Jill, said, "Tell me how the contracts work. Christopher knows he's got a hit out on him now, knows we're one of two, possibly more, parties looking to kill him. What would drive him to pursue us instead of hiding?"

Jill said, "Contract fulfillment."

Clare said, "A bounty on his head doesn't cancel payout on his own agreements. He probably thinks he's smart enough to get to you first, collect, and then reverse roles on whoever else is sent after him. He very well might be."

Jack shoved the last of what he'd removed back into his bags. "So do we run, or do we hunt?"

"You might not have a choice."

Jack stopped. Jill turned. They both stared at her.

Clare had said a lot of strange things in

the past, but nothing so strange as extricating herself from a scenario she'd caused and handing the fight off to them with the word *you*.

Jill said, "Where are you going?"

"Even if we win this one, it won't stop. There was big money behind the hit, and my escape creates a failure the Broker can't tolerate. He'll spread the word that I've surfaced. Bigger money will follow. We could divide up here, and I could draw the heat, but there are pictures of you circulating now, not great pictures, but pictures, and soon enough there'll be seekers looking in your direction. We'd win the first rounds and the legacy would grow and the prices would go up, and then the big-game hunters would come, the crazy ones who don't know shit about shit, and would cut a swath of destruction that makes it impossible to hide." Clare sighed. "I'm tired of running," she said. "I'm done. The only way to make this stop is to cut off the source before it gets out of hand."

Jack said, "Alone?"

"It's the only way."

He said, "You'll lose what you were chasing in the first place."

Clare smiled in wan self-chiding and pulled off the scrubs that worked as her top.

"Every decision has a cost," she said. She tugged the clean shirt Jack had given her over her head. "If I don't put this to rest now, it'll never end, which makes everything else meaningless. That's the trade-off."

Jack tossed a handful of one-way pagers on the bedspread.

Clare leaned over, picked one up, rolled the plastic between her fingers, and Jill followed her hand. The technology, big when they were babies, had mostly been put out of business as cell phones got smaller and cheaper, but it still had a thriving niche market supported by doctors, firefighters, and emergency personnel. Pagers were reliable in ways cell phones weren't, and the batteries lasted weeks, if not months. But that wasn't why Jack had reverted to old-school tech. Unlike cell phones, pagers didn't store information and couldn't be tracked. If Clare was going her separate way, he wanted to be able to reach her, and her to be able to reach him.

Clare handed the device back. "Can't take the risk," she said. "If I make it out, I'll post on Craigslist."

Jill struggled to produce an argument against Clare leaving. She finally had a mother, a real mother, had had her for a whole fucking hour, and just like that, everything she'd wanted her whole life was about to disappear in a fight against the impossible.

She opened her mouth in protest. A jolting buzz cut her words short.

They all three looked toward the nightstand, at the telephone beside the tattered lamp. Jill, closest to the handset, leaned over and picked it up.

Robert's voice said, "Sorry for calling this way. Your cell keeps going to voice mail, and I didn't have any other way to reach you. There's a problem with the car, something about them not wanting to take it back at this location."

Jill glanced at Jack.

He didn't need to be a mind reader, he already knew what this call was about.

She said, "You're a grown man, Robert. Figure it out."

"Jen, this is *your* problem. For God's sake, just come help me out."

"I'm busy," she said. "Call my cell in exactly ten minutes."

She dropped the phone into its cradle, and said, "Well, fuck."

CHAPTER 43

Holden
Age: 32
Location: Spring, Texas
Passport Country: Paperless
Names: Nameless

The miles ticked off in accusing silence, a slow dog-legged route past headlights and streetlights, away from the car rental return at George Bush Intercontinental, where he'd collected Robert, and into the outer stretches of suburbia. The kid sat beside him, jaw clenched, fists clenched, body poised somewhere between fight and compliance.

It hadn't taken much to get him into the car.

A nod. A welcome.

You know the drill. Don't make this more difficult than it needs to be.

They were nearly to the trip's midpoint when Robert, voice low and not quite flat enough to hide the mix of fear and anger, said, "What is it you want this time?"

Holden checked the rearview. "Need you to make a call."

Robert waited, tense with the expectation of more, and when Holden gave him nothing, he said, "That's it? I make a phone call and you let me go?"

His tone had way too much hope, the crazy kind of hope of a guy who'd blown a grand on scratch-offs and was down to the last ticket.

Holden put the blinker on and changed lanes. "Depends," he said. "Depends on how well you do on the call. Depends on what you'd do if I let you go."

Hope deflated.

"What *would* you do, Rob, if I let you go?"

The kid studied his knees.

"It's not a trick question."

"Go home," Rob said. "Keep my mouth shut. Pretend this never happened."

"Take it you've already had this conversation at least once tonight."

"Pretty much."

Holden waited for the light and turned into a Whataburger lot. "There's the phone call, and I also need a favor."

Robert coughed out a laugh. "Oh, a favor. That's rich. And by the way, while we're at it, that was a real dick move, making me believe I was wearing a bomb."

Holden parked the car in a bath of orange and white neon. He shut off the engine and glanced right. "Duly noted," he said. "Next time I'll use the real thing."

Robert went back to studying his knees.

Holden shifted in the seat, propped an elbow on the wheel, and waited until the kid looked him in the eyes. He said, "Let me explain how this usually works. I kidnap you, you see my face, listen to me talk, and you know too much. That makes you a threat. So I use you, and when I don't need you anymore, I kill you. Nothing personal. It's to protect myself. You with me?"

Robert didn't answer. Holden offered him a phone.

The kid didn't take it.

Holden said, "You've got to know you're not the first — not the first to die, not the first to plead or promise or beg or lie. You know I'm not stupid, and yet you're already prepared to say yes to anything you think will keep you alive, figuring you'll run as soon as my back is turned." He shoved the phone in Robert's hand.

The kid took it like it might bite.

"Call Jen."

"Are you going to kill her?"

"Not if I can help it."

"She's not going to do it. She won't walk into another trap for me."

"No," Holden said. "But she'll come for me."

Robert's expression clouded. His mouth opened in protest, and he stopped and went back to staring at his knees. "What about the favor?"

"First the call. Then we'll see."

Robert's thumb hovered over the pre-dialed number.

Holden cut off the last hint of rebellion. "I like you, kid," he said. "It's not your fault you got roped into this — wrong girl, wrong time — but if it comes to you or me, I won't lose a minute's sleep over putting you down. Follow?"

Robert gave him a side-eye glare and punched the call button.

Jen picked up — Holden knew she would — and Robert performed well enough, with bullshit about rental cars and problems, that she'd hear both truth and lie. She'd come. Holden took the phone back and set an alarm.

Jen had said to call again in ten minutes.

In thirty, a long enough time gap for anxiety to rise and Jen's questions to multiply, his new best friend would make one final plea.

Twenty was what it took to reach the room where Baxter slept, a room that was dark and quiet, exactly as it'd been when Holden left but for the quart of ice water, now a few inches emptier. That one small change gave Holden his own form of crazy hope.

Robert shuffled toward the bed. Voice thick, concern almost genuine, he said, "Did Jen do . . . ? Will he be . . . ?"

Holden said, "Wasn't her, and I hope so, but I just don't know."

Robert stopped by Baxter's side. His fingers reached toward the sheets and then stopped. "I should be glad," he said. "I should hate you guys, I really should, and this should make me happy." His brow furrowed. Sorrow mixed with disgust. "He never hurt me, never raised his voice. We just sorta chilled the whole time." Carefully, almost reverently, he touched Baxter's arm. "He'd have killed me, though, if it had come to that."

Holden said, "It's not —"

"Yeah, I know. Not personal."

Holden's pocket vibrated with the alarm's call reminder.

Baxter's eyes twitched behind their lids, and his lashes fluttered, and the first two fingers on his right hand rose an inch off the bed. He might as well have stood and grabbed Holden in a bear hug.

Crazy hope burned that much hotter.

Holden squeezed the big guy's shoulder.

The war wouldn't allow him to stay, and this was as close to a permanent good-bye as they'd ever get. He whispered, "See you on the other side, my brother."

Holden handed Robert the phone and followed with a slip of paper.

The kid glanced at the handwritten scrawl, comprising hours of scheming, scouting for a plan B location in case the play at the preserve failed to net them what they wanted, all condensed into a single address and a few lines of instruction.

Holden said, "Just read the script."

Robert dialed.

Jen's voice assaulted the air with irritation and questions.

Robert, in a monotone, pronouncing each word as if he feared she'd pay a price for him missing even one, spoke over her. The other end went silent. Holden waited until the kid reached the final line and, script unfinished, plucked the phone from his hand and killed the connection.

The first call, full of lies and pleas for help, had been the lure.

This second had set the hook.

Time itself would reel Jen and her brother in.

He didn't need the kid anymore.

Robert glanced up, expression stuck somewhere between fear and confusion. "You told me you'd let me go if I made the call."

Holden pocketed the phone. "There was also a favor involved." He nodded toward the bed. "Twenty-four hours is what I'm asking. Sit with the big guy, follow the dosing instructions on the pad over there, and if I don't make it back —" Holden swiped a sealed envelope from off the bedside table and flicked his fingers against it. "If I'm not back in twenty-four hours, open this. It's his mother. Call her. She'll come."

Robert took the envelope. His focus stayed on the bed. "This is messed up," he said. "You realize that, don't you?"

Holden nodded.

Didn't get more messed up than a kidnapper relying on the kidnapped to keep his best friend alive. Holden turned to leave. He paused at the door and looked back. He said, "That big guy right there is the best reason I have to keep you breathing. If I make it out and you're not here, I *will* find you."

Robert sighed and sat in the bedside chair.

Holden gave Baxter a final glance and

stepped into the hall.

If he'd predicted correctly, twenty-four hours was more than enough to get what he wanted. If he'd predicted wrongly, a widow who'd worked long days and hard nights to feed, clothe, and house six children, who'd kept them on the straight and narrow, in spite of hooliganism and brushes with the law, who'd always had room for him in her overcrowded apartment when Frank was away, would be forced to collect her youngest. And, through her howls of pain and protest and through her finger-pointing blame, Frank would learn that some promises would never be kept.

CHAPTER 44

Jill
Age: 26
Location: Houston, Texas
Passport Country: USA
Names: Julia Jane Smith

Hands to the windowsill, she boosted up, threaded her legs and torso between broken panes, and dropped ten feet to hard, empty floor on the other side. Diesel and metal and concrete aged by salt, humidity, and warmth rushed her brain, familiar with the chemical slick of Managua and Barranquilla and a dozen lightly polluted industrial zones before and since, comforting like homemade bread.

Sun blindness turned the dim room dark, made her vulnerable.

She skirted for cover behind a gouge-scarred slab that might have once topped a desk. Knee and fists to the floor, she listened and waited.

A flurry of wings scattered off a roost somewhere upstairs.

Rusted metal and broken switches stirred in the breeze, discordant wind chimes creaking to the distant rumble of shipping containers on flatbeds, warehoused goods in big rigs, and cars and smaller trucks shuttling the flow of day laborers and dockworkers during shift changes. All this, but no sound of Christopher.

Her eyes adjusted to the limited light.

Shadows and shapes morphed into broken shelves and tooling tables still lag bolted to the floor. Oil-slicked dust coated every surface the way it coated the transom windows. Soot stains and holes in the ceiling pointed to a fire. Best as she could tell, the machine shop had occupied over a quarter of the lower floor plan.

She searched surfaces for recent disturbance.

No sign of Christopher there, either.

She wanted to move, wanted to eliminate this location and get the hell on with the rush of the hunt and the chase. Training told her to hold, to hold until she was certain, and then hold again for just as long, because patience was a weapon and waiting spawned curiosity and curiosity had a way of flushing even the best from hiding.

She'd never had much use for patience.

She slipped into the open, taunting fate in a double-dog dare, insides rebelling against the likelihood that her effort to steal in undetected had been a pointless time waste because the address Robert had called to give her had been misdirection, and Christopher had never been here, and Rob would call again last minute with another location, and Jack, the golden boy, would be the one to see action — again — while she was left to wait and wait and wonder.

She crossed the room for the half-opened steel doors at the end.

Whatever Christopher's plans, he'd chosen the site well, she'd give him that: two lofted stories on the far end of a peninsula of sorts, a bulb of land that reached into the waterway and on which the only two roads — which threaded through acres of concrete and warehouses, railway yards and liquid bulk repositories, with their thousands upon thousands of gallons of crude — dead-ended just short of the water.

The limited entry points ensured a direct line on incoming traffic, the industrial zone made noncommercial vehicles easy to spot, and the noise guaranteed that whatever happened here wouldn't be heard. It was a perfect rendezvous for a close-up kill and a perfect lure for a shooter set up on a nearby tower or rooftop.

The multiple possibilities had turned strategy into question marks and forced them to stretch resources in opposite directions.

She'd had Jack drop her off at a truck stop on the Pasadena Freeway frontage, had hitched a ride with a long-haul trucker she'd sweet-talked into taking his eighteen-wheeler on a two-mile detour, and had rounded back on foot from the waterfront through a stretch of undeveloped land. Midmorning sun's reflection had turned barren windows into watchful eyes, and the broken panes had winked, as if in on a private joke.

There'd been no cars, no sign of Robert.

She'd climbed the chain-link under the shield of the building's windowless short end, skirting truck bays and warehouse doors secured by rusty padlocks on rustier chains. Knee-high thistle weed sprouting tall between cracks had decorated the bleached concrete.

It'd been too easy.

She'd seen what Christopher could do with a rifle.

Careful as she'd been, there'd been moments of exposure, and he hadn't even tried.

He wasn't out there. Didn't seem to be in here.

She reached the steel doors now, and stole a glance into the empty entrance hall.

Her front pocket vibrated.

Rebellion rose in response.

She'd left the burner with Jack so Christopher could track it, if he cared to, and so Robert, who'd hinted at the possibility of another location change, could call again if needed. And Jack, searching for Christopher from a distance in the same way she was searching up close, would alert her to any change in plans.

She pulled the pager free and read numbers off the screen.

The sweet, sweet trickle of pleasure began a slow drip from brain to veins.

Six-slash-two.

Jack had spotted movement on the second floor, had gotten a visual on Christopher. Another vibration offered another numbered code. Jack was packing up, would leave his vantage and head her way. He wasn't stupid enough to ask her to stand down and wait for him, but he'd certainly hurry to minimize the time gap.

She tucked the pager away and stepped into the entrance hall, avoiding the wide stairwell and keeping far back, beneath the overhang. She was on her own for now, just she and Christopher, one-on-one in this big, bad, empty building, in which he had the advantage of knowing the layout and owning the high ground.

She scoped the scarred industrial-green elevator doors and ruled them out.

Footsteps, deliberate and taunting, thumped across the floor above.

Her eyes tracked the movement. Her fingers released clasps, dropping a Czech-made CZ P-09 into each hand. Two weapons. Forty rounds. Of everything they'd found and taken from Clare's stashes, this was all she'd brought. More would have bulked her up, weighed her down, turned dexterity into clumsiness, and she'd never liked firearms for close-up work, anyway. Loud and dirty, they inevitably left trace evidence behind.

Garrotes, knives, and hands made for a quieter, cleaner dispatch.

She moved sideways, muzzles trained upward, feet taking her to the opposite doors, until her shoulder nudged them. They gave enough to indicate chains through the handles on the other side.

A building this size had to have other ways up.

The footsteps stopped just beyond the

machine-shop doorway.

A piece of cardboard dropped through a hole in the ceiling and fluttered to the floor. Christopher testing her twitchiness, she guessed, and giving away his position as a bonus. She side-stepped for the stairs.

His voice, traveling in both directions, said, "Your brother should be here soon."

The accent, years removed from its homeland and familiar in a way she could almost place, made her pause. Footfalls thumped from above the machine shop to the open area above her head. She retreated from the first step for the shelter of the landing, and shoulder to the doors, she tried again to budge them.

Christopher said, "I'd hoped your mother would be with him."

Those eight little words made the hair on her arms stand on end.

It made sense that he knew Clare had escaped. It stretched sense but wasn't impossible that he knew Clare was her mother. But that he knew all that *and* that the three of them had been together? He'd have learned that from Robert, and Robert was the issue that ate her and that there'd been no time to discuss.

Robert, Christopher, Robert, Robert, always back to Robert.

She'd changed out his clothes and shoes. She'd made damn certain there was nothing on him that Christopher could use to track her. Robert wasn't the link that would have led Christopher to them, it was the burner she'd refused to sacrifice. Rob had had nothing trackable on him when they cut him loose.

She stopped there.

Understanding hit with the awareness of spotting eyes peering into her bedroom window.

Christopher had been at the motel.

He'd been there when Jack and Clare arrived, he'd been watching when they sent Robert off, and this was his way of matching wits, telling her he could have fired blind into the motel room and taken them all, that he could have set this place up as a lure and used the safety of distance to score at least one kill, if not two, like he'd done to Ray. This was him telling her that just like with Jack at the preserve, he'd chosen life.

Silence filled the building. No footsteps. No words.

In her mind's eye, she saw him, short dark hair and broad shoulders, T-shirt and cargo pants, seated with his back to the wall and rifle across his lap, content to wait her out, even knowing Jack was on his way and they'd soon be going two against one in a close-quarter conflict.

Overconfidence or madness — she couldn't tell which — and it didn't matter, because *she* wasn't content to wait for Jack to steal the mission out from beneath her and have Clare award him credit by virtue of his mere presence.

To the ceiling, she said, "Where's Robert?"

"Safe, I assure you."

"The rental car?"

"Returned."

The voice moved, but the footsteps didn't. She crossed the entrance hall, following the sound. "I want to talk with Rob."

"Not possible right now."

"Proof of life, Chris. Can I call you Chris? You know how it works."

"Yes," he said. "That's how it *would* work if you cared about proof of life beyond its use in collecting intel and flipping control."

The words were harsh in their truthfulness, seductive in their lie, and stung just enough to make her defensive. She said, "You hurt him, I'll kill you."

Laughter echoed from over the machine shop. "And if I don't hurt him?"

She tried not to smile. "I'll kill you less painfully."

His voice reached out from the upper landing. "I don't want to kill *you.*"

She spun back in its direction.

He said, "Contractually, I do need you dead, but a little acting, a little cooperation, and we could end this with me paid and you alive."

She calculated her position against the probability of one of her rounds reaching him before his found her. She said, "I admire your ballsy overconfidence."

"You don't want to kill me, either."

She didn't, not really, not on any personal or emotional level, not any more now than she had once Clare had come walking through the motel room door, but she'd be damned if she let Jack be the one who satisfied Clare's order to get it done.

She said, "How about you come down and we talk about it?"

"Better view of the road up here. Come help me watch for your brother."

She crossed the entrance hall and peered through the crack between doors to get a bead on what kept them secured. "There's a long plank between danger and death," she said. "I'd prefer not to walk it."

"You already are."

She re-scanned the corners, searching for cameras she might have missed.

447

He said, "I'm the one in danger, not you. Like I said, I don't want to kill you."

He told the truth, she knew.

She'd lied to enough men and been lied to by enough men to recognize one from the other, but Clare wanted him dead, so he'd have to die. Wasn't personal or payback for the kidnapping or a matter of avenging Ray. Christopher had done a job, just as Clare had done jobs, and she'd done jobs — *favors,* as Clare had called them — and this was business, a self-preserving business in which Christopher knew too much and through which the big money would soon provide too big of a temptation to keep him from coming back.

He said, "You joining me up here?"

She shoved the handguns back into place. "Need to think about it."

"Take your time. You've got, oh, maybe another minute and a half till your brother gets here."

She pushed back through the doors to the machine shop.

He said, "Entryway stairs are the only way up."

That made her smile. For someone with dexterity and years of hard training, stairs were merely a convenience. She crossed the floor, walk turning to run, picking up speed, hitting full stride, and leapt from concrete to table slab to wall, moving fast to keep up momentum, utilizing each step as a spring board. She jumped for the transom-window ledge, hefted herself up, twisted, and threaded her head and torso back through the open panes.

Her fingers found purchase against the brick. She dragged herself upward, pulling and pushing from crack to crack to crack, free-climbing the distance as if it were a ten-foot rock face, and she punched through picture-frame glass.

Silence crept out of the room in which Christopher had been.

Heart pounding, lungs burning, she scanned the space.

Fire had eaten framing and devoured a third of the gypsum ceiling, exposing a metal roof through which heat vents, spinning in the breeze, pulsed sunlight across the footprints and smudges and the trail of a laden bag that had been dragged across the floor. Where double doors stood on the bottom floor, here a gaping hole opened to the stairwell landing. She balanced on the window ledge, grabbed the nearest joist, and pulled herself up into what had once been crawl space.

From the stairwell, Christopher's voice

said, "I know where you are."

She studied the dark recesses where ventilation ducts snaked between bracing and collar ties, and where what had once been insulation now played house to insects and rodents and bird nests, grabbed hold of a brace and moved, one joist to the next, toward solid footing. She never heard him, never saw him, all in black, hidden in the dark and angled with the roof pitch, never saw him until she nearly faced him, and his eyes, white against the darkness, met hers. Adrenaline jolted through her system. A lifetime of microsecond calculations and practice erupted into simultaneous movement.

Her body shifted. Left hand went up for attack, right hand lunged for the bowie strapped to her thigh. She was fast. He was faster. The rifle stock hit her square on the side of her head, hit with the unexpected force of disbelief, and knocked her off balance.

Pain seared into her brain, blurring vision.

Her footing slipped, and she fell.

Time rolled into weightlessness, and for a dizzy, disoriented second, she knew what it was to fall in love. Instinct sent her rotating in self-preservation against the danger of an uncontrolled crash onto the weakened, fire-burned floor below.

Her left arm hit a joist. Her hand caught hold.

She hung, arm straining, palm slipping, head cocked back, seeking her target while her free hand searched for, and found, a pistol grip.

Christopher waited her out, waited until gravity took hold and her fingers gave.

She fell again. Her feet hit hard. Her legs buckled.

The floor shook and splintered in a cough of termite dust, and she rolled from rotted wood to solid flooring, and up to her feet, and was running, running for the gaping hole at the end of the room before she had time to think, running to reach the stairwell and the ladder that led to the crawl space access hatch before Christopher could reach it, running to block his way. She raced the ladder rungs, hand over hand, popped back into the dark, and rolled away from the opening.

On her back, knife gripped tight, she fought to control ragged breathing.

Far to the right, Christopher said, "We have the same enemy."

She shifted her mouth toward the metal roof to distort sound direction. "That doesn't make you my friend."

"I'm not sure you've ever had a friend in your life."

The words pricked in their truthfulness. She kept quiet and rolled to a crouch.

Metal touching metal echoed through the shadows.

She paused, waiting, measuring.

From somewhere along the roof beams, his voice said, "I could be your friend, I think. We have a lot in common. We've both seen the world."

"We both kill for a living," she said.

"We both hate the Broker."

She honed in on the voice, couldn't see him, but knew where he was.

He said, "Is it hard for you being the perpetual outsider?"

"I deal."

"Not very well, if the things I've heard are true."

She sighed on the inside.

God only knew what Robert had told him about her.

Every story, every observation, would be a tool in his arsenal. Human intelligence — HUMINT was what Clare had called it — laid the groundwork for manipulation. He had everything, and she had nothing.

She blocked out the words and focused on his position.

He said, "Work with me, Jen. I can guarantee what I'm getting paid is more than what you're being offered for me, and I'll go fifty-fifty with you."

She pressed the blade between her teeth and crept toward his voice.

"I don't care that your mother's escaped. Don't care where you go or what you do from here. Help me settle this, and we can part ways in peace."

She recognized the accent now.

Clare's description turned around in her head.

He started young, real young.

Wasn't a lot to work with but was more than his bounty packet revealed, and that alone should be enough to throw him off guard.

She said, "Must have been rough for you growing up poor in Colombia, with no middle- or upper-class frills, nothing but what you took for yourself. Big ole USA must have been quite the shock. Not much of a relief, was it? Hard to relate when everyone around you is crying over first-world problems."

His breath caught, and his shadow slipped down to the crawl space floorboards.

She watched his hands, watched his posture.

He was too big, too strong to go at directly, and fast enough, she'd learned, to make close contact a genuine threat. But he didn't want her dead.

That was his mistake.

"Work with me," he said.

She gripped the nearest brace, swung to gain momentum, and launched her full weight feetfirst into his side. The blow should have knocked him over, should have put her on top.

His torso rotated before she hit.

He seized her leg and twisted, changing her trajectory, dulling the impact.

She grabbed hold of him and took him down with her.

They tumbled, propelled by motion, and rolled in a flurry of fists and blocks, rolled right over the edge, went falling, falling, just as she'd fallen minutes before, falling without the controlled landing, both of them toward the fragile floor.

She gripped his collar in an attempt to position herself above him, to use his body as a cushion for landing. His elbow powered into her, broke her grasp. She smacked down hard, feet, hip, shoulder, head. Couldn't breathe — had to move.

She groaned up from her side onto her stomach, dragging and clawing forward to put space between them.

The bowie was gone. His rifle was gone.

Her right arm wouldn't move.

She limped to her feet, blinking through the haze, shrugging her working shoulder against her face to get the sweat out of her eyes, and she fumbled left-handed for one of the holstered handguns and leveled the muzzle in his direction.

She should have fired, fired before he'd had a chance to move, fired with the clinical, cold detachment of business, but hands shaking, lungs sucking in whatever oxygen they could find, she hesitated in the intoxication of his defeat.

His eyes met hers.

He opened his fists and lifted his hands an inch off the floor in a show of surrender. She shuffled toward him, kicked his feet apart and, with the weapon pointed toward his chest and steadied as best as her shaking arm could manage, searched his legs and waist. He moved to sit.

She motioned with the muzzle for him to keep still.

Wincing, blood trickling from his lips, he said, "Your mother has something I need. Connect me with her. One phone call. That's all I'm asking."

She backed away for a better angle.

She said, "You're in no position to ask for anything."

"Work with me, Jen."

"The name's not Jen," she said.

She clenched her teeth.

This had to end. Clare wanted him dead, so he had to die.

She moved her finger toward the trigger.

CHAPTER 45

Jack
Age: 26
Location: Houston, Texas
Passport Country: USA
Names: Jason Francis White

He stepped over weatherworn chains and a recently cut padlock and nudged through paint-chipped doors into an entrance hall stagnant from abandonment and an almost silence broken by stirring rusted things. Voices that didn't belong, quiet voices amplified by emptiness, bled over the landing and down the stairs. Tweaked on sleep deprivation and fueled by adrenaline, he moved toward those voices, rifle to his shoulder, finger beside the trigger, up one cautious step after the next on dust-drenched, oil-slick stairs.

Every second's tick on the mental clock put him further on edge.

He turned onto the landing and slipped

left along the wall, past an elevator, toward a burned-out hole where wide double doors had once been.

He could hear the words now.

One phone call. That's all I'm asking. Work with me, Jen.

He quick checked the room.

Jill stood with her back to him, right arm and hand wounded and limp, handgun in her left pointed toward Christopher, who lay there, palms up, in a show of surrender, talking.

Jack lowered the rifle and swore in silent protest.

He'd confirmed Christopher's presence, had watched Jill begin the climb up the outside brick. He'd hurried from rooftop to parked car and driven recklessly, abandoning stealth, drawing attention he otherwise wouldn't have, racing time to ensure he didn't leave her exposed, all for *this*.

The enormity of the moment upturned reality.

Jill the badass, Jill the party girl, who'd never found a man she couldn't discard, didn't have it in her to pull this trigger.

He didn't need to see her face to know what her expression looked like, and didn't need to hear where the conversation had traveled to understand where it had gone.

Christopher alive, Christopher still talking, Christopher on his back, showing his belly like a too-comfortable, safe-feeling cat, said it all.

Present played against past and pitted Jill against Clare.

He'd have turned and walked away for no other reason than to give his sister a chance at whatever had stayed her hand, but he couldn't.

Life was cruel and bitter with its jokes.

Christopher had to die, and it fell to him to kill the man who'd spared his life.

He stepped into the room and strode across the floor.

Christopher's focus cut from Jill's face to his, and in that glance, the nature preserve, wet with blood and biting betrayal, sent memory rushing to the fore.

"For us, there's tomorrow," Christopher had said.

Jack's thoughts slowed. His skin flushed.

Clare smiled in his head and winked and repeated her mantra.

You need to know your opponent to outthink him.

Understand your enemy and you'll know his plans before he does.

Christopher had known, known that if they separated, Jill would be the one to pursue him. So he'd laid diversions, seeded a trap worthy of Clare's operational handbook, and bought time alone with Jill to incapacitate the stone cold in the killer and deliberately funnel death's decision into hands he'd already let live.

Comprehension mired down in traitorous respect.

It was difficult not to laugh and call this whole thing off as a joke just to find a way to spend a late night over beers, deliberating battlefields and scars with a worthy opponent, the way old men in parks and pubs played chess.

But no. Christopher had to die.

Jack slipped in beside his sister.

"Robert here?" he said.

She shook her head, confirming what he already knew.

He turned his shoulder toward Christopher, leaned for Jill's ear, and whispered, "Look, I know how it is with you and Clare, and I don't want to step into that. You've already pissed all over this. It's yours, right? But she wants him dead."

Jill's lips tightened.

Her finger massaged the trigger guard, but still no action.

Conflict bore down on him.

He reached for her hand to take the

weapon.

She jerked away and kept the muzzle leveled exactly where it'd been.

Christopher's expression registered the change in tone.

Jack studied the man laid out on his back, one killer fighting against two in a trap of his own making.

He'd gone to considerable effort to put his life in these crosshairs. Confident as he might have been in victory, he'd have had to consider the price of miscalculation, which meant that whatever he ultimately wanted, he wanted it badly enough to die for.

Christopher stayed focused on Jill. He said, "I get it. Really, I do. You have your mom back. Don't need me anymore. All that's left now is to clean up the threat. But I knew that before I got here. If I wanted you dead, you'd already be dead. I didn't come here to kill you any more than you wanted to kill me at the preserve."

Voice flat, Jill said, "You don't know what I want."

"Same thing I want. Same thing your brother wants."

"And now we all hold hands and sing 'Kumbaya.' "

"I've done the best I can to make my position clear. I'm not your enemy."

Jill said, "Why?"

Christopher sighed, as if the single word asked a dozen questions to which there was only one answer, and that answer was so clear the only reason she'd have asked was to play dumb, and he had no time for dumb.

He said, "For the same reason I need to talk to your mother."

"Which is?"

The sigh turned to exasperation.

"Obvious, don't you think, given what happened at the preserve?"

Jill's finger twitched, and she shook her head in slow contradiction. She said, "No. You made the no-kill decision before what happened at the preserve."

"True, but what happened there was observable, and you were a witness to it, which makes it easier to point to than trying to get you to take my word for anything."

"You're asking us to take your word right now. You — a guy whose entire skill set revolves around kidnapping and killing — want us to believe in a onetime, special just-for-you change of heart."

"Not a change of heart," he said. "A change of priorities. Killing you was never part of the contract. The Broker switched terms after you showed up, refused to pay contract fulfillment, and then stabbed me in the back. I have no personal reason to want you dead, no professional reason to want you dead, I've already fulfilled my obligations regarding your mother, and what happened after is none of my business. I'm going to zero out this balance sheet with the Broker, and your mother has what I need to find him."

"And you know that how, exactly?"

Christopher's eyes smiled like she'd offered him a long-sought-after gift.

If the circumstances hadn't been dire, if the man hadn't been one wrong word away from death, Jack would have sworn he was flirting.

Christopher said, "Let's grab coffee. I'll tell you the whole long story."

Jill said, "Doesn't matter, anyway."

"It matters."

"Not to us. Whatever you say, the fundamentals don't change. You know who we are. You know we're alive. The bounty on our heads will rise, and the temptation to collect on that will only grow."

"Not interested in the money," he said. "Not now, not ever."

Jill shrugged, as if to say words and promises were meaningless from a man in his position, but Jack saw beneath the tone and posture, saw what only someone who knew her the way he knew her would. She was struggling hard to feign indifference.

Christopher said, "Work with me to fake your death. We'll split my fee, disappear. All problems solved."

She said, "We don't need the money and can fake our own deaths. You've got nothing to offer that we can't get for ourselves."

"I offer our common enemy."

"You need us for that, not the other way around."

Jack stretched his hand over hers, and this time, she let him take the gun.

He didn't want to kill the guy any more than she did, but it had to be done. Not because Clare had said so, but because the only thing that mattered long term was keeping his family safe, and they had enough threats to worry about without the specter of someone like this hanging over their future.

Jack raised the weapon.

Christopher's gaze traveled from Jill to the handgun to Jack's face, traveled with the steady calm of a man who'd accepted death a hundred times and had no fear left to squander by arguing with fate. He said, "Killing me won't change the inevitable. Word will spread. They'll find you, and you'll end up running hard. You could use an ally, a friend. I'd like to be your friend."

Jack watched the words form, heard in them a siren's lullaby that promised belonging and brotherhood and offered kinship from another who knew what it was like to be them. He lined sights to forehead.

Christopher said, "The three of us, together, we'd be damn near invincible."

Every part of training warned against self-preserving lies. Every part of gut instinct insisted each word was truth. The strategy wheel flung through possibilities, searching for a way in which they might all walk out of this alive.

In that pause, Christopher inched toward his weapon.

His miscalculation broke the trance.

Doubt firmed into resolve.

Jack tightened his aim, and somewhere in the half blink between lineup and trigger pull, a ringtone stole finality from him.

Jill's breath hitched.

Christopher glanced toward his pocket. "It could be Robert," he said. "He's with my brother — that big guy you shot at the preserve. Rob was supposed to call if he took a turn for better or worse." He nodded toward the weapon. "At least let me know before you . . . you know."

Jill moved her hand over Jack's and nudged the muzzle toward the floor.

For her sake, for the sake of not turning a moment's reprieve into a three-way war, Jack didn't resist. Christopher kept one hand in the air, out and visible. He spread the fingers of the other wide, and, never breaking eye contact, working slowly to ensure every movement was clear and predictable, opened a snap, reached fingers into a pocket, pulled out the phone, offered it, palm forward, for inspection, and bought himself more time.

He squinted at the screen, answered, listened.

On his face bewilderment turned to confusion.

He said, "Yes."

And then, "Received."

And then, "Honored."

He pulled the phone from his ear, looked at it as if it were toxic, and stretched it toward Jill. "This call's for you," he said. "For the both of you."

CHAPTER 46

Jack
Age: 26
Location: Houston, Texas
Passport Country: USA
Names: Jason Francis White

The unexpected sucked oxygen out of the room and the unanswerable encased time in silence. Christopher held deer-in-the-headlights still, arm outstretched, phone in his palm, waiting for retrieval. Jill glanced at Jack, and Jack stared at the phone, sorting known from unknown in a rapid sequence.

Something had changed.

The call had come to Christopher's equivalent of Jill's Blackphone.

Whoever was on the other end wasn't Robert.

Probably wasn't the Broker.

Was even less likely to be Clare.

Whoever was on the other end had left Christopher authentically surprised.

A new variable had been added to the equation.

Jack said, "Take it. Put the call on speaker."

Jill plucked the phone from the outstretched hand, stepped out of Christopher's reach, swiped, tapped, and said, "Who is this?"

A male voice thick with a Slavic accent said, "London. Paris. Moscow. Rome."

She sighed. Her shoulders sagged.

Jack whispered, "What's that mean?"

She hit MUTE. "It's the kill code — a safe word. Every bounty packet has one. Gives the client a way to terminate the contract in case a sensitive situation changes or they get cold feet. Dead or alive, we get paid either way."

Jack nodded. She unmuted. Said, "Continue."

The accented voice deepened and, as if delivering an edict of life-altering consequence to an audience sure to understand its significance and be properly awed, said, "I call on behalf of Dmitry Vasiliev."

Jill cut Jack a sideways glance.

Twenty-four hours ago, that name would have meant nothing.

Clare's late-night tale had changed that.

She said, "Who's Dmitry Vasiliev?"

The question wrested control and shunted the conversation off its rails.

The voice, more restrained, said, "Your phone does not answer. You are sent photographs for introduction and connection. You must retrieve them."

Jack shrugged out of his pack.

"Blackphone," he whispered. "Get it on."

Jill unzipped the pocket and, struggling to work with one good hand, tugged the phone's Ziploc bag loose.

In that distraction, Christopher shifted another few inches toward his weapon, fast enough, subtle enough, that anyone else might have missed it.

Jack fired a round just shy of his leg.

The report thundered through empty space, shaking windows and scattering birds.

Christopher froze.

Jack searched him for a hint or tell — anything that might indicate this call had been Christopher's doing and they'd just leveled up into another round of Clare-crazy foresight and manipulation — and got nothing. He said, "That was a warning, not an accident. Next one will hurt."

Jill shoved the SIM and battery into place. She said, "We received a stand-down order. If you kill him, there'll be consequences."

Everything they did from this point on

had consequences, and consequence was a matter of degree. He said, "Any rules on maiming?"

"Kind of a gray area."

She snapped the case together and powered on for boot up.

Questions churned in the agony of the wait.

She navigated through passwords to the phone within the phone, drew a sharp inhale, and shifted the screen to where Jack could see it.

"There are pictures of you circulating now," Clare had said. "Soon enough there'll be seekers looking your direction."

The caller had sent four images. The first two were a series of his and Jill's faces — photos that had been taken at the preserve, enlarged, and cropped. They were blurry, but the sibling connection and the resemblance to Clare would be unmistakable to anyone who'd known her when she was younger. The next two were digital copies of physical photographs that had been manhandled by time: a younger Clare with a man her age seated on a couch in a room distinctly old East Bloc, neither of them fully smiling but bodies close enough to be intimate, and Clare again on the grass in the warm outdoors with the same man and the same intimacy. Clare before their earliest memories, a Clare they'd never seen before. A Clare who almost seemed happy and a man he recognized from the one picture Clare had shown them of their father when they were younger.

Maria Catalina and Dmitry. CIA and KGB.

Jack wanted to study their faces, wanted to let history swallow him, but couldn't afford the distraction.

Jill said, "Photos received."

The caller said, "Dmitry Vasiliev requests honor agreement, immediate payment for immediate contract termination."

Jill muted the call and answered the question before Jack could ask it. "The contract requires me to stand down on a kill-code order," she said. "Asking for an honor agreement means he's willing to take my word as bond and pay immediately, instead of waiting to close escrow through the Broker."

Inside Jack's head the strategy wheel spun.

For twenty-six years Clare had been searching for the father of her children, haunted by not knowing if he was dead or alive, wanting to understand what had happened in the days after she left Moscow and what had happened to him since. Each time she'd surfaced for answers, she'd faced capture or death. And now, out of the blue, someone using their father's name had made direct contact and offered bona fides through the man who'd been contracted to kill them.

This was rolling right off the deep end into the twilight zone.

To Christopher, Jack said, "What'd he say when you answered?"

"Same as to you. Gave me the kill code and asked for an honor agreement."

"No, after that. His exact words."

Christopher pitched his voice into an imitation of the accent and doused the syntax with sarcasm. "We do not call for you. We call for your targets. Transfer the phone to your targets please."

Jack held his stance, muzzle leveled, eyes seeing but not.

Two separate contracts, two separate kill codes.

There was no way, in any form of logic or insanity, that a single client had initiated both contracts. But both kill codes had arrived from a single source.

That was wrong.

To obtain both kill codes, the caller either worked with the Broker, held power over him, or had hacked into the Broker's system to work against him. Without knowing which, it was impossible to predict the traps ahead or the tangents each decision could take. He needed time to think, to pace, to puzzle through, and didn't have that luxury.

The voice said, "Please confirm contract termination."

To Jill, Jack said, "You have leverage. Get more."

Jill unmuted. She said, "Confirmation pending. Contract isn't yours. Who are you, and what do you want?"

The voice softened and, perhaps sensing resistance and the likelihood that events were about to scatter out of control, the man spoke plainly, without posturing or pretense. "On behalf of Dmitry Vasiliev, I bring news of your father," he said. "He wishes to meet you. Arrangements are made for your travel but can proceed only upon contract termination."

News of your father.

Can proceed only upon contract termination.

Jack's brain overheated, burning the span between reason and reality.

This call, the baited name-dropping and the invitation to travel, the elaborate extension of the shit storm that arose whenever Clare crawled out of hiding, was one thing. But raising the specter of a father he'd never known as a temptation into that trap? That crossed out of business into a deep and personal violation.

He fought off anger, brushed aside distraction, and grabbed hold of facts.

He didn't care about the money.

He didn't care about the contract.

He cared about protecting his family for the long term, and he cared about securing answers to the issue of Dmitry Vasiliev.

He couldn't have one with Christopher alive.

He couldn't have the other with Christopher dead.

The why of it all churned in a cauldron of trap-seeking, self-preserving suspicion.

Clare's voice was in his head.

You've got seconds, John. Act or die.

Instinct. Your gut knows.

You don't have time for perfection.

Congratulations. You're dead from a self-inflicted dumb-thought wound.

Information shifted and reordered.

Someone who knew of the connection between Dmitry and Clare, someone who knew she'd been pregnant, knew she'd given birth, someone who knew those kids were players and targets in a bounty war had just run out into the middle of the battlefield offering a crap load of money and motivation for a cease-fire.

The silence of indecision drew out into something long and uncomfortable, and Jack understood.

This was a forced truce to avoid the complications of a potential blood feud.

Jill backed out of the images and thumbed the screen.

"Two Lufthansa tickets. Dallas–Frankfurt–Berlin," she said. Her color drained. She looked up, and her eyes met his. "Last name Lefevre on both of them."

Pieces that shouldn't have fit slipped into place.

Lefevre.

Possibilities replaced the past to make sense of the present.

Clare claimed Dmitry had gotten her out of Moscow and then abandoned her. "As favor or manipulation," she'd said, "I still don't know." Maybe he'd done neither. Maybe he'd been delayed getting to Switzerland and had arrived to find her gone. Like Clare, he'd been a foot soldier in a war of ideology, low enough in the hierarchy that he might not have even known she'd kept coming back to find him.

An alternative time line formed, a parallel story to the one Clare had told.

Dmitry had tracked her to France.

He'd found their birth certificates.

He'd searched for her and searched for his children and found a dead trail, because those names had died the month after Clare had given birth. And in the years that she'd been searching, he'd been searching, too.

She'd been off radar a long time. Long enough that, as she'd said, agencies had changed hands and years had ravaged memories, enough time for Dmitry — whoever he really was, whomever he really worked for — to move up the chain of command, to be in a position of power that allowed him to act on his own, a position powerful enough that when the pictures from the preserve came calling and he saw the familial connection, he was able to step beyond his government's official position on Clare and intervene to stop the bloodshed and keep his children alive.

Jill, still scrolling, said, "Hotel reservations in Berlin four days from now."

Somewhere in the hazy distance, the voice said, "Please confirm."

Jack couldn't rule out wishful thinking.

The alternative, parallel story was a best guess.

But he wanted to know, needed to know, and the only way to sort truth from lie was to fling headlong into the mix. He signaled the go-ahead.

Jill said, "Accepted. Contract termination confirmed."

"Payment will transfer now. Next photographs will arrive."

Jill scrolled and tapped and shifted the screen toward Jack again.

A new set of images showed a flooded machine room where half-submerged bodies bled out into rust-colored water, a visual answer to how Clare had escaped last night, if ever he'd bothered to ask.

The voice said, "Regards to Maria Catalina."

The line went dead.

Silence filled the room.

Jill let out a long, slow exhale, and they stood there, he and his sister, facing the man whom they'd intended to kill and who, in turn, had been hired to kill them.

Broken things twisted and creaked in the vacuum.

Laden trucks rumbled in the far distance.

Jack said, "What happens if you renege on contract terms and kill him anyway?"

Jill's gaze tracked from him to the gun to Christopher.

"Bounty goes out on me, maybe both of us," she said. "Not that there isn't one already. If we're cool with that, it really becomes more a question of this. . . ."

She offered him Christopher's phone.

Jack took the device and pondered the weight it represented. To renege on the contract meant walking away from the possibility of answers.

He said, "Check your account. See if the agreement's legit."

Jill's thumb worked the Blackphone screen.

Jack tossed Christopher his phone back. "Open your ledger," he said. "I want to see."

Christopher moved to sit. Jack waved him back down with the gun.

The silence bore down with tangible heaviness.

A minute passed, two, five. Finally, Jill said, "Fully funded."

Christopher said, "Same."

And with that there was nothing but a hole of emptiness where action had been. They were done here, done with Christopher, done with running, one minute high on adrenaline and the next at a sudden stop.

The absence felt like a cheap hit, felt like getting robbed. Jack deflated. He was tired, uselessly tired.

The final words of the phone call rang in his ears.

Regards to Maria Catalina.

He'd have passed on the message to Clare if he'd had any way to contact her.

She'd refused to tell them where she headed — for their own protection, she'd said. In that, some things would never change. She was still Clare, still running. She was invisible and truly, utterly alone, and that was exactly what she wanted.

Christopher, on the floor, tucked the phone away with the slow cautious stretch of a man testing the ice of a recently frozen lake.

Jack watched but didn't react.

Christopher pulled himself to his feet, limped across the room, and retrieved his rifle. He paused there and glanced back. He said, "I'd twitch at you now just to mess with you if I didn't think that'd be enough for you to put a few holes in me."

Jack snorted. He almost smiled.

The almost smile faded to an internal sigh.

He'd gone into finding Clare adamant against reverting to the way things had been before, fully intent on returning to a shadowed half-life in a world that wasn't built for people like him. In the end he'd have both and he'd have neither.

There was no job to quit.

No one he cared about enough to call and say good-bye.

Nothing in his apartment he would miss if he never came back to get it.

He and Jill would be on that flight to Frankfurt.

They'd rendezvous in Berlin and start again on the hunt for answers that Clare had written off as lost just a few hours earlier. He had no idea what would come between here and there or what would happen after, but wherever they went or whatever they did, they'd never return to life as it'd been a week ago.

Maybe that was the silver lining, and maybe that was hope.

Jill pinched his cheek, and he batted her away.

Christopher said, "My offer's still on the table. Put me in contact with your mother, get me what she knows about the Broker, and I'll split my payout fifty-fifty."

Jack said, "You want the Broker dead, you're going to have to get in line."

"That's why she's not with you?"

Jill chuffed, snorted, and broke into an exhaustion-filled laugh.

Christopher's expression darkened.

Jack sighed on the inside. His sister had gotten her wish, hadn't had to execute the guy or watch her brother do it, and now that she wasn't trying to kill him, she was back to messing things up. He said, "Our mom's complicated. You'd have to have lived our life to get why the question was funny, but yeah, as far as we know, she's gone after him."

"You know where?"

"Wouldn't tell you if I did."

"She went after him on her own?"

Jack nodded.

"There's a good chance she'll fail."

He nodded again.

There *was* that chance, had always been that chance, and if it happened, the wee morning hours they'd shared with her would be the last. He'd have no opportunity for good-bye and no way to continue building the bridge she'd begun, but that had been the subtext of his entire childhood. Clare had left five dozen times, and even when they were certain it would be the last, she always returned.

He counted on that now.

He said, "She might, but her going it alone is the best shot you have at getting the job done. You'd have to know her to understand."

Christopher hoisted his gear and limped toward the stairwell. "I do know her," he said. "Just wish the circumstances had been different." He paused a few feet from where they stood. A shy smile crossed his face. He glanced toward the windows and then back at Jill.

He said, "Still have that long story to tell. You wanna get coffee?"

CHAPTER 47

Clare

Age: 54
Location: On the Louisiana Gulf Coast
Passport Country: Paperless
Names: Nameless

He was Boris Popov. William Mason.
Amaud Durand. He was Russian, American,
French. He was a dozen faces and a hundred legends, none of which mattered,
because for people like him, like her, names
were artifacts, constructs, clothing tried on
for size, worn, shed, and sometimes washed
and reused.

Tonight she'd find him as Alan Henry, but
she knew him for what he really was.

She was in Louisiana waters now, close
and closing in, riding low in a boat borrowed from a private dock in Baytown —
not so much a boat as a dinghy — loaded
with stolen jerricans and syphoned fuel.
She'd followed the coast from late evening

into the deep night black, guided by dwindling city light and winking shore light, engine vibrating from tiller down through her body while the rhythmic rise and fall soothed a week of deprivation and lulled her dangerously close to sleep.

Mental movies walked her through the labyrinth of the coming confrontation and warded off exhaustion in the long hours the same way they'd warded off insanity during times of captivity.

Tonight she'd finish what she should have finished long ago.

Tonight she'd ensure the Broker of Death faced a death of his own.

Rumors as to who he was and how to find him had existed since before she knew him as Boris. Speculation had only grown wilder as turbulence hit the USSR and the satellite states broke away and his influence increased.

Those who weren't inclined toward superstition placed him in Brussels.

She knew better.

Raymond Chance hadn't settled an hour's drive north of Lake Charles by coincidence any more than she'd been the only one to carry a decades-long grudge.

She'd pushed hard in the months after the twins were born to prove what she'd instinctively known about the events that had led to her leaving Moscow. The hunt had guided her to Raymond, and through him, she'd learned just how long she'd been compromised. The agency had known about Boris and had let her float, had sacrificed her to maintain an illusion of ignorance in their pursuit of a more valuable target.

Her little stunt with the recording had done nothing but speed up the inevitable.

Boris had seen the writing on the wall, had cut deals, and had slipped their grasp.

Ray, working in Prague, had been part of the fallout, just one of so many casualties. She'd reached him before his killers, had covered him, staged his death, given him a rebirth, and in exchange, had gained loyalty and kinship.

It had taken them seven years of trial and error and tensely close calls to find their quarry, and three more after that to circle surveillance tightly enough to monitor movement, document vulnerability, and ensure they wouldn't lose him.

Ten years they'd worked, until they'd held imminent death in their hands.

She could have killed him in numerous ways over numerous days and hadn't. Not because she hated him less, but because those years had allowed her to understand that Boris served them all better alive. He was the devil they knew — knew how to find, knew how he worked and the games he played, knew where they fit inside those games — and that knowledge had provided a measure of safety and allowed them to sidestep traps and pitfalls they might otherwise have fallen into.

His death would have created a vacuum.

Others far worse would've risen to take his place.

She'd have been content to let him die of sickness and old age if he'd been smart enough to simply broker her capture, as he should have. But no, he'd had to meddle, had to turn things personal. He'd taken Ray. He'd taken her heart. He'd threatened her children. He'd miscalculated and cornered an animal meaner than he was.

GPS guided her into the cove she'd travel tested on far too many bitter nights, and there, under a clouded quarter moon, she beached the dinghy and slogged through high-tide cordgrass for dry ground. She turned east, trudging around marshes and bald cypress groves, walking three miles as the crow flew, until she reached the clearing that marked the boundary of the coastal estate, home of the recluse who pulled the world's puppet strings.

The stone facade loomed large in the moonlight, upper-floor windows dark and only a few lights burning in the grand foyer and bottom right, thirty thousand square feet of dark and gloomy haunted house rising from the midnight foggy ground in a paranoid dream of interconnected halls and rooms and hidden passageways.

Unseen below the surface was that much more.

So many nights she'd stood here, observing from beyond.

So many days she'd watched and re-watched rare footage taken from inside.

Loss welled up, fueling the fire of retribution that had until now stayed muted.

Raymond should have been here. He was the one who'd studied the architectural drawings, the one who'd kept up with changes as they were made.

They'd never expected that he'd be the first one Boris got to.

That was her failing.

One ring to warn him that she was preparing to surface again.

He'd known what that meant and had chosen to stay, but he'd have been better off if she'd never called at all.

She continued forward, hands free and pockets empty.

Under other circumstances she might have scaled the fence, skirted the dogs and the armed foot patrol, bypassed the alarms, and let herself in.

Tonight called for none of that.

Tonight she'd walk through the front door.

Muck and weeds turned into manicured lawn, and manicured lawn led to tree-lined gravel road. She walked that road for the gate and from there could see the man inside the guard shack, feet up on the small desk, chin on his chest, while the colors of a small television danced across his sleeping face. In the dark, without headlights, she made none of the impression a vehicle would have made.

He didn't wake on his own, and she found no need to disturb him.

Hand over fist, boots to niche after niche, she scaled the wrought-iron gate, dropped down to the other side and, knee to the ground, waited for the loping rattle of dog tags and the thud of boots on patrol.

Sounds from the marsh filled the night.

Shadows in her peripheral vision charged toward her.

She spread her fingers and stretched her arms wide, allowing the breeze to catch her body's fragrance and carry it on. The shadows slowed.

She closed her eyes and welcomed them.

All those nights watching from the outside had allowed her to learn the dogs and feed them well. She knew their names, their individual quirks, had watched them grow and age. Noses touched her skin. Muscle bumped her body.

She ran her fingers along coarse Akita fur, bitter over the callous loss of her own pack leader. She missed Mack, loyal protector and constant companion, as much as she missed Ray, and she'd seen to it that the man who shot him had bled out and died that night, but retribution couldn't put air back into the lungs of the lifeless.

Raymond was gone. Mack was gone.

There was no evening the score when the dead stayed just as dead.

She waited until the pack lost interest, watched as the fog took them back to shadow, then stood and, wary of men on patrol, who seemed strangely absent, continued for the wide double doors. Hand against warm metal, she tested the latch.

Heavy wood on silent hinges opened to marble floors and cooler air.

The ravage of time filled her nostrils — wood polish and wax, and cleaning chemicals that did little to mask the must and mold, all riding on the stale filtration of overworked air-conditioning. No alarm sounded, but she knew well enough there'd been an alarm.

This wasn't the security of a man hiding from alphabet agencies the way she'd been hiding for the past half century. The men who ran the world knew where to find him, just as they'd known in Moscow and before Moscow and after Moscow. They'd used him then and were using him now, brokering out what they couldn't afford to have traced back to them, letting others sully their souls to keep their own hands clean.

He held too much collateral to worry about the powerful coming for him.

No, this monstrosity had been built to hide him from those he'd personally betrayed and to protect him from those who'd kill to take his place. Boris, in the control room, encased in concrete and behind bombproof doors, like a nesting alien lifeform whose tentacles reached into every room and hallway, knew she'd come.

She slipped into the circular foyer.

A low-light chandelier hung thirty feet above, and a polished staircase swept in a wide, majestic curve to the second floor and to doors that led nowhere. Hallways branched off right and left into darkened holes framed by sideboards bearing floral arrangements in three-foot vases. An ice pick rested beside the nearest vase, its tip pointing to the right, the way a compass needle pointed north.

Boris might as well have carved *welcome* into the sideboard lacquer, offered her a weapon, and begged her to take it. Her fingers hovered over the handle.

Laughter lilted through the foyer, crazy carnival-horror-house laughter, so faint and multidirectional, it might have been inside her head.

Footsteps pattered somewhere on the upper floor, a single set of steps, lonely and eerie in a house that should have had multiple servants and guards and far more ambient noise. Her fist closed around the ice pick.

The footsteps stopped.

She eyed the hallways and weighed them against the stairs. The ice-pick compass pointed in the same direction from which she'd seen light outside.

Debate marched its way through a multitude of choices.

She pulled her hand away, leaving the weapon as she'd found it and, hands twitching, senses on overdrive, turned out of the grand foyer into a mirror-lined hallway. Her image warped and stretched, a haunting shadow in the dark, and she dragged her fingers along the glass, smudging spotless mirrors, counting the seams between them.

Laughter and madness followed, bringing cliché to life.

She focused on the light at the end. The laughter grew louder and more frantic, echoing in a dizzying circle.

Laser pointers on the ceiling tracked her, projecting red dots on her chest, beams bouncing in endless reflection from mirror to mirror. A CCTV camera shifted on a robotic arm, moving with the pointers — no, not pointers, but sights . . . and not a camera, but a magnetometer.

She understood the ice pick. Understood the footsteps. A gun, a knife, a watch — anything metal — would have been enough to trigger the magnetometer that guided the sights.

Boris had known she'd come empty handed and had provided her a weapon to trigger the onslaught.

The mirrored passageway ended in a T.

The laughter stopped, leaving a sudden, jarring silence.

The sound of Brahms rose slowly from the left, and she stood motionless, listening. Over a quarter century since she'd last touched or heard the concerto, and still, she knew the music note by note, as her fingers had known it once.

This was Dmitry's music.

This was Boris taunting her, predator toying with its food before the kill.

She let go of logic and strategy, turned into the haunting and, fingers dragging against the wall as they had against the mirrors, followed the melody.

The narrow hall curved past unmarked doors.

Her fingers counted the space between ridges and interpreted them as placeholders that could be removed or shifted to close halls, open rooms, and reconfigure the floor plan by the push of a button.

She rounded another corner.

The passage dead-ended at a carpeted media room.

Empty leather entertainment chairs provided auditorium seating for twelve, and a theater screen played a live recording of a concert performance, which explained the music. She scanned the ceiling, the walls.

This room hadn't existed when she last saw the building plans.

She headed for the far wall, tracing her fingers across leather seat backs, and once there, ran them along the wood paneling until she felt the outline of a door against the molding.

The screen flickered.

The music shut off.

A face in shadow replaced the performance.

A voice, larger than life, said, "I'd expected you sooner. Years sooner."

Searching out the hidden door, she said, "Me? Or just any one of us?"

"Any one of you, I suppose, though I'd always hoped it would be you."

"There are less painful ways to commit suicide."

Boris choked down a laugh made garish by its mechanical delivery. "I'll give you a choice," he said. "Turn back the way you came, allow my men to take you into custody, and maybe you'll live."

"Not much of a choice."

"Continue this mad quest of yours, and you'll most certainly die."

She accepted the truth of the odds, and returned to tracing the door.

"The warning is a favor," he said. "For old times' sake."

Her fingers found the pressure point.

She said, "That's your cost to bear, not mine."

"You won't win. Whatever advantages you think you have, they're smoke and mirrors.

You will lose, and you will die. Those are the issues you should consider."

She nudged the panel. The door released and opened inward, and she stepped through the doorway into a tight, clinically bright between-the-walls passageway just wide enough to fit her. The panel door shut behind her back. A lock clicked.

The media room went silent, and hallway ends that had been open swung closed, shutting her into a box smaller than the vault she'd escaped from on the ship.

Claustrophobia filled her in the narrow space.

Laughter soared above her, around her, crazy, manic laughter.

"Wrong choice, Catherine," the voice said. "You're so pathetically easy to manipulate, always have been. Least you could have done is make your death a challenge."

The lights went out, and darkness swallowed her, complete and wholly black.

Time slowed. Memories yanked control of instinct and shoved her to the floor. Live fire screamed overhead, too steady and too ignorant of her position to be human controlled. She belly crawled through the pitch black in a race for the endcap.

The only way to win, to reach him, was through the back side of the maze, and the only way through the maze was to escape a trap he didn't expect her to survive.

That was the difference between manipulation and strategy.

CHAPTER 48

Clare

Age: 54

Location: Outside Lake Charles, Louisiana

Passport Country: Paperless

Names: Nameless

The voice boomed in like thunder over the weaponized chatter. Laughter picked up again, manic with glee. His words bounced round her brain.

So pathetically easy to manipulate.

She blocked him out, shut down emotion, shut down anything other than the objective at hand, just as she'd shut down to get through the years.

Her knuckles collided with a solid frame.

She flipped feet to the wall, pounded boot heels forward into the dark, kick after kick in a fight to break through before the weapons shifted and found her on the floor.

Drywall gave way between framing studs.

Wrong choice. Wrong choice. Wrong choice.

The whine of robotic arms crawled up her skin: weapons repositioning.

A gap opened between studs, large enough to wedge an arm and shoulder through, not wide enough to escape. She climbed, boots and palms against the narrow passage walls, heart thumping, muscles straining to hold her flush to the ceiling.

Bullets riddled the spot where she'd been.

She blessed Boris, blessed his lying, traitorous legacy.

The man who'd double-dealt and back-stabbed every person he'd come in contact with couldn't imagine a world in which others didn't do the same to him. Paranoid, he limited human contact, relying on technology to replace the henchman's hands.

Had there been a person behind the trigger, she'd have been long dead.

The shooting stopped.

She dropped to the floor and threw her shoulder into the gap between studs.

Sand bled from life's hourglass.

Behind her back, the whine started again. This time she had no way to predict in which direction the bullets would fly. The gap widened. She wedged her torso between the studs, forced the framing loose, and tumbled over a metal arm that had guided the end wall into place.

Rounds punched drywall, passed through the gap, passed through the wall.

She rolled to the side, hands over her ears, face tucked in against splinters and shrapnel. Laughter rose above deafness and picked up speed.

She swiveled to kick against the unfinished framing at her back, broke through, pushed into a crawl space, and squeezed toward the hydraulic arm. She traced her fingers over joints and bolts, found the release, and dismounted the Tavor SAR that should have killed her. Compact and agile, the fully automatic short-barreled rifle would have been perfect for tight-quarter protection if not for the hundred-round magazine protruding awkwardly from its body. She checked the ammunition.

Five rounds left.

She racked the charging handle, confirmed the chamber was empty, and snapped the high-capacity magazine back into place. Stock to her shoulder, she pushed back through the gap and, rat in a warren, re-entered the maze's second layer.

No gunfire. No footsteps.

Laughter turned into screams of nightmares and torture.

Lights switched on and off in motion sickness–inducing bursts.

She oriented to the map in her head, gauged distance by the seams and panels she'd counted to get to the media room, and moved corner to corner, hallway to hallway, in a web of walls designed to provoke panic, claustrophobia, and desperation, up a floor, down again, all the while screaming overlapped laughter that rose louder and more frantic.

She almost missed the footsteps.

There were two of them tracking her, moving faster than she was, jumping ahead and behind in a way that defied physics. With enough time, she could find the hidden doors and floor traps, but under these circumstances that would be a time-wasting diversion.

The walls, like the screaming and the lights and the laughter, were illusions.

She paused at a hallway junction, reversed with a slow backward count, flipped the rifle, and slammed the butt into the wall. Sheetrock caved, as it had in the passageway.

In response, footsteps pounded from the left and right, the sound of urgency and intervention moving fast and closing in.

Boris hadn't expected her to breach the second maze.

They'd be armed. She had only five

rounds, couldn't spare even one, and couldn't risk engagement in a kill zone. Beat against beat, she raced them in her assault against the wall, shoved through, and stepped out of the maze onto deep carpet.

She knew where she was now, knew how to find what she needed.

Every beast had a soft side, and this fortress, too, had an underbelly.

She ran along the hallway, past an empty library, skidded into a lifeless kitchen, and kept going out the rear, taking each turn according to the diagrams laid down by memory.

Footsteps followed above her head.

She reached the utility room and slipped inside to a temperature several degrees warmer. Shelving played host to computer servers, and fans kept the air moving. At the far end, set into the wall and leading to the outdoors, were the metal boxes she'd come for. She opened the second one and flipped the breakers, grabbed the nearest shelf, braced a foot against its leg, and tipped it toward the floor.

Gravity and momentum took over.

The servers slid forward until their power cords gave, and metal and plastic hit tile in a cacophony of dents and splinters, killing the camera feeds that Boris depended upon for sight.

Radio chatter filtered in to her from the hallway — three, possibly four, men communicating with their boss. They called to her by name.

"Maria Catalina."

"Catherine."

"Karen."

They ordered her out. She moved backward to the first metal box, rested the blade of her hand against a row of breakers, squeezed between metal filing cabinet and wall, and waited for them.

Bullets punched through the walls and door.

Seconds passed. The door opened.

She shoved the breakers. The world went dark.

She vaulted up onto the servers, counting precious seconds, and slid feetfirst into the doorway. Her boots connected with a body. Breath expulsed.

Muzzle flashes rolled into an arc of short burst fire.

She slammed the Tavor SAR into the enemy, hit after hit of adrenaline and anger until he went limp, and she tumbled beside him, and rolled his body on top of her.

The emergency system kicked on.

Soft LED running lights turned night into

dawn, and with the light, each body in the hallway formed a shadow. Hand on his rifle, fingers on his fingers, she pressed the trigger, firing burst after burst until the magazine emptied.

One went down. The other two disappeared behind corners.

Predictable and foolish they'd put themselves between her and the passage that led to the underground bunker, led to Boris. She shoved out from beneath deadweight and rushed in the opposite direction, guided by light running off the same emergency system that would prevent unauthorized access to the bunker.

Up the hallway, down a corridor, down a stairwell she went, past the laundry room where the LED lights stopped, into darkness, past water heaters and propane pipes for the workroom where underground cables entered the building from an off-site generator and fed power to the main electric panel. She traced the wall, searching beyond power tools and hand tools and between gardening tools, found the fire extinguisher, then the axe. And she crawled, following concrete and brick beneath workbenches, until she reached the conduit sleeve and she traced the rubber up to the electrical panel. The sound of pursuit rose behind her.

She measured distance in the dark, torso to brick, shoulders to conduit and, with all she'd lost at the Broker's hand crushing in, stepped aside and swung her soul into the sleeve.

The blade severed rubber and copper, throwing sparks.

The axe head chunked into brick.

On the edge of awareness, between hit and separation, she felt a twinge of power and let go. Scope sights cast scattered red beams into the room.

She grabbed the fire extinguisher and slipped behind a tool table.

Bullets and noise and gunpowder filled the air, feeding adrenaline and instinct. Darkness embraced her, darkness her friend, translating sound and vibration into mental images, the same way it had in the ship's dank hellhole. She pulled the pin.

The noise paused. She went up over the tool chest and onto the table, senses long honed for the dark, spraying foam, gumming scopes, clogging night vision, and turning the floor slick. Order turned into chaos, and silence into grunts, and she followed those grunts with the extinguisher's heel, off the table and into faces. Quiet returned.

She stood, lungs heaving, arms worthless.

She waited for movement and, when there was none, dropped to her knees.

Living rough on the land had kept her tough, she'd kept herself limber, stayed in shape, but this was so much harder than it'd been twenty years back.

Her fingers roamed over shirts and collars until she found the chain that would lead her to Boris. She yanked metal off neck, grabbed shoulders, and inched the guy farther into the workroom.

She splayed his right arm out wide, retrieved the axe.

Blade to his limb, she swung.

Wrist severed from arm.

Her fingers gripped fingers.

She carried key and amputated hand turn by turn back the way she'd come, and down to the cinder-block passage and the creeping ambience of soft running lights that brightened as she progressed, lights powered by the same backup batteries within the bunker that ran its ventilation and door locks.

In twenty hours they'd fail.

Steel doors and hydraulic locks were better protection than hired hands, but without intervention from inside or from without, Boris would be buried alive.

He was old and frail but not so far gone

into paranoia that he'd risk turning his safe room into a mausoleum. The fail-safe was keyed for a scenario like this.

She placed the severed hand to the digital pad, and the circular key into the fitted slot.

If she'd needed eyes for an iris scan, she'd have taken his head.

The hydraulic system pulled the foot-deep door into its recess.

She waited, allowing time and the unknown to raise questions and heighten tension on the other side. The minutes passed in silence: one, three, five.

Boris said, "You're a miserable coward, Catherine." The words came out ragged and whispered, without any of the monotone vigor bestowed by computerized speech. "Your old bosses and friends would laugh if they saw you now."

She leaned against the wall, fiddled with her nails, and let time march on.

He railed again. "You're weak, always have been, always will be. The new generation, those fools that believe in your fairy tale, they'd kill you in disappointment if they knew what you really were and had become."

She closed her eyes and rested.

He said, "Come into the light, where I can see you." Desperation seeped into his tone.

"You're afraid of an old man and shadows."

She slipped the severed hand around the door as if it was her own.

Suppressed reports responded.

She counted and then peeked around the doorframe.

Boris sat in a wheelchair ten feet in, blanket over his lap, darkened monitors around him, skin ghastly in the emergency green–tinged glow. She tossed the hand in his direction, waited until the shooting stopped, and moved into the room.

Aged, arthritic fingers swapped one magazine for another but struggled to pull back the slide. She pumped a single round into his shooting arm.

His body jerked.

He switched the weapon to his other hand and rested his fist on his knee to steady the tremors. The muzzle followed her.

She put a bullet in his other arm.

The gun dropped and clattered to the floor. His lip curled. "You're a disappointment," he said. The sound formed as much through the hole near his throat as his mouth. "I expected more from you."

She ripped the blanket from his lap and scanned atrophied limbs.

The shock of age washed over her. Boris was seventy-five, maybe, should have had another decade or more of decent health. Fallow color and hairless skin spoke of a body being destroyed from the inside out. She'd lost track of the men and women she'd deliberately targeted in this life of blood and death, but no matter what else those enemies had been, they'd been vibrant and strong, and she'd done herself, her children, the world a favor by ensuring they were gone. He was a corpse too bitter to die.

His shoulders heaved. He choked on saliva.

"Well, here you are," he said. "Do what you came for. Get it over with."

She said, "Where are the rest of your men?"

The hand in his lap waved dismissively from the wrist. He said, "Lost, stumbling about in the dark."

She ignored his words and watched his fingers inch down the outside of his thigh. "Don't," she said.

"Or what? You'll kill me?"

He moved faster than his frailty warranted.

She kicked his knee. The chair tipped sideways. The weapon beneath his leg skittered under the desk. She knelt and studied him.

Drool rolled down from the corner of his mouth. He choked again. "You've always been slow," he said. "Sentimental."

"You shouldn't have meddled."

"Oh, that's it, then? This is because I meddled? You're stupider than I gave you credit for." He laughed, and dragged in a rattling breath. "Dmitry never existed," he said. "The boy was a fabrication, a psychological ruse that CIA analysts fell over themselves to court, and you, dumb bitch, fell for him even harder."

She patted Boris's cheek, tugged the phone out from his jacket pocket, and plucked his dangling hand from across his lap. He watched, slack-jawed, confusion creeping across his face, as she pressed his thumb to the screen to unlock it.

She'd known the truth about Dmitry even before the trail led her to Raymond — the truth insofar as Dmitry, the student, had been nothing more than a KGB legend — but there'd been a living flesh-and-blood man behind that legend. Whatever his name, whoever he was, she'd laughed with him, learned with him, and had eventually borne his children. *That* Dmitry had existed. *That* Dmitry had vanished. *That* Dmitry may have even loved her. And whenever she surfaced to find *that* Dmitry, killers came

509

hunting. Boris said, "Stupid whore. The past doesn't forget. Not after a year. Not after twenty." His mouth curved in the sneer of triumphant gloating. "Word of your sighting started a bidding frenzy. You should have stayed in whatever hole you crawled out of."

She said, "Maybe."

His sneer faded slightly.

She said, "More than fifteen years, I've watched you. Watched you build this place, hired the architects who drew your plans and the contractors who put in your wiring, tracked the women who've shared your bed." She glanced at his legs. "When you still had a bed." She put the muzzle to his chest. "You shouldn't have meddled."

He mustered a shrug. "I'm old. Sick. Tired. I die laughing." The sneer returned. "I die knowing you're a pathetic fool still pining for a man who wants you dead."

The words slowed between his mouth and her ears.

Clarity rushed in, clean and cold.

Boris mistook that precision for pain.

His smugness thickened, and widened into a smile. "Yes," he said. "Your precious *Dmitry* was the one to outbid *all* the others."

Relief filled her lungs, and she inhaled the sweet, sweet stench of betrayal's victory. Of all the facts she'd held, and all the hopes she'd hoped, this was more than hope had ever granted, more than in this ghoulish hell, more than in all the grueling years when every search for answers returned as a killing card.

The kids had come first. They'd always come first.

For them she'd waited, biding her time as they grew, holding off until they no longer needed her, and longer still, until they no longer wanted her, long enough that she no longer had the time or connections to begin again on her own. So she'd sold information on her location and brought hunters to her door, had let the past take her, knowing that those who'd sought her would provide the quickest starting path toward those she sought, and that if she died in that pursuit, she'd die with the peace of knowing that what she loved most was safe and hidden forever. That had been the plan, anyway, until Boris's surrogates had placed pictures of her children in her hands and she'd abandoned hope of finding answers, but in that abandonment, Boris had gifted a finish beyond hope.

Your precious Dmitry was the one to outbid all the others.

Perhaps Boris really did think her *that* stupid.

If Dmitry had wanted her dead, the contractors would have come to kill, not to exfiltrate. No matter what else Dmitry had planned, he'd outbid the others to keep her alive. The relief of knowing didn't erase twenty-seven years of running and raised more questions than answers, but it answered *the* question.

She rolled a chair to the desk and sat, gun on her lap, muzzle pointed toward the old man. She'd cut the power and, in so doing, had cut access to the Internet, his archives, and the brokerage system, but his phone still provided all of that.

Her fingers scrolled and tapped.

He watched her in silence, and his expression shifted, confusion transforming to understanding, and understanding to anger. Anger told her that he'd finally grasped what had just happened, that she hadn't come to kill him, and that in his wrong belief, he'd inadvertently given her what she wanted — that he'd been the one manipulated, not her.

He said, "What are you doing?"

She didn't look at him. "Exactly what you think."

She'd come for answers. She'd come to protect her children.

Karen. Maria Catalina. Catherine. Clare.

Spy. Thief. Mother. Killer.

She was everyone and no one.

She'd paid for hits under one legend and had been the assassin from others. She'd completed missions, real and imagined. She knew his operation from both sides, and now she controlled the back end. She transferred money from his brokerage accounts to hers, used his phone to log in to her own private server, uploaded a pending dossier that had been updated over the course of a decade, and established a fully funded contract.

She accessed the full associate list from his account.

To killers one and all, she sent the link.

Target: Henry, Alan. Location: Lake Charles, Louisiana.

All-call, no confirmation, no check-in.

Eighteen million. Upon proof, winner takes all.

The assassins would come, from all over the world they'd come, professionals and wild cards alike, hurrying in a race against each other and in a race against time.

They'd kill each other to kill him.

There'd be casualties, so many casualties, in the clawing, scraping fight for the money. And in death, Boris would provide a measure of life.

Others far worse would rise to take his place.

And because she'd surfaced and because her children were now known, the past would come seeking revenge. But there'd be fewer killers left to fill the contracts, and this bunker, and the bloodbath to follow, would raise the cost of doing business and would stand as a permanent warning to anyone foolhardy enough to accept the challenge.

She pocketed his phone and knelt to look at him one last time.

He reached for her. She backed away.

Fear crept over his face like shadows up a wall.

He said, "You're leaving."

"You'll have company soon enough. You've paid well. It shouldn't take long."

Boot steps echoed down the cinder-block hall, someone running with the intensity of a man late for work. Boris hadn't been lying about having more men in the house.

She stood, hefted the SAR, three final rounds in the magazine, and turned and faced the door.

CHAPTER 49

Holden
Age: 32
Location: Spring, Texas
Passport Country: Canada
Names: Troy Martin Holden

He stood at the foot of Baxter's bed, equipment and weapons at his feet, toothpick in his mouth, grinding scattered thoughts and possibilities into pulp. The IV bag continued its steady hydration drip. Heavy curtains blocked streetlight and security light, and the air conditioner's hum held the room in reverent stillness, but optimistic hope had displaced the supplicant's pain and pleading.

He was at twenty-four hours, nearly to the minute, since first heading out in search of closure. He'd chased and found his ghosts. Revenge would have to wait.

Robert sat in the chair beside the bed, body language expectant, waiting for answers to unasked questions.

The kid had been head back, mouth slack, sleeping like the dead, when Holden had walked in, and woken somewhere between checking Baxter's vitals and checking his bandages. The kid had stood, then, and joined him.

Holden shrugged out of his jacket and tossed it on the chair.

He'd called hour by hour, grilling Robert for details, and had been assured there was nothing more he could do in person than from afar. But seeing Baxter now, color good and wounds infection free, was Christmas, Easter, and birthdays all wrapped into one.

The big guy had a long recovery ahead, but he'd live.

Holden said, "You did good."

Robert waited, hesitated, and said, "Did you find Jen?"

Holden nodded in answer, offering both truth and lie.

They'd gone for coffee, he and she and the brother, who'd joined them later, and morning had turned to evening with a speed that made a mockery of time. With humor, she'd given him a glimpse of a pain-filled past that rivaled his own, and with serious-ness, glimpses of a mother he'd have loved and hated. She'd told him her name was Julia, though that wasn't any truer than that her name was Jen, or that her brother's name was John, or that he was Troy or Christopher, because names were placeholders that imparted a sliver of life story within a discrete slice of time, and Julia fit this one perfectly.

So yes, he'd found her, but he hadn't found Jennifer White.

Robert could have found her, too, if he'd thought to look one floor up and eight rooms over. They'd closed down a bar, the three of them, and the siblings, needing a place to sleep, had invited themselves along to his hideaway.

He'd been in no mood to decline.

Robert said, "Did you kill her . . . ? Is she . . . ?"

"She's alive, still in one piece, not hurt."

A partial dose of tension drained from the kid's posture. He kept his face toward the bed and, avoiding eye contact, said, "What happens to me now?"

Holden put a hand on his shoulder and waited for him to look up. "You able to permanently forget and forever keep your mouth shut?"

Robert nodded.

Holden didn't doubt the sincerity, even if

the confidence was misplaced.

Silence under pressure was a learned skill that came from life experiences the kid could only pray he never had.

Holden pulled a few hundred dollars from his wallet and stuffed them in the kid's pocket. "You can finish the night out here if you want or leave now," he said. "It's entirely up to you."

Robert glanced at the door, as if trying on the idea of freedom, and unwilling to test fortune or risk waking to a change of plans, made a beeline toward escape.

Holden debated the need to warn him.

The kid would never truly be free.

The disappearance and suspected murder of Jennifer White would follow him for life, would always be there when employers, schools, and girlfriends searched his name, and any clarification of facts would be an afterthought or an unread footnote in a trial-by-Internet, guilty-even-when-innocent world.

Holden watched him go.

The kid was smart, headstrong, resilient.

He'd be as okay as okay could get.

The door closed, and its thud echoed with resounding finality. Holden sank into the sofa seat, slipped the envelope off the bedside table, and flicked the paper against his fingers. The emergency numbers were still secure behind the seal. Decisions bounced like pinballs, lighting up the bumpers in his tired head.

Vibration and an unmistakable tone interrupted the flow, set his pulse racing in the way only bounty alerts from the Broker could. Hatred rekindled anger and a deep, unquenchable need that he'd managed to forget for a few blessed hours.

He didn't want to look.

There'd be nothing good waiting, not when death was the only truce to satisfy the rage. That the Broker dared contact him at all, much less by an alert, only heightened the relentless thirst.

He retrieved the phone and thumbed through layers of obfuscation and passwords to get to the link that led to a newly released bounty packet.

The payout shouted like chest pains before a heart attack.

He mouthed the words into the dark. "Eighteen million Swiss francs."

Eighteen million free and clear upon proof of kill, no questions asked.

His thoughts bogged down, bottlenecked by questions.

The packet contained photos, multiple photos of a man who'd been surveilled over many unkind years, and a geographical marker, architectural drawings, and security schematics. Holden zoomed in for clarity and clicked for more.

All-call bulletin. Upon proof, winner takes all.

It didn't matter who made the kill, only who submitted evidence first.

Assassins would come in a race for that win, young and old, novice and hardened, killing to kill and killing to steal from one another, next to the next to the next they'd come.

He understood in a way most wouldn't.

He almost laughed.

This bloodbath in the making, initiated by the Broker, was a hit on the Broker himself. These pictures were of the man behind the voice, the schematics a map through his lair, and the bounty fee would likely be paid out of his own pocket.

"You want the Broker dead," John had said, "you're going to have to get in line."

Even he couldn't have known at the time how long that line would be.

Karen. Catherine. Catalina. Clare. This was her doing.

Her going it alone is the best shot you have at getting the job done.

You'd have to know her to understand.

He had thought he had, and hadn't come close.

The beauty and genius in this reversal, water to parched and desperate need, held enough payback to satisfy revenge for two.

Holden's gaze traveled up and settled on the ceiling.

The same all-call would have gone to Julia, and she'd recognize it for what it was just as he had. But her phone was in pieces. It'd be a long while before she knew.

He reached for the room phone to dial upstairs directly but stopped and returned the receiver to its cradle and the envelope to the table. He leaned back and closed his eyes.

In four days the twins would rendezvous in Berlin.

There were as many possible motives for the Russians to arrange that meeting as there were threats. Their mother had made a lot of enemies. There were buyers who'd want her children, as they'd wanted her, if for no other reason than revenge.

"They'll find you," he'd told them. "And you'll end up running hard. You could use an ally, a friend."

Decisions fell into place, made by life, as life sometimes did.

He had time to take Baxter home to his

mother's care, which was better than anything a hospital had to offer. He had time
to visit Frank, have a real visit, father and
son.

He had time enough to return.

Some iteration of John and Julia would
board that flight for Frankfurt, and he'd be
right behind them. They might suspect,
might even mark him, but he'd have them
in his sights when they met the past. He'd
have their backs.

The three of them together, they'd be
damn near invincible.

AUTHOR'S NOTE

If you're new to my books, thank you for being willing to take a chance on the unfamiliar! I truly hope you've enjoyed the read, and would love to hear from you if you have. If you're already a fan or a reader back for another round, thank you for being part of this ongoing journey. I can't tell you how happy I am to be able to share these new worlds with you.

I'm blessed beyond measure to be able to create fiction for a living. What many don't know — mostly because I'm bad at remembering to mention it — is that there's also a real-life component to the craft that includes a sizable amount of personal interaction and a whole lot of teaching others how to do what I do. So this here is me trying to make up for some of the forgetful times.

Fans, readers, and curiosity seekers who'd like more than what's available on the taylorstevensbooks.com Web site can connect with me through:

- Regular e-mail, via the contact information found at taylorstevensbooks.com.
- The Taylor Stevens Fan Club Group on Facebook.
- E-mail drip from www.taylorstevensbooks.com/connect.php, where you'll get monthly updates with the latest news, upcoming events, and details on where things are with each writing project, plus bi-monthly essays that include an insider's look at publishing, thoughts on overcoming adversity, personal insights, and everything I've learned on this writing journey.
- Special insider access to video on patreon.com/taylorstevens.
- And, rarely, twitter @taylor_stevens and facebook.com/taylorstevens.

Aspiring authors looking to improve their craft can access everything I've learned about writing and storytelling through:

- E-mail drip at www.taylorstevensshow.com/connect.php.
- Weekly podcast at www.taylorstevens

show.com, where, together with friend and cohost Stephen Campbell, we solve real-life-listener writing issues, do in-depth line- and story-editing show-and-tell, and generally kick writing in the butt one word at a time.

- Patreon.com/taylorstevens, for Q&A and *Hack the Craft* writing tutorials.

ACKNOWLEDGMENTS

Writing can be a long, solitary experience, but turning a manuscript into a book certainly isn't. To that end, *Liars' Paradox* would never have become what it is without the many hands that've helped carry it from its frustrated beginning to its polished end.

To my editor, Michaela Hamilton, thank you for believing in this story. To my agent, Anne Hawkins, I treasure your wisdom, experience, and guidance. To the many unsung heroes within Kensington Publishing who put so much effort in on my behalf, don't think for a minute I'm unaware of all that goes on behind the scenes. You guys are rock stars.

To my friends, family, and children, who endure the strange hours and long disappearances that come with the writing process, thank you for your patience and also for sometimes cleaning the house. To the Muse, thank you doubly so for bringing stability to the chaos in ways that allow creativity to flourish. To my fans and readers, thank you for continuing to let me work at a job that doesn't require getting out of pajamas. And to my Patreon supporters, you've turned love and encouragement into tangible, life-changing action and opened my world to possibilities I never thought existed. Thank you for believing in me.

ABOUT THE AUTHOR

Taylor Stevens is a critically acclaimed, multiple award-winning, *New York Times* bestselling author of international thrillers including the breakout hit *The Information-ist.* Best known for high-octane stories populated with fascinating characters in vivid boots-on-the-ground settings, her books have been optioned for film and published in over twenty languages. In addition to writing novels, Stevens shares extensively about the mechanics of storytelling, writing, overcoming adversity, and the details of her journey into publishing at www.taylorstevensbooks.com. She welcomes you to join her.

The employees of Thorndike Press hope you have enjoyed this Large Print book. All our Thorndike, Wheeler, and Kennebec Large Print titles are designed for easy reading, and all our books are made to last. Other Thorndike Press Large Print books are available at your library, through selected bookstores, or directly from us.

For information about titles, please call:
(800) 223-1244

or visit our website at:
gale.com/thorndike

To share your comments, please write:
Publisher
Thorndike Press
10 Water St., Suite 310
Waterville, ME 04901